PRAISE FOR THE NOVELS
OF JEN LANCASTER

HERE I GO AGAIN

"This is the only book in twenty years that made me wipe my eyes. Jen Lancaster's like a modern-day, bawdy Erma Bombeck. It's so relatable—it's a novel about a girl who grows up such a bitch, but she has to relive her life as a nice, decent human being. I couldn't wait till the next chapter. I couldn't put it down!"

—Lisa Lampanelli, *New York Post*

"Entertaining, humorous, and well-written, and the characters are perfection; those of you who grew up in the eighties will be transported back there as if it was only yesterday. Like Lissy Ryder, Jen Lancaster has gotten a fiction do-over, and she's nailed it."

—Examiner.com

"A whimsical twist on the *Back to the Future* scenario . . . a fitting and none too treacly close. Quantum physics was never funnier. A great read." —*Kirkus Reviews* (starred review)

"A charming comedy in the vein of movies like *Big* and *13 Going on 30*. . . . Readers will find it easy to root for the frank and funny heroine of this winsome, whimsical tale. Lancaster's downright fun novel is chick lit at its best." —*Booklist* (starred review)

"*Mean Girls* meets *Back to the Future*. . . . Lancaster's as adept at fiction as she is at telling her own stories—no matter what she's writing, it's scathingly witty and lots of fun."

—*Publishers Weekly* (starred review)

IF YOU WERE HERE

"If laughter is a great tonic for the spirit, then Jen Lancaster's debut novel is a double dose of what's good for you . . . a perfect summer read." —*USA Today*

"Witty and hilarious even for non-Hughes fanatics."

—*People* (3½ stars out of 4)

continued . . .

"Jen Lancaster is one of the funniest writers I know . . . a hilarious debut." —Jane Green, author of *Promises to Keep*

"Jen Lancaster tackles fiction with the same humor and wit as she does memoirs. *If You Were Here* needs no renovations; this book is nearly perfect." —Karyn Bosnak, author of *20 Times a Lady*

"A snappy and hysterical love letter to John Hughes, HGTV, and we poor deluded souls who fell in love with a fixer-upper house."
 —Quinn Cummings, author of *Notes from the Underwire*

PRAISE FOR THE MEMOIRS OF JEN LANCASTER

MY FAIR LAZY

"Hilarious . . . *My Fair Lazy* does not 'suck it.' It rocks it."
 —Examiner.com

"Light and fun and full of pop-culture musings."
 —*Chicago Sun-Times*

PRETTY IN PLAID

"Like that dreamy pair of heels that [is] somehow both comfy and chic . . . a hilarious tribute to her early fashion obsessions."
 —*People*

"Scathingly witty." —*Boston Herald*

SUCH A PRETTY FAT

"She's like that friend who always says what you're thinking—just 1,000 times funnier." —*People*

BRIGHT LIGHTS, BIG ASS

"A bittersweet treat for anyone who's ever survived the big city."
 —Jennifer Weiner

BITTER IS THE NEW BLACK

"She's absolutely hilarious." —*Chicago Sun-Times*

Other Titles by *New York Times* Bestselling Author Jen Lancaster

JEN LANCASTER

Here
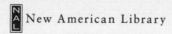 I Go
Again

New American Library

New American Library
Published by the Penguin Group
Penguin Group (USA) LLC, 375 Hudson Street,
New York, New York 10014

USA | Canada | UK | Ireland | Australia | New Zealand | India | South Africa | China
penguin.com
A Penguin Random House Company

Published by New American Library, a division of Penguin Group (USA) LLC. Previously published in a New American Library hardcover edition.

First New American Library Trade Paperback Printing, January 2014

 REGISTERED TRADEMARK—MARCA REGISTRADA

NEW AMERICAN LIBRARY TRADE PAPERBACK ISBN: 978-0-451-41685-8

THE LIBRARY OF CONGRESS HAS CATALOGED THE HARDCOVER EDITION OF THIS
TITLE AS FOLLOWS:
Lancaster, Jen, 1967–
Here I go again/Jen Lancaster.
p. cm.
ISBN 978-0-451-23672-2
1. Self-realization in women—Fiction. 2. Suburbs—Illinois—Chicago—Fiction.
I. Title.
PS3612.A54748H47 2012
813'.6—dc23   2012021417

Printed in the United States of America
10 9 8 7 6 5 4 3 2 1

Set in Sabon
Designed by Spring Hoteling

For Stacey, the reigning queen of a good idea

Here I Go Again

PROLOGUE

Every high school has a Lissy Ryder—you know, the girl who's absolutely untouchable. She goes by many names, but you might have known her as the Prom Queen.

The Head Cheerleader.

The Mean Girl.

The Bitch.

She was the richest and the prettiest, with the blondest hair, the thinnest thighs, and the hottest car, and she never let you forget it. Nothing made her happier than stealing *your* boyfriend, just to see if she could.

And she could.

Of course she could.

She was Lissy Ryder.

Lissy Ryder spent her teen years making yours miserable. She's the one who "accidentally" tripped you on the bus, mocked the sweater your sweet old Nana knitted, and told the boys you stuffed socks in your bra, despite being the one who taught you how to do it. (Ankle socks. The trick is using ankle socks.)

Every time she looked at you, sighed, and rolled her eyes, a little piece of you died inside.

You hated her.

You wanted to destroy her.

But you were satisfied just to graduate and get away from her.

So you went to college, grew up, and now live a successful, fulfilling life, vaguely wondering if that thing called "karma" ever comes for the Lissy Ryders of the world.

Hmm . . . let's find out.

CHAPTER ONE
Perfection Is Overrated

Oh, honey, no.

I scan the woman's outfit up and down. A thong-bottom leotard worn over neon tights? With high-top Reeboks? Seriously? I'm sorry, were you possessed by the ghost of 1983?

I sigh into my Bluetooth. "What are people thinking when they come here dressed as extras in an Olivia Newton-John video? This is the *West End* Club, not some nineteen-dollar-a-month Boys Town storefront, full of old StairMasters and HPV germs. So shameful. So inappropriate."

I glance at my properly clad self in the mirror across from where I'm paused on the elliptical machine. Lululemon Wunder Groove cropped capris paired with a Back on Track tank in Heathered Pig Pink?

Check.

Long blond layers of honey and ash (never platinum—I

mean, who am I? Holly Madison?) pulled into a messy yet attractive high pony?

Check.

Smashbox O-Glow blush and a swipe of MAC Lipglass in Early Bloomer?

Check.

I continue. "The West End Club is a sophisticated place and you're pretty much nobody in Chicago if you don't belong. I mean, Oprah's a member, for God's sake. I wish the Big O were here right now, because she'd be all, 'My friend Jane Fonda called and she wants her leg warmers back.'"

Nicole is my go-to person for phoning when I'm working out, because she's always home. I'd urge her to get a life, but frankly it's kind of nice being able to chat with her whenever I want. She hesitates on the other end of the line, finally saying, "Um . . . Lissy, I thought you weren't allowed to come within five hundred feet of Oprah."

I slowly begin to pedal. "That was a *suggestion*, Nicole, not a law. Like it's *my* fault she thought I was too aggressive for sneaking into her massage room. I mean, the world of PR is all about differentiating yourself. You'd think she'd *want* to work with the publicist who tried something different to catch her attention." I begin to pedal harder. "Whatevs. Doesn't matter anyway, because she's totally passé now that her show's over. Enjoy your obscurity!"

Okay, the truth is that unpleasantness with Oprah still stings even though it was years ago. I know I'd have done an outstanding job for Harpo, Inc., but she wouldn't even hear me out, which is rude, considering I forked over ten thousand dollars I didn't have back then (thanks, Daddy!) to join this place to get close to her.

To be fair, she didn't have my club membership revoked. I grudgingly give her credit for that.

I blot my face with a thick Turkish towel and pat the area around my Bluetooth so I don't, like, accidentally electrocute myself. Theoretically I'm not supposed to use a cell phone in here, but I think that's because the management wants patrons to keep both hands on the machines. Liability and all. A couple of the regulars are shooting me dirty looks, but if they can't multitask while getting their cardio on, that's not my prob.

"Who else is there today?" Nicole asks gamely.

"Um . . ." I scan the room. "There's the Chris Colfer doppelgänger who lip-synchs to the *Glee* sound track and is always talking about his 'girlfriend.' You're not fooling anyone, sweetie! The closet's wiiiiiide open! Come out already!" I take a swig of filtered water from my skull-print SIGG bottle. "Let's see . . . Hey, there's Cougar Town who takes Pilates with me. She told me she can wrap both her ankles around her neck. I'm all, 'Really? Did you do porno back in the sixties or something?' And there are the two fake-titted twentysomethings who date Bulls players. They're totally fat."

This, of course, means they're totally thin.

I don't tell Nicole that, though. Don't want to shatter her illusions about me. But how could they *not* be in perfect shape? These bitches have no responsibilities save for workouts and waxing. I mean, SOME of us aren't a size two anymore because SOME of us have day jobs.

"Uh-huh . . ." Nicole sounds distracted. She's got three rug rats under the age of six and they're always screaming in the background when we're on the phone. Not cool. Plus her husband brought a stepdaughter into the marriage, and I swear I want to slap the smug right out of that brat. Last time I was over, Charlotte was all, "Wait, you guys were alive *before the Internet*? How old *are* you?!" I told Nicole to go all Snow White's wicked stepmother on her, yet for some reason she's got a soft spot for the kid. I don't understand it.

Actually, I'm less than thrilled with a lot of Nicole's decisions. For example, she traded her adorable Audi coupe for some hideous, multirowed family truckster with automatic sliding doors and built-in video monitors. I was like, "What's next, mom jeans?" I won't ride in it on principle. I wait for her to say something else, but she's quiet, possibly because of all the banging and shuffling in the background.

"Nicole! Are you even listening?"

"Oh, gosh, I'm sorry! Bobby Junior just poured his own milk for the first time. He's so independent lately!" Her voice goes up a couple of octaves. "My little man, I'm so proud of you; yes, I am! Lissy, you won't believe it—he pulled up a chair and got the fridge open all by himself, and almost every drop made it into his sippy cup! Every time he accomplishes something on his own, I feel this incredible surge of—"

I've found that if you give a mother an opening, she'll yammer on about her boring offspring all damn day. Like I care that little Madison or Isabella can wipe her own ass. I feel it's my job as a friend to keep Nicole from spiraling into the Mom Zone, where it's nothing but sensible haircuts, soapbox derbies, and organic carrot sticks. "That's just *super*, Nic. But let's talk about tonight instead."

That shut her down right quick.

Nicole exhales a little loudly on the other end of the line. "Okay, Liss, so what are you doing later?"

"Tonight's our anniversary dinner!" I gasp. It's not that I'm all pumped about the evening. Rather, I'm slightly winded from having ratcheted up the resistance on my machine after watching the stunning red-haired Bulls consort sprint on the elliptical like a goddamned gazelle.

"Where's he taking you?"

"We're going to MK on Franklin Street. I made Duke book us in the private room. I don't really want the Great Unwashed in the regular dining area horning in on my joy."

If you want to be all nitpicky, Duke and I have been together off and on since our junior year of high school, but we've been married for only three. Yes, before you say it, we're that "breakup" couple. We know. We've had more splits than *Real Housewives'* Taylor has had lip injections, but we always find our way back to each other. I mean, yes, I dated all kinds of people when we were on a break—and even when we weren't, like when I hooked up with my neighbor Brian for a few weeks—but ultimately we were fated to be a couple. Our not being together is like a manicure without a pedicure—sick and wrong and not of the Lord.

Also, his real name is Martin Connor, but everyone started calling him the Duke of Hurl back when we were seniors at Lyons Township High School in La Grange, Illinois. His clueless family still believes it's because he was a quarterback with a golden arm, and not due to the night he mixed Jack Daniel's, Jolt Cola, and Jägermeister. Seriously, do you know long it took my dad to get the smell of vomit out of my car? I had to drive with the top down for a solid month!

While I mentally cycle through my wardrobe for the perfect dress, the timer dings on my machine. "Woo, one point five hours! Yay, me! I just burned one thousand and eighty-three calories!"

Which should make up for the three lattes I had this morning.

(I hope.)

"Listen, I want to catch a little peak tanning time, so I've gotta bounce."

"Shouldn't you get back to the office soon?" Nicole sounds characteristically worried. If fretting were a sport, she'd be a gold medalist.

"Um, thanks for your concern, *Mom*, but it's fine. I told my boss I was going to a meeting, and that's not really a lie. This place is filled with potential clients." I glance over at the Bulls girls. "I mean, escort services need publicists, too, right?"

"Still, maybe you should make an appearance."

I blot the thin sheen of sweat from my unlined brow . . . TGFB! (Thank God for Botox.) "Please, I can do whatever I want in that place. They love me there. I'm kind of a legend." After all, I brought in so much new business during the dot-com era that they hired me an assistant.

Of course, that assistant eventually became my boss, but that's only because I refuse to be an ass kisser. "Later!"

I hang up and step down from the elliptical, staggering for a second before I get my legs back. One of the Bulls sluts smirks and I may or may not make an obscene gesture back at her. I head to the locker room to change into my bathing suit (a tasteful tankini, natch) covered with the sheer floral sarong I bought in Bora Bora on my honeymoon, and I run up the stairs to the rooftop pool.

This is my favorite spot in all of Chicago. I love being here during the workday because it's practically deserted. The deck's all done up in just-bloomed hibiscus bushes and prairie grass and there's nothing but empty loungers as far as the eye can see. The pool is placid, with wisps of steam rising from it, making it warm enough to use even though it's still early summer. The sky's an impossible shade of blue today, and because the club's next to the river, none of those pesky office buildings casts shadows and blocks my sun. It's heaven . . . if heaven served cocktails. (*Of course* there's a bar in this gym. You think Oprah would join a place that didn't boast every amenity?)

I arrive at the check-in area and present my club ID to the buff teenager working the desk. "Hey, James, I'll be in my regular seat. Bring me extra towels, a piña colada, and an order of fries." He taps in my information and an odd look crosses his face. "Oh, please, I'm not going to eat them all. I just want a few." ("Moderation" is so the new "binge and purge.")

James gets all flushed and flustered, and he keeps a kung fu grip on my card when I try to grab it back. "Um, Mrs. Ryder—"

"Ms.," I correct him. "It's *Ms.* Ryder." I've always been hesitant to let go of the name I had in high school. Otherwise how would anyone even know who I was? Were I to call myself "Melissa Connor" on Facebook, everyone would be all, "Who?" But Lissy Ryder? Queen of the Belles, the best clique in school? No one forgets her.

James clenches his jaw. "Ohhhh-kay, Ms. Ryder. There seems to be a problem with your membership."

I nod. "Um, *yeah*, the problem is I'm standing here without a cocktail." He continues to tap in information for so long that I attempt—and fail—to wrestle my card back. Listen, we're burning daylight, and if I don't get color on my shoulders I can't wear my new Akris goddess-sleeve dress tonight. So I may or may not lunge at him to speed the process.

"Ms. Ryder! Please! Stop that!" he exclaims, launching into bitch-panic mode.

A steroid-addled trainer waddles over to us. His legs are so muscular he moves in tiny, mincing steps. "What is going on over here?"

"What's going on is that I'm losing my tan by the minute! And he won't let me have my French fries!" James turns the computer monitor toward the side of beef in gym shorts standing next to him. I bet this guy hasn't seen a carb since the Clinton administration. Or his nut sac.

Then, in a manner far less gentle than merited, Captain 'Roid Rage takes me by the arm and escorts me to the membership service desk three floors down. I suspect the manhandling might be due to my inquiry on exactly how small his marble bag is. (Hey, I watched the MTV *True Life: I'm a Juicehead Gorilla* special, and I'm well versed in exactly what anabolic steroids do to your junk. I can't be blamed for merely stating what everyone's thinking.)

When we get to the membership office, some minimum-wage desk monkey tells me my membership hasn't been paid in three months.

Oh, I know *someone's* accountant who's about to be fired.

(Do I have an accountant? I should check with Duke.)

I slap my well-worn Visa on the desk. "Put whatever I owe on here. But make sure my fries are ready when we're done with this nonsense."

The desk girl runs my card. "It's been declined."

Um, that's an awful lot of smug coming from someone who makes six dollars an hour. "Run it again," I demand.

"I already did," she replies.

Is a shit-eating grin appropriate at this time, really?

In the next ten minutes, I'm a lot less haughty as each of my cards is systematically rejected. And when she takes out an enormous pair of scissors and snips my prize gold AmEx, I get a sinking feeling in the pit of my stomach.

Um, what's happening? Duke makes plenty of money, despite the current economy, and we're always on top of our finances.

I mean, aren't we?

I kind of can't be bothered with all that stuff. Numbers. Ick. My mom always said I was too pretty for math. But this has to be a mistake. I keep dialing Duke's office number, but each time the phone goes straight to voice mail.

I'm summarily escorted out of the club without even being allowed to change from my bathing suit. When I get down to the parking garage, my Infiniti is missing. The parking attendant blathers something in Mexican about a tow truck.

What the *hell*?

I immediately dial Nicole and tell her to come get me. I give her explicit instructions not to drive the van, but when she arrives twenty minutes later the family truckster is full of little bastards watching a show about a big gay dinosaur.

The side door swings open and I'm suddenly overwhelmed by the stench of Cheerios. I point at her demon spawn. "Why are they here?"

"Because I'll end up on *Dateline* if I leave them home alone," Nicole cheerily replies. "Hop in!"

I attempt to climb in the front, but Charlotte's already stationed herself in the shotgun position and makes no indication that she plans to move. She pretends I'm not standing there while she busies herself sending texts about important shit like Justin Bieber's most recent haircut. When I try to nudge her out of my seat, she plants herself and rolls her eyes while Nicole grins at me like there's nothing wrong with this scenario.

Really? We're letting the fourteen-year-old stepchild run the show now?

Fine. I'll just get in the backseat like some snot-nosed little asshole on her way to T-ball practice.

I attempt to launch myself into the back of the hateful van, which is almost impossible with this slim-cut sarong. I hike it up and try again. Ugh. This place smells like juice box and desperation. As I attempt to clamber into the far back row in order to avoid the sticky hands coming at me from car seats on all sides, I catch a glimpse of an enormous blob in the side-view mirror.

Upon closer inspection, I realize the big, fleshy moon eclipsing the mirror is actually how my ass looks while I'm bent over.

Perfect.

CHAPTER TWO

Lissy Ryder and
the Bummer Summer

"Lissy?"

I pull my pillow over my head to drown out the tapping on my door.

"Lissy? Honey?"

I shrink down under my covers, rationalizing that maybe if I ignore him, he'll go away.

The knocking gets louder and his voice more exasperated. "Lissy, please. Lissy." My door swings open and soon he's jostling the bed. "Lissy! *Melissa Belle Ryder!* Wake up! It's one p.m.!"

"I'm awake, okay? Jesus, you shook me like a British nanny," I grouse. I yawn and stretch and scrub at my eyes. He hovers by my bed for a minute, and when I don't say anything, he takes it as his cue to exit. As he retreats, I remember something crucial.

"Is there any coffee, Daddy? If not, make me a cup?"

My father returns to stand in my doorway. He's all duded up in his Sunday golf gear, with his silly red-and-green-plaid pants and a white alligator shirt. In the harsh light of early afternoon, his face seems a lot more lined than I remember, and when did his hair go completely gray? He clenches his lips and they turn all pale and puckered. "Melissa, I made coffee when I got up. *Five and a half hours ago.*"

I say nothing in return.

I think I'm supposed to feel guilty here.

Yet I can't feel anything without first having my coffee, so you can see my dilemma.

He sits down at the end of my canopy bed and softens his tone. He gently pats me on the back and begins to wax all philosophic. "I know times have been trying, honey, but life does indeed go on. People face adversity all the time. Rise to the occasion and I guarantee you'll be a better person for it. You're stronger than this. Remember, the sharpest steel is tempered by fire."

I consider his advice for a moment. "So you're telling me that I should be hot metal."

He sighs and his expression bothers me. I can't tell if he seems more mad or frustrated, which is not fair, because *I* am the victim here. "This can't go on. It's been two months. When are you going to pull yourself together, Lissy?"

"Um, I don't know," I snap, swatting away his hand. "Maybe when I get my job, my home, and my husband back?"

To bring you up to speed?

Worst. Summer. Ever.

After Nicole drove me home from the club that day, I made an appearance at the office, and my fat-ass boss had the nerve to fire me. I mean, how does that happen? Fired by the secretary who used to fetch my cappuccinos? Granted, I may have taken a few liberties with company time recently, but come on! It's swimsuit season! Also, did I not land the industrial plating company's account? Sure, the owner's in my dad's golf foursome, but I did an excellent job for them on my own merits. Like, do you know how hard it is to make a press release about a new anodized coating on decorative carabiners sound sexy? *That*, my friends, takes skill.

And then—then! I met up with Duke for dinner and he looked so handsome in his blue blazer with his sandy bangs flopping onto his forehead. I was amazing, of course. I had my hair all upswept to highlight my strong jawline, and my cheekbones were like knives! My almond-shaped blue-green eyes were practically emerald due to the color of my dress and careful shadow application. My bow-shaped lips were extra-kissable due to a recent round of injectables. Seriously? I was the hottest bitch in the whole restaurant, at any age . . . and yet none of that mattered. I was recounting my horrible day and we hadn't even finished our appetizer when he told me, "I want a divorce." I almost fell out of my chair.

Um, hello?

The twenty-six times we've broken up in our relationship were all at *my* behest. *I'm* the one who decides when we're done. Since when is he allowed to break up with me, especially on the most awful day of my life?

You don't break up with Lissy Ryder, okay? She breaks up with *you*.

The worst part is that he's intent on staying in our Gold Coast condo. Apparently the prenup I made him sign entitled him to keep the assets he came in with, which included the apartment. Maybe it was *his* house, but *I* made it a home. (I mean, Restoration Hardware and me.) He didn't even have a towel-warming rack before I moved in!

While I contemplated stabbing him in the eye with an oyster fork, he was all, "Blah, blah, blah, we're not functioning as a team, your spending is out of control, you're going to bankrupt the both of us, you're the *Exxon Valdez* of financial planning, etc." But do you know how expensive it is to keep up this face and body after you hit the downside of thirty-five? Placenta-based wrinkle creams and eyelash extensions and personal training aren't free, you know. And that doesn't even take into account the cash I've spent bleaching things on this body, and I'm not talking about my teeth.

I mean, sure, he mentioned something about my paying my own credit cards from my personal accounts, but I figured it was one of those heat-of-the-moment ideas, like when you drink too much tequila and suddenly everyone wants to go somewhere terrifying, like Tijuana or Harlem or Denny's. I had no idea he actually *meant* it.

So here I am, drowning in credit card debt and back in the time capsule known as my childhood bedroom. Which doesn't make me feel like a failure *at all*.

Nothing about this place has changed since I left for college, either. From the white wicker furniture to the French bulletin board plastered in pictures from my senior year, it's like a portal to the past in here. Look at me in that photo wearing my trapeze dress next to my brand-new, custom-painted convertible. I was at the top of the world *and* the high school food chain. I mean, how do you divorce (or fire) a dead ringer for Jennie Garth? Makes no sense.

My walls are still covered in Gerbera daisy–print wallpaper my mom surprised me with when I turned fifteen, and the posts of my bed are topped with my vast collection of *Blossom*-inspired hats.

(Spoiler alert: Mayim Bialik does not grow up to be cute. Like, at all.)

The bookshelf is lined with all my old treasures, like the diaries I meticulously kept back then. Life was so fabulous that I didn't want to forget a thing. I spent twenty minutes every single night before bed journaling the day's happenings. Many exclamation points were used. And merited.

The next shelf down houses my collection of *Sweet Valley High* novels. (Jessica Wakefield, you're my hero!) After the shelf of books are all my trophies and ribbons. I've got memorabilia from student council, tennis, gymnastics, powder-puff football, and cheerleading. I mean, how could they *not* do a three-page spread of me in the yearbook? Oh, and on my bulletin board there's a clipping of me in the town paper from the night I won homecoming queen, right next to the photo in my sparkly rhinestone crown at prom.

I was *the shit* back then. The perm . . . the Clinique Rose Gold lip gloss that used to cement little strands of my hair to my lips . . . the overall pinkness of everything. My fuchsia tea-length prom dress had a massive tulle bustle, and I paired it with my funky white Doc Marten gladiator boots. (RIP, *Sassy* magazine. Thank you for defining a decade of outstanding personal style.) Of course, I changed into some chunky satin heels the minute I saw that everyone had copied my choice of footwear. Lemmings. Fortunately for them, no one dared to wear my signature shade of hot pink.

To avoid seeing the disappointment all over my dad's face, I turn and settle my gaze on a life-size poster of David Coverdale from Whitesnake, circa 1988, and I'm quietly comforted. The poster depicts Coverdale in all his feathered and oiled glory. He's dressed only in sweaty leather pants and motor-cycle gloves. Sigh. I used to tell the Belles I kept the poster for the irony factor. Total fib. Truth is, when everyone else was getting into Seattle music, like Nirvana and Soundgarden, I was still deeply in love with late-eighties metal.

I never understood how the rest of the Belles worshiped those filthy grunge boys when rock gods so clearly still ruled. Who in their right mind would opt for Eddie Vedder over Bret Michaels? The man had an eight-pack and his eyes were the color of the Aegean Sea! Kurt Cobain? He didn't even use hair product!

My mother huffs up the stairs in four-inch wedges and a cloud of Chanel No. 5. "Leave Lissy alone, mister! Don't you go fillin' her head with notions that she did anythin' wrong. She's the injured party here and she needs time to heal! I mean it now, git! Go!"

Mamma pushes past my dad before turning back to look him up and down. Her lips purse like she's smelled spoiled milk, and she shakes her head. "And change your clothes right this minute, George! You're dressed like Santy Claus on casual Friday." Then my mother shoos—literally shoos—my father out of the bedroom. Defeated, he slinks out and retreats to the sanctuary of his law book–lined library, the one place in this big, overly decorated house that Mamma lets him have for himself.

My mother places a silver tray on my lap. There's a garde-nia bud in a vase, and the whole thing's piled high with plates and glasses. There's shrimp and grits, fluffy buttermilk bis-cuits, rashers of bacon—chewy, never crisp—café au lait, fresh grapefruit juice, three kinds of jam, and a slab of butter the size of an anvil. Interesting thing about my mother—she'll cook anyone (except usually Daddy) a million-calorie breakfast, but will she take a bite of it herself? Never. She exists largely on rice cakes and gin martinis.

She smoothes my hair back from my face. "How are you today, darlin'?" Despite moving north of the Mason-Dixon line when she married my (damn Yankee) father in the early seventies, she still sounds exactly like Scarlett O'Hara.

"Surviving," I say, before amending it with "barely."

I examine the meal with equal parts revulsion and ecstasy. Much as I adore my mother's Southern cooking, my waistline despises it. I've taken to wearing yoga pants daily because I can't slide my Rock & Republic jeans past my thighs anymore.

Oh, yeah. Life's just *awesome* right now.

I stab a piece of shrimp with my fork while my mother recounts the conversation she had with my dad earlier today. I guess all the arguing I thought I dreamed was real. Apparently not only is Daddy opposed to settling my debts, but he also wants me to do more with my day than mope. He thinks I should take a job, any job, like maybe working retail, until I find another PR gig. My mother reassures me: "I insist you hold out for an executive position. The mall! Can you imagine? My li'l girl is not workin' behind a tacky makeup counter jus' to pay some pesky charge card. We'll cover whatever you need, sugar."

Which is outstanding, because I think American Express is about to *send some guys*.

She keeps me company while I pick at (fine, inhale) my breakfast. The breakfast thing is still kind of a novelty, actually. I swear the woman wouldn't let me ingest a single morsel that wasn't green or cruciferous until I got married. As I gorge, she fills me in on all the local gossip. Apparently Mrs. Brandywine's new face-lift is so tight she can't turn her head, and her tennis partner has been dallying with her pool boy.

And Beth Ann Carter's feckless husband? B-A-N-K-R-U-P-T, my mother reports with more than a little delight in her voice.

When I finish, Mamma stacks up my empty plates and, just as she's about to go down the stairs, she remembers something. "This came for you today." She slides an envelope out of her bra and hands it to me.

I glance at the return address. It's local and familiar, but I can't quite place it. Using a butter knife, I slice open the envelope and an invitation flutters into my lap. I scan the page and I suddenly start to terror sweat.

"Lissy, sugar, you look like you've seen a ghost! What's the matter, is that no-account husband of yours tryin' to take even more o' what's yours? You gave that worthless pissant your whole youth!" My mother snatches up the paper and begins to read aloud. " 'The LT Class of 1992 cordially invites you to your twenty-year high school reunion.' Well, isn't that lovely? I bet you're so excited for everyone to see you and—" Then she stops herself, eyes lingering on all my puffy parts and problem areas.

"Is it that bad, Mamma?" I ask.

She quickly composes herself. "Oh, honey, *no*, you're perfect just the way you are. Just perfect. But . . . perhaps you would like to consider takin' a shower. And a ten-mile run."

So now I desperately need a life, a job, a smaller ass, and a shower.

I'll start with a shower.

I open my laptop. Instead of visiting Monster.com, like I promised my dad as he stonily wrote enough checks to cover the GNP of Botswana, I pull up the reunion's Facebook page. As senior class president I was supposed to be in charge of organizing this thing, but I couldn't be bothered, rationalizing that I was already in touch with everyone worth knowing. But I guess someone else spearheaded this effort, because the planning is in full swing.

I'm debating whether I should attend, because I'm not presenting my best self right now. There are expectations for me, you know? And up until two months ago, I was fulfilling all of them, from stem to (perfectly bleached) stern!

Damn you, Duke!

After swallowing my feelings in the form of an entire package of Oreo Double Stuf, I feel my attitude improve. I mean, the years can't have been kind to everyone. Surely all my classmates have gotten older and fatter and poorer since high school.

I scan the page's fans and start clicking on familiar faces. I tab over to Nicole's profile and am dismayed to see eleventy-billion photos of her rotten crotch fruit, including many of bad Charlotte, and not a single shot from our glory days. Seriously? She was second in command of the Belles! She was the top of our cheerleading pyramid! I feel like this is an act of betrayal, and we will definitely be having a conversation about this at our next friendship performance review.

Who else is on here? Ooh, here's that weird hippie Debbie, who was always smudging the gym with burning sage before home basketball games. She claimed it removed "negative energy." Like some lame hocus-pocus was going to be more effective than my leading the Belles in a "Be aggressive! B-E aggressive!" cheer? I guarantee we did not win regionals that year because she made the gym smell like soup first.

Anyway, looks like she's now . . . a new age healer?

Oh, honey. Of course you are.

Now, who's this? She seems familiar, in a nerdy, overly eager kind of way. Hmm, Amy Childs. *Dr.* Amy Childs? Oh, sweetie, what are you, a chiropractor?

I pull up her profile and I suddenly feel like I've been kicked in the stomach. One of the first shots I see is her and Oprah sitting in big, squashy chairs on an elaborate wooden deck by a lake, wearing matching jammie pants and roasting marshmallows. The caption reads, "Best neighbor ever!"

That can't be right.

Thirty minutes of Googlestalking later, I find that Dr. Childs is indeed a famous plastic surgeon who spends half her year helping disfigured third worlders and the other half nipping and tucking society women on the North Shore. Well, I guess that explains why I didn't recognize her. Clearly the first thing she did was fix her heinous beak. Yeah, well, you may borrow cups of sugar from Oprah, but I made out with the captains of the football, basketball, baseball, hockey, wrestling, and lacrosse teams.

I win.

Moving on.

The beefy girl who spent all her time in the library has . . . *damn it*. Has been to Jenny, apparently. She must have dropped a metric ton before she sold her pilot to NBC. And, wait, won an Emmy? Argh. Wait a minute, I've seen her show! Come to think of it, Blake Lively plays a high school villainess who tools around in a hot-pink convertible. You don't think . . . no. That's crazy. Total coincidence.

The loser orchestra geek is . . . on tour with Maroon 5.

I grit my teeth and keep clicking.

The mathlete is . . . proud to have served on the crew of the space shuttle *Atlantis*'s final expedition.

The girl who always brought her creepy sprouted-bread

sandwiches from home is . . . a food critic for the *New York Times*.

That swishy kid has . . . just debuted his collection at Bryant Park. After winning *Project Runway*.

Argh!

I punch my keyboard in frustration.

Great. Now I'm mad *and* my hand hurts.

I wonder what my old neighbor Brian Murphy's up to? He's not listed on the RSVPs yet. He had quite the crush on me, which may or may not have been mutual.

Okay, fine.

The crush was totes mutual.

Brian gave me the kind of butterflies in my stomach that Duke never inspired, probably because he was so very sweet and genuine. He was as interested in what I had to say as what I looked like, and that was such a refreshing change from my usual meatheaded paramours.

Naturally I had to break Brian's heart, but what choice did I have? Like I was going to dump the captain of the football team for a dork in the computer club . . . despite his being the only other guy I've ever entertained serious feelings about?

Again, *fine*.

Maybe I considered bucking the social norm for a minute, but then I was all, "Wait, what is this, a John Hughes film?" News flash—no one actually gives the popular chick the slow, standing clap when they find out you're dating down. People don't rally around you and praise your open-mindedness. This was *real* high school and not some far-flung, romanticized eighties-movie concept of it. The truth is I'd have committed social suicide in dating him, and I did not work my way to the head of the Belles to throw it all away for some guy who was more into George Lucas than Troy Aikman. Thank you, *no*.

Anyway, that was a million years ago. I'm sure he's forgotten those few weeks we spent together twenty-one years ago.

I consult Mr. Google to help me find him. I insert search criteria. Pages of information come up and I begin to peruse.

Well, now, *this* is interesting. . . . Brian's running a company called I Don't Have Time for Coupons™ (d/b/a NoCoup. com), and if the *Wall Street Journal*'s to be believed, they're going to be bigger than Groupon. There's a rumor of an IPO, too.

My professional brain kicks into gear and I imagine how lucky some PR firm will be to land that business. There are so many compliance issues in terms of regulations, and one misstep during the SEC's mandatory quiet period can cost a company millions in valuation. (Which I know, because I totally watched a YouTube video about this right before I was so unfairly canned.) Point is, handling the corporate communications for a pre-IPO gig would be a license to print money, back like we used to do in the late nineties.

Hey . . . wait a minute.

I'd like a license to print money.

It's not like I don't understand the publicity game—I've been doing it since I graduated, and I worked with a million start-ups back during the boom. Maybe no one's hiring right now, but what's stopping me from starting my *own* company and trying to get the business? Sure, maybe I lost my passion for my old job, but that's because I was working for some big corporate entity, not for myself. If I were to create a firm and win Brian's account, I'd be back in the high life again. I could have a *town house* in the Gold Coast and not some stupid one-bed-plus-den like stupid Duke. I could buy Akris goddess-sleeve dresses in every color! I could finally get one of those vintage Jaguar XJs like Tawny Kitaen cartwheeled all over in Whitesnake's "Here I Go Again" video!

This could work. This could *so* work.

I make a chart of all the pros and cons of starting my own business. The only con is that I wouldn't have that much time to watch Oprah reruns. (Know thine enemy, I always say.) In terms of pros, I'd make enough money to get my dad off my back and buy my own place before my mother's cooking makes me so fat I'll need the Jaws of Life to get me out of this bedroom. Plus, if I were financially independent, Duke would be so happy with me!

We could get back together!

Then I could dump that sorry son of a bitch on my own terms!

I mean, possibly.

Maybe I'd keep him around. I guess I'd have to see.

Not having an office is a minor glitch, but I can probably set up shop in the garage until I find a space. (Mamma would never allow me to sully one of her numerous, perfectly appointed guest rooms with a bunch of ugly file cabinets and four-color copiers.)

Oh, my God, I *knew* I was a genius! My life is fixed!

Except for the stupid reunion, which . . . you know what? I'm looking at this all wrong. So what if I've put on a few pounds? Who cares if I missed my last Botox injection because I was busy drowning my sorrows in a Gotta Have It–size Birthday Cake Remix sundae at Cold Stone Creamery instead? I'm still Lissy Ryder, former head of the Belles and new president and CEO of Lissy Ryder Communications, Inc. (d/b/a LissCom) and every single person at that party is a potential client. This reunion isn't my greatest nightmare; it's my best opportunity!

I mean, I've worked on tons of campaigns for bands and designers and authors. I could help the guys in Maroon 5 work on their image. (Two words—hair spray!) I could help the math-stronaut book engagements on the lecture circuit. I could make Dr. Childs an international brand and hook her up with makeup conglomerates. Under my tutelage (and, duh, for a share of the profits), I could help her launch a line of cosmeceuticals!

Best idea ever!

All I need is my old Rolodex and some business cards.

I glance at my bloated visage in the mirror.

And some Spanx.

CHAPTER THREE
Party Like It's 1992

"You're late. And you're driving a minivan. Strikes one and two."

Color floods Nicole's cheeks. "So sorry about the van, Liss. When we planned the night, I forgot Bobby was taking his car. Then Charlotte was delayed at swing choir, and she's babysitting the little ones, so I couldn't leave till she got back. But I'm here now, right?" She flashes me a toothy smile, like that's supposed to excuse her lateness.

I simply scowl in response as I stand outside the open door.

Nicole leans across the center console. "Would it help if I tell you how pretty you look?"

"No." *Yes.*

I am semihot right now, less because I've been able to shake off any of this excess poundage and more because I'm wearing multiple girdles. My mother and her martini kept me company while I got ready, and by the time I sucked myself into the third pair of extra-thigh-controlling shorts, she asked whether I was going to a reunion or deep-sea diving with Mr. Jacques Cousteau. It's possible I overdid it with the shapewear, as breathing's really not an option and my whole body pulses in time with my heartbeat. But *you* try losing weight in a house where lard is its own block on the food pyramid.

I remove a handful of free-range LEGOs and brush the remnants of an entire school of Goldfish crackers from the seat before I ease into it. The Spanx make it almost impossible to move from the calves up, but I manage to wedge in anyway. I contemplate not wearing a seat belt, since I'm already wrapped in the equivalent of four hundred tourniquets, but I err on the side of caution. I glance over to the driver's side and note the dashboard on this thing looks like the cockpit of a 747. I warn Nicole, "God help you if this heap doesn't have satellite radio."

Nicole quickly tunes in to the nineties station on XM and we're off to the city for the reunion. Unbeknownst to me, Nicole was part of the planning committee (strike two and a half) and they decided to throw the event at the same location as senior prom, so instead of hitting the high school, we're heading to the Drake Hotel downtown.

"Why isn't Bobby here?" I ask.

What I really mean is, why isn't Bobby driving us to the event in his shiny, expensive, Goldfish-free sedan?

Nicole begins to bob her head in time with Color Me Badd's "I Wanna Sex You Up." Because nothing says "sex you up" like a former second-grade teacher surrounded by side-curtain airbags. Yet I can't help but notice how defined her collarbone is in her portrait-collar dress and I'm instantly jealous. She doesn't even try to watch her weight and routinely finishes whatever's on her children's plates. Her regular diet is supplemented by grilled cheese crusts, spare chicken nuggets, Oreo cookies minus the cream filling, and GoGurt tube dregs. Yet the bitch hasn't gained an ounce since our glory days. She says she keeps fit by chasing after her kids, which sounds like the worst weight-loss plan ever.

Nicole's definitely getting lines on her forehead, and the parentheses on either side of her mouth are starting to deepen. I keep trying to drag her to my aesthetician, but she claims she wants to "age gracefully" and "set an example" for her children. But the only example she's setting is what happens to a grape when you let it dry out in the sun. I mean, look at my mother! She's pushing sixty, yet everyone routinely mistakes us for sisters. (I'm far less thrilled about this than she is, by the way.)

Nicole tucks a stray wisp of hair behind her ear and glances over at me. "Bobby's had a fishing trip with his brothers planned forever, so I didn't want him to cancel once we set the reunion date. Besides, it's not like he went to school with us or knows many of our people. I figured he'd be happier at the lake. He just called and he told me the walleye are practically jumping in the boat—"

I begin to paw through Nicole's bag. "Guest list in here?"

Nicole cuts her eyes back to the road and, if I'm not mistaken, seems suddenly anxious. "Um, why don't we just enjoy the scenery?"

I'm supposed to enjoy . . . what? All the smokestacks and water towers? The stately Sanitary and Ship Canal, which is the preferred body dump for local mobsters *and* drug lords? Billboards advertising paternity tests and personal injury attorneys? To my left, there's a crumbling hospital for poor people, and to the right, an abandoned warehouse.

"I-55 is universally known as the armpit of Illinois. What aren't you telling me, Nicole?" Not waiting for an answer, I dig around until I find the list and begin to scan as Nicole suddenly becomes very interested in the traffic.

Who's worth speaking to on here? Looks like NoCoup. com's Brian Murphy's most likely a no, which completely bites. Approaching him about business tonight would have been way less formal than going through his assistant. Not impossible, by any means, but definitely a wrench in the works. And what if we find we still like each other? A corporate boardroom's decidedly less flirty than the flattering light of a ballroom and the lure of an open bar.

None of the rest of the Belles is coming, either. No huge loss there. Kimmy kind of hasn't been reasonable since I went to Puerto Rico with her boyfriend Chet back in the late nineties. I *told* her he was cheating on her. She didn't believe me, so it was my job to prove it. Six times in one long weekend I proved it! (Would have been more if he hadn't chugged all that watermelon sangria on our last night there.) Yet when I related this information she acted like *I* was the bad person in this scenario.

God, some people can't appreciate the lengths I go to in the name of friendship.

April was unforgivably bitch-panicky after I kidnapped her and brought her to the Derek Lam sample sale. I mean, her Nana's not that old. She'll have plenty of other ninetieth birthday parties, and how often is there a sample sale of that magnitude in Chicago? (A lot less often, I'd imagine.)

And Tammy? I did her a massive favor when I changed her dress order. She would not have looked back on those pumpkin-colored nightmares fondly, let me tell you. Plus, I suspect she was putting us in them on purpose so she'd look better next to us. That shade of orange is a blonde's worst night-mare, so clearly I had no choice if I didn't want to be forever pasty in her wedding photo album. Yet you fix someone's bridesmaid dresses and they shit all over you.

And please, like the bitch wouldn't have done the same thing to me. She spent her whole high school career trying to oust me as leader; why would my wedding have been any different?

Whatever. I'm glad they're not coming. The Belles are *supposed* to be my ladies-in-waiting and not just a group of thirty-something women who tend to shout at me.

Lots of people I Googlestalked have RSVP'd yes, though. I might not land them all as clients, but even a couple would make a huge impact on my bottom line. Currently the only business I've lured to LissCom is the industrial plating manufacturer. I'm working on a scintillating campaign to raise awareness of the lubricity of chrome plating, which is used to prevent corrosion. Hot, right? (And don't even get me started on the bennies of cylindrical grinding!)

I run across Duke's name. There's a note next to his RSVP, asking to be seated with his date, who is, apparently, a member of our class, but her name isn't specified.

And that's fine.

No, I mean it.

It's *fine*.

Seriously, who's he going to find that's better than me? I'm sure he's just escorting some rent-a-skank to make me jealous. Or maybe he's bringing Elyse, that bloodsucking divorce at-torney of his who graduated with us. Either way, what's going to happen is he'll see her and me in the same room and there'll be no question of who's cuter.

And yet . . .

I feel a twist in my stomach, maybe from nerves. Of course, that could just be Mamma's gumbo. That woman does not skimp on the andouille.

While Nicole drones on about something called Gymboree (don't know, don't care), I mentally prepare my pitch for the evening. When we arrive at the Drake, I insist we stop for a drink in the bar of Palm Court before we hit the reunion. Nicole's all, "Blah, blah, blah, missing dinner in the ballroom," but I tell her that Lissy Ryder likes to make an entrance.

"You're not going to start talking about yourself in the third person, right? Oh, God, it'll be tenth grade all over again." Nicole shudders.

Ignoring her, I down my first skinny-girl margarita, followed by another. I pretty much have to keep my hand clamped over Nicole's wrist while we're at the bar, because she keeps claiming she needs to manage the registration table. I tell her if our classmates are too dim to figure out that they're supposed to take the tag with their own name and photo on it, then they need a helmet, not a facilitator.

At eight thirty-two p.m., one hour and thirty-two minutes after the reunion starts, I release Nicole and she sprints off ahead of me. I'm not in love with how cut her calf muscles are as she fifty-yard-dashes into the party. (Note to self: Encourage Nicole to eat more carbs.)

As I push through the doors of the ballroom, the deejay begins to spin Right Said Fred's "I'm Too Sexy." Not my favorite jam by a long shot, but definitely a fine, fine song for making an entrance.

I stand and bask for a moment and wait for my minions to rush me. The gracious paneled ballroom is a couple of stories high, and there's a stage decked in a banner stating WELCOME BACK, LT LIONS—CLASS OF 1992. There're lots of old photo collages on the sides of the bar, and over by the deejay booth there's an enormous poster of our school's most famous alumnus to date . . . David Hasselhoff.

Oh, yes.

Let the (lion) pride of *that* sink in for a moment.

Dozens of white-draped tables line the parquet dance floor, and they're all topped with flowers in our school colors. Really, Nicole? Gold and blue carnations grouped around a tiny stuffed lion clad in a football jersey? Strike two and three-quarters.

Still, tonight marks my relaunch into life. Yes, things were bumpy during the summer, but that's all over now. LT, get ready for Lissy 2.0!

I bask a little longer, enjoying the solitude before the onslaught of those hoping to catch a ride on the Lissy 2.0 Express.

I continue to bask as the song ends and Kris Kross's "Jump" begins. Clearly every person in this room will notice me as soon as they stop hopping up and down like a bunch of cracked-out kangaroos.

Basking, basking . . .

When "Achy Breaky Heart" comes on, the crowd shrieks and storms the dance floor, like they have absolutely zero shame in two-stepping to Miley frigging Cyrus's father. Open bar, indeed.

I continue to bask.

Nothing happens, save for a group of moderately attractive people squealing, hugging, and grooving on the other side of the room.

Um, *hello*! I'm basking over here!

Then everyone completely loses their shit for "Smells Like Teen Spirit." I have to roll my eyes at how everyone's banging their heads as though they were onstage with Kurt and company. Er, pardon *me*? You're all on the wrong side of thirty-five and air guitar stopped being cute, like, two decades ago. Also, am I the only one who's disturbed that this song is technically an infomercial about girls' deodorant?

When Def Leppard's "Let's Get Rocked" plays (finally something decent!) and the dance floor empties, I make my way to the bar. Ah, looks like everyone's enjoying fine, fine boxed wine. Strike two and four-fifths, Nicole.

I take a belt of my sauvignon blanc and put on my best Belle smile. The first familiar face I see is that of Debbie, the former—scratch that, current—hippie. She's all done up in some kind of bizarro caftan and head wrap, and I want to ask if Maya Angelou is suing her for likeness rights. But I stop myself, remembering the article about Debbie's booming new age boutique on Oak Street catty-corner from Prada. Growing retail outlets need crazy-big amounts of publicity, and I hear that crystal therapy is the new faux fur vest for society chicks.

Oh, Jaguar, I can feel the purr of your V8 engine as we speak!

"Hey, there, it's Lissy Ryder. How are you, Lissy Ryder?" Debbie not only approaches me, but positions herself approximately six inches from my face. Wow, violate my personal space much?

I take a step backward and I force the new, more professional Lissy 2.0 to answer, which is why I don't deliver a devastating burn about the bit of grape leaf from the dolma lodged between her incisors. "Fine, thanks. It's Debbie, right?"

Her face is wreathed in smiles. "Actually, it's Deva."

"Um, no, I'm pretty sure it's Debbie." Listen, Lissy 2.0 did not study that goddamned yearbook in vain. You *are* Debbie Mitchell or the LTHS *Tabulae* is full of filthy lies.

She continues to moon at me. "Debbie is who I was. Deva is who I am now." I must look as confused as I feel, so she continues. "Deva is my spiritual name."

"All righty." I say nothing else for fear of making a hilarious yet career-limiting comment. I take another step and stumble back into a potted palm.

"Lissy Ryder, how are you?" She grasps my left elbow between her large, meaty palms and assists me out of the plant.

I think, *Ready to pass out from lack of blood flow to my waist, Man Hands*, but I say, "No problem, just a little dirt." I brush a bit of soil off my skirt.

"Lissy Ryder, really, how *are* you?"

I arrange my mouth into what I hope looks like a grin but really is more a matter of baring my teeth and pulling back my lips. "Did we not cover that with the 'fine' business? I kind of feel like we covered that."

Debbie—rather, *Deva*—moves in even closer, and I can smell the onion from the dolma. "Lissy Ryder, your words say fine, but your aura disagrees. Are you in a dark place? I'm seeing an ominous cloud all around you. And your chakras! Oh! Do not start me on your chakras! Your soul is crying out for clarity and purpose and inner peace."

I bite my tongue in order not to retort, *And* your *soul's crying out for Listerine*. I consider this Lissy 2.0's first official victory.

But can I just note that this?

Right here?

Is exactly why I didn't consort with losers in high school.

After Deva-Does-Dolmas floats off into the ether, I run into Dr. Amy Childs, plastic surgeon to the stars and hoped-for client. "Amy!" I greet her effusively. "How are you?"

Instead of returning my kind salutation, she cocks her head and looks at me like I spoke Klingon or something, like, *interested*, but not quite understanding. She's stonily silent, which I interpret as excitement at finally having the attention of the head of the Belles. That's right, Dr. Amy Childs. Dreams do come true!

"Amy? It's me! Lissy Ryder!" I attempt to hug her and she kind of just stands there. "Long time no see, huh? Listen, I read about all your success—congratulations! I have to know how you're managing your busy, busy life. And I have to wonder if, with all that you do, you're really making the time to build your brand. Now, this is just a suggestion, but what I'd like to see is someone—maybe me—pitching you for a recurring spot on WGN's morning show as a health and beauty expert, with an eye toward eventually parlaying that into a gig on *Today* or *GMA*. But not *CBS This Morning*, because, really, who watches that?"

Amy just stands there in what must be rapt attention, so I continue. Not surprised, of course. I really am at my best in front of an audience.

"With an eye toward the future, the way I see you maximizing your brand and, of course, your revenue, is to come out with a line of cosmeceuticals. I mean, quality stuff with antioxidants and hyaluronic acids and placentas and shit. I think manufacturers can produce eye creams without blinding bunnies and monkeys now, if that's a concern, but that's a few steps down the road. And then you could get a celebrity endorsement from someone like—and I'm just spitballing here—Oprah, and I'm telling you, your product would be behind the counter in fine department stores around the globe! Isn't that exciting?"

Clearly Amy is so excited she's speechless, so I press on.

"We could call the line Childslike, because that harkens to baby-soft skin, right? If this sounds good to you—and I suspect it does—why don't we sit down this week and figure out how the right publicity campaign can put you on the road to fulfilling your wildest dreams. Sound good?"

Finally, Amy speaks.

"That is unbelievable."

I reply, "I know, right? So exciting! So many possibilities!"

Amy's face is very serious. "No. Not exciting. Unbelievable. That you have the nerve to stand here and speak to me like we're peers, like we're *friends*, after what you and your asshole minions did to me. You know, they all apologized eventually, but you? You just blithely went about your senior year, cheering at games and running student council and driving around in your fucking hot-pink convertible like you didn't have a fucking care in the fucking world, like your casual cruelty didn't almost destroy me. So, no, Lissy fucking Ryder, I don't think your little plan 'sounds good'; nor will I be 'sitting down' with you. Ever. Now, if you want to do me a favor, if you really care about me and how I'm 'managing everything,' you can get out of my way and never dare to speak to me again."

I let her words sink in while I struggle for the appropriate response.

Lissy 2.0 must have left the building, because I suddenly hear myself shouting, "Maybe we should talk when you're not having your period. Hey . . . *hey*! *If you were a proper plastic surgeon, you'd have better aim!*"

I stomp to the ladies' room to blot off the club soda she threw at me. Well, no wonder I didn't like her back then. I hope Oprah realizes exactly how volatile her stupid neighbor is.

I dry off fairly quickly—I suspect the Spanx possess water-wicking properties—and I smooth escaped bits of hair back into my chignon. Then I apply a fresh coat of MAC Lipglass in Desire to remind myself of my purpose here tonight. As I'm tossing the tube back into my (actually, Mamma's) sparkly lemon-slice Judith Leiber bag, I recognize another face in the mirror.

"Brooks? Brooks Paddy?" I ask. Yes! Brooks is here! In her RSVP she said she might be needed on set for rewrites, since her show's back from hiatus, but she made it. Excellent. Maybe I'll just exchange some pleasantries and warm her up before I begin to talk about business.

"Don't you mean 'Books Fatty'?"

Uh-oh.

"If you're talking to me, you must mean 'Books Fatty,' because that's certainly what you called me twenty years ago." Brooks narrows her eyes and languidly leans back onto the sink. She's all slender angles and catlike grace now. Which I don't love.

The public relations business is all about damage control. Clearly this person thinks I did her wrong in high school, so I'm going to learn from Dr. Premenstrual and spin this to my advantage. I place my hand on her (bony) shoulder so I come across extra sincere. "Did I? I'm so sorry. You know how girls can be. We were, like, bears or something, stalking an injured elk. You can't blame us; it was just our nature, and elk are delicious and stuff. But come on! That was so long ago and no one remembers! Surely you've gotten over it. I mean, look at you! You're all tall and thin and perfectly highlighted! You have a show on television! And is that an Herve Leger bandage dress I spy? Amazeballs!"

Brooks pulls a fresh pack of cigarettes and a fancy gold lighter out of her clutch. "Oh, sure, of course. I'm so over it, because clearly no one bears the scars from high school."

I sigh in relief. "Whew! I'm glad you're being cool about it. You know Amy? Dr. Amy Childs? Is she on the rag or what? She couldn't get past some nonsense from twenty years ago and she threw a drink on me!"

"That's practically criminal," she coolly observes.

"I know, right?" Brooks seems plenty softened up, so I begin to pitch her. I tell her all the proactive things LissCom can do in terms of her social media presence, and she nods appreciatively the whole time I'm talking. Brooks is actually so amenable that I feel really confident that I've gotten through to her and I go in for a soft close.

"I would love to do business with you," she tells me, turning my business card over in her hand. "There's just one thing I need."

She bought it! Woo-hoo! Town house, here I come! But I try to maintain a poker face and reply, "Of course! Just name it." I'm already mentally moving my desk out of the garage and into some hip space down in the South Loop or River North. The next time I need a file, I'm not going to have to navigate around a pile of old cross-country skis and golf clubs to reach the drawer!

Brooks takes a long, thoughtful drag on her Virginia Slim. "I need for you to go back in time and change the past. I need you to have not relentlessly bullied me. Like the time on the class trip when you stole my suitcase and showed the guys the size of my underwear? And you flew them out the window because you said they were as big as a flag and you made everyone salute? That needs to have never happened. I need to have not been tormented. I need to have not gone home every day and cried into a half gallon of strawberry Breyers. I need to have not been so ostracized that I didn't spend every waking minute in the library, because I knew that was the one place you wouldn't go. Can you do that for me? Can you change history? If so, we have a deal."

I sputter, "Are you deaf? I just apologized!"

Brooks takes my card and uses her shiny lighter to set it on fire. When it's halfway burned, she drops it in the sink, where it curls and disappears into a pile of smoking ash. "Twenty years too late, bitch. You're twenty years too late."

When I exit the bathroom, I run smack into Duke and his date, who's a dead ringer for a younger version of Sofia Vergara. I feel like I've been kicked in the heart with a really pointy boot.

I need a drink.

Correction: I need many, many, many drinks.

CHAPTER FOUR
McFly Girl

I try to open my eyes but it's virtually impossible.

Whether that's because of the hangover or due to false lashes cementing my eyes shut is yet to be determined.

I sit up and manage to peel them open, and only then do I catch a glimpse of my surroundings. I expected to rise under the glossy visage of David Coverdale, but instead I'm somewhere entirely different.

Where the hell am I?

I peer around the space and determine I'm in someone's apartment.

No, no, that's not it.

The word "apartment" doesn't adequately describe the four thousand square feet of vast windows and twenty-foot-high timbered ceilings. I'm in some kind of loft and it's filled with odd artifacts and old books. There are multicolored tapestries and dream catchers and crystals hanging all over the place, and the whole area's infused with the kind of earthy spices I always smell in the backseat of taxis. I spot beaded curtains and tribal art and hand-hewn furniture. Maybe I've landed in Jerry Garcia's afterlife?

When I glance down, I see that I've been passed out on a nest of body pillows and animal skins, and I'm wearing a strange kind of . . . bathrobe? Poncho? Serape? One of those scratchy, stripy blankets every frat guy buys in Cancun and keeps in his apartment until his girlfriend finally sneaks it into the trash? I can't really say. I'll simply add this Technicolor Dreamcoat to the list of questions I'm not entirely sure I want answered. I try to stand, but gravity gets the best of me and I buckle and drop.

"Oh, good, you're awake. Namaste!" Debbie pops out from a kitchen area that's a solid half mile away from where I'm sitting and heads toward me. "Here, break your fast with this." She hands me a pint glass filled with a neon green concoction interspersed with black dots.

I'm desperately thirsty, so I take a healthy sip and immediately gag. "*Blergh!* Why does this taste like lawn clippings?"

Debbie nods like I've paid her a huge compliment. "Probably because the wheatgrass was just picked."

I blink hard a couple of times. "You just gave me a glass of *grass*?"

"Juiced grass. I grow it myself on my roof garden. Don't worry; it's all organic and pesticide-free. I keep a supply of lady beetles called mealy bug destroyers, and they allow me to maintain a poison-free environment."

"Congratulations." I roll my tongue around in my mouth and note an even worse aftertaste that's all fishy and primal. "What is that other horrible, horrible flavor?"

"That's the spirulina I added for protein. Spirulina was one of the ancient Aztecs' dietary staples. They called it *tecuitlatl*, and they believed in its healing properties."

"Tastes like pond scum."

"Spirulina is a type of algae harvested from the surface of lakes."

"So it is pond scum."

Debbie bobs her head and looks all beatific and pleased with her bang-up entertaining skills. Somewhere a shudder just ran down Martha Stewart's back at the notion of serving a guest a glass of moldy grass.

Debbie launches into a series of bizarre stretches before finally folding herself into a sitting position in front of me. I didn't know people could bend that way. As I process the whole scene—the art, the outfits, the joint-defying movements—I realize I've fallen into some kind of new age *Alice in Wonderland* rabbit hole. The only way out is figuring out how I got here in the first place, so I ask the most obvious question.

"What kind of drugs are you taking and can I have some?"

Debbie laughs and says, "Lissy Ryder, you're still such a card." When she takes a gulp of her drink, I notice it leaves a chlorophyll mustache.

I point at my mouth. "You look like you just blew the Incredible Hulk."

Debbie responds with more beaming and less wiping. "Lissy Ryder, I sense that you have questions, so please untrouble your heart."

"You got that right." I gesture at myself. "For starters, what am I wearing?"

Debbie does a shoulder roll before answering, and I can hear every vertebra in her back pop. "You're dressed in a Central Asian Ikat robe. Interesting fact about the Ikat process—

the act of dyeing each strip of fabric was an ancient art, and craftsmen kept their techniques secret, which accounts for all the color variations. In the oasis towns of Central Asia, prominent men would wear these items as a showy display of their wealth. That sort of thing seemed right in your wheelhouse."

I have no frigging idea how to respond to this.

"Also, my pajamas were too small on you."

"Aces." I'm superdehydrated, so I take another tiny sip of the wheatgrass, hoping that the flavor has improved. Nope, still tastes like Jolly Green Giant ass. "Number two, where are my clothes? And three, why did I take them off in the first place?"

Debbie circles her head, nods, and rests her chin on her tented fingers. "Your dress is in the bathroom. When we got here, you cried that your underwear was 'murdering' you, and you stripped down."

Ah, yes. Spanx are a harsh mistress. "Where's *here*?" I gesture at the space around me and knock over a wooden figurine. I pick it up by the handle to right it and, upon closer inspection, I see that it's twelve inches of wooden man and six inches of wooden man's woody. Argh. As I focus on other objects, I note a decidedly naked bent to many of the artifacts. I feel like I'm touring Larry Flynt's Museum of Mayan Porn.

Again, this is why we weren't friends in high school.

Debbie places her great ham hands together and does an odd little bow. "You're in my home, Lissy Ryder. Welcome. I live above my store. I bought this building so I'd never be far from my work." So . . . the Ethereal Girl owns thousands of square feet of prime Mag Mile–adjacent real estate, yet the Material Girl can pretty much lay claim to one David Coverdale poster? How is this possible?

I shake my head to clear the cobwebs and instantly regret the sudden movement. I brace myself on the pillows in an attempt to keep down the vertigo. "We're on Oak Street, then?" I ask, trying to MapQuest the location in my head.

"Uh-huh. We walked over from the reunion—I'm only two blocks away from the Drake. That's the preferred hotel for many of my international clientele." I vaguely recall fresh air last night, but everything's still so fuzzy. "Now tell me, Lissy Ryder, did you enjoy the sleeping pit?"

"I always sleep my best when curled up with a yak's pelt." Debbie beams. Apparently they don't have sarcasm on her planet. "Wait, where's Nicole? She was supposed to drive me home."

Debbie taps a long finger to her chin and focuses on the ceiling. "She said . . . what were her exact words? Oh, yes, she said, 'That hateful bitch is going to puke in my Odyssey and I'm not having my kids smell her vomit for the next month.' She dumped you on me."

Strike three, Nicole.

I rest my face in my hands and try to remember. Suddenly the night's events come rushing back to me and I'm all nostalgic for two minutes ago, when I didn't know what ancient Aztecs ate for breakfast.

Oh, God, last night.

When I used to imagine what hell might be like, I pictured flames and pitchforks and a lot of screaming. I envisioned hell as the scene from the Adam Sandler movie where Hitler faced an eternity of having pineapples shoved up his ass.

Of course, I know better now.

Hell is an open bar and boxed wine.

Hell is three complicated pairs of Spanx and a tiny bladder.

Hell is a deejay with a penchant for Sir Mix-A-Lot.

Hell is being accosted by women I'm not sure I ever met telling me exactly why they despise me.

Hell is being ignored by the very people who used to worship me.

Hell is making choices two decades ago that will completely impact my ability to do business today.

Hell is four hours of watching the guy who pledged to forever honor and cherish me dirty dancing to "Rump Shaker" with someone thinner and hotter.

My head throbs as I replay my conversation with Duke.

Debbie seems to pick up on my thoughts. "I take it from last night's display that you're no longer with Martin."

That? Is an understatement.

After I choked down the bile from seeing Duke with someone else, someone painfully fit and attractive, someone who hung on his every word, *damn it*, I decided I'd be the bigger person and break the ice. He seemed to not want the ice broken, and that made him ten times more attractive than when I had him and didn't want him.

Seriously, no girl digs the guy who actually wants her back. Where's the challenge? Where's the anticipation? Where's the thrill of the hunt?

When I tried to cozy up to him at the reunion, I moved in real close and was all, "Duke, why is everyone being so meeeeeeeeeeean to me?" and he completely lost his shit.

"First, my name isn't Duke. It's Martin, okay? M-A-R-T-I-N. The only person who's called me Duke since leaving high school is you. The name Duke isn't cute; it's not endearing; it's not a pet name." His eyes were all hard and he spoke to me in a tone I never heard before.

I was completely gobsmacked (and a little turned on). "What are you talking about?"

"*Duke* is my badge of shame from one unfortunate night when I drank too much *because you kept daring me to*, and you've never let me live it down. Remember that? The 'only-pussies-can't-do-Jägermeister-shots' night? Then, after I over-indulged? *You* thought it would be funny to do doughnuts in your new car and the centrifugal force got the best of me. I threw up and I'm sorry. I've been sorry for more than twenty years. But were you sorry? Were you empathetic? Did you take any ownership of the situation whatsoever?"

Where was this coming from? I interjected, "Oh, please, I totally—"

He pressed on and the little veins in his forehead got all bulgy. "No. No, you weren't. Instead, you made out with my best friend to punish me for having 'puke breath' and then spent two weeks after that macking on your nerdy neighbor. For the rest of my life, you've delighted in sharing the origin of my nickname with everyone—college roommates, coworkers, neighbors, bosses, bankers. You even told our dry cleaners, and each time I see them, they greet me with 'Herro, Duke!' Well, that stops now."

I placed a hand on his jacket lapel. "Come on, Duke, you have to admit it's kind of a funny story. Who mixes Jolt, Jack, and Jäger?"

Holy cats, I thought, we are going to have the best makeup sex!

Yet Duke wasn't reading from our usual playbook. Instead, he practically levitated to get away from my touch. "You know what, Lissy? Duke is dead, gone, no more. As for everyone being mean to you? They hate you. All of them. If you can't figure out why, Lissy—I mean, *Melissa*—then there's no hope for you." With that, he returned to his date and the two of them bent their heads together at the table, deep in conversation.

So, no makeup sex, then?

I recount his words to Debbie and ask her, "I wasn't really that bad back then, was I?" expecting her to reassure me that clearly Duke's the dickweed here.

Debbie doesn't even hesitate. "Absolutely."

"Absolutely?"

"Yes. You were the kind of girl Tina Fey writes movies about."

This is news to me. "Huh."

She leans in, all sympathetic. "Is that difficult for you to hear?"

I nod. "A little. I mean, I'd always pictured Charlize Theron or Cameron Diaz in the role of Lissy Ryder, but I guess I could imagine Rachel McAdams starring instead. She was excellent in *The Notebook*."

Debbie drains her glass, then, mercifully, wipes her lips with a woven-bracelet-covered wrist. "I'm so intrigued by what *you* consider a compliment. Now let me ask you something, Lissy Ryder—are you finally acknowledging the person you were in high school? Because that's the first step to making a change."

It's my turn not to hesitate. "No, I'm not acknowledging shit. I couldn't have been so bad, if for no reason other than basic time management. Between cheering and tennis and student council and my rigorous social schedule, I never had time to crack a book."

I don't add, *Which is why I barely got into college*, even though it's true.

I press on. "Plus I'm here with you, right? If we weren't cool, you'd have left me at the Drake."

Debbie practically erupts, and her voice echoes through

the cavernous space in her loft. "Ha! You're the worst person I ever met."

Ha?

Really?

I merit a "ha"?

How is this possible? I never even thought about her unless she was in front of me doing something bizarre. I didn't, like, seek people out to criticize them intentionally, but if they were right there with, say, hairy pits and a tank top, it was kind of my duty to mention it. You know, as a friend.

"What'd I do to you?"

I'm not being oppositional; I really don't remember. Sure, with her herbs and her Stevie Nicks dresses, I thought she was queer as a soup sandwich, but for the life of me I can't recollect any direct negative interaction.

"Debbie Does Deep Throat."

"Beg pardon?"

Debbie's expression darkens. "*Debbie Does Deep Throat.* The day the cafeteria served corn dogs? You don't remember shrieking in front of the entire senior class, 'Oh, my God, she's fellating her lunch'? Like it was so goddamned easy to eat food on a stick in a back brace and I had another choice. Then to be stuck with that nickname on top of it? *That's* what you did to me."

Debbie pauses, places her hands on her thighs, and takes a couple of deep breaths. She exhales for a solid thirty seconds. "I apologize for that outburst, Lissy Ryder. I'm centered again. Anyway, the reason we are 'cool,' as you say, is because I'm *not* Debbie anymore. *Debbie* wants to punch you in the motherfucking face."

She pauses to breathe again and clears her throat. "*Ahem.*

I'm Deva now. I've devoted my adult life to transcending negative emotions like anger and resentment. I channel all that's
bad into positivity and light. Trust me when I share that your
actions eventually produced a *shitload* of positivity and light."

I fall back into the sleeping pit's pillows. "This is all too
much for me to process. I had no clue."

"I'm very sorry if my painful teenage memory troubles
you."

Seriously, this is kind of news to me.

"What you're telling me is that I did all kinds of damage
to you in high school." I tend to repeat what people say to me
when it sounds important. It's a great PR trick I picked up
years ago. Makes people believe they're really being heard.
Only . . . half the time I used to parrot stuff back in meetings,
I'd be reminding myself that I needed to schedule a mani and
a wax.

"Again, *ha*! Not just to me! You left a string of wounded
in your path."

"Really?" I thought I was just being funny. Everyone used
to tell me how hilarious I was. Well, the cool people, anyway.
"But I can't consciously recall trying to hurt people's feelings.
I was just being me."

"Who you were wasn't nice. Understatement. Who you
were was Satan."

Ouch.

"Okay, if that's the case and I was all Regina George, then
why didn't people accept my apologies last night?"

Deva coolly appraises me before answering. "I imagine
they doubted your sincerity. Were your words coming from
your heart or were they motivated by something else, like
greed?"

Damn.

"Lissy Ryder, if you reflect on your evening, what message is most clear to you?"

Oh, I know this one!

"Never drink boxed wine."

Debbie—no, *Deva*—grits her teeth and inhales so hard, I'm afraid all of her ancient booby statues are going to fly off the shelves from the suction. Then she exhales so hard she blows my hair back. "Beyond that. If you listen with your head and your heart, what is the message that you received?"

I scrunch my eyes shut and I come up with an answer I don't particularly like or agree with. "That if I want to live a happy life now, I need to have not been Lissy Ryder in high school?"

Then, in a flash, everything falls into place. I bet that's why the bank manager in the class behind me wouldn't advance me a line of credit for LissCom, even with my dad cosigning. And the girl I cut from the squad because her hair was too shiny? Elyse, Duke's reunion date and divorce attorney. No wonder she went for my jugular. No wonder she wore that slutty dress.

My mind races through all the slights I've suffered in the past twenty years—drinks "accidentally" spilled on my new Tory Burch shoes, elevator doors not held, paperwork misfiled, parking spaces stolen, and all the vaguely familiar faces attached to the perpetrators.

Is it possible I've generated an entire universe of bad karma?

That thought is far too overwhelming to consider before coffee, so I vow to shove this realization to the back of my mind the second I leave this place. Like Scarlett O'Hara says, I can't think about that right now because I'll go crazy. I'll think about everything tomorrow.

Deva taps a meaty digit to the tip of her nose. "Bingo."

Now I'm mad. Anger's a way healthier emotion than guilt. "Bingo. Bingo? What is *bingo*? What are you saying? That I need to find Doc Brown and build a DeLorean and go back to the future?" I throw my (delicate, adorable) hands in the air. "I'm not even sure how I'm getting back to La Grange."

This is where Deva's deep and abiding spiritual guidance comes into play. "There's a ten twenty-five Metra train, and you can grab a cab to Union Station right out front," she offers.

"Thanks," I retort, failing to keep the sarcasm out of my voice. "That takes care of my future. What about my present?"

"Lissy Ryder, if you turn yourself over to the wisdom of the universe, you'll find things have a way of working themselves out."

I level my gaze. "People really pay you for this kind of spiritual guidance?"

She nods. "Enough to buy vacation homes in Maui, Aspen, and Sagaponack."

"Sweet." My wheels start to turn and I'm trying to come up with a reason that Deva might need to bring me along to the Hamptons or Hawaii when I notice that she's staring at me. I mean, she really, really sizes me up, like she's checking me for blackheads or nits or something. I feel self-conscious all of a sudden. I touch my face. "Do I have boogies?"

With the hint of a smile, she continues giving me the whale eye. Seems like she's having a debate inside her own head. After sixty extremely awkward seconds, she appears to have come to a conclusion. "I may have something that will help. If I give it to you, you must promise to use it carefully."

I shrug. "Sure, whatever." The more amenable I am here,

the more likely she is to let me camp out in her extra bedroom in Aspen. I haven't been skiing in years! But I'll probably need new snow pants, so that's a dilemma. Not insurmountable but—

"Give me five minutes." While Deva goes downstairs to her shop, I find a palatial bathroom where I dry-heave a couple of times. When I'm done, I inspect myself for damages. Oh, my Lord, I could go swimming in my pores right about now, and my crow's-feet have crow's-feet! Also? I have a not so fresh feeling that I'm hoping stems from having slept under a yak pelt. I splash cold water on my face (and other areas) and then blot with a big, nubby piece of cloth I assume is a towel, although maybe it's some kind of ancient fertility rag; it's not so clear in a place like this. My dress is in here, too, so I slip out of the Ikat robe and leave it by the side of the massive sunken tub. The Spanx are in shreds. She can keep those.

Deva greets me when I exit the bathroom. She hands me a small brown vial about the size of an airplane bottle of gin. Ugh, gin. I do not want to think about liquor right now. "What is it?" I ask.

Deva cups the bottle like it's some kind of precious gift. "This is a powerful elixir. You should only drink a drop at a time. Do you understand? It's crucial that you're very, very careful."

"What does it do?" After the whole wheatgrass debacle, you can't blame a girl for being skeptical.

"This is an ancient Incan tonic that, when used properly, will imbue you with a sense of clarity, purpose, and inner peace. An old shaman taught me how to blend it on my last spiritual quest to Machu Picchu. The fluid's distilled from the seeded flora indigenous to the high jungle, such as the *Lupinus mutabilis* and pteridophytes, which, now that I'm thinking about it, isn't a flower or seed so much as a vascular crypto-gam, in which case—"

Noting that she's losing my attention, Deva tries to press the bottle into my hand. I must seem dubious, so she grudgingly adds, "This will cure your hangover and help your complexion, Lissy Ryder."

I grab the vial and stuff it in my bag. "Sold!"

As I have many things to avoid thinking about, I decide it's time to motor. When I get to the front door, I turn and tell her, "See you later, Deva. Thanks for everything and . . ." I suddenly feel a flash of empathy for the weird little hippie girl with the stringy hair and the back brace and the big mitts, just trying to eat her lunch in peace. ". . . I'm sorry about the corn dog thing. That was uncalled-for and I apologize."

The damnedest thing is?

I think I actually mean it.

My mother picks me up at the station, greeting me with an enormous tumbler of sweet tea. Even though my thirst is Saharan, I take tentative sips for fear that I'll see it again all over the seats of her Volvo SUV. When we arrive home, she wants to help me plot revenge against everyone who shunned me. (As it is, I suspect Books Fatty's mom is about to be iced right out of the garden club.) I appreciate Mamma's enthusiasm but I'm desperate for a nap, so I escape to my room instead.

I try to lie down but the bed's spinning, so I sit up again. My thoughts are racing, despite my attempts to avoid thinking about the night. I cue up my Whitesnake playlist and dock my iPod, hoping that music will soothe my soul and quiet my head. David Coverdale's mournful wailing on "Ain't No Love in the Heart of the City" perfectly captures my mood right now. Ain't no love for Lissy. I'm trying not to be all "Self-Pity, Party of One," but the past twenty-four hours have been more mind-altering than Jack and Jäger.

When I recounted events to Mamma, she said the problem was that everyone at the reunion was jealous of me. I like the sound of that, but if I'm being brutally honest with myself, I can't fathom how that might be true. Three months ago, yes, absolutely, but now?

Especially given the awesome lives they're all living?

What do they possibly envy? My best friend who bails on me? My loving husband and his hottie? My newfound ability to pack on half a pound per day? The four hundred dollars LissCom has thus far raked in?

Before I can ponder further, I have to dry-heave again. As I race to the bathroom, I knock into my bookshelf and I hear all the touchstones of my glorious youth clatter to the floor as I hug the bowl.

When I return to my bedroom, I begin to right the fallen items. One of the pieces on the floor is an old diary. When I pick it up, I notice Debbie's name, and right there in black and white, I've recounted the whole corn dog incident. I'm all self-congratulatory on the page, like I accomplished something really great that day. I sink onto my bed and start to read while David Coverdale croons over whether or not this is love.

Six hours later the sun is low in the sky and I feel sick. Only this time it's not the boxed wine. I understand now what everyone was so mad about at the reunion. These events are going to be forever burned in my mind now.

Deva's right—I wasn't nice. To anyone.

The things I thought were hilarious at seventeen are decidedly less so at thirty-seven. I'm not sure I even meant to be so cutting half the time; doling out well-timed retorts was the easiest way to hold on to my power. As my mom told me on more than one occasion, "Fear's more powerful than love." She may have been even more concerned about my social status than I was.

I lean back against the headboard and I catch a glimpse of myself in the mirror, all hollow-eyed and middle-aged beneath a poster of a greased David Coverdale.

Pathetic.

I'm about to call to Mamma and invite her to my pity party, but then I remember what Deva gave me. Bad as I feel both mentally and physically, I'm willing to try anything right now.

I dig around in my purse until I find the vial. I take a tentative whiff and I smell . . . root beer schnapps? I carefully unscrew the lid and tip it back. The rubber stopper permits only one tiny bead of fluid to struggle free and land on my tongue.

Whoa!

The drop travels through my system with the intensity of a rifle blast and the fire of nine thousand tequila shooters.

Definitely not root beer schnapps.

I wait a few minutes for my clarity, purpose, and inner peace, or at the very least, to stop wanting to pray to a porcelain god. Yet there's something strangely appealing about the fluid, so I take another wee swig. My mouth feels oddly alive and my shoulders less tense as I swallow the second drop.

I repeatedly ingest minute amounts of the potion, and each time I do, I feel less queasy and my thoughts are quieted.

Maybe I'm being hypersensitive about the night, and maybe what's in my diary isn't so bad after all. Kid stuff. No big deal.

Each time I look in the mirror, the image is somehow softened and my edges seem smoothed. This shit's got to be a hallucinogen, because I swear I look younger. Too bad Dr. Amy Childs is a jerk who doesn't want to grow her business. The three of us could sell the bejesus out of this stuff to cosmetic manufacturers. The notion of Incan Pepto-Bismol/Xanax is genius.

Deva, I say to my reflection, *you've completely redeemed yourself for the wheatgrass.*

Over the course of the next hour, I end up chugging about half of the bottle. I'd have finished the whole thing, but I'm so, so sleepy. I'm not sure I've attained inner peace, but I'm borderline euphoric. Plus, the bed has stopped spinning enough for me to take a nap.

So there's that.

CHAPTER FIVE
Time May Change Me

I wake up to the sun illuminating a swath of David Cover-dale's bare chest, just like God intended. I feel a million times better than I did yesterday. I've noticed that as I get older, my hangovers tend to last more than a day, which is completely unfair. You'd think with age and experience one's liver would function more efficiently, but, sadly, that's not the case.

I sit up and try to work the kinks out. Surprisingly, there are no kinks. None. I'm not even bothered by my high-maintenance elbow, which I screwed up from so many years on the tennis court. I practice a couple of backhands and I have total freedom of movement. This is great! Maybe I'll lob a couple of balls against a backboard today at the park. Or, more likely, play Wii Tennis. Either way, it's nice for my joint not to be sore for once.

I immediately begin looking for the Incan tonic I placed by

the bed last night, but as I search, I realize I'm not actually nauseous and I don't need it. I'm not spinny, I'm not achy, and my head's no longer hosting a ten-piece brass band composed entirely of fourth graders. My hangover is officially Audi 5000! Yay!

When I hop out of bed, my pants fall down. Oh, nice job, Lululemon. You shell out ninety-eight bucks for a pair of bottoms and they don't even last a year? Granted, I may have been taxing the elastic lately, but still. Double-plus uncool. I end up rolling the top and having the waistband rest on my hips.

While I poke around for my iPhone—where is that damn thing?—I hear the familiar sounds of my parents fighting. They're extra-shouty today. Something about a car? I sigh. Just another day in paradise.

I hear the consecutive slamming of front and side doors, meaning my dad's off to a twelve-plus-hour day practicing patent law and my mom's off to . . . well, probably Oakbrook Center. Every shopkeeper at the mall knows her by name. Seriously, it's like she's a conquering hero when she walks through Neiman Marcus with minions running up to her displaying jewelry, handbags, and calfskin boots. I used to be so impressed by that, but now I'm not sure it's so great.

I sort through the covers and look under the bed for the phone. Nope, not there. I can't seem to find my Louis bag (not a Birkin, but not bad, thanks to Mamma) and I suspect it's in there. So now I have to go for the nuclear option—calling myself from a landline to find my purse and my phone.

My perfect pink Princess phone still lives on my desk, so I pick up the receiver and dial my cell. I don't hear my ringtone (Warrant's "Cherry Pie," of course) and my voice mail doesn't kick in, either. I probably forgot the whole shootin' match on the train yesterday and by now some little jackass like Charlotte has sent nine million texts about how Justin Bieber makes her feel tingly in her underpants.

Fucking Bieber.

Can someone explain to me why music icons have changed so dramatically in the past twenty-five years? When I was Charlotte's age, Jon Bon Jovi made me swoon, largely because he looked like a *man*. The way he moved . . . the way he sang . . . Maybe he had long hair, but there was no mistaking the testosterone that simply oozed out of him. He was a true rock star. Girls threw their underwear at him when he was onstage. What do they throw at the Biebs? Their retainers? Their Girl Scout merit badges? That little boy is probably still smooth as a Ken doll down there. I mean, there were no LesbiansWhoLookLikeBonJovi Tumblr accounts back then.

Okay, there might be now, but definitely not then.

Speaking of music, where's my iPod? Maybe I'm still a *little* hungover, because I seem to have misplaced everything. I toss the room and still can't find it. I do run across Duke's old class ring that I lost a million years ago, though, and it gives me great pleasure to throw it in the garbage. The ring lands with a satisfying thunk.

Fortunately, my room is a living time capsule, so I quickly locate a metal mix tape and snap it in my Hello Kitty cassette player. Jani Lane comes blasting out of the old speakers sounding as fine as he did twenty years ago. (RIP, you magnificent bastard.) I feel a world better today than I did at this time yesterday, so I dance around while I make the bed.

I'm your sweet cherry piii-iii-iie, yeah!

As I boogie I have to keep yanking up my pants, and I still can't find a damn thing in here. I bet my mother had her housekeeper clean my room while I was asleep—she's famous for orchestrating that kind of thing, like that time she sent her gardener to rip out all the daisies I planted on my condo balcony because she thought they were "the kinda flowahs poor people grow."

I figure I'm probably not going to wake up fully until I wash the stink of yak pelt off me, so I quit searching. I peel off my clothes and step into the shower, letting the warm water rinse all of Saturday's shortcomings right off of me.

Oh, how funny is this? Mamma must have found a bottle of Gee, Your Hair Smells Terrific on the Internet to cheer me up. (I recently introduced her to eBay, and Daddy? *Not happy.*)

God, I've missed this shampoo. I squeeze a big glob into my hand and work it into a rich lather. One whiff and I feel like I'm back in the day, rollin' down the hall with the Belles at my side and crowds parting like the Red Sea, exactly like they depict in so many cheesy teen movies. It's curious how one little smell can trigger such a rush of memories, isn't it? I inhale deeply and can't help but smile. The Lissy Ryder whose hair was scented like gardenias and saffron and cinnamon would never have a drink tossed on her. No one would set her business card on fire. Nobody dared ignore *that* Lissy Ryder . . . no matter how much she might deserve it.

I'm hesitant to rinse and come back to the present, but eventually the water gets cold and I have no choice. Yet as I hose off, I notice how much better my skin looks today. Note to self: Call Deva. Whatever that potion was, I want more.

I wrap myself in a gigantic pink towel and run a comb through my damp hair. The shampoo must contain some stripping chemical that modern products lack, because I swear I look more blond right now. My hair seems longer and curlier too, but that's probably because I'm desperately overdue for a trim.

I wipe the steam from the mirror and I have to blink a few

times. Is it just me or is my complexion extra creamy and rosy right now? The pores are smaller and the lines are practically nonexistent. I must have desperately needed fourteen hours of uninterrupted sleep, because I feel thoroughly refreshed.

Back in my room, I slip into a simple cardi and T-shirt. I rummage through the laundry basket and find a pair of jeans. I know I haven't worn anything denim in a few months, so I suspect my mom bought me some in a bigger size and slipped them in here so I wouldn't feel like an abject failure. But I'm working in the garage today and I don't want to get chilly, so I'll give them a try. As I slide them on, I'm dying over the criminally high waistband, which hits me about an inch below the bra line. I've seen Jessica Simpson embracing this trend in magazines lately and I just can't get behind them. They're total mom jeans, which, ew! Hello, AC Slater called; he wants his Cavariccis back!

And yet . . .

I regard myself with a critical eye.

Is it just me or do these mom jeans look *frigging fantastic*? I check myself out from the front and back. I could wear the highest thong in the world in these pants and no one would ever see a whale tail, no matter how far over I bent. (Not that I currently fit into any of my thongs, but still. Nice to have the option.)

There must be something about the hilariously dated cut, though, because I'm not kidding when I say these shave off thirty pounds. Hell, if I'd known, I'd have worn these to the reunion. I always thought mom jeans gave you butt belly and camel toe but these are outrageously flattering. To think I'd been turning my nose up at Chico's all these years. Suddenly the *Sisterhood of the Traveling Pants* movies make perfect sense—denim *can* possess magical qualities!

I preen for a few more minutes before I finish dressing. I can't find my fringed Burberry scarf (suspect it's being worn to Neiman Marcus today), so I opt for a silly knit one in my old school colors and loop it around and around, hipster style. I toss on a pair of socks and loafers to complete the look.

My makeup bag's in my missing purse, so I duck into my mom's dressing room to help myself to her cache. A few swipes of eyeliner, mascara, blush, and gloss and I'm ready to face the day. I can't believe all the times I've dragged her to Sephora, yet she's all about the old-school stuff like Merle Norman. I guess you can lead a horse to Latisse but you can't make it stop using Great Lash.

As I dust a layer of powder on my nose, I marvel over how tiny my pores seem. Deva just earned herself two free press releases and one Twitter social media campaign.

When I arrive downstairs, I'm pleased to find there's coffee left. As it's a gorgeous fall day, I decide to drink it on the front porch before I start working. I'm pretty sure the industrial platers can wait an extra hour for me to send out the press release on a stunning new breakthrough in torque and tension performance.

I'm two sips in when I see Tommy Barker tooling down the street on his ten-speed. Is he . . . is he delivering newspapers? Oh, dude, I'm so sorry. I feel a real flash of empathy that he's somehow ended up in his old high school job. I'd heard that he'd been killing it on Wall Street after college, but clearly the recession's gotten the better of him if he's back here doing this. No wonder he avoided the reunion.

He tosses the paper on my porch, but I pretend to be very interested in my coffee so we don't have to make eye contact. We're both less embarrassed that way.

I jog down the steps to retrieve the paper and return to the big Adirondack chair. I'm having a little trouble concentrating on the news, because I can't stop peeking at Brian Murphy's parents' house across the street. When he lived at home, he used to sit out front and read the paper every day when weather permitted. I still can't believe I was ever into someone who read the newspaper in high school! Voluntarily, and not just to find movie listings! Seriously, if he and I had ever gone public, I'd have been ousted as head of the Belles faster than you can say "shunned."

I wonder what kept Brian from the reunion? I guess that's a good thing, though. He didn't witness my entire social implosion. Of course, there's a possibility he's got bad blood with me, too, as our brief dalliance ended so badly. I'll probably need to rethink my strategy in discussing business with him. Maybe I'll ask Deva how she'd approach him.

I scan the headlines of the *Chicago Tribune*, looking for mentions of NoCoup.com. I don't see anything about the IPO, but I do notice that Clinton's announced a run for the Democratic nomination for president. Good for her. Yet I hope she does something with her hair if she's elected. I mean, really, should the leader of the free world be running around in *velvet headbands*?

I idly page past the news of another Clarence Thomas hearing—what did that old perv do now?—and editorials on the war, which frankly give me boredom cancer. I skip those entirely.

I'm about to pull open the sports section when ancient Mrs. Camarelli's cat, Snowball, walks across the paper. Why is it that cats can't stand the sight of you until you're reading? I attempt to shoo him off my lap but he keeps nuzzling me and getting fur all over my sweater. He's a sweet cat, but come on!

"Snowball! Snowball, please!" I'm in the process of placing him on the ground when it occurs to me that Snowball went to the Big Litter Box in the Sky about ten years ago.

This is weird.

"You're not Snowball, right? You're some other annoying cat keeping me from getting my news on." I read the tag on his collar. *Snowball Camarelli, 708-555-9989.*

Well, I'll be damned. I guess Mrs. Camarelli somehow found a replacement Snowball, right down to the two different-colored eyes and half a tail.

What are the odds?

But didn't I hear that Mrs. Camarelli herself went to the Big Litter Box in the Sky last year?

Um . . . am I suddenly living an episode of the *X-Files*?

I slowly flip back to the front page of the paper and I read that it's, in fact, *Bill* Clinton who's seeking the presidential nomination. And the paper's dated October 15, 1991 . . . the day before my seventeenth birthday.

What. The. Fuck?

I dash back inside the house, looking for clues or possibly Scully and Mulder. The kitchen calendar is open to October 1991. According to today's entry, my mother's having her hair "frosted" this morning before hitting a noon "Jazzercise class."

Okay, someone is messing with me.

Clearly.

And yet Jodie Foster's on the cover of the *Time* magazine in the half bath, with an article on her directorial debut in the film *Little Man Tate*, which I saw with Kimmy's boyfriend Chet on a night I was mad at Duke during my senior year. (Told you he was a cheater.)

Well, Mamma did discover "the eBay," so it's possible she could procure these items. *Why*, I couldn't say, but it's possible. Maybe she wants to remind me of better times? That's lovely, but kind of esoteric. I don't really understand the no-longer-dead cat business, but snaps for creativity, yes? Was she in the bushes while I read the news, all, "Cue the cat! Cue the cat!"

The *TV Guide* in the den features Sharon Gless and Ar-senio Hall on the cover, both having topped Mr. Blackwell's "Worst Dressed" lists. Michael Westen's mother is done up in clown pants and a tapestry vest, and Arsenio's wearing a tie the color of baby poop. (I know this because Nicole made me try to change a diaper once.) (*Once.*) These two deserve to be on the naughty list, for sure, but I don't have time to parse out the specific nature of their fashion crimes right now.

I'm thoroughly confused and possibly a tiny bit creeped out. This isn't outside of the realm of what Mamma would do to cheer me up, and she's known for being an elaborate plot-ter. Like the time she threw that massive surprise party for Daddy's fiftieth birthday and she hired Frankie Valli to sing but then she forgot to have anyone actually bring Daddy to it. I'll say he was surprised . . . at breakfast the next morning.

Okay, I can see maybe how she'd enlist the services of a not-dead cat, an i-banker, and maybe an auction site to buy a few old magazines.

I guess?

I look around the room, trying to piece this all together, and my eyes come to rest on Daddy's big square Magnavox. (Clever attention to detail, replacing the plasma screen my fa-ther bought before the 2010 Super Bowl.) (Geaux, Saints!)

Still, it's not outside the realm of the possible that Mamma set this all up. I don't quite understand why, and that's a puz-zler, because usually her motives are clear, like when she'd buy me designer jeans a size down from what I normally wore when she was at the height of her passive-aggressivity while I was in high school. (I certainly don't miss her doing *that*.)

But is all of this really her doing?

As I stare at the television, I realize it holds the key. My mother can't control what's broadcast, right? So if this is all one big (confusing) ruse, I'll turn it on and see Matt Lauer and Ann Curry. Easy enough.

I search for the remote and the television slowly fires up. *Today* is indeed on NBC, featuring a prepubescent Katie Couric and a fat Al Roker.

There's no way Katie and Al are in on this, too.

OMG!

WTF!

IDK!

I bolt into the garage, expecting to find my desk, a bunch of balloons, and perhaps a very confused Frankie Valli, but instead I run directly into a hot pink BMW convertible, topped with an enormous red bow.

This car is my birthday present.

In 1991.

Deva, what was in that bottle?

Shell-shocked, I make my way back into the driveway. I'm standing there all dumbfounded when Nicole pulls up, not in a hideous family truckster, but instead in her mom's battered old Ford Taurus.

Did I mention she's *clearly* seventeen again?

I stand there trying not to gawp when Nicole cranks down her window. "Hi, Lissy! We've got to fly or we'll be late for homeroom!"

I slide into the seat next to her and I say nothing, as words currently escape me.

Nicole self-consciously smoothes her miniskirt and poufs her perm. "You look really pretty today, Liss. But, um . . . I thought you said we weren't allowed to wear jeans on Mondays."

That's when it finally sinks in.

This is it.

This is my chance!

Somehow, some way, I've been granted an enormous do-over. I don't know why this happened, but it *did* happen and I'm here now. I have no choice but to roll with it. If I'm back in time, that means all the bad stuff in my future never actually happened. I'm not old, I'm not fat, I'm not dumped, and no one's mad at me.

And maybe all those diary entries that make me seem like the Meanest Mean Girl Who Ever Meaned don't actually exist?

Grappling with this new reality, I search Nicole's face for some kind of clue as to what's next. Yet as I seek her confused brown eyes, I can't help but remember her abandoning me in my hour of need at the reunion. I have no clue if this means that the reunion actually happened or not, but you know how sometimes you wake up from a bad dream and you're all pissed off at the person who wronged you in it? And despite its being a dream and even though, say, your mom's sister Aunt Sissy never *actually* wrote a scathing review of the trendy new Italian bistro you opened, claiming your mozzarella sticks are "on par with the Olive Garden" and that your wine list is "uninspired," you still spend the whole day stewing at her for something that never, ever happened?

That's how I feel about Nicole right now.

"No, Nicole. *I'm* allowed to wear jeans on Mondays. You're not. Now get this heap moving."

Just like that, I slip into the skin that's been waiting almost twenty-one years for me to return.

And it feels so very *right*.

The last twenty-one years were all a dream.

Obviously. That's the only explanation.

All those memories from college and working as a junior-level publicist and getting dumped over MK's pan-Asian twist on scallops?

Just your garden-variety nightmare brought on by mixing Jägermeister and Dexatrim Max over the weekend at a football party. Granted, a highly detailed, Ghost-of-Christmas-Future dream, but one nonetheless. It's like the universe is giving me a heads-up of what's to come and it's not too late! Here's a silver dollar, boy; go buy me a big, frigging goose!

When I see Duke—I mean *Martin*—in the hallway, I don't greet him as enthusiastically as I might have last week, because I'm still pissed off at him for taking that slutty lawyer to the reunion in my dream future.

"Hey, babe." He tries to kiss me as I work my locker combination. I always have used 34-24-26, my ideal measurements. (Why did chicks ever want big hips in the olden days? *So gross*.)

I shrug away from his embrace. "Whatevs."

"What's the matter, Liss?"

He tries to touch my hair and I wriggle away from him and start to walk to English class, with him trailing behind me. Because I've been cold to him all day, he's been nervous and attentive and I can sense a delicate yet important shift in our balance of power. In my awful dream future, he started to lose interest when we were seniors, so I'd get him jealous by breaking up with him and making out with other guys. But now that I sense I can have authority over him by *just being bitchy*? I can do that! I am so going to flip the script. Dismissively, I tell him, "I've got to get to class."

He's all puppy-dog eyes. "Can we talk later?"

I wave him off. "In-box me."

He stops in his tracks and stares at me. "Do what now?"

"Hit me up on Facebook."

"Huh?"

"Or you can just text."

His confusion reminds me that none of this technology is on the market in 1991!

Holy crap, I could invent Facebook before that Michael Cera–looking douche and *I'd* be the scrillionaire! Oprah would have no choice but to be my friend! I vow to pay more attention in my computer class.

Anxious not to give away my get-so-freaking-rich-quick scheme, I tell him, "I said 'I'll smell you later.'" I punctuate this statement with a toss of my gloriously scented hair. I leave him in a cloud of flowers and Tahitian spice.

As I make my way to Miss Beeson's class, I notice all the junior girls admiring how I knotted my scarf. Ten bucks says they show up wearing them that way tomorrow. I give them the vaguest hint of a smile and they all start acting like they just won both showcases on *The Price Is Right*.

Damn, it feels good to be a gangster.

When I get to English, all the Belles are surrounding my empty desk. The whole crew is here—Nicole, Kimmy, April, Tammy—and they're each clad in some variety of pastel miniskirt, slouch socks, and oversize blazer. They take in my jeans and knotty scarf, and when Kimmy starts to ask about them, Nicole makes frantic neck-slashing motions. Kimmy slinks into her chair like a scolded puppy.

Class begins and Miss Beeson instructs us to take out our Jane Austen books. Apparently we're studying *Emma*. Ha! I know *Emma*! I never read it, of course, choosing to cheat off of know-it-all April during the exam back in the dream past. But Gwyneth Paltrow is a national freaking treasure in the dream future and she starred in *Emma*. She won an Oscar and everything! (Yeah, she ruined *Glee* and also that CeeLo song at the Grammy Awards, but that's not important.) Plus, there's no one I love more than Cher Horowitz in the modern-day version called *Clueless*, which I DVR every single time it's broadcast.

(Note to self: Invent DVR. And do it soon, because *90210*'s on at the same time as *Cheers* and no one in my house can figure out how to work the timer on the VHS.)

Miss Beeson asks us, "What's the significance of Mr. Elton framing Harriet's portrait?" She sweeps the room with her gaze. "Anyone? Can anyone answer?"

No one raises their hand, not even Books Fatty. Should I be calling her Books Fatty, I wonder? According to my diary, her nickname didn't go mainstream until the week of the homecoming dance. Plus, she seemed awfully touchy about it in my dream, so maybe I'll just let that one go.

Miss Beeson seems particularly disappointed that no one's participating. She's all deflated in her dumpy skirt and nurse's shoes. (Cher Horowitz would give her a makeover.) (But I don't actually care enough to try.)

"Really, no one knows? Oh. I thought you guys might like this one. Austen's sensibilities normally translate so well into modern times."

Wait . . . isn't that when Elton put Tai's photo in his locker, not because she was classically beautiful, but because Cher snapped the shot? My hand flies up into the air.

Miss Beeson is taken aback by my sudden enthusiasm, but calls on me nonetheless. She seems to be bracing herself. Really? Having to brace oneself? Am I that much of a loose cannon? Is this because I don't want to give her a makeover? Regardless, I say, "The significance is that Emma misinterprets this as a symbol of Elton's, I mean, *Mr. Elton's* affection for Harriet, when really he treasures the portrait because it was Emma's work. It's one of the main conflicts in the movie, er, book."

Miss Beeson looks like she's going to bust her oh-so-polyester buttons. Okay, fine, if I were to give her a makeover—which I won't—we'd start with natural fibers and a keratin treatment. "Very good, Lissy! Very, very good!"

I feel a flush of pleasure that registers somewhere between a strawberry margarita and half a hit of Ecstasy. Wow. Who'd have guessed that positive attention's even more of a rush than negative?

"Who can explain what happens when Emma realizes she's in love with Mr. Knightley?"

I raise my hand again; I'm about to *own* this class. I rattle off a dozen more answers (I have a PhD in Paul Rudd, natch), and when the period ends, everyone's looking at me like I'm a rocket scientist/supermodel and it feels glorious.

That's right, bitches. Beauty *and* brains.

Lissy Ryder just made being smart cool.

Believe it.

Wait until I invent Facebook.

Then we'll see who *truly* reigns over the twentieth reunion.

CHAPTER SIX
But I Can't Trace Time

I kick serious academic ass in all my classes. I zip through questions on the sinking of the Titanic *in World History (thank you, James Cameron), and I completely blow away my speech teacher in a practice debate. (Sixteen dream-future years of spinning bullshit for a living will do that.) What really gives everyone pause is when I detail the process for copper plating in my physics lab.*

Of equal importance is that I'm able to teach the other cheerleaders an amazing hip-hop routine that I call the Super-Liss, which looks suspiciously like that from Soulja Boy, whose baggy pants I'll be suing right off in about nineteen years.

Watch me crank it, watch me roll! SuperLiss, now whoa!

I may not have been the best teenager *before* last week's weirdness, but now I've got this new life on lock. I'm going to capitalize on all that I gleaned from my dream future.

First I plan to take this crazy psychic knowledge and use it to get into a better college than the University of Central Illinois. *Playboy* magazine ranked UCI first in the nation for partying, but academically? They fall somewhere between Hamburger University and barber college. The UCI mascot is a *sloth*, for God's sake. Sloth pride? Um, no. The worst part is that in the dream past I was accepted to UCI only because Daddy called in a favor from his law school buddy who's on the board. So shameful.

"Whatcha doin', honey bunny?" Mamma asks, hovering in my doorway.

What I'm doing is writing down every bit of information I can remember about the dream future, because I plan to find a way to make it pay off. One word . . . Sportbook! I can't wait until I'm eighteen and old enough to go to Vegas!

But . . . even though I'm extra-close with my mom, it's probably best not to share this information for fear of being sent to a shrink. That's always her home-run swing whenever I don't do exactly what she wants—she threatens to enroll me in therapy. Well, that or fat camp.

For now I tell her, "Studying for my Italian test tomorrow." In the dream future, I spend a whole summer bumming around Italy after graduating from UCI and I come back semi-fluent. My teacher was so impressed today when I could say, "*Il mio fidanzato non ha bisogno di sapere*" ("My boyfriend doesn't need to know") with a flawless accent!

She saunters into the room, cocktail in hand, and then putters around, straightening pictures and adjusting trophies before she comes to perch on my bed. She sips her drink and intently watches me. "Well, finish up, 'cause the *Dynasty* reunion is on. Don'tcha want to find out what happened to Alexis and Dex?"

Actually, I already know. Ooh, ooh! Write that down, too!

I say, "I'll be ready in a few."

Mamma doesn't get up. She takes a long pull on her drink. "I jus' worry about you, darlin'. Study too hard and you're gonna get you some wrinkles."

I jot, *Item #37—Invent Botox.*

"I'll be fine," I reply.

She sets her glass on my nightstand and idly fingers the fringe on my bedspread. "Y'all in any classes with June Childs's daughter? Name's Amy? Smart as a whip, but the poor thang's been beat in the face with an ugly stick. Her nose?" She leans in all conspiratorially. "It's shaped like a P-E-N-I-S. Her mamma had to drop out of Jazzercise because she's savin' up for plastic surgery."

At this news, my stomach knots just a little bit. I give her an almost imperceptible nod.

"What about this girl named Brooks? Brooks Paddy? You know her? She's about y'all's age."

There goes my stomach again. I say nothing, keeping my eyes on the page.

"Well, her mamma is in the Junior League with me. Good Lord, that child is fat as the day is long. When the family flew to Washington, D.C., this summer they had to ask the stewardess for one o' them special seat belts. You know, for the O-B-E-S-E. Awful, just awful."

I put down my pen. "Which part, Mamma? The fat part or the being embarrassed on the flight part?"

My mother bristles. "Young lady, I do not care for your tone. All's I'm doin' is tryin' to help you, because you do *not* want to be lahk these girls." When she gets rattled, the South really comes out. Once when Daddy tried to cancel our country club membership because he said the dues were too high, she went from zero to Atlanta burning in point five seconds. (The membership stayed.)

I try to maintain my temper, because trust me, no one wins a fight with my mother; it's best not to even try. Yet I can't stop myself from saying, "What's your point, Mamma? That I don't want to be like them because they're on the honor roll?"

What I don't say is that these girls have committed the cardinal sin of not being pretty enough for Virginia "Ginny" Cavanaugh Jefferson Beaulieu Ryder, top debutante at the Savannah Christmas Cotillion, circa 1971.

From the time I was old enough to hold my own hairbrush, my mother has been grooming me on the importance of grooming. She's always said it doesn't matter what you're like on the inside if folks can't get past your outside.

When I was in grade school, no matter how late I might have been running, I wasn't allowed to leave for the day until my ribbons were tied, my shoes polished, and my cheeks pinked. I remember saying, "Why do I need rouge? I'm six!" and she'd simply reply, "Trust me, darlin'. This is an investment in your future." She even hooked me up with a cheerleading coach in seventh grade to make sure that by the time high school rolled around, there was no way I wouldn't make the squad.

At no point did she ask me if I wanted any of this.

For the most part, I did and I do, but it's nice to be consulted, you know?

She waves her hands in front of her face like she's trying to dry her long, expertly manicured talons. "Oh, honey! Nobody gives a fig what your grades were in high school! What everyone 'members is what you drove and who you dated and if you won you some crowns! And once you get to college, it's all 'bout being a Kappa or a Tri-Delt, 'cause that's how you land the best husband. The right man'll set you up for life!"

I roll my eyes—like I haven't heard a million times how she was the belle of every ball and how she dated the lieutenant governor's son. Instead of engaging, I concentrate on my list. What am I missing? I do a quick, seated Pilates stretch to help my blood flow. Hey . . . Pilates! I pick up my pen and write, *Item #38—Invent Pilates*.

I chew on the tip of my pen while I concentrate.

Item #39—Invent GPS.

What else might make me rich, rich, rich in the future?

Item #40—Invent LOLCats.

"You're getting all squinchy again right there." She taps me above the bridge of my nose with the lip of her glass.

I duck away from her. "That's because I'm thinking."

She brushes my hair out of my face. "Well, maybe you should think less, darlin'. After all, your job as a young lady is to be attractive, not smart. Trust me, boys do not line up for the clever girls. No one ever says, 'Oh, my—check out the big IQ on that one!' "

At some point during our conversation my dad materialized in the doorway and now he's hopping mad. "Really, Ginny?" he sputters. "It's one thing to insist on rewarding piss-poor academic performance with *a brand-new sports car*, but to hear you actually *encourage* our daughter not to try? To say it's more important to be attractive than intelligent? What kind of message are you sending?"

Mamma deliberately sips her drink before she responds. "The right one." Which comes out sounding like *raaaaaaaaaaht*.

Daddy is seething mad. "What do you want, for her to still be living here twenty years from now because she never learned how to work hard enough to hold a job? Help me out,

Ginny, because I really don't understand your warped set of values."

My mother leans back against my David Coverdale poster and crosses her arms. She draws back into herself, not unlike a cobra about to strike.

In a voice as chilly as the little shards of ice floating on top of her martini, she says, "George, soon as anyone in this household gives one hot goddamn about what you *thank*, we'll be sure and let you know." Then she winks at me.

It's the most terrifying wink anyone has ever seen.

All the blood drains from my dad's face, and for a second I kind of hope he'll fight back. But instead of exploding, he takes a few deep breaths before retreating to his library.

My mother turns back to me and gives me a victorious smile. "Now, honey bunny, let's talk about homecomin'. Forget your silly ol' test. I say we go shoppin' for gowns tomorrow!"

S ave for the usual tension with my folks last night, this has been one of the best weeks of my life. The Belles are looking at me with newfound respect, Duke/Martin's mooning over me like he's completely lovestruck, and I've aced every single test, quiz, and homework assignment. And my new (old?) convertible? Every girl wants to be me and every guy wants to be with me.

I am unstoppable.

So, if and when I hit my twenty-year reunion, I'm showing up with an amazing job, a fat checking account, a doting husband, and Michelle Obama arms. Bank on that.

I'm in the ladies' slicking on one more coat of the same shade of bloodred lipstick Donna Martin wore on last week's *90210*. Debbie (I mean Deva—no, I mean . . . crap, this is so confusing) comes into the bathroom and makes a beeline for a stall. We don't have any classes together and it's a huge school. I only ever run into her when she's burning herbs in the basketball gym. As we're smack in the middle of football season, this is the first time I've seen her since my dream.

I monkey around with my hair and give serious deliberation to having bangs cut. I'll focus-group the Belles on this, with the caveat being if I opt for them, there's a moratorium on anyone else having a trim for at least a month.

Yes.

That's exactly what I'll do.

I forgot the rush that comes from wielding this kind of influence. I'm the trendsetter, the tastemaker. What I say goes. I even have enough cachet to make everyone listen to hair metal again if I were to publicly deem it cool. Seriously, if I came to school in a Van Halen tee tomorrow (which I totally own) it'd be 1984 all over again. At the moment, no one can shut up about the local band the Smashing Pumpkins, whose lead singer, if my dream future is correct, is cue-ball bald and wears no eyeliner whatsoever! Blech.

Somehow, though, I kind of want to keep Axl and Tommy and Kip and David and the rest of them all to myself. So much of what I do lately is subject to public scrutiny that I'm starting to feel oddly private about a few things.

I guess what I'm saying is, I have the power to make "fetch" happen . . . but I choose not to exercise it.

I hear a toilet flush and Debbie meanders out in one of her oddball kimono shirts, all rigid and upright in her back brace. I give her a quick nod—a serious social coup for any non-Belle—and then I brush on another layer of Great Lash.

Debbie grins back at me. She methodically washes her big

hands and then dries them on the scratchy brown paper towels known exclusively to public lavatories everywhere. Then she just stands there real close to me, waiting to catch my eye. When I glance over, she says—all matter-of-fact, like she's asking me about the math assignment—"Have you achieved clarity yet?"

The only sound is that of my mascara clattering into the sink. Every ounce of my blood has completely frozen. "*Excuse me?*" I whisper.

"Your journey, Lissy Ryder. How's it going? I've been meaning to catch up with you all week, but ironically chemistry's giving me trouble this time around."

"What? I mean . . . how?" I feel my knees go weak and I have to steady myself against the wall. Because if this isn't Debbie doing the usual talking out of her ass, I have just fallen into a massive metaphysical wormhole. (One of the *Real Housewives of New Canaan* has a metaphysics coach, which is why I'm familiar with the concept.)

"The Incan tonic, of course."

I gasp for breath as the wind rushes out of me. "Are you telling me that was all *real*? That I didn't have some bullshit dream like on *Dallas*? Are you Patrick Duffy or something?"

Now Debbie seems confused. "No, Lissy Ryder. I'm *Deva*. We've met. Don't you remember—I brought you to my place after the reunion? The wheatgrass? The Ikat robe?"

I nod numbly as I slide down the wall and sink to the floor. "The tonic did more than fill in crow's-feet."

"Far more."

I rest my face in my palms for a moment, not even considering what that might do to my makeup. The whole room feels like it's swirling around me in a blur of baby pink and mint green tiles. I try to focus my eyes on the paper-towel holder while I collect my wits. I'm not sure if I want to barf or scream.

"Does this mean I don't get to invent Facebook?"

Deva shrugs. "Can you do it in the next couple of weeks?"

"Probably not. The squad's got to learn three new routines before homecoming, and I have an English midterm."

Deva pats my shoulder. "That's unfortunate. By the way, I saw your squad practice the SuperLiss. Derivative, but I like it. Reminds me of a Zulu dance I saw in sub-Saharan Africa. Here's a thought—what if the girls bared their breasts like the tribeswomen? That would feel more authentic for me. Maybe go with a beaded skirt? Oh, you've not lived until you see Zulu beadwork! So intricate! So colorful! So—"

I stand up and begin to pace. "Are you planning on explaining what happened or should we keep making small talk? 'Nice weather today! And how 'bout them LT Lions? Think we'll beat Hinsdale Central at the homecoming game?'"

Deva shakes a large finger at me. "You're still funny, Lissy Ryder."

"And *you're* still freaking me out. Can we discuss all of this"—I sweep my arms around the ladies' room—"before I have a panic attack and then find out Ativan's not yet been invented?"

It takes a good half an hour of tangents, diversions, and exotic travelogues until I finally wrestle the whole story out of Deva. Basically, the fluid she gave me has the ability to alter time. Each drop of the tonic is equal to one hour in the past. With the amount I ingested, I should be here in 1991 for two more weeks, as I've already been here a week. When the potion wears off, I'll wake up exactly when and where I was when I drank it.

"How could you know I'd drink half the bottle? You told me to use it sparingly," I protest.

"Lissy Ryder, you're as predictable as the tides. Since when do you listen to what anyone tells you?" Deva gives me a playful chuck on the arm.

Touché.

"But what am I supposed to do for the next two weeks?" I ask. "If I'm just going back to my miserable life, what was the whole point of this exercise? To show me how awesome everything used to be? To make sure I don't have enough time to invent Facebook?"

Deva seems a little disappointed in my question. "How many times do I have to tell you, Lissy Ryder? The point is to achieve clarity, purpose, and inner peace." She narrows her eyes. "You do realize your journey's not about ripping off that nice Mark Zuckerberg, right?"

I shrug. "I was still kind of hoping I could make it work."

This succeeds in finally rattling her. "Do you need me to spell this out? Lissy Ryder, we're here—*you're* here—because you're soul-sick. There's a dark cloud around you. I went out on a limb for you because I've never seen anyone who generates worse karma."

Likely because she's never met Mamma.

"Well, what am I supposed to do about it?"

"You're meant to take a long, hard look at your past. What do you notice? What might you change about yourself? What works? What doesn't? What's the source of why you are the way you are? Right now, it's not too late to make a difference. Consider this, Lissy Ryder: A spaceship can go one degree off course and that's nothing, right? Just one small tilt of the space steering wheel and you're right back on track. But the farther the ship travels from where it veered off course, the harder it is to recover the original orbital trajectory. At thirty-seven, righting all your old wrongs is an almost insurmountable obstacle. But at seventeen? That's nothing. Bear in mind, though, that the nature of time is fluid, Lissy Ryder. Place one finger in the water and the ripples impact the whole lake. Aim for subtle, not grand gestures, okay? Please don't try to assassinate any presidents or anything."

I feel like Keanu Reeves learning about the Matrix. My brain is throbbing and I still may or may not revisit the Cheerios I had for breakfast. "Let me get this straight—what you're saying is, if I want to have a good life in the future, I have to make small changes to what I screwed up in the past?"

"Bingo."

"Bingo?" What is it with her and "bingo"?

"Bingo. It's exactly that easy."

"Whoa."

Deva begins to walk to the door. "Any more questions? Because I should probably get to calculus now. No matter how many times I return, I never can quite master antiderivatives. Very embarrassing in my line of work."

I catch up to her. "The tonic—how'd you know how to make it? The shaman taught you?"

Deva has to nod with her whole body to compensate for the brace. "Right. Bob at Machu Picchu is highly skilled with ancient Incan potions. He's a real mixologist. You should try his lime rickeys! He says the secret is using fresh juice, but I—"

"The shaman's name is *Bob*?"

"It may be a nickname. I'll ask him next time."

Then I remember some boring History Channel show that Duke/Martin insisted we watch right before he dumped me. "I thought the Incans vanished entirely in the fifteen hundreds. They all died out or something."

Deva pats me on the shoulder. "The Incans aren't dead; they just went home."

"Hey!" I bark. My voice echoes off the tile. "You swiped that line from Tommy Lee—not the hot one—in *Men in Black*. That movie's not out for another six years! I thought we weren't supposed to steal stuff from the future."

Deva chuckles. "No, Lissy Ryder. *I'm* allowed to steal stuff from the future. You're not."

CHAPTER SEVEN
Turn and Face the Strange Changes

"Lissy? Are you okay?"

"Huh?

I snap out of my reverie and glance up into the concerned face of Brian Murphy. He's standing next to my car, yet I didn't even notice him walking up to me. My heart inadvertently speeds up for a second until my head reminds me that dorks are *not* sexy-in-a-bookish-sort-of-way.

"I asked if you were okay. You've been idling in the driveway for a while. Saw you from my bedroom window and couldn't figure out what you were doing out here." When he smiles, I notice how white and straight his teeth are. I guess all those years of wearing his Nerdzilla headgear finally paid off.

"Oh, I was . . ." I've been in a complete fog since my conversation with Deva. Honestly, I don't even recall the drive home. Last I knew, I was ditching seventh period and heading to my car. I got in, popped the top, cranked the tunes, and then just drove for a very long time.

Brian's all attentive and expectant, so I have no choice but to answer. "I was just listening to some . . ." I stop myself before I finish the sentence.

Brian nods appreciatively. "*Slip of the Tongue?* Not bad, but not Whitesnake's best. They lost something vital when Vivian Campbell left the band in 'eighty-seven."

I don't respond, so he takes that as an invitation to continue. "Is Whitesnake still a rock powerhouse? Yes, of course, but Vivian? He brought such an interesting element to the guitar riffs, a complexity. Real layered sound, you know? Here, listen to this." Brian leans across the open passenger side and fast-forwards to "Kitten's Got Claws." "Lacks the nuance of previous work, right? It's missing that certain something that makes them quintessentially Whitesnake."

I sit up straight in my seat. I instantly forget to be distracted about what Deva told me and I disregard the fact that I'm too cool to admit to loving this music. "I know, right? Steve Vai's talented, but he's no Vivian Campbell."

Glancing over both shoulders, he crouches down and I catch a hint of the sweet tang of his Ralph Lauren aftershave. If the nineties had a scent, it would be the woody, mossy whiff of Polo, applied liberally, and then applied again for good measure. "I hear he's been talking to Def Leppard. Rumor has it he may join."

"*Shut up.*"

Holy crap, Vivian's been with Lep now for so many years that I forgot there was ever a point he *wasn't* with them.

Brian leans against the passenger side, all chatty and casual-like. Other than Deva, he seems to be the one person I don't intimidate. Hmm. "My uncle works for Geffen and he's in on all the dirt. Total insider. Speaking of, I have some news that'll blow your mind. Ready for this? David Coverdale and Jimmy Page are secretly working on a collaboration. My cousin just got back from the Abbey Road studio in London and he brought me a track."

I throw off my safety belt and fly out of the front seat. *Coverdale/Page!* I love that album! It's one of my favorites and it doesn't even come out until 1993! "Then what are we waiting for? Let's go give it a listen."

Brian seems taken aback, but pleasantly. "Er . . . sure! Let's go."

In my dream future, which I guess is my actual future, this is the time of year when Brian and I had our little fling, only the circumstances were slightly different. Originally, last weekend was when Duke/Martin was sick in my car and he came over that Sunday and got kind of shouty and aggressive. Which made me like him all the more, according to my diary. (I'm really starting to question my teenage value system, FYI.)

Brian came out to calm everyone down and then he made Duke/Martin leave, politely but firmly. I was so impressed with Brian's fearlessness and command of the situation that we ended up hanging out for a couple of weeks, until I realized being with him would send me to social no-man's-land.

But I didn't even *see* Duke/Martin over this last weekend, because I'm still kind of mad at him for his behavior in my dream future, which is actually my real future. Regardless, that means that he never *actually* threw up in my car.

Ergo . . . I didn't saddle him with "Duke," so he's not going to resent my giving him a nickname for the next twenty-plus years.

Which means I've *already* made strides to fixing my future!

Yes!

Maybe this whole time-travel dealie really is a blessing and not some cruel joke perpetrated by a meddling hippie with large paws and an unhealthy amount of nudie art in her apartment. (I'm still probably going to call him Duke in my head, though, because every time someone says "Martin" I assume they're talking about Martin Lawrence.)

We cross the street to Brian's house. His place is decorated so differently from my house, even though they're laid out pretty similarly . . . which I discovered the last time, when I'd routinely sneak up to his room in the dark to make out with him. (But that's not happening this time because I'm all Team Duke.)

Whereas our central-stair Colonial is all about big vases of silk flowers and fussy couches and oil paintings, his central-stair Colonial looks like a Toys "R" Us on Black Friday. There are balls and army men and Barbie dolls on almost every surface. Crumbling LEGO kingdoms top each coffee table, and scattered bits of puzzles poke out beneath the tall pile of the living room shag rug. It's not dirty, but it is total chaos.

We step into his cheerful kitchen and I spot Brian's mom outside with a couple of the smaller kids. Their backyard is overrun with swing sets and sandboxes. I watch her shoo Snowball away from the sand, shouting, "No! That's not for you! Bad kitty!"

Brian grabs a couple of Cokes out of a fridge that appears to be constructed entirely of shitty finger paintings.

Looking back, I recall him living in a houseful of siblings. And I recall being superannoyed by them, particularly when they'd run through the sprinklers and squeal. Like nails on a chalkboard, that sound.

"How many brothers and sisters do you have again?" I ask.

He's puzzled for a second, but I play it off like Lissy Ryder can't be bothered to know the comings and goings of this sleepy little burg, even though we've lived across the street from each other since third grade, rather than the truth that Lissy Ryder just got here from the future and struggles to remember anything that wasn't explicitly posted in her diary, so please don't call the authorities. Brian replies, "Four. I'm the oldest. The first set of twins—Diana and Holly—are nine, and the younger set—Paul and Greg—are six."

I shudder inadvertently. "Your poor mother."

Brian cocks his head and when he does, his eyes catch a swath of afternoon sun. I thought they were brown, but with the light on them, I see they're more of a lake-water green with tiny speckles of gold. Did I ever notice this before? I suspect I may have. "How do you figure?"

"She's got to deal with all those brats! My God, what a nightmare! I mean, they're sticky and loud and they ask a million questions. Ugh. Who wants that?" My skin crawls at the notion of being saddled with so many progeny.

Brian grins again. "I'm pretty sure my parents like their kids. They're a little worried about paying for five sets of college tuition, so they're careful how they spend, but otherwise, we have no plans to sell 'em on the black market."

"That's a damn shame," I reply. "Healthy Caucasian kids like that would fetch enough to fund an Ivy League education."

Aw, crap, what'd I just say? I'm supposed to make small changes and be nice, and the first thing I do is suggest he sell his siblings into white slavery. Smooth, Lissy. Real smooth.

But Brian just laughs and the moment passes. While he

fills a couple of glasses with ice, his two brothers run screeching through the kitchen to the family room like a thundering herd of asshole buffalos, LEGOs toppling in their wake. I clamp my hands over my ears but Brian is completely unaffected. "We call that 'joyful noise' around here. You learn to tune it out." I smile and nod, hands still firmly in place over my ears. He peels a hand back. "But you're clearly not into it, so let's head upstairs."

We gather up our drinks and a bowl of butter pretzels and exit the kitchen. We arrive at the landing in front of his door on the third floor and he opens it with a flourish. "Welcome to the jungle."

Brian's room is still exactly the way I'd described it in my diary—organized and meticulous without being sterile or lacking in personality. It's kind of cozy in here, with slanted ceilings, and it's refreshingly clean for a boy's room. Unlike Duke's room, which smells like sweat socks and is plastered with bikini sluts lounging on Lamborghinis, this place is populated by neatly aligned books and model airplanes and *Star Wars* memorabilia. (I'm glad he has a solid eight years of bliss before the whole enterprise is ruined by Jar Jar Binks in *The Phantom Menace*.)

There's a hilariously boxy Macintosh computer on his desk and he seems very proud of it. Oh, honey. Wait until you see the iPad. For a moment I consider asking him how one might go about building a complex social networking site but I'm not sure how to describe it except that it involves "likes" and "dislikes" and something called Farmville.

His desk overlooks the street, and now that the leaves are falling off the (huge, pre–Dutch elm disease) elm tree, I notice he has a view right into my bedroom. I'm not sure how I feel about that.

Half of Brian's room is devoted to high fidelity—he's got a turntable, a CD player, a dual cassette deck, and, what really impresses me, a reel-to-reel, all wired through a stereo receiver and cabled to a pricey pair of Bose speakers with a subwoofer. "That's some setup you have here," I tell him. Duke has only a Walkman, a boom box, and an unfortunate boy band fixation. (Color Me Sadd.)

"I'm really lucky," he tells me. "I could never afford all of this on my allowance. My uncle gives me all his castoffs and the swag he gets from vendors. Even used, his equipment is better than most consumers could buy in a store right now."

"Lemme check out your collection," I say, brushing past him. The whole wall by the desk is filled with music on various mediums, too, including lots of genres outside of metal. "Elvis Presley? Lame!"

Brian arches his brow. "You are so wrong."

Well, *that's* refreshing. No one tells me I'm wrong. Ever.

He points to various albums, explaining. "You can thank Elvis for being the grandfather of rock and roll and for blurring the color lines in popular music. Without Elvis, you wouldn't have had blues go mainstream, which led to R and B and eventually hip-hop. More important, without Elvis, there'd be no Beatles. Without the Beatles, no Rolling Stones; no Stones, no Zeppelin; no Zeppelin, no Aerosmith; no Aerosmith, no Van Halen; no Van Halen, no grunge. Shall I continue?"

"Only if you want to bore me to death." But I say it kind of nicely and he seems amused. Brian launches into a whole genealogy of popular music, demonstrating which sounds spurred new music, and when he's done, he's mapped out an entire tree with most of the limbs stemming from Elvis. I grudgingly give the King of Rock and Roll some props.

(But not for the teddy bear song. Tell me that wasn't beyond creepy.)

We listen to his uncle's bootleg and it's everything I remember, too. We spend the afternoon waxing poetic about
music, with me sprawled in his beanbag chair and him at his
desk so he can access his neatly categorized wall of sound. His
deep and abiding love for Elvis/his pelvis aside, I'm surprised
at how similar our tastes and opinions are, like how we both
prefer the Scorpions to Ratt (despite Ratt's glam-metal fa-
cade), and how Mutt Lange's vision is why Def Leppard's *Hys-
teria* sold as many copies as it has. We're both passionately in
love with the movie *Spinal Tap*, too, and in the middle of entirely different thoughts, we keep shouting, "No, we're not
going to fucking do Stonehenge!"

After Brian plays a retrospective of all my favorites, he
starts sampling clips from the "second wave" phenomenon out
of Norway that his uncle sent him. Scandinavia's having a real
hard-rock resurgence here in 1991. The music's more thrash/
speed punk, and way, way darker than the candy-coated, sexy
hair metal that I prefer. While I'm not a huge fan of the beat,
I'm charmed listening to Brian gush about the Viking-black-
death rock ten feet away from where he sleeps on sheets patterned with Wookies and droids.

Our tastes truly diverge only when we broach the subject
of Nirvana. And, trust? In 1991, *everyone's* talking about
Nirvana.

"How are you not enthralled by them?" he argues. "The
lyrics, the raw emotion, the power behind the guitar licks, the
way they're so stripped down—they're the very essence of
rock and roll without having to rely on theatrics."

I counter, "Pfft, I'm all about the theatrics. Plus, how are
you able to get past that each one of them is in desperate need

of a shower? Or if that's not anarchy or punk rock enough for them, maybe they could jump in a fountain or something."

Brian tsk-tsks me. "Lissy, hate to say it, but you're way off on this. Nirvana's going to be one of those bands everyone's still talking about in twenty years. Cobain is the father of an entirely new genre and no one's ever going to forget him. I'll wager in fifty years, some other nerd will find himself with a pretty girl in his room and he'll impress her by explaining the cultural significance of *Nevermind*."

He is *so* not winning this argument . . . even if he did just imply that I'm pretty. I mean, I know I'm way cute, but it's lovely to hear those words coming from him. So I say, "Ha! And then when the nerd ends up taking his cousin to prom, he'll be all, 'How'd I blow it with the hot chick?' "

The phone rings and thirty seconds later someone comes chugging up the stairs. His mom, Priscilla, bursts through the door wearing a dirty apron and carrying a drippy wooden spoon.

"Oh, thank God!"

Brian jumps out of his seat. "What the *heck*, Mom? The kids okay?"

She has to catch her breath for a second before blurting, "Lissy's mother"—*gasp*—"called and said she saw her come over here a couple of hours ago." *Gasp, gasp.* "She said to make sure you kids weren't having sex because—and this is a quote—'If your son makes me a grandma, I will kill each and every one of your no-necked monsters.' She actually said 'keel' but, still, I understood what she meant." *Gasp.*

"Mrs. Ryder is pretty funny. I'm sure she was joking," Brian declares, trying to make me feel less mortified. Which is not working.

His mother paces around his room, splattering bits of icing

from the spoon as she gestures. A glob hits a scale model of the *Millennium Falcon*. "Are you? Because I'm not. That woman terrifies me, no offense, Lissy. Do you remember the block party where I made German potato salad instead of regular potato salad?" She flails and more frosting flies onto a Han Solo action figure. "I still have flashbacks from her reaction. Your father fought in 'Nam, yet *I'm* the one having flashbacks. Once in a while I wake up in the night screaming, 'No hot vinegar!' I thought we'd have to sell the house for a while. Do me a favor: Don't have sex with Lissy."

"Not really an issue, Mom," Brian assures her calmly, even though his ears have flushed bright red.

She's appeased, but barely. "Maybe leave your door propped open, too, while you're up here. Oh, Lissy, dear, you feel like staying for dinner? It's taco night and I'm making Bundt cake with lemon icing for dessert."

"I should probably take off soon," I tell her, not mentioning how I'd like to go home and properly die from shame in my own bedroom. I may be thirty-seven inside, but mortification knows no age limits.

"Okay," she says, exiting the room. "If you change your mind, remember there's cake! No sex! Just cake!"

"I'm so sorry about that," I tell Brian.

"No need to apologize," he says. "If anything, *I'm* sorry. Your mom didn't come in here brandishing a loaded wooden spoon. But no-necked monsters? What's that about?"

"Sometimes Mamma forgets she's not Blanche DuBois."

Brian frowns. "Okay . . . but you realize that line comes from Maggie in *Cat on a Hot Tin Roof*."

"Really?"

He nods. "Unless my English teacher was lying about the collected work of Tennessee Williams."

"Huh. Well, please don't tell my mother. She swears it's Blanche DuBois who was always bitching about them, and she's, um . . . not a fan of being wrong. And my whole point was, she's also not a fan of children, either. Like, at all." Clearly, Brian is confused by this statement, so I'm compelled to elaborate. "She digs *me*, obviously—actually, she's a little bit obsessive in that regard—but she equates the concept of kids with death."

"Why's that?"

Brian's so sincere that I find myself sharing something I never mentioned to Duke. "She got pregnant in college and had to get married. Of course, this is a big, tragic family secret and no one will actually admit it, but I can do basic math. I was born five months after the wedding and I wasn't premature or anything."

When my parents met, my mother was a junior at the University of Georgia and my dad was just finishing law school down there. From what my aunt Sissy says, my parents weren't at all serious about each other. Actually, my mom had been dating this wealthy football player named Bo, who was the lieutenant governor's son, but he broke up with her because she was all in his grille about getting married. That may be the first—and last—time she didn't get her own way.

To make Bo jealous, she dated my dad. She figured that seeing her on the arm of some poor Yankee Democrat lawyer would incense him. And it did, but by then she was knocked up and it was too late. My grandmamma (you want to talk scary women? Let's just say the terror apple didn't fall far from the terror tree) gave her no choice but to marry Daddy and to stay married and the rest is history. He moved her back up to his hometown in Illinois shortly thereafter and she's been making him pay for it ever since.

You know what? Brian is Duke's polar opposite, too, and Mamma knows I've been aggravated with Duke lately, even if she doesn't know why. She probably thinks I'm over here having revenge sex, but the truth is I don't discover *that* until college.

"Listen," I say, "I'd better go home and calm her down. She can be a little high-maintenance."

I exit the beanbag. Rather, I attempt to haul myself out, but it's like trying to limbo when the bar's at knee height. Brian reaches for my hand and when he touches me, I swear I feel a spark of electricity. But maybe he just dragged his shoes on the carpet first.

"Here you go," he says, helping me to my feet. "This was fun."

"Yeah, it kinda was," I agree, before adding, "even though you're wrong about Kurt Cobain. And Elvis, for that matter."

He snorts. "Ooh, stubborn, eh? If you want to come over tomorrow, we can discuss the folk branch of the tree. I'm talking all Bob Dylan, all the time."

"I just might take you up on that," I curtly reply.

As I cross the street, I consider what I wrote about Brian in my diary. Back in the day, I felt very comfortable with him very quickly. If today's any indication, I can see why. We weren't together long in 1991, but now that I've been reminded of how I felt back then, all sorts of sweet memories have returned. Like the night we drove to the quarry and listened to "Every Rose Has Its Thorn" a dozen times on a loop. Brian brought a little telescope and pointed out all the constellations unique to the fall sky. We had a real *Can't Buy Me Love* moment. (FYI, Patrick Dempsey's still smokin' twenty-five years after that film was released.)

Until right this minute, I hadn't considered how different my life would be in the future if I hadn't been so afraid of what everyone would think about my dumping the quarter-back for the computer geek. Like in the scheme of things that would have been such an issue? Brian's even better-looking than I remember in a nerdier–Ryan Gosling kind of way, and I appreciate how he never once mentioned sports or the prospect of getting into my pants. When I'm with him I feel . . . less angry at violations in the social hierarchy, as though it's really not a huge deal if some random classmate wants to wear my signature color of pink.

Like I said, I find him refreshing.

None of which matters, of course, because I'm technically thirty-seven and he's seventeen and statutory rape is no laughing matter. Although . . . Edward has no problem hooking up with Bella and he's, like, a hundred years older than her and no one's pressed charges yet. Also? He's a *vampire*. In this case, I'd simply be the mayor of Cougar Town. Still, this isn't a conversation I'd like to have with a judge, particularly since I'm here in the first place to right karmic wrongs, so the whole point is moot.

When I arrive home, I have to talk my mother down from the ledge, convincing her that we're just friends and that nothing happened, nor would happen. And yet I find myself glancing over at his window all night and I don't stop until I see his light go out hours later.

I've not yet achieved clarity or purpose, yet I feel a little bit of inner peace.

Weird.

"Hi, Liss! Saved you a seat next to me!" Tammy waves and shrieks when I exit the cafeteria line, like I wouldn't spot her and her stop sign red hair without all the histrionics.

"Settle down, Beavis," I tell her, and then instantly regret it when I realize the show doesn't premiere on MTV until halfway through my freshman year of college.

Here's an interesting discovery this time around—except for Nicole, I don't actually like any of my friends. Further—except for Nicole—I'm not sure any of them particularly care for me. I suspect we've only been palling around as long as we have because if we didn't, the entire social fabric of the school would disintegrate.

Fortunately, Kimmy's dumb as a bag of hair, so she lacks the intellectual capacity to conceive of a power play. April's no slouch, but she's a hopeless kiss-ass, so conducting a social junta goes against her very nature. Really? April's the very definition of a herd animal.

(Note to self: I invented frenemies twenty years ago! Have Daddy look into copyright infringement when I get back to the future.)

As for Tammy?

I'm keeping my eye on that one. Ol' Fire Crotch has been angling to take over the Belles ever since she had her braces removed. Like a little less tin in her maw would make everyone forget she's a ginger. She makes no overt moves, mind you; she's too slick for that. Rather, it's the little stuff I'm starting to notice, like how she flirts with Duke, and how she's always trying to get together with Nicole outside of the group. Divide and conquer? Not on my watch, Opie Cunningham.

If I could prove it was Tammy who slapped the I BREAK 4 MONSTER BOOTY bumper sticker on my shiny new car, she'd be out of the group so fast her ugly crimson head would spin. Nicole's all, "Blah, blah, blah, benefit of the doubt innocent until proven guilty," but I know the score. (Also, Nicole's probably too sweet for her own good.)

Can I mention Tammy's a stepchild with red hair, yet no one has beaten her like that old expression promises?

Let's rectify this, universe, and soon.

Tammy nods at my Beavis comment, as though I've somehow said something meaningful. I slide in across from her and place my tray on the linoleum table, which is in the prime position, as we can see the entire room, while at the farthest point from the garbage cans, dishwashing conveyor belt, and teachers' corner. The eastern light lands just shy of the table at this time of day, meaning we're well lit but not squinty, and we're spitting distance from the soda machines. When the Belles skip school, our six-top is left vacant, as no one dares sully our seats.

I regard the lunchtime bounty in front of me. How did I turn my nose up at school cafeteria offerings twenty years ago? Iceberg wedge salads? Square slices of pizza? Grilled cheese? Goulash? Food trucks are making a killing today selling old-school comfort foods, but back then I'd suck down three Diet Cokes and one bite of Duke's ice-cream sandwich, followed by a double Dexatrim Max chaser. No wonder I was perpetually crabby.

(Note to self: Invent food truck.)

Today's exciting because lunch feels extra-retro—Tater Tots and sloppy joes and chocolate milk. I've died and gone to trans-fat heaven!

"Ohmigod," Kimmy exclaims. "You're *eating lunch*?!"

I pause in midbite, lips parted and Tater Tot hovering somewhere between my mouth and my plate. Icily, I reply, "You're not?"

Duly chastened, April and Kimmy hustle up to the hot food line and they gaze at the offerings with the wonder and fear of an aborigine having witnessed a Coke bottle falling from the sky.

Nicole's busy with a project for her child-development class, so it's just Tammy and me at the table. She's all poised and anticipatory, like she's waiting for me to say some words so she can hang on them now before using them against me later. I notice girls at the other tables are all leaning in to hear me, too.

Truth? This idol-worship business is becoming a little played out. Two weeks ago it was a real ego boost, but now? Not so much. Take yesterday, for example. I was in a total haze after hanging out with Brian until late the night before. He synched up Pink Floyd's *Dark Side of the Moon* and *The Wizard of Oz* and it blew my mind. Then he tried to explain his Usenet newsgroup (basically an online *Star Wars* bulletin board) that he accesses with his modem. I didn't want to ruin the surprise for him, but seriously—he's just going to die when he finally gets a broadband connection.

Boy, I wish it weren't illegal in twenty-nine states to make out with him.

Still . . . I *do* have a boyfriend who's eventually going to be my husband. Whether or not he *stays* my husband is yet to be determined, but maybe if stuff in our relationship doesn't get broken, we won't have to fix it. Plus, I'm hoping Brian's business will make me rich someday, so I'm trying not to lead him on, much to my mother's relief.

Anyway, my point is, when I stepped into the shower yesterday morning, I was tired and daydreamy and I ended up washing my hair with conditioner. Because I was already halfway to straight hair after that, I gave myself a proper blowout. Then I pulled my industrial-strength curling iron through each section to make it smooth, because, let's face it—a perm does no one any favors. Then, today? No fewer than nineteen girls, including Tammy, have attempted the same thing.

I suspect that if I were to go Britney-on-a-bender and buzz my hair clean off, they'd be all, "Can we borrow your clippers?"

Kimmy and April approach the table with, hey, what do you know? Trays of sloppy joes, Tots, and chocolate milk. I consider messing with them by dunking my Tots in my milk before eating them, but that seems pointless and icky. Also, the Tots are golden and salty and magnificent and I don't want to mar this experience for one minute. I figure I'm going to be in this bod for only the next week, so I may as well enjoy it. Too bad camera phones aren't out yet. I'd definitely take some underwear-clad, MySpace-type photos to keep on file, because my derriere will never be tighter, smaller, or higher than it is at this moment. I'd like to memorialize it, maybe put it on a Christmas card.

(Note to self: No reason to invent MySpace.)

The rest of the Belles gamely chew and try to hide their grimaces over the influx of empty calories. I have no doubt they'll be revisiting their lunches as soon as they can sneak away to the ladies' room. Oh, ladies . . . bulimia is so 1990.

I'm falling madly, truly, deeply in love with these Tots when Tammy elbows me. "Check it out," she hisses. She gestures to the side of the caf with the unflattering light over by the dish room. I follow her pointed finger until I see the object of her derision. Deva's trying to navigate around her corn dog with her back brace and the results are . . . kind of pornographic.

I'm not going to sugarcoat it: She's working that nitrate on a stick like Jenna Jameson, all tongue and bared teeth and tilted head. I'm starting to realize that I didn't always make the best choices in my past, but come on! Deva's practically begging someone to mock her.

I'm not advocating bullying (I'm totally about "it gets better," after all), but for Christ's sake, if you don't want to be teased, then stop sending everyone an engraved invitation!

I beg of the kids today, please don't show up for school wearing an ascot or your grandfather's smoking jacket or guyliner (unless you're Nikki Sixx). Save your budding individuality for college, where you won't get your ass handed to you for requesting a glass of sparkling water at a kegger. For now, stay with the herd! The herd's way safer than being out there all by your lonesome with your pink hair and nose ring! Eccentricity is great . . . but wait until you graduate.

I'm slowly beginning to understand that a lot of the time I don't even *want* to mock others, but there they are in their *Mork and Mindy* suspenders and crocheted hats more suitable for hiding extra toilet paper rolls than wearing, and they give me very few other options. High school is a battlefield, and no one wins the war wearing Moon Boots. It's kill or be killed up in here; thus it's imperative to strike the first blow.

I want to laugh at Deva's performance, but then I catch myself before I actually say what I'm thinking.

Wait a sec: *This* is one of those opportunities to make a future fix! Everyone's going to follow my lead regardless of what I do, so if I'm not intentionally cruel in this instance, it stands to reason that no one else will be, either.

Tammy's virtually vibrating from the scent of fresh prey. She likes to fancy herself my "second," like if I can't fulfill my Belle duties, she'll take over.

Pfft. She's fourth at best.

Tammy pokes me again. "Look! It's like she's giving her corn dog a whoomp-whoomp!"

I lean back in my seat and cross my arms, focusing all my attention on Tammy. "A what?"

Tammy giggles nervously and waggles her eyebrows. "You know, a *whoomp-whoomp*."

I'm purposefully dim. "I'm sorry; I don't understand what you mean."

Tammy starts to panic. A while back she was all, "You swear too much, Lissy, so I'm going to set an example and never use dirty words," to which I replied, "Knock yourself out, motherfucker."

But now she's finding herself in an unwinnable sitch. She can curse and go back on her big declaration, or she can be cagey and continue to flounder.

After sputtering and making some hand gestures that assure us all that she's never satisfied a boy once she got his pants off, she must figure that she's dug herself into this hole and the only way out is through. She clears her throat and then whispers, "She appears to be giving that corn dog a . . . *ahem* . . . " following up with an openmouthed wink.

"Tammy," I say slowly and deliberately, "are you too chickenshit to say 'blow job'? What are you, twelve?"

Tammy flushes deeply, and her freckles, skin, and (now straight) hair are instantly the same shade of ruby red. "Well, no, it's just . . . she was . . . come on! That was way gross, Lissy!" I can see the kernel of an idea forming, and she quickly tries to turn the situation on me. "Aren't *you* going to say anything about it? Maybe *you're* the one who's chickenpoop."

Okay, I mentally brace myself, doing the right thing in three . . . two . . . one . . .

"Oh, honey," I tell her, patting Tammy's hand, "if it makes *you* feel good to mock the handicapped girl, then have at it. But I? Have better things to do. Now have some Tots; they're delicious."

Tammy, who should be duly chastened by what's a heroic

burn on my part, mistakes my kindness for weakness and attempts her first overt power play. Her cheeks are still pink when she swivels around to point at Deva and exclaims, "Oh, my God, she's fellating her lunch!"

Except Tammy's never actually *used* that word because of her faux–good girl act, so it comes out, "Oh, my God, she's inflating her lunch!" and then April sprays chocolate milk all over Kimmy, who in turn knocks her sloppy joe onto Tammy's lap, who then pulls April's hair in frustration. Our table erupts in screaming and spilled comfort food. The entire cafeteria begins to laugh and the Belles turn on one another.

"You effing bee! There's sloppy joe all over my mini!"

"Oh, like no one's going to notice this chocolate milk bull's-eye on my shirt?"

"You got sauce in my hair!"

Wonder if Nicole will be sorry she missed this?

The three of them begin to tussle like a bag of kittens, so I eat my last Tot and leave them to their catfight.

As I walk out of the cafeteria, Deva throws me the horns, better known as "metal hands," and first used by Mr. Ronnie James Dio shortly after joining Black Sabbath.

Rock on, she mouths in approval.

Indeed I will.

CHAPTER EIGHT
Back to the Future

According to my diary, I inflicted the deepest psychological damage during Spirit Week, the five days leading up to homecoming. No one was safe from my wrath, likely because I didn't consume anything that entire week save for sugar-free Mentos and a handful of Funyuns. What can I say? Starving people aren't predisposed to being friendly. If they were, you'd see a lot fewer Somali pirates on the news.

What sparked my own personal Dispirit Week was shopping for my homecoming dress. The first time around when Mamma and I were about to drive to the mall, my dad popped out of his library. "You ladies care for some company?" he asked.

Before I could say, "Of course, Daddy!" my mother shot him a chilling look. "Wouldn't your day be better spent generatin' billable hours? You're nevah gonna make partner if you don't buckle down."

My dad dismissed her callousness. "It's Saturday—I can afford to take the morning off to be with my best girls. Besides, I'm a shoo-in for the partnership." Then he ruffled my hair and wrapped an arm around me. Daddy always smelled of Royall Lyme and Wint-O-Green Lifesavers, and to this day, those scents make me feel safe and calm.

My mother began to tap her heel. "Really, George? So you'd say beyond the shadow of a doubt that the partnership's in the bag? And that you'll have no trouble sendin' Lissy 'n' me to join Aunt Sissy and Augusta in Paris in June? We're all set? In that case, here we go."

My dad visibly deflated and mumbled something about a trademark infringement case he'd been meaning to look into, and we were off to the mall without him.

Once we arrived at the mall, Mamma had distinct ideas on my dress, too.

"Bring her a size four," my mother instructed the saleslady, who was holding an off-the-shoulder, emerald green sheath that was tight to the knees before fishtailing out. I'd look like the world's sexiest mermaid in this gown!

"Your daughter has a lovely figure, but she may be a smidge bigger than a four. Plus this one runs small," the clerk countered. She had reading glasses perched on the edge of her nose and measuring tape looped around her neck. Considering fitting dresses was what she did all day, every day, I was inclined to believe her.

"Mamma, you know I take a six," I added. For one glorious month in my sophomore year, I was a size two, but only because of mono. Yet Mamma bought me diamond stud earrings to celebrate. I'd since "ballooned up" to a six, which were her words, not mine. Actually Dr. Watts had told her at my last sports physical that for my height I was actually underweight, and my mother responded that there was no such thing.

Sensing her commission was on the line, the clerk returned with the smaller size. I fought my way into it, and it took both of the women to work the zipper. The top part wasn't too horrifically tight, but I was bulgy from the waist down. A six would have fit like a dream.

"We'll take it!" Mamma declared.

"That's crazy! I'm going to have to starve between now and then to fit in it!" I groused.

Mamma pursed her lips. "What's your point, honey bunny?"

I was incensed. "This is how girls get anorexia!"

My mother seemed to be considering this very real possibility. "If you're plannin' on being one o' them anorexics, please do so before we see my spiteful sister in June. Tired of her and Grandmamma always throwin' Gussie's success in my face. 'Oh, look, Gussie got into Kappa at Ole Miss; hey, Gussie's drivin' a brand-new S-class Benz; my goodness, Gussie's dating the president of Co-Cola's son.'"

Yet when faced with the prospect of a week without Eggo waffles and frozen yogurt, I didn't care about avenging her decades-long sibling rivalry. All I wanted was permission to digest on occasion.

My mother had been riding me about my weight since my sixth birthday, when I asked for a second piece of birthday cake. She badgered me so relentlessly that I began to resent any item of food that actually tasted good. Milk shakes made me angry, and may God have mercy on whoever dared put cheese or dressing on my mixed-greens salad.

"I take it lunch is out of the question?" I asked.

"You got that raht!" She laughed. "Besides, wouldn't you rather have shoes? Let's see what's new at the Nine West."

When we walked past the food court on the way to the south side of the mall, I took a big breath and was overwhelmed by heady scents of baking pizza and fried egg rolls. "Will I ever be allowed to eat what I like?"

She stopped in her tracks and stood in front of me with both hands on my shoulders. "Oh, Lissy, yes, baby. Course you can. Eat whatever you want." Before I could even sigh in relief, she added, "Soon as you're married."

True to her word, she never said boo about what I put in my mouth from the minute I walked down the aisle. Sometimes I worry that's why I finally forced Duke to propose.

Anyway, pretty much the same thing happened while shopping for a homecoming dress this time around. However, I'm in a lot better state of mind now, largely because I discovered that Lycra bicycle shorts serve the exact same purpose as a pair of Spanx. I've since been enjoying Tater Tots with impunity. (And ketchup!) I'm a kinder, gentler Lissy when not in a caloric desert.

As for Spirit Week, each day encompasses a different theme, such as Fifties Day, and the school goes whole hog. Even the teachers and the lunch ladies and the janitors wear costumes. (Can I tell you how weird it is seeing Buddy Holly pushing a big mop down the hall?) Junior year, the Belles came as the Pink Ladies from *Grease*. Because no one could argue that I wasn't the perfect Sandy, Tammy insisted on being Rizzo, like somehow that was a bigger deal.

The excitement of wearing costumes every day during homecoming week is supposed to culminate in a Lions victory on Friday night. I don't really understand the science that translates Crazy Sock Day into a win, but apparently there's a lot about metaphysics I've yet to learn.

(Side note: My cousin Augusta went to Catholic school in

Savannah and they had a Dress as Your Favorite Saint Day during [Holy] Spirit Week. Gussie was sent home for wearing a St. Pauli Girl costume . . . but not before every single starting-five basketball player asked for her number.)

Anyway, on Monday the theme was to "Rock and Roll over the Hinsdale Central Red Devils," meaning come as your favorite musician. All the guys wore ripped jeans and flannel shirts. So, pretty much business as usual, only with more air guitar. Brian was Roy Orbison, and everyone kept asking him if he was Johnny Cash. He was an excellent sport about it, though, and black suited him. Tammy caught me admiring the fit of his jeans and I had to totally lie about what I'd been looking at. I really have to keep an eye on Tammy. If she can't stab me in the back, she's going to try to stab me in the front soon.

The Belles and I did ourselves up like the dancers in Toni Basil's "Hey, Mickey" video, not because any of us had a great passion for the song, but largely because we already had the cheerleading uniforms and Nicole could French braid.

Having lived through this week before, I knew what was to come. So, first thing Monday morning, I stationed myself by the door to the parking lot, ready to spring into action. The second I saw the dead ringer for Madonna vogueing her narrow ass down the hall, I threw a blanket over her cone-bra-corseted self and wrestled her into the ladies' room.

"What are you doing?" Madonna shrieked through perfectly crimsoned lips.

"What should have been done long ago," I replied. "Now wash your face and don't make me tell you twice."

I stood over Madonna while she used lavatory hand soap and brown paper towels to scour off the layers of freckle-hiding pale foundation, black liner, and expertly arched brows, bitching and moaning the whole time. "I woke up at

five a.m. to get my costume ready! You're just jealous because
you don't look as hot as I do! You're such a hag! I don't know
why everyone lets you get away with everything. This is so not
fair!"

"Yep, life sucks and then you get a minivan," I replied, all
philosophical-like. "Keep scrubbing, Madge. The fake mole
goes, too."

I positioned myself between the sink and the door so she
couldn't escape. If she'd tried to bolt, I was capable of stopping her, because even though my seventeen-year-old body
was lean, I was extra-strong from having to basket-toss-and-
catch Tammy's big ass every day at practice. (Dollars to
doughnuts, that bitch gained weight over the summer specifically to injure me. Well, too frigging bad, Porky. You lose
again.)

"Why are you doing this to me?" Madonna huffed.

I didn't answer.

She wouldn't have believed me if I told her.

When she was finally fresh-faced, I demanded she hand me
her Marilyn Monroe wig. I took the squeeze bottle I'd filled
with vegetable oil and gave it a healthy douse before pulling a
comb through it. The previously pristine locks now fell in
blunt, greasy, dirty-blond chunks, exactly the look I'd hoped
to achieve.

I handed Madonna a plain T-shirt, ratty cardigan, jeans,
and a pair of Chuck Taylors before forcibly removing the
pointy bra. "Put these on over your leotard."

"You've ruined my costume, you hateful cunt!"

I shrugged. "I sure did. Put 'em on. And take this." I
handed her a cigarette to tuck behind her ear.

For the finishing touch, I used spirit gum to attach a scraggly goatee. Once the transformation was complete, I stood

back to admire my handiwork, and it was even better than I'd hoped.

"You look exactly like Kurt Cobain!" I said proudly.

Ex-Madonna stomped and screeched. "I don't *want* to look like Kurt Cobain! I hate Nirvana! They sing about antiperspirant! I want to look like Madonna and you ruined everything because you are the suckiest suck whoever sucked!"

I smiled beatifically. "You'll thank me someday, Robert."

I knew that the only thing I'd ruined was his trip to the ER with a broken nose and a fractured rib from my inadvertently whipping a couple of football players into a frenzy over his cross-dressing.

I thought about his winning on *Project Runway*. "It gets better, but not today," I told him. "Now go to class."

Tuesday was Fifties Day, and not so dramatic (the fifties were a simpler time, after all), but I made a number of small but crucial changes then, too. For example, instead of ridiculing the future food critic, I had everyone try her taro chips, and she, in turn, tasted my Tater Tots. Turns out she was a big fan!

I did all kinds of other good-karma stuff over the course of the week, like getting the mathstronaut to explain a trig principle so no one would be distracted by his massive flood pants on the Red Devils Can't Top Us or Our Outrageous Hats Day. On Backward Day, I chatted with the orchestra geek about how both Eddie and Alex Van Halen were first classically trained musicians, and he seemed superintrigued.

Earlier this week in English class, the substitute was taking roll, and when she called out Brooks's name, Tammy was all, "Don't you mean *Books Fatty*?"

Seriously, Winona Ryder was right in the movie *Heathers*.

(No relation, unforch.) I cut the head off of Heather Chandler (myself), and Heather Duke's head (Tammy's) has sprung right back in its place. However, I was dealing with real life, not the movies, so I quashed her little rebellion right quick. My head spun around all Linda Blair–like and I replied, "I'm sorry, did you have something to contribute, *Hammy*?"

Trust me, no one was talking about Brooks after that.

Deva's been remarking on my progress all week.

"Your aura! So changed! So light yellow and pale green!" she gushes.

We're chatting in the bathroom while I slip out of my Show Your School Colors Day outfit and into my cheerleading uniform before the pep rally.

"Is that what my aura's supposed to look like?" I step out of my blue leggings and into my cheer bloomers before pulling up my skirt. (To answer everyone's burning question, yes, *of course* cheerleaders wear undies beneath their bloomers.) (Unless you're a whore, *Tammy*.) When I spin, the pleats billow out and then snap right back into place, all tidy but still swingy. You know what? This needs to be the year fashion brings back the pleat, because I am patently adorable in this skirt.

"Your aura colors are stupendous, Lissy Ryder! Such an improvement! When I saw you at the reunion, your natural glow was almost completely marred by blackness, but today you're all light and love. Well, mostly light and love. There are a few spots here and there, because you're still intrinsically you, but still, well-done! Up here!" Deva holds up her hand for a high five and then smacks me so hard with her catcher's mitt that she almost dislocates my shoulder.

"*Ow!*" I exclaim, shaking out my arm.

"Sorry," she says, all sheepish. "The Mayans play a game with a nine-pound rubber disk called an *ulli* and I'm quite skilled, because I can really palm it, you know? Sometimes I forget my own strength."

Three weeks ago, I'd have been deeply annoyed by Deva's casual mention of yet another Mesoamerican Fun Fact, but now I'm charmed, especially with how she's all present tense with the Mayans, like she might go visit as soon as she's done with 1991. (Which, I guess, she actually might.) She's so much more interesting than I ever imagined, and I wish I'd given her a chance back in high school. Surely I'd have enjoyed her conversation more than Tammy's daily treatise on *Saved by the Bell*. It's been all I can do to not mention that Screech eventually releases a sex tape.

"Hey, real quick—you said I should be heading back tomorrow. How does that work?" I'm bent over my K-Swiss, tightening my laces and slouching my socks.

Deva replies, "Simply go to sleep and you'll wake up within a few minutes of when you left three weeks ago."

"That's all there is to it?" I gather my hair in a ridiculously high pony, adorning it with a massive white ribbon. (The tight pony—the next-best thing to Botox, you know.)

"That's it."

I smooth my hair and swipe on some gloss. "Easy enough. All righty, all set. I guess I'd better head to the gym. They can't have a pep rally without all my pep." I wedge my stuff into a hot-pink Vera Bradley tote and make my way to the door. "No time like the present, right?"

Deva shoots me a lopsided grin. "I prefer to say there's no present like time."

"We've got the spirit now, it's all around us now, we've got the spirit now, 'cause it lifts us off the ground!" At the "lifts us off the ground" part, the Belles and I take three big hops to the right. We repeat this over and over, until we succeed in coaxing the crowd to participate in taking three little hops in their own seats as well. Each clattering hop fills the stadium with the sound of thunder and it's awe-inspiring.

It's a perfect night for a football game, too. Chilly without being too cold, and the air's crisp, but scented with the slightest tang of a hardwood fire. We haven't been hit by the cold November rains that Axl will sing about next year, so there's been no dampness to speed the decay of the fallen leaves. The whole night feels magical, and even though I already know our team will lose shortly after Duke gets sacked, I've had a blast being here.

"Which cheer should we do next, Liss? Let's make it our best ever!" Nicole says. She's as excited to be out here as I am, color high in her cheeks and breath coming out in little white puffs.

I started off this experience furious with her for bailing on me at the reunion, but as I've observed her over the past few weeks, I'm struck by what a kind person she is. She talks to everyone, regardless of their social status. If some nerd's struggling under a load of books, she's right there to retrieve those that fall. If some stoner girl needs a tampon, she doesn't hesitate to dive into her purse. She doesn't gossip and she doesn't mock and she doesn't judge. I can see now why she chose to work with children as a career—her patience is infinite and being helpful is second nature to her.

That she still chose to be my friend for the past twenty years is nothing short of miraculous and speaks to her gentle soul. In retrospect, I haven't been the best friend. I can think of a million instances when I bullied and steamrolled and negated her feelings.

With this new sense of awareness about Nicole, I've noticed that when the other Belles get all catty, she excuses herself to hit the restroom or study for an exam.

I have the feeling she appreciates the changes I've made, and we've grown so much closer than we ever were in the first 1991. I even confided in her about my parents fighting and all the pressure my mother puts on my dad and me. Nicole simply listened without judgment and I felt better afterward. She said she suspected my parents' marriage wasn't perfect, but never wanted to say anything.

When I return to the future, the first thing I'm going to do is apologize for everything. Somehow I must have thought I bought her complicity when I treated her to all those Good Humor bars so many years ago, and I've been taking advantage of our disparity in power ever since. The time has come to make amends for three decades of pushing her around and not showing her the respect she so richly deserves. And I'm going to keep saying I'm sorry until she believes me. Then I'm going to prove to her that I'm worthy of being her friend. I'll make a real effort to be better to her kids, too. I'll even find a way to bond with awful Charlotte. (Maybe I'll teach her a little something about real music! Kids love anything retro, right?)

My heart feels all happy and unburdened and I want to share the joy with everyone, starting with Nicole. "Maybe you should captain the cheer this time, Nic." Her whole face lights up and she throws one pom-holding arm around me before deftly leading the squad in a rousing chant about the importance of touchdowns. What's ironic is, it really is our best cheer ever.

I'm scanning the crowd during a Gatorade break and I spot Brian. I give him a little nod and he returns a melancholy salute before focusing his attention back on his computer club buddy. I guess I can't expect him to be all moony over me after our conversation earlier today.

After the pep rally, I drove him home so that we could talk. Once we climbed into the car and selected our sound track (David Bowie, as Brian's been educating me on the origin of glam rock), he asked, "What time do you want to work on your essay tomorrow?"

In addition to my musical education, Brian's been helping me with my college applications over the past few weeks, too. Determined to create a key future fix, I've been pouring all my effort into them. We've been together every day, and I'm at the point where I can barely keep from jumping on him, but karma demands that I not break his heart, so I'm following a hands-off policy. And besides, I don't know what my future holds with Duke, but I can't risk going back with this kind of dangling thread. Yes, Brian and I have had an intense couple of weeks, but I miss Duke. A fortnight of breezy fun and puppy love is no match for twenty-plus years of history. I'm pretty sure I want to be with Duke, or at least have the opportunity to figure that out, which means I need to head back unencumbered.

I had to end things with Brian. And the fact that no one had touched anyone's goodies yet made everything way less dramatic than the first time around, which, frankly, got a little shouty and a lot mean.

I kind of don't like to think about how it ended, because no matter how I spin it, my words and actions were inexcusable. I went for his jugular, and he was too much of a gentleman to do anything but allow me to unload. Much as I try to live my life with no regrets, I've never quite stopped regretting that day.

But today was much easier, because instead of crafting an elaborate lie about my feelings, I simply told him the truth.

Not the *whole* truth, mind you, but enough for it all to make sense.

I pulled over by the park so I could give him my full attention. "Listen, Brian, we have to stop hanging out like this, at least for now."

Concern was etched all over his face. "Why? Have I done something wrong?"

Oh, God, why is he so damn supportive? I hope that the Duke in the future is like this.

I took a deep breath and proceeded. "No, of course you're a perfect gentleman, Brian. . . . You know I have a boyfriend and that nothing can happen between us, but if we keep spending time together, it will. I'm afraid that I've been leading you on, and that's not okay. You're an awesome person and you deserve better than to be yanked around by me."

Brian toyed with the seat belt until he finally replied, "Don't I have a say in this? What if I want you to yank me around?"

"You don't," I said, suddenly very aware of how quiet my dad gets every time my mother runs roughshod over him. "Trust me on this."

He handled my not-really-a-breakup breakup like a champ, and we agreed to be cordial albeit distant friends. To prove that he was fine with whatever our eventualities, he insisted on buying me some frozen yogurt before we went home to get ready for the game.

I take comfort in having let him down as gently as I could, as opposed to the histrionics of the first time. I'll miss him, but ultimately I'm confident I've done the right thing for my present and my future.

Mostly confident, anyway.

Close to the end of the game, there's a problem with the

fancy new electronic scoreboard, so there's a delay in the action on the field. I watch as our computer teacher nabs Brian to enlist his help.

We cheerleaders are kind of standing around, unsure of what to do. Do we chant something about the scoreboard repair? *Go, fight, reboot?*

As we're all grouped together in front of the bleachers, I notice Amy Childs sitting right up front. I don't recall her attending many games before, and I assume she's in the cherry fifty-yard-line spot this time only because she received some big science award at halftime.

I'm not sure if Amy's been hit with a bad cold or if it's the chill in the air, or if maybe she just needs one good swipe from her Cover Girl compact, but whatever the circumstances, her nose is so red that it's extra-noticeable, to the point of being a tad phallic. And by "a tad" I mean, for the love of all that's decent, put a black censored-for-TV box over that thing.

Shit.

It's last time all over again. I immediately turn away so no one else sees what I've spotted, in the hope of not repeating an unfortunate piece of history.

"Holy doody," Tammy exclaims, "Santa called Amy Childs—something about guiding his sleigh tonight?"

Kimmy and April giggle while Nicole suddenly becomes very interested in a mosquito bite on her shin. I simply roll my eyes in the hope that it ends this line of discussion tout suite.

It doesn't.

Tammy presses on. "Check out the full frontal nudity of Childs's nose! She needs to slap a condom on her face!"

Amy sees that we're watching her and she begins to shift in her seat, making eye contact with everyone but us. I guarantee her inner monologue's repeating, *Please don't look at me, please don't look at me, please don't look at me.*

I feel enormous pangs of guilt over my behavior last time. What happened was not okay and I'm ashamed at having been so harsh. What could I have been thinking? Why would I ever be so deliberately awful?

Now it's time for me to flip the script.

I smile and nod at Amy, officially granting her the Lissy Ryder Seal of Approval. I can see the relief washing over her and that makes me happy. Maybe we'll become friendly this year. Bet she's less of a drag than Tammy—of course, how hard could that be? Maybe someday she'll invite me to her lake house and then I can be BFF with Oprah, too. Surely the Big O will have forgotten all the West End Club foolishness by then. Maybe we'll even laugh over it while we eat s'mores.

I turn away from Amy to face the field. Nicole follows suit. The players are starting to run back onto the grass, so the scoreboard problem must be fixed. When I spot Duke, I shake my pom-poms at him and give him a high kick, because I'm positively effervescent right now at having skirted all the un-pleasantness. Had I known the rush from doing the right thing previously, I'd have been on board years ago. When Duke spots me doing my Dallas Cowboy cheerleaders impression, he offers me a huge grin and I can see his mouth guard. He looks like he's eating a navel orange slice the way we used to do when we were kids.

The teams start to play and I assume that Tammy's issue with Amy has passed. Tammy, however, senses another op-portunity to assert herself as the Belles' true leader. As it turns out, my acknowledging Amy was actually an invitation for Tammy to cause trouble. She starts her cheer off low and slow, but soon Kimmy and April join in and the crowd begins to shift their attention from the field.

"It's crooked! It's long! Amy's nose looks like a schlong!"

Okay, I did not just hear that.

"It's crooked! It's long! Amy's nose looks like a schlong!"

Oh, no she di-in't.

"It's crooked! It's long! Amy's nose looks like a schlong!"

Listen, did I not just bend the space-time continuum specifically to prevent this from happening?

No. No frigging way.

Amy turns chalk white. Instead of running away like any sensible person, she's frozen in her seat in horror.

"Shut up, Tammy," I demand. I try to grab her arm, but she's jumping up and down so much that I can't quite keep my grip on her.

"It's crooked! It's long! Amy's nose looks like a schlong!" Tammy and company turn their sound up to eleven.

Amy's friends begin to creep away from her, anxious to not claim her social annihilation as their own. You know what? High school girls are *lethal*. We should send them to Afghanistan. A couple of passive-aggressive Facebook status updates, three unflattering photo tags, and a well-timed unfriending and those godless hordes would lay down their arms in a hot minute.

But I can't worry about world peace right now, even though I make a mental note to myself about contacting the UN with my idea.

"Tammy, *I will end you*. Understand? Stop. This. Now," I shout. But, spurred on by having finally gotten a reaction from me, she keeps on chanting.

"It's crooked! It's long! Amy's nose looks like a schlong!"

People as far as ten rows back are starting to stare at Amy, who's sitting stiff as a statue, save for the tears threatening to spill over at any minute. Nicole's shell-shocked by the depth and breadth of Tammy's petty assholery, but she's not strong enough to fight them on her own.

This all comes down to me.

I need to drown out these bitches, but how? Do I tackle her? Throw a punch? I suddenly wish I were my future size so I could put a little weight behind a right hook.

We're moments before Duke throws the desperate pass that in 1991 cost us the game, and I'm suddenly struck with an inspiration. Turns out having Brian instruct me on the roots of rock and roll is about to come in handy.

"Follow my lead," I call to Nicole.

According to Brian's lecture last week, "Gene Dixon and Earl Edwards had already experienced some success on the R and B scene back in the early sixties, but they didn't have a number one hit until 'Duke of Earl,' their crossover doo-wop single, dropped on January thirteenth, 1962." Though I could give a flying fart about that *American Bandstand*–sounding nonsense, his lesson stuck with me, and now it may be exactly what saves Amy.

To the cadence of the song, I begin to chant, "Duke, Duke, Duke of Hurl! Duke, Duke, Duke of Hurl! Duke, Duke, Duke of Hurl! Quarterback is the Duke of Hurl! Nothing can stop the Duke of Hurl!"

I clap and bounce and shout even louder for the second round. My calves burn and the balls of my feet kill, but I keep leaping higher and higher as I chant. This time, Nic joins in.

"Duke, Duke, Duke of Hurl! Duke, Duke, Duke of Hurl! Duke, Duke, Duke of Hurl! Quarterback is the Duke of Hurl! Nothing can stop the Duke of Hurl!"

Tammy ratchets her voice up even louder while Kimmy

and April pause, anxious to see who's going to win this power struggle so they can follow the true leader.

They're going to follow *me*, though. Bank on that.

After all, I'm still Lissy Ryder.

"Duke, Duke, Duke of Hurl! Duke, Duke, Duke of Hurl! Duke, Duke, Duke of Hurl! Quarterback is the Duke of Hurl! Nothing can stop the Duke of Hurl!"

At this point, the only one chanting with Tammy is Tammy, and that's just until Mrs. Colecheck, our cheerleading coach, yanks her off the field by her flaming ponytail. Spell broken, Amy Childs is whisked away by her friends and the crowd returns their attention to the game.

Spurred on by our enthusiasm, or possibly by the prospect of having earned a way-cool new nickname, Duke throws a Hail Mary pass. This time around? The wide receiver actually catches it, the Lions clinch the victory, and every one of us (except those being scolded in the locker room) loses our damn mind!

"Lions, Lions, that's our name, ask us again and we'll tell you the same! Lions, Lions, that's our name! Check out the board, 'cause we won the game! *Lion pride, woo!*"

I know this is some no-matter match and that today's really twenty-one years from where I'll be tomorrow, yet the excitement I feel from the victory of this moment is absolutely genuine.

I'm still on an endorphin high an hour later, when the Belles and I arrive at the dance, sans Tammy, who's since received a three-day suspension. Ha!

The gym has been magically transformed from a sweaty, gross, vaguely-smelling-of-soup place into a sweaty, gross, vaguely-smelling-of-soup-but-now-with-bonus-streamers place. Yet I don't mind. I'm in the moment, and the moment feels fantastic.

I spot Duke coming out of the locker room. His hair's still damp and I can see the comb tracks in it. He rushes over to me amid claps on the back and shouts of "Duke!" "Hey, it's the Duke of Hurl!" A couple of juniors try to lift him over their shoulders, failing miserably and spilling him onto the floor. Instead of getting mad like usual, Duke simply laughs and lets them help him up. Then he sweeps me up, my mermaid tail flying out behind me.

"Did you see that pass I threw? That was a million-to-one shot! I can't believe it!" He's intoxicated with the excitement, as opposed to last time, when he was drunk on Meister Bräu.

"That was amazing!" I gush. "You're a regular Peyton Manning—I mean, Troy Aikman!"

"I can thank you for that. Your cheer got the crowd to its feet and I fed off that energy! Duke of Hurl! That was awesome!" Duke's as animated as I've ever seen him. I forgot how boyishly charming he is when he's content. I wonder if I haven't seen this side of him in a while because I haven't given him anything to be happy about. (Note to self: Fix that, like, now.)

"Coach says there was a scout from U of I here tonight. Glad I gave him something to remember!" He starts simulating passes to teammates, who leap and pretend-catch.

In 1991, I cemented myself to Duke's side, sure he was going to dance with other girls the second I turned my back. But tonight I tell him, "Why don't you go talk to your friends? Bet they're not quite done rehashing the game."

He looks at me as though he's trying to figure out my angle, or like I'm testing him and he's about to fail. "Really?"

"Of course! Tonight's all about you, not me. You're the conquering hero! Now go bask in everyone's admiration. You earned it."

I finally realized that Duke needs his moments in the spotlight as much as I've always demanded mine. (See? People like to bask.) For us to make it work, I have to be able to take a backseat when it's his time to shine, because it can't be all about me.

This night is a turning point for us; I can tell. What's so weird is that right now is the most affection I've felt for him of any time since we've been married. We've been a couple by force of habit for so many years—yet I suspect this do-over might possibly bring us to the place where we're together by choice.

"You sure, babe?"

Wow. I really must have been overbearing.

(And we weren't even doing it yet!)

I give him a little shove. "Go! Have fun!" Then he takes my face in his hands and gives me the kind of kiss that I feel all the way down to my hot-pink toenails. I'm struck with a longing for him that's almost a physical ache. I can't remember another instance when we had this kind of simple, heartfelt moment. Mostly I remember fighting with him and breaking up and then getting back together again. But we must have had hundreds of magic moments like this in the two decades we've been together . . . right? Regardless, I'm suddenly glad I made the appropriate decision with Brian.

What's so strange is that tonight we truly feel like a couple, like together we're more than just the sum of our respective parts, and I realize that what he brings to the table is equally important as what I contribute. It's never been like this before; our relationship has been a perpetual power struggle, and I've always tried to bend him to my will. I had no clue that the minute I stopped playing games, he would, too. If I'm able to miracle myself back into his life in the future, I'm going to start taking care of him and not vice versa.

Although Duke spends a portion of his time goofing off with his teammates, he returns to dance every slow song with me, not because I make him, but because he genuinely wants to. And when we're elected homecoming king and queen (a lot more enthusiastically this time than last, I might add), he doesn't even balk when I suggest we dance to "Love Bites."

Bliss. Every second of the night is bliss.

When I arrive home, I find my parents asleep on the couch in front of the big old Magnavox. Their heads are tilted toward each other and their shoulders are almost touching. This is the least oppositional I've seen them in years, and I stand back, trying to save a mental picture. I feel a lump rise in my throat, like I'm going to miss them when I'm gone in the morning, even though I'm likely going to wake up in their house beneath my David Coverdale poster.

I kiss them both and then quietly climb the stairs to change into my pajamas.

When I wash my face, I give my seventeen-year-old countenance one last, wistful look, admiring the smooth, clear skin. I hope Lissy-at-seventeen starts using moisturizer with SPF, like, yesterday, because that convertible top is doing my epidermis no favors. As for my hair? Its 100 percent real highlights are perfectly blond from the sun and not by some snippy queen who calls it "our hair," mocks my grays, and charges four hundred dollars for the privilege. (In case you were wondering? The carpet actually matches the drapes right now, or at least it will until I tear it out and install hardwood.)

I place my hands on my waist and admire its small span before practically kissing my unblemished thighs good-bye. I swing my arm around, reveling in my elbow's freedom of movement. Then I do a back walkover, just because I still can.

I won't lie—I'm going to miss the package that seventeen-year-old Lissy Ryder came in, because gravity takes no prisoners. Yet I'm equally excited to find out where thirty-seven-year-old Lissy comes out, not just with Duke, but in all aspects of my life—professionally and with my friends and family, too. I accomplished everything Deva told me to do, and now I'm ready to go back to the future.

I drift off to sleep feeling an overwhelming sense of clarity, purpose, and inner peace.

(Note to self: Send Deva a fruit basket upon reentry.) (Organic, if possible.)

As I nod off, my last thought is . . . Here I go again.

CHAPTER NINE
Back in Black

First thing I see when I open my eyes is a bare chest.

And this time it doesn't belong to David Coverdale.

In the pale pink predawn light, my eyes trail up from the six-pack to the face, which belongs to Duke.

Whew.

I tiptoe out of bed and try to get my bearings in this entirely strange place. I don't know where I'm going, but I sure know where I've been. (Yeah, Whitesnake lyric; I went there.) I can say with certainty that this is not my parents' house or my old condo. Outside of that? No clue.

I wander into the first open door and I find myself standing in a walk-in closet. It's not quite a Carrie-marries-Big closet, but it's still pretty damn swanky.

I ease the door shut behind me and flip the light switch and when I do, I see that I'm surrounded by racks of neatly stored, highly polished shoes and row after row of suits and dresses, all of which are in shades of gray and black. Really? Not even a hint of fuchsia? That's not like me. Still, these garments are high-quality; that's patently obvious.

I peek at the label on a severe black dress. Armani.

Very nice.

Then I see it's a size four.

Very nice!

I continue my tour of the closet, dismayed to see a dearth of denim. I grew rather fond of my ol' high-waisters and I'll need to rectify this situation immediately. I wonder if I have credit cards that aren't maxed.

Judging from an overall lack of casual clothing, I have the feeling I spend a lot of time in an office. Where do I work? Considering all the somber colors in my wardrobe, I hope it's not a funeral home. Or a law firm. Ugh, what if I'm my dad's secretary?

I run across a mountain of exercise gear, which explains not only the size-four wardrobe but also how I spend my free time.

Am I a humorless fitness Nazi now?

I step out of my teenage cotton nightgown and throw on yoga pants, a tank, and a zipped fleece before I continue the tour. Everything fits beautifully.

Oh, Lululemon, let's never fight again.

I'm just about to pass into the bathroom when I spot something that takes my breath away—a Birkin bag! No! Could it possibly be real? Holding the bag to the light, I give it the ten-point inspection and it checks out everywhere, from the perfect seams to the interior chèvre leather. The zipper, the accent over the E in Hermès, the impeccable skin of the outside—this is the genuine article!

Ohmigod!

A real live Birkin bag! And if it's in here, that means it's *mine*! I hug it to my chest and say a little thanks to my mom, because how else would I own one?

I walk into the attached bath and flip on the lights. Holy cats, this is the bathroom of my dreams! Everything seems ultramodern and hip, although that may be due to my having spent the last three weeks in bathrooms that were stylish twenty years ago. (Mauve, you shan't be missed.) Even without the comparison, this room's pretty spectacular—the tub's a massive freestanding unit in the center of the room and it's both deep and wide enough to seat two, boxed off in a rich, wide-plank mahogany that matches the cabinets.

The shower's across from the bath and you could wash a minivan in this stall! Two ginormous rain showers extend from the ceiling, and a dozen different body sprays are located in key points up and down the sage green, sand, and pale powder blue glass-tiled walls. The commode is enclosed in its own frosted-glass booth and it's next to a bidet. Heh. I could give myself an ass bath in here.

I'm surprised to see there's only one sink . . . and then I notice the mirror image of this bathroom out the door. Sweet child o' mine! I thought that *was* a mirror, but no! This is a real his-and-hers set of baths. Duke's doesn't have a tub, but, hey, he's welcome to use mine!

At this point, I figure I'd better check out the damage to myself, but when I pull up a lighted makeup mirror, I'm delighted to see how much better I've been at fending off the ravages of time. I was hyperconscious of engaging in antiaging rituals once I turned thirty, but maybe starting to use UVA blockers at seventeen made a big difference. Sunscreen! Genius! Kurt Vonnegut was right!

I run my fingers through my hair and I'm thrilled with the color, even though the cut's a bit short and severe for my liking. Since when do I opt for a chin-length bob? Who am I, Anna Wintour? How am I supposed to give my high pony a condescending toss when someone says something stupid?

Oh, wait. I kind of don't do that now. My bad.

Walking through a sitting area, I get to the main hallway. I close the bedroom door behind me so as not to wake Duke before thoroughly inspecting the massive corridor. The hall leads to a landing where I find staircases made of metal and mahogany, and they go down at least two flights and up one. Not only is this a single-family home—it's monolithic, to boot.

Holy moly, Duke is *rich*!

I wonder if my boosting his self-esteem at the big game is what spurred his success? In my past-future (I assume that's what I should call it), he was a midlevel processed foods sales executive. He must have gotten a serious promotion!

I run up the stairs first to find a professional-grade home gym. This area's a mini West End Club, encompassing everything from treadmills to rowing machines to weight machines to a Pilates bench!

Maybe Duke invented Pilates!

The glass walls of the gym open onto a huge roof deck surrounded by boxwood hedges, but they're not so high that they obscure the skyline. Judging my proximity to the Sears Tower and the Hancock Center, I'm in the dead center of Old Town, which borders the Gold Coast. The Gold Coast is a little trendier, but hey, the view's a lot better here than in my La Grange bedroom, amirite or amirite?

I inspect every inch of the deck, from the Sunbrella-cushioned teak couches to the outdoor shower. Outdoor shower! I live for an outdoor shower! It's so nice to have access to one when sunning myself. I glance down at my skin, which seems awfully pale. Huh. Looks like I don't tan too often. Well, I'll fix that next summer!

I correct myself—*in moderation*, of course.

I scope out the scenery from the roof deck. The weather's still decent, although the leaves are starting to come down, so I must be back in time at the exact point Deva promised I'd go. Was the reunion last night? If so, did we go?

The gym's across from a media room that boasts a seventy-two inch television. That thing is the size of a bay window! Sleek leather chairs line up in front of the screen, and there's a complicated system of speakers and sound bars and subwoofers. Yet even with all the tasteful decor, the room feels a bit unlived-in. Don't you worry, Mr. Gigantor TV, I'ma have me a film festival very soon with everything Reese, Jennifer G., and Sandy B. ever starred in. Girls' night in! (Do I have any girls for a night in?)

I chug past the master bedroom's floor and down to the next level. There's an en suite guest room and a couple of bedrooms set up as offices. One of them must be mine, so I'll come back to it. I imagine that's where I'll find the most clues to my life right now.

I'm blown away when I see the floor-to-ceiling glass window on the main floor, which showcases perfectly appointed living and dining rooms comprised of sharp angles and shiny metal and white leather. White, huh? Never really fancied myself as someone who'd buy white furniture. Not sure how or why I went all J. Lo, but the look is chic, albeit chilly. I congratulate myself on my interesting new taste. I'd been much more into squashy couches, pretty patterned rugs, and an overall feeling of warmth in my past-future, but I guess circumstances have led me here. Nothing about this place says "hearth and home."

Rather, it says *Architectural Digest*.

But that's cool, too.

The kitchen is past another bath and a butler's pantry, where I notice we own an unholy amount of crystal barware. We must do a lot of entertaining. Perhaps we're drunks?

The kitchen's done up in the same style as the front of the house, only with tons of open shelving and white subway tile. Would a little accent of red kill me? The stools pulled up to the breakfast bar are the same silver Seats of Shame the bottom three on *American Idol* have to sit on before they sing for their lives. They look as comfortable here as they do onstage, which is to say not at all.

I open the fridge to find all kinds of healthy items, like fat-free milk, Greek yogurt, a crisper full of vegetables I don't recognize, and—seriously? *Spirulina powder?* I must be friends with Deva.

Off the back deck, there's a decent-size yard, especially for the city. The area contains lots of Buddhas and shiny rocks in tidy formations. It looks very Zen. And like it might be improved upon with a few flowers—geraniums, maybe. But otherwise, very Zen. There's a garage beyond that. Fingers crossed my old Infiniti's in there!

Off the breakfast nook are the stairs to the basement—that's where I find the house's mechanicals, the laundry area, and tons of storage. Okay, this is weird. I think I just unearthed some of our old furniture. Here's a big Crate & Barrel chair-and-a-half next to a matching couch, and there's a gorgeous red Persian rug rolled up on top of it. Actually, I'd hoped to redo our den in pieces like this before Duke and I broke up—why aren't we using them now? They're too . . . comfortable? I get why we'd want the living room to be a showpiece, but even the TV room? Why are we so formal?

I have much to learn about the past twenty-one years, so I can't dwell down here. Fortunately, I spot a bin labeled *Melissa's Journals* on my way back up the stairs.

Melissa? Who the fuck is Melissa and why is she— Oh. Heh. I grab the plastic tub and haul the whole thing up to my office.

Once in my office, I'm not sure where to begin. It's still pretty early, so I'm hoping to figure out the basics before Duke wakes up. Otherwise? *Awkward!*

Clues abound in here already, though. The framed wedding invitation tells me we've been married for—I do the math, using the fingers on both hands as well as a couple of toes—fourteen years!? I was married at twenty-four? Child bride alert!

As I poke through the cabinets, I find our wedding photo album. Holy puffballs, Batman! I imagine my newfound taste in minimalism stems directly from having worn this hoop-skirted, mutton-sleeved, is-anyone-buying-it-that-I'm-still-a-virgin monstrosity. And my bridesmaids are . . . Nicole (yay!) and three girls who are definitely not the Belles. Ha! Bite me, Tammy!

My office is slightly less forbidding than the rest of the house, even if my desk is mostly glass. A glass desk—who buys a glass desk? I wonder if Duke works for the Windex people?

I notice all kinds of music memorabilia on the shelf across from my desk. Backstage passes and drumsticks and guitar picks and a crazy platform shoe that looks like something Elton John might have worn in the seventies all fight for space on the shelf. I peruse the photos of me with people who look like they're in a band, but I don't recognize any of them. You know what? Duke must do something in the music industry. Maybe he's an exec for the Allstate Arena or the United Center. That's way more badass than when he peddled oatmeal for a living.

As I scan the shelves, I see a superhuggy photo of a college-era Nicole and me and the girls who were in my wedding. We're in matching Greek sweatshirts. Hey! I got into a college with a Greek system! And I was in a sorority! Take that, Cousin Augusta! And screw you and the sloth you rode in on, UCI! Next to that, I see my diploma from Indiana University. That's where Nicole went. I love that we experienced college together. Oh, I can't wait to dig into these journals now!

Seeing these pictures makes me so happy. Aw, there're Duke and me somewhere tropical. And look at how I fill out that bikini top. I peer at the shot more closely and then I look down at myself. Um . . . I press my hands to my chest and give myself a tentative squeeze. Unless gravity's no longer a factor in this century, I had a boob lift! I lift my shirt to get a closer look. Oh, yeah. Those are way perkier. (And yay, me, for not getting implants, because I'm pretty sure I'm not a stripper in my new and improved present.)

Tons more pictures hang on the wall next to the shelves. Look, there's Mamma and me with the Eiffel Tower in the background. Here I am with Cousin Gussie and we're in matching dresses. Bridesmaids, I guess? Whose wedding? Cousin Lydia? Oh, this one's cute. Look at that little girl with her hoodie and her hair in her face. How do I know an adorable little lesbian? Yay, diversity! It gets better! Wait, no . . . WHY AM I HUGGING JUSTIN FRIGGING BIEBER?

I need answers and quick. I sit down at my computer and use the touch pad to bring it to life. Password protected?! Shit!

I try the most obvious ones, like "Belle" and "Lululemon" and all the permutations of my mom's maiden name. No luck. I input variations of my social security number and my parents' phone number. Nada. Then I just type everything that's at the front of my mind.

"DukeofHurl."

"IkatRobe."

"Jägermeister."

"TaterTot."

"Beemer."

"NoSexCake."

"TammySucks."

Damn it! Think, self, think! What would stay with me for twenty years? What's a constant in my life? What's the one word or phrase that I simply can't forget? I snap my fingers. I've got it!

"Coverdale."

I'm in!

Let's learn a little bit more about me.

In the words of Jerry Garcia, what a long, strange trip it's been.

The most interesting part?

Duke's not rich.

I am.

Not because I invented Facebook, though.

Condensed version? After high school, I went to IU to study communications, and while I was there, I took some music theory classes. Moved to L.A. when I graduated (four years, bitches!) and did publicity for a couple of record labels. Duke came with me and worked for a tech company. After 9/11, we wanted to be closer to family, so we came back to

Chicago. Duke did sales for Kraft Foods whereas I started my own PR firm . . . only not in my parents' garage this time.

Ten years later, MCPR (Melissa Connor Public Relations) is a full-service public relations firm, although my personal specialty is working as a music publicist. (I know, right?!) I oversee satellite offices in New York, L.A., Nashville, and Atlanta and dozens of employees. Best part? David Coverdale sends me Christmas cards, because apparently I helped him on a project in '09.

Eight years ago, Nicole quit her job and now she's my number two in the Chicago office. She says managing a bunch of twenty-five-year-old PR girls isn't that different from teaching second grade. Pretty much she's still refereeing equal amounts of petty playground antics, like crying and hair pulling.

I've been in the swing of my awesome new life for about a week. Between my journals and Facebook and Google, I quickly came up to speed on my past. I wish I could access all the best parts in my memory (especially Coverdale), but just being in this life now is pretty damn spectacular. I keep making the most awesome discoveries, like when I realized the impeccable vintage Jag in the garage was mine.

I could not have plotted out a more perfect future for myself if I tried. Professionally, I'm at the top of my field, and that's without having to beg a bunch of old high school classmates for their business. Personally, Duke and I seem happy and the tables are all turned now—he's dependent on me. I like that. A lot. And did I mention I was rich? I couldn't remember who won any games, so I didn't do Sportsbook, but I did make a couple of wise investments.

Oh, please.

It's not technically insider trading, and it's not like the SEC could prove that time travel's why I invested in Apple and Cisco. Like Warren Buffett wouldn't have done the same, given the opportunity. Plus, I spent lots of the money I earned, so really, I've been helping the global economy. I'm kind of a hero, if you think about it.

Most important? I look really, really good. I guess because I didn't endure the stress of what happened in my past-future, I didn't live through three months of the second coming of Paula Deen at my parents' house. If I had any Rock & Republic jeans now, they'd fit great!

(Note to self: Take a day to go shopping, like, immediately.)

Plus, people seem to enjoy my company. They don't fear me like they did in high school, but that's really okay.

I must bring Deva up to speed, but when I call her shop, I find out she's at her place in Hawaii. Her employee gives me a contact number, so I text her instead.

> **Me:** hey, deva! lissy here! back in the future, baby!
>
> **Deva:** outhouse, lassie roadhouse! everything worked out for yoo-hoo?

I quickly realize that texting is not Deva's forte. Big fingers.

> **Me:** couldn't be better! happy marriage, real friends, fab job. small ass, huge house—all good in my hood!
>
> **Deva:** you've achieved chlorine, porpoise, and inner pieces?

Oh, honey, I think, you have no idea how much chlorine, porpoise, and inner pieces my snappy new black AmEx can buy.

> **Me:** totes. still trying to get used to how everyone calls me melissa connor, but otherwise, aces!

> **Deva:** how are ur parrots?

> **Me:** ?

> **Deva:** parrots

> **Me:** ??

> **Deva:** pantaloons

> **Deva:** apartheid

> **Deva:** ptarmigan

> **Deva:** parentheses

> **Deva:** NO!! HATE AUTOMOBILE!

> **Me:** ???

> **Deva:** argh! parents. how are yon parents, lucy rye bread?

> **Me:** had dinner with yon parents on tuesday—r fine

That's the truth. They're fine. My mom naturally commandeered most of the conversation, so, business as usual. I didn't love instantly seeing twenty-one additional years on their faces, although Daddy's showing his age a lot more than Mamma. He's still doing crazy hours at the firm, but I guess he's kind of a workaholic. Nothing new there.

Deva: oaky, just checkout

Deva: checker

Deva: check in mail

Deva: dam! checking!

Me: new client coming in 5, gtg—talk when u get back

Deva: cunt

Me: i'm sorry?

Deva: oh, deer, no! NO! c u later, lacy romper! argh! hate autocorrect!!

Me: take care and say hey to the mayans for me

I turn off my phone and pull up the meeting brief one of my assistants prepared. (Assistants! Plural!) We're trying to woo a new pop sensation away from our competitors and today's our first sit-down.

According to my notes—did I mention that Future Lissy—
I mean, Melissa—has been working on a memoir?—"I normally approach a new client interaction by really staying quiet.
I let them do all the talking. I find in so doing, they'll tell me
exactly what's most important to them and I can build my
strategy around their wants and needs." Wow, how smart was
my future parallel-universe self?

According to the brief, this kid we're pitching, known to
her legion of fans as ChaCha, became an overnight sensation
due to some YouTube videos. Unfortunately, I've not watched
any of them yet. My stupid computer's making me batty—
every time I try to access streaming media, I buffer and never
load. Seriously, I can slip through a wormhole in the cosmos
with no issue, but can I access a video of a bear bouncing off
a trampoline? Negatory. Fortunately, there's an IT guy coming
to take a look at my laptop later today.

I glance at ChaCha's CD cover. Hmm. The photo caught
her in motion, so her features aren't real clear, but she looks
thirty with all the hair and makeup. She seems familiar, but
that's likely because this little girl is what would happen if
Britney and Ke$ha had a baby, sprayed her with glitter, and
sent her to work the main stage.

But her songs are incredibly popular, even though they're
so bubblegum/electropop that they make me want to stab myself in the ear with a letter opener. Is she talented? No clue.
Couldn't tell you what her actual voice sounds like, because
her tracks have been Auto-Tuned to death. The bulk of her
audience is between eight and fifteen years old, and every time
ChaCha goes to a shopping mall, riots ensue. And yet David
Coverdale can hit Whole Foods in Lake Tahoe and be completely unnoticed, at least according to his recent Christmas
card. That seems so wrong.

Regardless, ChaCha's first single, "Fruck You," has been one of iTunes' most downloaded songs in history, and her follow-up, "No Frucking Way," from the new *Motherfrucker* album, is on a similar trajectory. I wonder what Brian's take would be on her music? Would he be all, "Give her some pants, slap a guitar in her hand, and she's a baby Janis Joplin," or more like, "So *that's* what three cats in a blender sounds like."

My first assistant, Mandy, intercoms me. "Melissa? They're here. Everyone's in the south conference room when you're ready. I put out coffee, soda, juice, tea, Red Bull, fruit, and assorted pastries, so they should be in fine shape if you need a second."

"Great, thanks!" I reply. I find now that I actually have responsibility, I've risen to the occasion. Honestly, it's not like I didn't know a lot of this stuff in my previous-future. PR's not exactly brain surgery. (No offense.) If you've amassed decent media contacts, if you can compose a sentence, if you're not afraid of using exclamation points, and if you possess the ability to bullshit/talk your way out of trouble/occasionally deny everything despite overwhelming evidence to the contrary, you're three-quarters of the way to success. Throw in motivation, determination, and a continental breakfast? Boom! Done.

I grab a notebook and a pen and stride down the hallway. I catch a glimpse of myself on the glass wall in front of the conference room. I come across as confident and happy, and the clothes and hair lend a certain gravitas that I've never had before. Clearly these aren't the sartorial choices I'd have made in my previous-future, but they sure seem to be working in this case.

I spy ChaCha and her team before they see me. Their

backs are to the glass wall and they're all hovering around the buffet. I'm guessing the one in the fishnet top, shorty-shorts, and army boots who's scooping cream cheese out of the Danish center and sucking it off her fingers is ChaCha. Charming.

I peg the guys in the shiny suits as her manager, agent, and attorney, and smart money says the mountain of a man in the untucked oxford with the shaved head is her security detail. The two trashy women (not judgey if it's true) are likely her hair and makeup people, and the guy in khakis who's standing really stiffly is her dad. I wonder if I'm used to teenagers with entourages in my new future.

I open the door and announce, "Hello! Welcome! I'm Melissa Connor of Melissa Connor Public Relations! Thanks so much for being here. I'm really looking forward to finding out what we can do for you."

Everyone turns around, including ChaCha.

Who, under all the makeup and truck stop waitress uniform, is actually *Charlotte*.

What the fruck?

CHAPTER TEN
Ripples

My thoughts immediately begin racing. Why is Charlotte here? When did she become a pop star? Why didn't anyone tell me? And does Nicole know her stepkid owns such obscene shorts?

The first person to speak is Bobby. He steps forward and extends a hand. "Ms. Connor, hello. I'm Bobby Paulson, Charlotte's father, and we'd—"

"My name is *ChaCha*, all right? ChaCha," Charlotte spits. "Get it right, *Bobby*." Then she digs out a crystal-studded iPhone I've never seen and begins to furiously text with her smudgy digits while Bobby shrugs sheepishly.

Um . . . why are they acting like I'm a stranger? Duke and I have spent every Thanksgiving with them for the past six years. We went to Puerto Rico together and New Orleans, and I've been to his little cabin in Wisconsin a dozen times. Maybe

I don't see him all the time, but I talk to his wife every day. I was maid of honor at his wedding. I was there when his babies were born.

Okay, I wasn't *there*, per se, but I sent lovely gift baskets. Or I meant to, anyway. Thoughts count.

Regardless, my hair's not so different, and I'm not that much thinner than I was before my postbreakup breakdown over the summer, so why is there zero flash of recognition? "Bobby, it's Lissy."

"Have we met before?" he asks politely.

"What's a *Lissy*?" Charlotte demands. "What, is that like a combination of 'lick' and 'pussy'? Ha! Seraphina, did you hear what I said? That means this bitch eats at the Y! Ha! Haa!" The one with the Bettie Page neck tattoo, presumably Seraphina, nods in appreciation at ChaCha's scathing wit. Charlotte responds with a profoundly vivid fingers-and-mouth gesture.

Oh, *hell*, no.

According to Nicole, Bobby's never been a disciplinarian, so I'm not surprised at this heinous brat's behavior in his presence. Actually, Nicole's parenting style is a tad indulgent for my taste, too, because when did it become okay for children to be seen *and* heard? Still, Nicole has some standards and clearly this teenage terrorist is violating all of them. The earth would open up and swallow Nicole whole before she allowed this kind of chatter from a kid . . . even if said kid can sell out Madison Square Garden.

My mission is clear.

"I'm so sorry—I just realized there's someone missing. Please excuse me while I grab her. Have some more coffee. Perhaps you'd like to disembowel another Danish, ChaCha?" I flash an icy grin before I spin on my heel and dash down

the hallway to Nicole's office. I drag her back to the conference room and hustle her through the door. I'm not even
going to tell her what's going on. I'm just going to let her
witness it so she can fix it. Maybe getting a good old ass-
whoopin' in front of her attorney is just what this junior Girl
Gone Wild needs.

Undaunted, Nicole steps forward and offers her hand.
"Hi, there. I'm Nicole Golden. Pleasure to meet you. Melissa
asked me to sit in on the meeting, if you don't mind."

I'm desperately confused. What's with the introductions?
Why are they not hugging? Or laughing? How come the she-
devil's face didn't light up like it always does when Nic walks
in the room?

And, wait a hot minute, since when is she Nicole *Golden*?
She's been Nicole Paulson for more than six years, and this is
her husband and booty-short-wearing, beating-needing, wicked
stepdaughter. I glance at Nicole's ring finger and notice she's
not wearing the big rock Bobby gave her three months after
they met.

Slowly the pieces begin to come together. If Nicole's been
working here with me for eight years, then . . . that means she
didn't meet Bobby seven and a half years ago at a PTA event,
so . . .

Holy guacamole!

If they never met, then they certainly didn't get married. If
they weren't married, then they didn't churn out enough sticky
progeny to require the purchase of a minivan. I guess that'd
explain why she hadn't plastered her office with their photos.
Shit! I thought she was just being professional by not yammer-
ing on about potty training and playdates and being all in my
face with class pictures!

Unable to handle the gravity of the situation, I land in one of the conference room chairs with a thump. Everyone else follows suit.

As I'm too stunned to speak coherently, Nicole adroitly takes over and starts a round of introductions. Although I've not actually seen her in action this time around, I have a feeling that Nicole's a better second than I am a first sometimes.

As we go around the room saying who we are and what we do, I learn I was right about everyone except the two women. Seraphina is Charlotte's swagger coach.

(Note to self: Google "swagger coach.")

(Suspect it has something to do with Bieber.)

(Fucking Bieber ruins everything.)

The other bimbo with all the purple hair extensions and a skirt the size of a hankie is named Tawny. She's Charlotte's *stepmother.*

I suddenly hate everyone and everything.

More so than usual, I mean.

I guess it stands to reason that if Nicole and Bobby never met each other, he's allowed to be with someone else, but, really, *her*? What attracted him to this cut-rate Pamela Anderson? An uncanny ability to tweeze her brows into twin pencil-thin mustaches? A deep and abiding love of small swaths of unnatural fibers? Her exemplary parenting skills? Them together makes as much sense as when Tiger Woods banged that Waffle House waitress instead of his Swedish bikini-model wife. Opting for her over Nicole would be like considering ordering a filet and instead eating a Band-Aid off a public toilet.

As Team ChaCha discusses expectations and goals, I steal glances at the new Mrs. Bobby Paulson. Were I forced to describe this woman in one word, that word would be . . . herpes.

While Nicole expertly explains the way our company handles online campaign management, Tawny interrupts with a question. "How much you gonna pay ChaCha for this?"

ChaCha's manager pokes the agent under the table and her attorney rolls his eyes, while the bodyguard makes a small moue of disgust. Gamely, Bobby volunteers, "This is a publicity firm, Tawny, baby. If we choose to work with them, we'd be paying them for their time and effort."

Tawny snorts. "That don't sound right. You should be giving us money if you want to be associated with my little ChaCha."

Pfft. More like her little *cha-ching*. There's no way Charlotte isn't her meal ticket.

ChaCha glances up from her phone, nods, and then gets back to her game of Angry Birds, currently being played at full volume.

Tawny continues. "ChaCha's an international megastar. Everybody wants her to promote their stuff. Just yesterday, we heard from a manufacturer out of Japan who wants to pay her boo-koo bucks to be the face of their product."

Nicole replies, "We would absolutely find your daughter opportunities to cross-promote, because that can be a powerful brand-builder. Look at what Rihanna's done with Cover Girl and Michael Jordan with Hanes, just as two small examples. With proper execution, the celebrity becomes even more iconic, she's exposed to new audiences on a variety of platforms, and product sales soar." She grins and all at the table follow suit. Nicole has a way of making everything sound so nice. "Everyone wins. May I ask, what does the Japanese company want ChaCha to promote?"

"Condoms with Hello Kitty on them."

While I choke on my water, Nicole smoothly suggests,

"Perhaps we should weigh all her opportunities before part-nering with any brands."

Charlotte's attorney and manager both mouth, *Thank you*, in unison, while Tawny pouts and bangs the table, spill-ing Bobby's orange juice. Without missing a beat, Nicole hands him a stack of napkins. It's like it's impossible for her *not* to act like someone's mom.

"Well, fuck me sideways. That's why this one won't let ChaCha do any club promotions in Vegas." Tawny points an inch-long French-tipped nail toward the agent, who currently appears to be biting his own lip hard enough to draw blood. Then she gestures toward the manager. "And you! Thought you Jews were all about gettin' paid, but, noooo. It's all, 'She can't sell condoms; she's a kid,' and, 'Maybe we should wait till she's outta ninth grade to pose topless.' Buncha Baptists, all of you. 'Cept for the Jew, of course."

The attorney keeps glancing at his watch. Oh, buddy, I really, really hope your hourly rate is worth it.

Eventually, Nicole's able to wrest control of the meeting away from Tawny and moves on to discuss crisis management. Somehow I suspect ChaCha's going to need a contingency plan sooner rather than later with Discount Dina Lohan at the helm.

Every time Tawny opens her maw, the differences between her and Nicole become more pronounced. What on earth does Bobby see in Tawny, outside of her overt (to the point of gro-tesque) sexuality? Nicole's all petite and athletic and adorable, with glossy brown hair and lashes that look fake but totally aren't, a lot like Natalie Wood in *Splendor in the Grass* before her character went batshit over young hotty Warren Beatty and was admitted to a mental institution.

You know, that's probably not the best example.

What I'm saying is that Nicole is lovely and light and lithe, all big eyes and high cheekbones and taut muscles. She's elegant and thoughtful and moves like a dancer, always swirling around in full skirts and ballerina flats. In the five minutes since Mrs. Tawny Paulson stopped trying to extort money from MCPR, she's thrust her hand in her blouse twice to reposition an enormous melon, and she's presently panning for gold in her ear canal. With my pen.

When she tries to hand it back, I wave her off. "That's okay. I have plenty more back at my desk."

Nicole leads the discussion while I attempt to make sense of the situation. Deva did explain that any changes in the past would impact the future, but it never occurred to me that *this* might be one of the changes. I'm all conflicted by the questions this meeting has raised.

Is awful Charlotte saddled with this terrible fame whore of a stepmom because of me?

Further, does Nicole not have kids because I changed the past? I wasn't a fan of her brood, per se, but I never meant for them *not to exist.*

Then again, if she never had her children or that life, she wouldn't specifically miss them, right?

I really need to speak with Deva.

I hope she's back soon.

Our meeting with Team ChaCha lasts an hour, and when we're done, I'm less concerned with rips in the fabric of time resulting in one unholy pairing, and more concerned that Nicole talked this hateful child's team into working with us.

"Shall we grab some lunch and discuss?" I suggest.

"Yay! I'd love to. I need to answer a few e-mails and I want to check in on Facebook real quick, but I'll meet you by the elevator at noon." We part and head back to our respective offices on opposite sides of the conference room.

Ah, Facebook! Yes! That's where I need to go. I'll look at her page and find out what's going on with her, because clearly things aren't like they were before. Whether or not that's for the better is still to be determined. At no point in the past week did I consider that changing my past might drastically alter anyone else's in any way but positive, so this is a bit daunting.

I settle into my desk in the corner office, with the entire Chicago cityscape behind me. But I'm not distracted by the view for once, because I'm on a mission. I boot up my laptop and make a mental note again to check on the tech appointment because this damn thing still isn't running correctly. If Nicole posted any streaming videos, I can't access them, but otherwise I should be good to go.

I decide pictures really are worth a thousand words, so I pull up her photo page first. In the previous-future, she had a million shots of holidays and playdates and birthdays and other toddler-related firsts. I was always very careful not to "like" it when she'd post a photo with a caption such as "Bobby Junior's first bite of sweet potatoes!" showing a kid smeared with orange goo, because A) gross, and B) I saw no reason to encourage her to share more of the same. You've seen one toddler in the bath, you've seen 'em all. Plus, if she puts up kid pics, someone else will think it's fine to put up kid pics; then everyone puts up kid pics and it's suddenly anarchy. There should be a whole Facebook for people who don't have children, much like there should be child-free restaurants. Ooh, or airlines! Seriously, how much would nonbreeders pay to ensure a screaming-baby-free flight? A lot, I'd imagine. I could publicize the shit out of any place that barred children and—

Ahem.

Anyway.

I still see a bunch of kid pictures on here, but it looks like they all belong to her brother, which is confirmed by her *Number One Aunt* T-shirt she's sporting in this shot from the Lincoln Park Zoo. Okay, so she has no children herself, but at least she's an aunt, right? That's kind of the same, except your house stays clean and you don't get hideous stretch marks.

So . . . her future is definitely different now, but am I to blame? It's not as though I forced her to work for me, like, held her at gunpoint or anything. She made the choice that ultimately took her out of the situation where she'd meet Bobby. That's not my fault . . . right?

I dig deeper into her profile. I click over to her wall. Looks like she's "in a relationship" with someone named Emcee Peere of Chicago. Sounds like a swarthy club promoter, but hopefully he makes her happy. Seriously? Whew! For a second I worried she was alone with a bunch of cats in her altered life. Let's have a look-see at Mr. Peere. I click and land on the MCPR Chicago page.

Oh. Pun on being married to her job. That's not cute.

I can't believe she's not married, or at least dating someone. She's a total catch! Now I'm really distressed—am I such a hard-ass that she feels like she's married to her job? Or is she married to her job because there's not a lot of stuff, like a husband and family, filling out the rest of her life? Beads of sweat break out over my lip as I begin to panic, so I try to talk myself down.

Nicole is upbeat and positive and happy, and she's in control of her own destiny, not me.

I'm sure her life is fulfilling and I'm just being silly.

While I peruse her page a new post appears in her timeline, and it's a shot of a black-and-white cat with a little spot over his lip that makes him look like Hitler. The caption reads, "Mr. Muffin—the number one man in my life!"

Well, fuck me sideways.

I tab through page after page of Nicole's life and I find more of the same. There's Nicole at an office party; there she is at a client event; there she is in another city on MCPR business. How's she supposed to meet anyone when she spends all of her time in an office and an industry that's comprised almost entirely of chicks and gay guys? More important, am I to blame?

What do I do here?

What's my obligation?

Am I supposed to fix this?

Do I try to help her meet someone?

Deva, these aren't ripples in time; they're tidal waves.

"All set!" It's noon and I'm waiting by the elevator as planned. Nicole sashays up to me in her swingy jacket and grabs me for a quick hug. "I'm so excited! We never have the chance to just hang out and talk! What are you in the mood for, sushi or salad?"

I realize that future me is all trim and toned and healthy, but I haven't quite gotten over my recent discovery of how comfort food reduces stress, and trust me, I'm stressed right now. Trying to figure out if I screwed up my best friend's life is definitely ratcheting up my anxiety level, so the last thing I want is lettuce or raw fish. I'm going to broach some heavy subjects at lunch, so I need to be girded by as many fat grams and calories as possible.

"What about Prosecco?" I suggest, thinking about the wonderful Italian place in River North. "I'm buying."

Come on. It's the least I can do. *Hey, bestie, sorry I altered your fate—have some bruschetta on me!*

"Sounds fabulous. We haven't had carbs in ages. Want to cab it or shall I drive?" Nicole asks.

I'm probably going to need a cocktail, particularly if I determine that I laid ruin to her life. "Let's take a taxi," I suggest.

Upon arrival, we both order glasses of wine and peruse the menu. Such is my state that I pretty much want to order one of everything. I want steamed mussels and clams tossed in saffron cream sauce with chunks of *pane italiano* to sop up the drippings. I want burrata, the mozzarella that's so fresh that it's semisolid, and I want to pair it with salty prosciutto. Oh, or carpaccio so rare that it's still a little blue. I'm in the mood for pasta with truffle oil and asparagus, and I want to wash it all down with something bubbly, because maybe food will tamp down my guilt.

What I don't want is to have this conversation, but after Nicole saved my (chewy, smoky) bacon from the fire today, I feel like I have no other choice.

We order our first course—avocado and poached lobster salad—and I broach the subject. "Some meeting today, right? How much did you hate the kid?"

"Charlotte? She was adorable!" Nicole protests.

"Were we in the same room?" Charlotte, or rather Cha-Cha, was many things . . . but adorable? No. "Did you not witness her breaking wind and then fanning said fart toward Seraphina to determine if she could 'smell the Chipotle in it'? Not adorable."

For the record, I was also not charmed when she burped the alphabet (at Tawny's behest), blew her nose on her manager's napkin before tossing it back on the table, or called me "what's-her-tits."

"Aw, Liss, she's sweet underneath it all, just a little misguided. Right now the whole world is bending over backward for her and that has an impact, especially at her age. I'm sure fame took her by surprise, and as she gets used to it, she'll settle down."

So Nicole's Team Charlotte even without knowing how linked they were in the previous iteration of our lives? Super.

"Besides," she continues, "I think Tawny's overzealous, not evil. I saw women like her all the time when I was teaching. They didn't achieve what they wanted in their own lives, so they placed the burden of success on their children. There's a lot of stage moms out there, and not just for those trying to get their kids into the entertainment business. Sometimes they're just as bad about sports and academics. Like, remember that Texas cheerleading mom who hired a hit man to kill another cheerleader's mom so her daughter's rival would drop out of the competition?"

I nod. Back in the day, Mamma was all, "A li'l extreme, but I lahk her style."

Nicole nibbled a piece of lobster before blotting her lips with a linen napkin. "Certainly Tawny's not that intense, but the thought process is the same, all about advancing her kid. Time after time, I've seen moms so intent on making their children well-rounded that they'd drag the poor things to jujitsu followed by Mandarin lessons in between soccer, gymnastics, cello, and Irish dancing and then not understand why Junior didn't have time to get his math assignment done. I'd tell them, 'Give him a break; he's seven!' "

I pick at a piece of bread, smearing it with an olive tapenade. "Would the moms listen to you?"

"Once in a while yes, most often no. Charlotte's stepmom's no different from most. A bit more colorful, perhaps, but ultimately I feel like she's trying to balance her own need for approval with what makes Charlotte happy."

"You're a frigging saint."

Nicole simply shrugs in return.

"How would you do it?" I ask. I'm not sure I want to look her in the eye for this, so I pay close attention to the patterns I'm tracing on the tablecloth.

Nicole sets down her fork and leans forward. "Do what, exactly?"

"Go about the whole being-a-parent thing. I mean, you never went that route, so maybe it's not important to you?"

Please say it's not, please say it's not, please say it's not.

"Funny you should mention that." Except, judging from Nicole's expression, it's far from funny. "I had a doctor's appointment last week. I'd missed my last couple of periods and I was hoping for good news."

"Wait, I thought you weren't seeing anyone seriously right now." So now Facebook is a lie, too? Great.

"I'm not. I . . . tried artificial insemination. I've been trying to get pregnant ever since my thirty-fifth birthday."

Did I know this? I'm not sure if I was supposed to know this, but I keep my yap shut as she continues. "Thirty-five. That's supposed to be the age you reach when you're more likely to be killed in a terrorist attack than to get married and have a family. I didn't mention it because if it worked, then it would be obvious soon enough. And if it didn't, then no one would pity me. I missed a couple of periods and I wasn't feeling well, so I made an appointment with my obgyn."

I brace myself in my seat, because I have a feeling this isn't going to end well.

Tears begin to brim in Nicole's eyes. "But I'm not having

a baby. No, I'm not. Nor will I. According to Dr. Bates, I've hit menopause and I've stopped producing eggs."

"How can that be? You're still way young! People have babies well into their forties! I know, because I bump into them in the Lincoln Park Whole Foods all the time." And how bossy are they, all gray haired and self-important, stocking up on organic vegetables. *Hey! Look at me! I don't buy shit with preservatives!* Like that'll make a difference when their baby's in college and they're wearing white shoes and eating dinner at three thirty p.m. But I stop myself from saying all this, because I fear it may not be helpful. Instead, I say, "What's going on?"

"I guess I just won the genetic lottery," she replies with an uncharacteristically bitter laugh. "Dr. Bates says this can happen in women with a genetic predisposition, especially if they're particularly athletic and have a low body weight. So, I've been hyperconscious about my health my whole life. I run five miles every day, and I've minded each bite I've taken since I was fifteen, and because of that, I can't have a baby. It's just . . . so unfair. I thought I had time. I thought I did everything right and yet I feel like I'm destined to spend my life surrounded by cats." Nicole dabs at her eyes with her napkin and exhales deeply. "But what am I going to do? It's not like I can change the past."

I fold my napkin and place it on the table, suddenly bereft of appetite. "Yeah," I echo, "no one can change the past."

Nicole, what have I done?

CHAPTER ELEVEN
Rhymes with "Bedazzled"

I change the subject away from what might have been, and Nicole's mood lifts. She seems okay with the concept of adopting from somewhere third-worldly, so maybe saving some poor kid from a warlord or tainted water or banana spider bite or something is really her destiny?

And maybe she's actually superhappy and feels bummed only when she dwells on the negative? Stands to reason that setting myself up in the best life ever would really have been a good thing for Nicole, yes? (That would certainly make me feel better.)

Once I grab a cab to go home, I text Deva.

> **Me:** need to talk! can u pick up?
>
> **Deva:** y and n. can text, not talk. on retreat in Maui—have taken bowel of silence

Please let that be another autocorrect.

Me: i may have wrecked Nicole's life

Deva: again?

Me: no! 1st time! never wrecked her life before

Me: possibly made it less pleasant

Me: not wrecked

Deva: oak tag—what harpooned?

Me: she didn't meet her husband because I changed past. waited 2 long to have kids & now can't

Me: can I travel back to 2004 & not hire her so she gets the guy & the kids & van?

Deva: so sorry, sissy rodent. ink potion doesn't work that way. only full resets possible. porthole very pacific—all or netting

Me: shit. when will u be back?

Deva: whenever shamwow says we're dinner—maybe 2 tweaks

Me: PLEASE call when you're here

Deva: a-hole

Me: ?

Deva: no! aloha!

Me: aloha til then

Even though Deva says there's nothing I can do to specifically fix this situation, I'm not someone who takes no for an answer. Also, her texts are kind of a Mad Lib anyway, so who knows what she really meant? Perhaps there's a way to make everything right without altering my superb present and we simply haven't stumbled across it yet.

At least, that's what I'm telling myself.

At some point over our second bottle of pinot grigio, I had broached the subject of a class reunion. I assumed we hadn't had one yet and turns out I was right. I thought doing so would be an excellent idea, partially because Nicole needs a project to distract herself, and partially because I want to verify that there aren't any more surprises with my graduating class.

(Not because I want to brag.)

(Much.)

(But seriously! My house is incredible! I know David Coverdale!)

The more we talked (read: drank), the more excited we both were at the idea. Nicole called in a favor from a friend at the Drake and we found out about a last-minute cancellation on the Friday after Thanksgiving. As former class officers, we have the authority to unilaterally decide if there's to be a re-union, so now it's official. The reunion is on like Donkey Kong. Nicole went home to build a Facebook event page.

Or possibly pass out.

She wasn't quite sure.

When I arrive home from our long, liquid lunch, I'm struck again at the grandeur of my house as the cab pulls up to my address.

"Nice place, lady," the driver says.

"I know, right?" I hand him a ten and tell him to keep the change.

I stroll slowly to the front door, taking it all in. Every time I look around, I feel such a rush of pride. I can't believe I ended up here; it's beyond my wildest dreams. I let myself in and throw my Birkin (yep, still exciting! I have a Birkin, bitches!) on the counter and kick off my shoes. I go to grab a bottle of water from the fridge and, finding none, I opt for wine.

"Duke? Duke! Where are you-*ou-ou*?" This place has a wicked echo because it's so huge and open. I should probably buy more stuff to fill up the house. Not for me, of course. For sound absorption.

Duke's not on the first floor, so I assume he's in his office. I climb the stairs and pad down the hallway. I don't turn on the lights because there are a whole lot of complicated switches I've yet to figure out, and also, I might be a little drunk.

I spy Duke alone in his office. He's not on his computer or resting or listening to music or anything. He's just sitting there, zoning out in front of his wall of old trophies and foot-ball pictures. Duke played college ball at Northern, but a torn rotator cuff ended any hopes he might have had at making a career of it after his junior year. I guess he was pretty broken up about the injury, but let's be realistic—how many players have actually gone pro after graduating from Northern? I can tell you, because I looked it up—from the years 1992 to 2000, the NFL drafted exactly four guys from Northern. It's not like he was coming out of a football powerhouse like USC or Ohio State. Even without the bum cuff, it's not like he was going to be fitted for his Super Bowl ring anytime soon.

You'd think he'd have been pleased when I informed him of those statistics—yay, me, for having shared interests!—but instead of discussing he decided to run on the treadmill for a really long time.

Totally doesn't matter, because he's really the big winner in this whole altered-destiny business. I mean, he doesn't even have to work anymore. Who wouldn't love that? Turns out I had him quit a few years ago when the demands of my business became too much. Now he lives a life of luxury and leisure, traveling with me and managing our household.

"What's up?" I ask, startling him. He jumps, which makes me jump and slosh a little of my wine. He clicks on the light at his desk and the room's washed in a golden glow.

"I didn't hear you come in." He seems somber. What's that about?

I settle into the love seat in the corner of his office and lick the wine off the side of my glass. "Nice day? Mine was kind of all over the place. We have a new client—total train wreck of a tween pop star and her music is shit. Although given your taste you'd probably love her."

Duke's passion for cheesy tunes has not abated since high school. A couple of days ago, I'm pretty sure I busted him watching a Jonas Brothers show, and I found a Hanson CD in his collection. *MmmBarf.* From what I've gleaned, everyone at the office still talks about how Duke lost his mind at the Backstreet Boys/NKOTB reunion show, which we attended *only* because MCPR worked with their promoter. Total fan boy. In the pictures, he was there in an original T-shirt from their *Step by Step* tour. Duke even knew—and thus performed—all the choreography for "Hangin' Tough." So glad I have no direct memory of that, because it gives me secondhand shame.

Duke nods absently. "Nicole's in charge of most of the hand-holding and the team will run her campaigns, so I should be fairly distanced. And thank God, too, because the mom is this silicone nightmare and the kid's an after-school special waiting to happen. Huge retainer on the deal, though, so if you feel like going somewhere awesome for the holidays, say the word! I hear Vienna is ah-*may*-zing at Christmas." In our old life, we rarely traveled because Duke was always, "Blah, blah, blah, my job is important and I can't just take off." Now he rolls as though he actually were an NFL baller!

"Hmm." Duke's started flipping through his old photos online. "Hey, remember when we beat Hinsdale at homecoming? That was some night." He sounds awfully wistful, which is weird. I mean, hello, best life ever! Would he rather be busting his hump all day, like he would be if I hadn't gone back and redetermined our future? Either way his cuff would have torn. Plus, right now he'd probably be stuck in Kansas City or Pittsburgh, trying to sell pallets of macaroni and cheese to Costco before coming back to our one-bedroom-plus-den hovel. Please. In this life he has all the time in the world to do any damn thing he wants. He's a lucky, lucky man, thanks to me.

I kick my legs out in front of me and my arms above my head, doing a full-body stretch. I'm kind of sore. Drinking all day is harder than you'd think. "What'd you do today, babe?"

His mouth twists in a wry smile. "Let's see, I had coffee and watched *Today*, picked up your coat from the dry cleaner—your button is fixed—I watered the plants, I had a haircut, I played a pickup game of basketball at the gym with a bunch of stay-at-home dads, and then I vacuumed. Very fulfilling. Not a waste of my degree or talent at all. I'd much rather be here than working what you used to call my 'sales job a macaroni-eating monkey could do.'"

"Excellent!" I declare.

Then what he said starts to sink in.

I must be a little slow on the uptake from all the wine.

"Vacuumed? Don't we have people to do that?"

Duke starts to say something, but then snaps his mouth shut. "I'm cooking dinner now. Swordfish in caper sauce sound appetizing?" He pushes himself back from his desk rather quickly and rises. The sudden motion makes all his pictures and trophies teeter for a second.

Well, that's all wrong. "Hey, babe, you worked your cute little behind off today. Relax! Treat yourself! Let's just order dinner in," I tell him. Without a word, he leaves the room.

I congratulate myself on my thoughtfulness.

Some days it's like I'm the greatest wife in the universe.

After dinner from Old Town Thai, Duke spent some time hitting the punching bag extra hard. You'd think from all that vacuuming his arms would be tired, or that it might bother his rotator cuff, but he was supermotivated. Probably because he's full of bliss. I mean, he's way more cut now than back when he was working all the time in our other life, so how could that not be satisfying?

Inspired by his motivation, I tried riding the recumbent bike but decided I was probably still too buzzed, so I sat on the bike and shopped online instead. Everything in my Bloomingdale's cart was some shade of pink and all my Sur La Table items were red. There's no reason we can't have a little color up in here. No offense, future-universe Melissa, but your taste is way beige.

After my failed workout and shopping extravaganza, I settle in to watch television in the bedroom. My teeth are brushed, my face is washed, and I'm wearing enough placenta-based eye cream to ward off crow's-feet until the next century. I just finished viewing *Real Housewives of Shaker Heights* and now I've switched over to the local news while I decide which jammies to wear.

I'll be ready to get in bed shortly, so I click on the intercom (I have an intercom system!) to see if Duke's coming up soon. He banged around the gym forever but he stopped half an hour ago. I was all, "Settle down, Hercules! You're already a fab trophy husband!"

I press the button and move close to the speaker. "Hey, what are you doing down there?"

"Making myself a drink." Apparently since he never puked in my car due to Jack, Jolt, and Jäger, he still has a taste for Tennessee sipping whiskey, and his preferred method of delivery is straight up. Blech. I'd rather swill turpentine. But at least his choice of libation is less girly than his taste in tunes.

"Are you coming to bed?" I purr, as come-hither as the intercom will allow. Not to be all TMI, but the new and improved Lissy/Melissa rocks the sheer chemise. I have a whole drawer of super-sex-goddess wisps of fabric and lace from La Perla and I'm not afraid to use 'em. We were all in flagrante delicto last week and I couldn't help but admire how ripped my back is when I caught a glimpse of myself in the mirror. I'm talking Madonna shoulders here. So buff!

Something must have been lost in translation, though, because Duke is all, "Maybe later."

Footie pajamas it is, then.

I'm smoothing on a coat of Kanebo Sensai Premier the Body Cream (four hundred dollars/tub, but I'm worth it!) when something on the news catches my attention. I wander into the bedroom and press the back button on the DVR.

I rewind too far, and then I forward ahead too far, so I rewind again and just sit on the tufted ottoman at the end of the bed while I wait for the mattress commercial to finish. (Note to self: If I'm ever in a position of power, all mattress commercials will be pulled from the air immediately due to their giving me boredom cancer. Also? Any feminine protection ads utilizing clear blue fluid. Seriously, if I start leaking something out of my blowhole that looks like antifreeze, my concern will *not* be for my tennis whites.)

WGN anchor Micah Materre, all striking in a festive fuchsia suit, reports, "Investigators are looking into the automobile accident that occurred on Saturday, involving an Elgin-area science teacher and three of her students who were returning from an academic decathlon in Whiting, Indiana. Marcella Raymond's on the scene to tell us more."

The news cuts to a cute reporter standing out on the side of the Dan Ryan who seems none too happy to be spending her evening in the dark and cold, two feet away from semis blowing past at eighty-five miles per hour.

"Thanks, Micah. Although no one was seriously injured in Saturday's crash, investigators are pursuing allegations that the teacher had been under the influence while transporting students." While Marcella reports, accident footage of a dented Chevy Malibu being towed rolls on-screen. When the camera cuts back to Marcella, a couple of thuggish teenagers in stupid low-hanging pants have since pulled up and are working their way into the shot. They begin making faces at the camera and are either waving or flashing gang signs.

(Note to self: Again, when I rule the universe, anyone caught loitering in the background while a news crew is attempting to report will be summarily kicked in the face by the reporter without fear of repercussion.)

Marcella's lips tighten into a frown when she realizes she's not alone on-screen, but she quickly recovers and continues with the story. (Seriously, how much would she like to kick those kids right now? Especially wearing something steel-toed?)

"A spokesman for Amy Childs of Bartlett, Illinois, claims these charges are unfounded. However, Childs was arrested on the scene and school board officials have since put her on administrative leave."

Oh, no wonder this caught my attention. Amy Childs isn't that common a name. Of course, it's not like this is *the* Dr. Amy Childs, plastic surgeon to the stars, maker of s'mores, and talk-show-host bestie.

I'm about to turn off the television when another picture flashes across the screen.

"Childs, seen here at a 2010 student jamboree, has faced similar charges previously. In 2003, she was arrested for failing a field sobriety test that showed her blood alcohol at point ten percent, which is above the legal limit to be considered intoxicated and . . ."

But I don't hear whatever Marcella says next, because I've paused my DVR. I can't stop staring at the photo of teacher Amy Childs.

Who's a dead ringer for *Dr.* Amy Childs.

Am I still drunk?

I fly down the stairs to my office and immediately Google

"Amy Childs." The first entry to come up is that of an Amy Andrea Childs, a British reality television star who's most renowned for bringing the word "vajazzle" into the public lexicon.

That's probably not her.

I find a Facebook page with the right Amy's picture, but when I pull up the account, it's set to private, so I can't tell anything about her. The online news articles show the same shot I saw on WGN and that doesn't answer any questions. Then I have the idea to do an image search and I find a (non-vajazzled) shot of her on the North Elgin school Web site, followed by a bio.

Amy Childs has been with North Elgin High School since her student teaching days. Miss Childs attended Lyons Township High School, graduating in 1992, before pursuing a degree in secondary science education at University of Central Illinois. Miss Childs is the faculty sponsor of the NEHS Academic Decathletes and a member of the National Association of Biology Teachers. In her spare time, she enjoys knitting and collecting stamps.

Um, no.

No, no, no, no, no.

Amy is supposed to have attended college at Michigan. She went there on some science scholarship. And then she went to Cornell for med school before doing her residency at the University of Chicago. What is this biology teacher bullshit? And what about her lake house? And her famous friends? Knitting? Stamp collecting? What the *hell*?

I spend an hour scouring the Internet for any evidence to the contrary and find none. (To be fair, I did get sidetracked on the vajazzling.) (Note to self: Try.)

As for Amy? What I'm finding makes no sense whatsoever. Looks like I'm going to have to take my stalking off-line.

CHAPTER TWELVE
Lion Pride!

"Hey, Mandy, it's Lissy—I mean, Melissa. I'm not coming in today. Tell Nicole to hold down the fort until I get back. Bye!"

I hang up the kitchen phone just as Duke walks in. "You're taking the day off?" He flashes me a wolfish grin and stands behind me, wrapping his arms around my waist while I work the espresso maker. "Something special in mind?" He's all enveloped in scents of spicy aftershave and fabric softener, which, when mixed with the aroma of strong coffee, is almost completely intoxicating. This is what heaven smells like.

"Special project, if that counts." I pour a few shots of espresso in my travel mug. I screw the lid on, reconsider, and then screw it back off, throwing in heavy cream and a couple of spoons of sugar. I take a sip—mmm, like hot coffee ice cream! Perfection!

Duke kisses the back of my neck. "You work so hard."

Ha! No one ever said that about me before.

"Why don't you let me help you out, Liss? Shoulder some of your workload? I'm at your service—what do you need? You know how quick I am with research. Maybe you need me to run a cost-benefit analysis? Remember how detailed my sales forecasts used to be? Best in the company, my boss would say. Or, if you don't need office work, maybe I could drive you somewhere? We should spend some time together."

Pfft, if he wanted to spend time, he could have done that last night. But it's nice to see him chipper this morning after all his moodiness. He didn't get in bed for hours, and when he finally did, he smelled like Mardi Gras.

I say, "Nah, I got it. There is something you can do for me, though." I spin around so we're face-to-face and he's holding me, looking all expectant. I smooth his hair back from his face. After all these years, he still has the floppy bangs and the boyish freckles. I trace my finger around his jawline, which is still totally firm.

I feel like I should get credit for his holding on to his rugged good looks, because he lives such a low-stress lifestyle. In the previous future, he had big squinty lines, and the parentheses around his mouth were supernoticeable, and he wouldn't get injectable fillers, no matter how many brochures I brought home about them. He was always in such a rush to get to the office in the mornings that inevitably he'd miss a patch when he shaved. Plus his hair had started to gray on the sides. But now? Still sandy blond with light ends from all the time he spent running and golfing with my dad over the summer. His long-standing hotness is my gift to him . . . and the world!

Because I adore him and because I want him to be content,

I suggest, "What you can do for me is pamper yourself! Make today a spa day! I'm talking the whole nine yards—mani, pedi, facial, seaweed wrap, massage. I mean, I'd kill for a spa day, but someone's got to pay for this place, right?"

Duke drops his arms and I plant a kiss on his forehead before collecting my purse from the living room. I pass back through the kitchen on my way to the garage and give him a playful swat on the backside.

"Love you lots, mean it!"

I'll assume he didn't tell me he loved me until the door had already shut, which is why I didn't hear it back.

When I open the garage, I decide to take Duke's SUV. My XJ, while impeccably restored and *so* much fun to drive, lacks a GPS unit. I'm not quite sure where I'm going, so I need a little help.

Once I input the address, I pick some appropriate road music from the CD case I grabbed from my car. How about . . . Mötley Crüe's "Girls, Girls, Girls." I love the concert footage from 2006's *Carnival of Sins* tour currently floating around the Internet. In it, the boys take the stage on choppers, so this feels like an excellent choice of driving tunes. Hey, I wonder if we've done business with the Crüe. (Note to self: Check into that.)

I'm driving only thirty-three miles, according to the GPS, but it takes me well over an hour to reach my destination with rush-hour traffic. I field a couple of calls from the office while I'm in the car. According to Mandy, a certain Mr. Coverdale is going to be in town the first week of December and he'd like to get on my schedule, as he's hoping to hook up for lunch!

Oh, my God, I love my life! Daiquiris for Deva whenever she gets back!

Given the fortuitous news and my constant stream of

traffic-directed cursing between my house and my destination, it never occurred to me that I might need a game plan upon arrival. That could be a problem.

I pull into an empty parking space between two rows of squat, identical buildings and I take a careful look around to make sure it's safe. I assess that this place isn't dangerous, but I will say it's depressing.

The apartments all have air-conditioning units hanging askew from their windows. The buildings are long and made of that awful yellow brick so popular in the late-fifties housing boom, and even with a second floor, they're so low that I can't imagine the ceilings are higher than seven feet. These units must feel like tombs.

Outside, someone made a hopeful attempt at landscaping long ago, but a hot, dry summer and lack of care has negated these efforts. The few bushes that survived are scraggly and half-bare, and the lawn is bald in some spots and brown in others, with lots of old cups and wrappers and plastic bags clinging to the perimeter of the building. The trees are overgrown and loom perilously close to the apartments, one violent fall storm away from limbs crashing through roofs into living rooms.

I jump out of the car and double-check the receipt on which I scribbled the address. Unit 2D. I follow the cracked cement path to the apartment on the end, where, lacking a better idea, I ring the bell.

When no one answers, I put my ear against the dirty steel door. I hear the sounds of the TV and smell coffee, so I believe someone's home. I ring the bell again, longer and harder this time, following up with insistent knocking.

After about thirty seconds, I hear shuffling followed by a series of locks being opened. Then the door swings in and I come face-to-face with the bathrobe-clad resident.

"What are you, another reporter? Well, *go away*. Leave me alone. Talk to my lawyer if you're so anxious for a story. Or anyone on the city council. They're superchatty."

As I take in the ratty bathrobe, the dirty hair, and the skin like ten miles of bad road, I'm not even sure I have the right apartment at first. I stare into her face, searching for similarities to the girl I knew twenty-one years ago and the impeccably polished woman I met in my past-present. Gone are the buttery highlights and the flawless skin. In their place is an inch of gray roots attached to listless Miss Clairol–gone-awry ends. Her forehead is furrowed, and instead of cheek implants, her face is sunken and hollow.

If you told me this was Amy Childs, I wouldn't have believed you until I saw the full Owen Wilson of her nose. Why is that not fixed? It didn't, like, grow back, did it?

Amy begins to close the door, but I stick my foot inside like I've always seen people do in the movies without incident.

"Ow! You just smashed my foot!" I yelp, clutching my Manolo-clad hoof.

"Why was your foot in my door where it doesn't belong?" she shouts back. "Besides, I told you vultures to go prey on someone else. Piss off."

Wait, wait, wait. This isn't how this was supposed to go down at all.

"Amy! Stop! It's me. Melissa, I mean, *Lissy*. Lissy Ryder. From LT. Remember? Lion pride! Please, I want to talk to you."

Amy's chin drops. "Lissy? Are you a reporter?"

I shake my head.

"Then what . . . Why . . . I don't understand why you're here." She slumps against the side of the door.

Well, I don't understand why you're not fishing for perch

with Oprah or sucking fat out of every high-end rump in Glencoe, but I can't really verbalize that. I quickly try to come up with a cover story. "I saw you on the news and I thought you might need a friend, so I brought you something."

Okay, I really didn't think this through. What did I bring her? I should have stopped to pick up a candle or flowers or maybe some wine. Although judging from the Sutter Home fumes currently wafting from the apartment, maybe not wine. But something.

I desperately dig into my purse, hoping to come up with an adequate offering. My fingers close around a thin, square object and I yank it out of the bag and thrust it toward her.

Amy quizzically examines the object. "You brought me a signed *Motherfrucker* CD? Thank you?"

"My pleasure," I say, pushing past her into the cramped, dark living room. Her furniture is all secondhand-store stuff, and not in the cute, vintage way. A rickety table ringed with coffee cup stains is surrounded by mismatched chairs. The dining nook abuts the microscopic galley kitchen on the other side of the room. The floor's made of sad, stained linoleum, accented by a threadbare rug. I know teachers don't make a ton of money, but come on! This isn't shabby-chic; it's just shabby.

With a tiny bit of trepidation, I plant myself on her oddly fussy, harvest gold mushroom-and-hummingbird-print sofa. The springs are shot and my butt sinks down past my knees. This couch is like trying to sit in a teacup, or a toilet seat with the lid up.

"Amy, can we talk?"

"No, please, I insist," she says all deadpan from her spot by the door. "Come in. Make yourself at home. May I fix you some breakfast, perhaps?"

I can't tell if she's being sarcastic or not. "You're sweet to offer but I had Burger King's French toast sticks in the car. Have you tried them? They're genius! They come with a cup of syrup for dipping! Plus, the hash browns? They're little round Tater Tot coins and they are phenomenal. I'm talking the perfect hangover food." Then I take in the rest of the scene, noticing all the empty wine bottles in the overflowing kitchen garbage. "Perhaps you've already discovered that?"

"Why are you here and how can I convince you to leave?"

I'm here on a mission from the future, sort of, but not really. But I can't say that, because it sounds cray-cray. Instead, I respond, "How've you been?"

Resigned to the fact that I've planted myself, Amy folds herself into the recliner across from the couch. "How the fuck does it look like I've been?"

"Wait, that came out wrong. Let me try again. *How* have you *been*?"

Amy crosses her arms tightly in front of her. "Doesn't matter if you emphasize different syllables; it's the same goddamned question."

Okay, think, self, think. You're here to get answers. You need to find out what went wrong. And she's not going to answer you if there's nothing in it for her. What can you offer her? How can you help?

"Do you want some money? I'm kind of rich." Amy eyes me suspiciously, so I scramble to make my offer sound less tawdry and obnoxious. "I mean, for your legal defense. I'm sure you're innocent and stuff and I totally want to help you. I figure on a teacher's salary, you're not . . . flush. And we're the LT Lions and we need to stick together. We roar as one! Lion pride!"

Amy continues to glower at me, so I keep pitching. I always say the most successful publicists never shut up when they're in a pinch. As long as words are coming out of your mouth, you're still in the game. "See, my friend Nicole— remember Nicole Golden; she was a cheerleader with me?— Nicole and I are trying to put together a twenty-year reunion for next month and we're pretty busy, so we thought maybe we could hire you to assist us, what with you on administrative leave and all. I mean, yeah, you have to prove your innocence at some point, but maybe by me paying you to work on the reunion, you'll be able to do so."

Amy responds with a sound that's somewhere between a laugh and a hiccup. "Innocent. Yeah. That's what I am."

I'm having a lot of trouble equating this wretch with the apple-cheeked nerdy girl from the front row of my classes who raised her hand for every question, and with the poised, polished woman who'd have scalped me given the chance. I liked it better when she hated me, because this is kind of heartbreaking. "All a big mistake, right? You'd never endanger the life of a student. That doesn't make any sense."

Amy pushes her hair off either side of her face. "Really doesn't, does it? Yet here we are."

Then she starts to cry. Big, fat tears roll down her face. She doesn't try to stop them or blot with a Kleenex. She just lets them flow.

I really, really did not think this through.

I give her a conciliatory pat on the knee, because I'm not sure what else to do. "What happened?" With the decathlete kids, with college, with Oprah, with everything. "Last I knew, you were winning science scholarships and planning to go to Michigan State. How did you get here?" I gesture around the room and then, as if on cue, her high school graduation picture falls off the wall.

"University of Michigan."

"Huh?"

"It was U of M. I was supposed to attend U of M."

"They aren't the same place?"

"No."

"Really? I always thought they were the same, because the University of Michigan is in the state of Michigan. You can see why that'd throw someone off. I bet it's a common mistake. Maybe one of them should call themselves a college and the other could say they're a university to cut down on the confusion factor and—"

Amy cocks her head. "Are you here to debate the differences in the Michigan higher-education system?"

"Oh, sorry. Go on." I pat her knee again.

"I won the Sanderson Sciences Grant, and that was going to pay for U of M. I guess you hadn't heard my grant was later taken away."

"How come? That's so wrong! You were such a smarty!"

"Do you remember homecoming night?"

I nod solemnly. "Like it was only last month."

"Then you remember that awful Tammy and her cheer. What a fucking bitch. My friends took me to the bathroom to calm me down and by the time we were finished in there, the game was over and we'd won."

I inadvertently shout, "Lion pride!" What can I say? Terrible habit. But Amy doesn't even seem to notice the interruption. She's all far away in thought.

"Some kids were celebrating in the parking lot and they asked us to join them. We figured we shouldn't be out there with open containers, so we went back to their house—one of the kids' parents were out of town. That's when I had my first drink. My friends weren't into it, but the first sip of beer was like coming home. I can't describe how amazing it made me feel, how different, how relaxed. I was so tightly wound in high school, but with liquor, I felt like a whole new me. That night changed everything. A real beginning of the end."

No. No, no.

Please don't say that the unexpected win at homecoming changed your trajectory. I cannot be responsible for this. I mean, I was *helping* her!

Or, at the very least, righting karmic wrongs.

"A lot of us drank in high school," I offer.

Amy picks at the pilled fabric on her robe. "Most of you didn't have a history of alcoholism in your family. Most of you weren't predisposed to becoming addicted, but my grandfathers on both sides of the family were drunks. Anyway, after that, I started drinking pretty regularly. My grades slipped and I lost my grant. Suddenly U of M didn't want me. The worse I did in my classes, the more doors closed for me. No college let me in except for UCI. The bitch of it is, I saw it all happening and I felt powerless to stop myself. Almost like being miserable was somehow my destiny."

Please stop saying the D-word. This isn't destiny; this is bad choices, right?

"College was a decent time for me—it was easier to manage my schedule around my drinking, and I tried hard in my classes. Well, maybe not as hard as I could have, in retrospect. I was premed for a while, but I was booted from the science department. At UCI. Sloth pride!" she spits.

I'm not sure what to say, so I just stay quiet. "I wanted to be a plastic surgeon; did you know that, Lissy? I dreamed of being able to travel to the third world and fix kids with deformities in my off-time. What a pathetic joke that is now. Instead I decided to teach science. That way I'd still have some involvement with what'd been my passion, at least in a cursory way."

Amy stands and begins to pace. She unties her robe and then wraps it more tightly around her narrow waist before retying it. (This would probably not be the right moment to compliment her for keeping her high school figure.)

"My parents were, oh, God, so unhappy. They didn't understand why I wasn't living up to my potential. To motivate me, they said they'd pay to get my nose fixed if I could just pull it together." She gingerly touches her proboscis. "Obviously that didn't happen."

"Then what? How'd you end up here?"

"North Elgin was the only district that would take me, and that's only because my uncle was on the school board and his was the deciding vote on a bond issue."

"But as a teacher—you must have liked parts of your job, right? I mean, you signed up to be an adviser for the mathletes, right?"

"I enjoy teaching more than I thought I would. But I'll be honest: I've struggled with my drinking every day, and once I've had my first cocktail, rational decisions fly out the door. Believing I'm fine to drive, for example. My first DUI was thrown out of court on a technicality, and my uncle was able to keep the whole thing on the down-low with the board. Not so lucky the second time. After that incident I went to rehab in lieu of being fired."

"Where's your family been in all of this?" I think back to the nice lady who gave up Jazzercise in order to afford her daughter's rhinoplasty and I hope that they're supportive. I can't imagine what it would be like not to have the galvanizing force of Mamma behind me.

Amy exhales long and hard before answering. "My family

totally disowned me after that. They said it was too hard watching me systematically deconstruct my life after what they lived through as kids. They started going to Al-Anon and the group encouraged them to try tough love. Anyway, I'm not getting a third chance from anyone. I don't deserve it either. I did what the news said I did. I endangered those kids. I thought, 'Oh, just one little sip to get me through the competition.' I guess I had more than one. I always do. The kids' parents are out for my blood—rightfully so. You should read the letters to the editor about me." Amy falls back into her recliner and hugs her knees to her chest.

"Are you going into treatment?" I've heard about the concept of bottoming out and it seems to me that if she's not there, she's close.

Amy wipes her eyes with the cuff of her robe. "The ironic thing is, I *want* to go to rehab. I feel like I'm ready to check into a facility, finally. This is rock bottom, and I'm so thankful none of those kids was hurt. Thing is, my insurance has been suspended while I'm on leave. I can't pay for it myself. I want to get sober, and doing it alone won't work. I'm so, so screwed."

I'm not sure what else to do, so I hug her.

Then I write her a check.

Yet I have a feeling that no matter how many zeroes I add, it won't be enough.

I begin the drive home in silence. No amount of glam rock is going to soothe my soul, so I embrace the quiet.

I'm having a hard time trying to differentiate between Amy's poor choices and my culpability. Did altering my own personal timeline create this situation?

What if everything about the past was exactly the same

except that one of the Lions ran a couple of extra yards for a TD at homecoming that night—would Amy have still headed down the path to alcoholism, whether or not I'd been nice to her? It's certainly not my fault that she has a family history. Much as I like to consider myself the center of the universe, a part of me knows that's not the case. Possibly I was the domino that started them all falling, but I wasn't the one who arranged the chips in such a manner.

When Deva explained the butterfly effect to me, she said the theory is that the air displaced from the flapping of one pretty bug's wings could start a chain reaction that eventually resulted in a tsunami across the globe. But the question that plagues me is this: Is the butterfly at fault for simply trying to propel itself from one flower to another? Were the butterfly to be aware that by flying, it's setting up an apocalyptic chain reaction, is it obligated not to move around and take sustenance? Is the butterfly compelled to sacrifice itself for the greater good? And even if the butterfly does cause a cataclysmic event, what if the aftereffects are just as important?

I mean, look at the Great Chicago Fire that burned down the whole town in 1871. Hundreds of people died and three square miles of the city were destroyed. But if the city hadn't burned then it wouldn't have been rebuilt at a time when civic planning had become a reality. The fire stripped the city down to nothing, and when it was rebuilt, it was on a solid foundation for the first time. The slate was wiped clean—not without a cost, of course—but that enabled Chicago to start over and rebuild so much stronger than would ever have been possible on a shaky foundation.

Drive down any street in Chicago today and you'll see very few of the "urban canyons" that make New York seem so dark and forbidding and patently impossible to find an address in if you don't know the cross streets. Chicago's simple to navigate because it's laid out on a grid. (New Yorkers will argue their city's on a grid, too, yet their streets don't perfectly coincide with latitudinal and longitudinal coordinates; ergo Chicago wins the arbitrary travel-ease contest I set up in my head.)

Point is, the city was built with a service level down beneath, so the streets are never choked with delivery trucks and mounds of garbage. The city functions now like it never could have had it not been granted a massive do-over. I have to wonder, would Chicago be capable of its present level of commerce and industry had it not suffered such a tragedy? I bet not.

I'm lost in thought when my phone rings. Anxious to get out of my head for a few minutes, I click the Bluetooth to connect, but before I can even say hello, my mother begins squawking.

"That man is crazy, hear me? He's lost his damn mind!"

I should probably be more concerned here, on the rare chance that my father actually has gone off the reservation. But every time Daddy makes a decision that Mamma doesn't care for, she attacks his state of mental health. Opting against an inground sprinkler system? *Insane!* Deciding to take a staycation rather than bring Mamma to Montreal? *Cuckoo!* Choosing to drive his old wheels for one more year instead of upgrading? *Unhinged!*

"What's he done, Mamma?" I ask, trying to sound more patient than I feel. I mean, I just spent the morning with someone having an *actual* crisis. I normally indulge my mother, but I'm really not in the mood for it right now.

"*That sonovabitch says he's going to retire!*" The whole car reverberates from the sounds of her shrieking.

This? *This* is her crisis? Oh, I am so not entertaining this.

"He's sixty-five, Mamma, and he's been working eighty-hour weeks since I was born. I'd say it's time for him to take a break if he wants."

You would not believe a woman of her age and social status could be capable of the string of profanity that happens next.

(You would be wrong.)

I do my best to put a positive spin on the situation. "Mamma, Mamma. Mamma! Calm down! The world's not coming to an end. Isn't there something appealing about the idea of Daddy being home all the time? You can go to lunch whenever you want or take off for the weekend with no notice. You'll be able to spend so much time at the club! This might be really wonderful for both of you!"

She's still fuming. "That is the whole problem! He doesn't wanna retire so he can be retired! He wants to retire so he can write a book! The man reads three John goddamn Grisham novels and fancies his damn self an author!"

Actually . . . that's not the worst idea I ever heard. My dad's been retreating to his library for years, so I can hardly picture him *not* standing in front of well-stocked shelves filled with everything from classics to Clancy. Daddy once told me that he'd read every single thing in there. Plus, the bulk of his time as a patent attorney is spent writing and researching, so it makes sense that he might gravitate to being an author.

As persuasively as I can, I tell her, "Mamma, a lot of authors were lawyers first, like Scott Turow and John Grisham. What about Emily Giffin? You like her books and she was a lawyer first. So was the girl who wrote *Legally Blonde*. This isn't without precedent and it might be very satisfying for him."

Oh. So. Much. Swearing.

"Mamma, I'm so sorry, but work's on the other line. Why don't you e-mail me and tell me how much Daddy sucks, okay?" I mercifully disconnect and click the other line. "Lissy, I mean *Melissa* speaking."

"Liss, hey! It's Nicole."

"Hey, rock star, how are you feeling today?"

"Physically, so-so."

"Next time, try a Burger King breakfast. All that fat and grease and sugar set me straight right away."

Nicole giggles. "We're really not seventeen anymore, are we?"

"That's the truth." Nicole sounds upbeat, but I'm concerned it might just be how she talks when she's in the office. She's the kind of girl who, no matter what's going sideways personally, will always have a kind word and a big smile when you run into her in the hallway. "How are you doing, like, emotionally?"

I'm relieved to hear her say, "A lot better, so thank you. You were right: A project was just what I needed. That's why I'm calling—the response to the reunion has been overwhelming! More than a hundred people have already RSVP'd yes! When you get a minute, check out the Facebook page—I sent you a link. You'll never believe where some of our classmates are now. I can't even tell you; you'll have to see it for yourself."

Having just seen for myself where one of our classmates is now, I'm not quite as fired up as she is.

"Woo! Lion pride!" Nicole cheers.

Wryly, I repeat, "Lion pride."

CHAPTER THIRTEEN
What Goes Up

"How's it going, Daddy?"

My dad rises from his seat at the table to plant a quick kiss on my cheek. We're meeting covertly, because I want to hear his side of the story about retirement without Mamma interrupting every five seconds.

We've been meaning to get together for weeks, but each time we make plans, my mother finds out about them (like a St. John–wearing bloodhound, that one) and insists on joining us. I suspect she doesn't want me supporting him in his decision, so she's done her best to keep us apart. We're having lunch in the executive dining room of his law firm, the one place she can't just show up unannounced.

I haven't been here in years and I'm impressed all over again about how swanky it is! Even though we're in the middle of an ultramodern twenty-first-century city, this room feels like a throwback to a different era, when men wore hats and smoked at their desks and called one another Mr. So-and-so, and a three-martini lunch would get you promoted, not fired.

The ceilings are impossibly high and the room's anchored by a gigantic marble fireplace surrounded by ornate wooden carvings. The walls are paneled in gleaming cherrywood and the windows are individually paned leaded glass. If I were a potential client, I'd absolutely hire Daddy's firm on the merits of this place. Fortunately, use of this magnificent room is one of the perks of Daddy's having worked so hard for his company.

"Hello, sweetie. Please have a seat." His table is located directly underneath an oil painting of one of the firm's founders.

I point at the art. "Are they going to put your portrait up there, Daddy?" As he glances up, his face catches the muted light of the room. He seems kind of pale today and he looks a little skinny under his impeccably tailored suit.

He shudders and replies, "God, I hope not."

"Really? Don't you want your legacy to live on once you retire? I thought you loved it here."

"Then you thought wrong, kiddo." Before he can say any more, a tuxedo-clad waiter materializes beside us with two crystal glasses of iced tea. My dad gestures toward the waiter's tray. "Is this still your poison? I took a guess."

I grin. "It is." I busy myself squeezing lemons and distributing sugar cubes while my dad places our order. We're having lobster bisque followed by the chef's special crab salad croissants and sweet potato fries. Yum!

After the waiter leaves, Daddy asks, "How's everything with Duke? And the office?"

"Duke's great and he says hello."

I don't mention that Duke urged me to have my dad really consider his decision to retire. I have no idea why.

"Excellent. Send him my love. Tell him we have a date on the links next spring."

"I'll do that." I can't help but smile when I think about how alike Duke and my father are. "As for work? Couldn't be better!"

Actually, work could be a tiny bit better. Apparently revenue's down since I returned from the past last month. I guess I was the one responsible for developing new business. I wouldn't say I've lost my touch so much as I'm not sure where I found my touch in the first place. I kind of figured this knowledge would translate across the space-time continuum, but as yet, not so much. I know how to land an electric plating account and dot-com idiots, but real clients? I probably need to figure that out.

Because of our newly (slightly) diminished returns, somehow I've been roped into meeting with Team ChaCha again this afternoon. Nicole was all, "Blah, blah, blah, your name on the door, make an appearance, blah-di-blah," so I don't have much of a choice. Really looking forward to that meeting. Not.

My dad takes a long pull of his tea. "Glad to hear it. Knowing that you're doing so well on your own takes a tremendous amount of pressure off of me."

"Meaning?" My stomach does a tiny backflip. Jean from accounting was rather stern about the state of our new receivables, which may or may not have coincided with my having recently discovered the company checkbook. Anyway, I plan on giving this an awful lot of thought. Later.

"Meaning that I don't have to take care of you. I don't have to worry about what's going to happen to you when I pass." Daddy suddenly seems superfascinated with his tea glass. He wipes a bit of condensation onto his napkin.

This is a surprise to me. "Were you and Mamma concerned that you'd have to provide for me?"

On the one hand, I'm insulted that my parents don't believe in me, and on the other, I'm grateful that they want me to have a security blanket. In the back of my mind, I've always accepted that failure is *absolutely* an option, because my parents would be there to bail me out.

Daddy snorts. "Me? No. You're an adult and it's your responsibility to succeed on your own merits. I'm a self-made man and I have little respect for those who've had their fortune handed to them. Your mother, on the other hand, insists that we have a substantial nest egg set aside for you. In turn, I've spent your whole life economizing on the things I want so that one day you'll get the keys to my empire. How fair is that?"

I'm not sure if I should feel relieved or afraid. "Don't I kind of have my own empire?"

"Sure hope so, kiddo. Because I'm about to start living on my terms."

I swallow but I can't seem to get rid of the lump in my throat. "Daddy, you're making me nervous."

He reaches across the table and takes my hand. "Don't be nervous, kitten. But do understand this—I'm done. I'm checking out of the corporate rat race. I'm finished making sacrifices. I've spent almost forty years doing what everyone else wants me to do, following their lead, toeing their line. I'm sixty-five years old and I'm ready to start calling my own shots."

Our soup arrives, but neither of us touches our spoons.

As tired as Daddy seems, there's a set to his shoulders that I've never before seen. I'm wavering between pride and fear.

"What's next, Daddy? How does this all shake out?"

My dad glances at the ceiling and counts off on his fingers. "My last day is the twenty-first, the Wednesday before Thanksgiving. The firm wants to throw me a retirement party. Considering I never want to see most of these bastards again, I may or may not attend. And then? Freedom. Absolute, pure, unadulterated freedom."

Daddy takes a bite of his soup and is suddenly reenergized. Whether it's the bisque or discussing his new life, I'm not sure. But the color has returned to his cheeks and he speaks with a confidence I rarely hear.

He leans in toward me and says, "I plan to sleep late and golf more often than once a week on Sundays. I want to do everything I've put off for the last four decades. First up? I'm going to learn to prepare that Bolognese sauce that Chef Mario used to make before he retired. You remember when he was here?"

I surely met him at some point in the past twenty years, so I simply reply, "Oh, yeah. He was great."

"Damn right he was. On his last day, the chef let me in on the secret to his sauce. It's cognac. Told me it doesn't take much more than a drop, but a drop is enough to make all the difference. I've had his recipe for seven years, but I've never had the time to try it myself. Seven years I've longed for this sauce and I never had it. Kiddo, those days are over."

The more he describes his future, the more excited he becomes. "Then I'm buying a vintage thirty-eight-foot Chris-Craft and I'm going to refinish it myself. I've been scouring the Internet for months looking for the perfect boat and I believe I found the right one in New Buffalo. Heading to Michigan the Sunday after Thanksgiving to look her over. Hope you've got yourself a decent retirement plan, because I'm about to blow your inheritance. And I love you, kitten, but I don't care, because this money is mine and I earned it." He chuckles.

Umm . . .

"Best of all, I'm finally living my dream of being an author. I've been kicking around a manuscript for twenty years and it's high time I made it into a real book. My golden years will be all about me, my boat, and my writing. I can't wait." When he says this, his face is wreathed in a smile that takes ten years off his weathered face.

I swallow hard. Nope, lump's still there and getting bigger. "What about Mamma?"

"Your mother can climb aboard the *Hull Truth*—that's what I'm naming her—or be left behind at the dock. I've made my peace with either eventuality. If that means we go our separate ways and I wind up with half my money? I'm willing to take that risk." He shrugs. "I'll live on the boat if need be. That's why I picked one with a double stateroom. Whether or not Ginny likes it, this is happening. Bank on that." He gives the table a tap to emphasize his point.

My soup has formed a skin, and as I poke my spoon into it, I find I'm not hungry for once.

"Daddy, you realize we're about to have the worst Thanksgiving ever."

He takes a bite of his soup before answering with more resolve than I thought possible.

"Don't I know it, kiddo. Don't I know it."

I leave my father's firm more confused than ever. Suddenly I don't have a choice on whether or not I want to put in the effort of making my business work. My safety net's just been yanked out from under me.

I return to my office and see that Nicole has sent me a link to the video presentation that she put together for Team Cha-Cha. I'm not sure why the kid doesn't just shut up, sing, and allow the grown-ups to discuss business without her, but she seems intent on being present for every step of the process. Shouldn't she be in school? I have no frigging clue what she plans to glean from today's discussion of SEO (search engine optimization), but to appease her, Nicole's prepared a video that breaks the whole process down into idiot-size bits of information.

Actually . . . I could probably brush up on my SEO knowledge before everyone gets here. I have a cursory understanding of it from my previous lifetime, but probably not enough to merit the fee they're paying us. I pull up the video link and press PLAY.

Nothing happens, save for an endless loop of buffering.

Argh!

I thought the tech guy fixed the stupid thing!

You know what? Screw it. I realize the company's having some minor cash-flow issues right now, but I'm the CEO (or am I the president?) (note to self: Check), and if I need a new laptop, then I'm buying one for myself. I probably have someone who does my purchasing around here, but I don't have the desire to figure out who that might be. I'm stopping at Best Buy the next chance I have.

I'm already in no mood for shenanigans when I arrive in the conference room. ChaCha's manager and attorney are in the hallway taking calls and I saw her father head toward the bathroom. Apparently these gentlemen are the glue that keeps the whole crew from going all Jerry Springer, for when I step into the room, shenanigans await. ChaCha's lying on the table while Seraphina Tarzans from the light fixtures and steps on her back. Tawny's with them but she's not paying attention, as she's preoccupied shoving my tiny espresso mugs from the buffet into her bag.

What the fruck?

I grab a chair at the head of the table. "Hello, Tawny," I announce. "I see you've helped yourself to the coffee . . . cups."

Tawny seems awfully pleased with herself. "Yeah! They're the perfect size to do shots without using your hands. See? Your mouth goes right around them." She clasps her hands behind her back and then, like Deva with so many corn dogs, she bends over to demonstrate.

That's when Nicole enters.

I beam at her. "Good news, Nicole! Our cups are the perfect size for doing shots."

Nicole pinches me as she passes, as if to tell me to cut it out. Oh, this is rich—the client's giving our glassware oral and *I'm* the one who's out of line? While we wait for the adults to join us, I pretend to look busy with my BlackBerry. I have a message from Jean in accounting.

Delete.

Nicole engages in small talk with the moron on the table and her posse while I make fists and imagine punching all of them.

"What happened to your back, ChaCha?" Nicole asks in a tone that indicates she's sincerely concerned about ChaCha's welfare. If so, that would make her the one person in this room who actually is. I glower at Tawny, who's now pilfering our entire assortment of LUNA bars and Bavarian pretzels.

"I had, like, a rilly, rilly bad injury and stuff," ChaCha replies.

"Ah," Nicole replies. "New choreography? I was a dancer and I know how hard it can be on your body with the repetition of learning a new move. One summer at cheerleading camp we spent a day practicing cradle catches for basket tosses and I couldn't lift my arms for a week. Melissa over there had to help me brush my hair and teeth!"

I can't help but grin at this shared memory. That was the summer after our freshman year, when we were still at LT South. Our high school was divided into two campuses—one for the freshmen and sophomores and one for the juniors and seniors. At South, the clique lines hadn't yet been drawn and everyone was still friends with everyone, because we'd all grown up playing Barbies and army and freeze tag together. Membership in our club had one requirement: living geographically adjacent. The Belles didn't even form into a unit until we all hit the North campus. In retrospect, those days at South were simple, happy times and—

"The doctor said she got hurt from texting," Tawny volunteers.

Oh, my God, who is parenting this child?

"I'm so sorry!" Nicole gushes. "How does that happen?"

Tawny shakes her head, yet her big blond bombshell of a hairdo moves entirely in unison with itself. "Well, Bobby 'n' me checked her phone and she sends something like four hundred texts a day. I was all, 'Keep it up, kid! You're gonna get the Arthur-itis.'"

"Then you took her phone away, of course," I suggest.

Tawny's perplexed, like I just asked her to name the square root of pi to the tenth decimal. "Why'd we do that?"

"No one's touching my frucking phone," ChaCha declares with her face pressed into the table and her arms folded up underneath her chest.

"You would die!" Seraphina adds. She braces herself by holding on to the track lighting as she traverses ChaCha's legs.

I nervously eye the fixture. I can't imagine they're installed to handle any weight. They creak, but for now, fortunately, they're staying put.

ChaCha snorts. "I know, right? Like, if I can't tweet and shit? Then how are my fans going to know what I'm wearing and eating and when I poop?"

I'm about to interject when I notice that Nicole's giving me the mother of all stink-eyes. Okay, fine. Let your not-stepdaughter get the Arthur-itis. I don't care.

Nicole tents her hands and rests her chin on them so she can gaze directly into ChaCha's face. "Sounds like this one has an excellent grasp of the importance of engaging in social media."

"Um, *duh*," ChaCha huffs. "Justin Bieber follows me. Actually, gimme my phone right now. I'ma DM him a picture of this!"

Tawny reaches into ChaCha's bag, which I now realize is a Birkin.

Of course it is.

Of course it frucking is.

"One blingy ringy-dingy, baby gurl," Tawny sings, sliding the phone down the length of the table, leaving many, many scratches in the fine wood.

I'm really, really trying not to come across as aggravated but does no one else consider this whole table-walk thing a problem? Also, those lights aren't equipped to handle Slutty Spice yanking on them.

I say, "ChaCha, no one's discounting the importance of building your brand via digital platform. But it stands to reason that if you're injured, perhaps you could temporarily turn your texting and tweeting duties over to someone else, say, Seraphina."

"If she's texting for me, then how would she text for herself?" ChaCha asks.

That's it. I officially give up.

"You good?" Seraphina asks, hopping off ChaCha's back with a dismount that involves her supporting her entire body weight on the fixture. I hear an ominous creak. Seraphina then sits cross-legged and sockless on the table. ChaCha rights herself and joins her. Every time ChaCha moves, her vertebrae make the sound of microwave popcorn. I try not to wince. (I fail.)

"There're plenty of open chairs if you'd be more comfortable there," I offer, but no one listens.

"What kind of treatment plan are you following for your back?" Nicole asks.

"Doctor said he wanted me to do some physical therapy bullshit and he wouldn't give me any drugs. Then Seraphina was all, 'If I, like, walk on your back, you'll be better,' so that's whassup. Still hurts, though."

"You don't say," I interject. "That's so funny. Personally, I, too, have always found my swagger coach to be more skilled at providing treatment than an accredited medical professional."

Nicole, your foot had better have just connected with my knee by accident.

Shortly, mercifully, the men join us and the meeting officially begins. We're about two minutes into Nicole's explanation of real-time searching when we hear a creak in the ceiling, which is immediately followed by the shriek of metal pulling apart, and then the entire string of track lights comes crashing onto the conference room table inches away from Seraphina and ChaCha.

To say that chaos ensues would be an insult to the very

nature of chaos. I'm talking a shit storm of such proportion that it makes disasters such as the *Titanic* sinking, the *Hindenburg* crashing, and all ten plagues of Egypt seem like a jolly old spin around the maypole.

Despite having not been touched in any way, shape, or form by the falling fixture, ChaCha screams about how we've broken her back and she's hustled out the door amid multiple promises of pending litigation.

While Nicole coordinates conference room cleanup, I excuse myself to head to my office, as I should probably prospect for new clients sooner rather than later.

I boot up my computer to discover no less than forty thousand poorly spelled, profoundly indignant tweets about how MCPR almost murdered a national treasure.

I should probably track down whoever handles crisis management around here.

But first I need to buy a new laptop, as it would appear that I've just thrown this one against my office door.

CHAPTER FOURTEEN

Strange Fascination, Fascinating Me

I'm pawing through Best Buy's (frankly pathetic) metal CD offerings when a voice behind me says, "Lissy? Lissy Ryder?"

I turn around to find someone clad in a cornflower blue polo shirt and rumpled khakis. The guy seems to be about my age, and from what I understand, no one's called me that name in years, which is a crying shame. Why did future me stop using it? Melissa Connor is so commonplace, but Lissy Ryder? There's a certain panache and musicality to that name. Melissa Connor is your ophthalmologist or your neighbor or the name after yours on the phone tree, but Lissy Ryder is someone special. Melissa Connor returns her library books on time, whereas Lissy Ryder's too busy living it up to read. Melissa Connor remembers to recycle all the bottles Lissy Ryder emptied. Melissa Connor can do your taxes, but Lissy Ryder? She can rock your world.

Anyway, by this person's knowing me as Lissy, my assumption is that this is an LT alum. (Lion pride!) His outfit says, *I work here*, but the rest of him says, *Mom lets my band rehearse in her garage*. His long, wavy hair is held back with a leather thong (not the underpants kind), and his tattoos, while both graphic and abundant, are strictly amateur. Each finger is wrapped in a silver ring, some shaped like skulls and some like pentagrams, and his wrists are stacked with all manner of woven, studded leather bracelets. His forked beard is an homage to either Scott Ian of Anthrax or James Hetfield of Metallica. (Possibly both.)

I'm trying to place his face. He's familiar and yet he's not. LT didn't have any rockers like this; trust me, I'd have made it my business to know them. But this guy seems tickled to see me and I appreciate that. Between my dad's big news and the hit my professional liability insurance is about to take, I could stand a little positive interaction. I muster as much fake enthusiasm as I can. "Hey! Yeah, it's . . . you! It's been too long!"

He claps me lightly on the shoulder, then throws the horns. "Right? Lissy! Lissy 'Rock Star' Ryder!"

Do you see what I mean? He gets it. Lissy Ryder is a patently stupendous name.

He eyes me appreciatively. Again, see? This is the kind of difference adding a splash of hot pink can do for someone's outfit. "Serendipitous to run into you, girl! I haven't seen you since graduation! What dirty business have you been up to?"

Okay, definitely a Lion. But which one? Even though we were in a class of almost a thousand, everyone still knew everyone, which is both the privilege and the curse of living in suburbia.

I rattle off the *Reader's Digest* condensed version of my life and he's very excited when I mention that I'm a music publicist.

His whole face lights up. "No way! I'm a musician!" He looks over his shoulder all conspiratorially. "Best Buy is just a day job to pay the bills and I'm out of here the minute things break for me."

"How long have you worked here?" I ask.

"Seven years. But I'm in a Metallica tribute band called the Metallicats. Got a regular gig at Durty Nellie's in Palatine on Tuesday nights—hey, you should come and check us out! We do a version of 'Enter Sandman' that fuckin' wails. *Rock!*" To demonstrate, he launches into a rather extensive air guitar solo.

Yeah, there's a hundred percent probability that I'm never going to Palatine for any reason, but I don't want to sound snotty, so I say, "That sounds great, um . . ."

"It's Steve," he supplies. "Steve Ramey. Or Steeeeeve-o, like the rest of the band calls me. Wow, Lissy Ryder."

"In the flesh." I give him a little curtsy.

"Funny seeing you after all this time. I mean, since you changed my life."

I already don't like the sound of this.

"Yeah, man. I was such a fuckin' tool in high school. 'Oh, look at me; I'm in the orchestra wearing my gay tuxedo shirt!' But then . . ."

He keeps talking while I process this information. Wait, Steve Ramey! Of course! The guy who couldn't come to the reunion because he was on tour with Maroon 5! Steve—I mean *Steve-o*—was the classically trained pianist who went on to be a huge studio musician in L.A. He's laid tracks with everyone from the Rolling Stones to Christina Aguilera. The general public may not know his name, but they've certainly heard his melodies.

Except that he's standing here in a Best Buy shirt, so . . .

". . . and that's when I gave up the piano for the ax. Best decision I ever made. Come on, the lead guitar gets exponentially more mad naked ass than the keyboard player. If you hadn't educated me on *real* music, who knows where I'd be?"

Sweet child o' mine, I know where you'd be . . . famous in your field, well paid for doing what you love, and mad naked ass-deep in Adam Levine's castoffs.

We exchange a few more pleasantries and I promise Steve-o I'll see what I might be able to do for him and the Metallicats. I give him my business card (noting that I'm president *and* CEO) and he throws me the horns again.

"Sleep with one eye open, Lissy, girl!"

"You've got it, Steve-o." As I head back to the computer section, I hear him attempting to talk a tween out of a Taylor Swift album in favor of Pantera.

I buy the first laptop that catches my eye and I drive home, so lost in thought I almost miss the turn to my street.

My mind is racing with possibilities, none of them good. *Why* does this keep happening? First Nicole, then Amy Childs, now Steve-o? Who else has gone precariously off-track due to my ripples? I mean, Steve-o seems content hustling CDs at Best Buy and playing hard rock in tiny venues, but if he knew where he could have been, he'd probably want to kill self-comma-others.

If I had any idea that changing my past would have impacted others, I'd never have done it.

Wait, *Melissa Connor* would never have done it.

But Lissy Ryder?

She'd have done exactly what was in her best interests and wouldn't have ever looked back.

But maybe now I'm some odd confluence of both of them, because I would and did, yet now I feel racked with guilt about it.

New laptop? *Check*.

Lyons Township High School Class of 1992 Facebook reunion page? *Check*.

Bottle of wine? *Check*.

Backup bottle of wine? *Checkity-check*.

Let's do this.

I scan the list and see dozens of familiar, albeit older faces. You know what's interesting? Every person who's had children looks categorically older than those of us who didn't. Fact. It's like children suck out everyone's life force or something. Yeah, you may have a little someone to wear matching sundresses with and write braggy Christmas letters about, but the trade-off is, you're going to look like the Crypt Keeper long before your time. So not worth it, if you ask me.

Anyway, who should I click on first? Let's see, here's Meredith Falcone's RSVP.

Oh, bummer, she's not coming to the reunion for un-specified reasons, but she's probably tied up with *New York Times* food critic business. Now that I have my own impressive career, I'm not overwrought with jealousy over her success. Actually, I'm happy for her . . . and for me the next time I need a restaurant hookup in New York. But just to be safe, let's make sure that all is well in her world before I book a flight.

Let's see, her Facebook picture is a bowl of something beige and the page links to a Web site. Lemme click it and that takes me to . . .

WhatsInMeredithsMouth.com

Ha! That's clever! Her Web page is professionally laid out and it's ringed in neutral-colored photographs of food. I don't see any obvious links to her business details but maybe that's how it works when you're a restaurant critic. They're oddly secretive in some ways, like they wear disguises out to dinner and stuff.

Anyway, I begin by reading the top blog entry.

"Hooray for oatmeal! I love oatmeal so much! It's soooo good for me and healthy and nutritious and it makes me feel like I'm being hugged from the inside! If I had a best friend, it would be oatmeal!"

Um . . . that must be some high-end, gastronomic, small-batch, local, organic oatmeal. What, does Bouley do breakfast now or something? And are microgreens involved? Every time food is overly fancy for no apparent reason, microgreens seem to come into play. Or arugula. All the top chefs are big on arugula again, except they call it rocket. I don't really under-stand why. It's still arugula, right? And what the hell is celery root and yuzu jelly? If I connect with Meredith in NYC, I'll have to ask her these questions.

"Today's batch is super-duper special. After I made the base, I added sooo many taste-licious mix-ins! As you can see, I sprinkled on butterscotch nibs, a handful of granola, a crum-bled cinnamon-chip muffin, some peanut butter, some apple butter, chocolate-covered cashews, and lots of shaved coco-nut!"

So, you're clearly not diabetic, Meredith. But maybe "craft oats" are all the rage now and comfort food trucks are over?

Damn it, why do I keep hitting these trends at the tail end? If everyone jumps back on the exotic raw-fish train, I'm going to be sorely disappointed. I was just getting my macaroni-and-meatball groove on.

"Woo!!! This is the creamiest, doughiest, bestest batch ever! I'm überexcited to put it in my mouth! Get in my tummy!"

Okay, maybe Meredith doesn't have time for lunch and isn't reviewing a new restaurant until really late and this is the only chance she has to eat for hours. Otherwise, I'm not sure why she's so psyched to be taking in twenty-five hundred calories of bland multigrains at breakfast.

Vaguely confused, I scroll down to the next entry.

"Give me an O! Give me an A! Give me a T! Give me an M! Give me an E! Give me another A! Give me an L! What does it spell? OATMEAL! What are we eating? OATMEAL! What do we love? Oatmeal! What do we put on our oatmeal? Jam and cream cheese and chia seeds and blueberry trail mix and sunflower butter and crumbled Girl Scout Samoas and Starbucks' frosted maple scone chunks!"

Wait, this is her *lunch*? After *that* breakfast? Did she have oral surgery? Is she only able to gum her meals? And what the hell is she planning to eat for dinner?

I keep reading.

Hey! Guess what! It's more oatmeal, only this time she's added two pulverized bananas, White Chocolate Wonderful peanut butter, a handful of hazelnuts, and a healthy sprinkling of *candy corns*.

What is going on here?

Does Meredith really have oatmeal for every meal outside of work? And if she's going to write about food, wouldn't she be . . . better at it? And I'm no one to judge, based on my new taste for comfort food, but what's up with all the sugar-laden toppings?

I keep tabbing.

Good Lord, she's covered this oat-y batch with *circus peanuts* and crushed *Jolly Ranchers*! Is she *insane*? Is this some kind of foodie inside joke? And why isn't she talking about the gourmet repasts she's having in New York's finest eateries?

I scroll down some more.

Oh, honey, you didn't really just slap a slab of Boston cream pie on your oats, right?

Unless this photograph is a lie.

Whoa, now you're blending your oats with spinach and topping them with s'mores and pine nuts? That makes me want to throw up a little in *your* mouth! Meredith, I thought you had a refined palate!

Unless . . . she's been another victim of the universe shift.

Argh! Not Meredith, too!

I tab through page after page, desperately hoping for something other than Meredith's salute to the humble oat, and I start to feel sick . . . and not just because she served sardines on top of her oatmeal in this last photo. (Although that isn't helping.)

Let's figure this out right now. I pull up the *Times* Web site and input her name.

"Your search 'Meredith Falcone' did not match any documents under 'Past 7 Days.'"

I try again.

"Your search 'Meredith Falcone' did not match any documents under 'Past 30 Days.'"

What are the odds she's on some colon-cleansing vacay and she'll be back to reviewing all New York's übertrendy bistros shortly?

"Your search 'Meredith Falcone' did not match any documents under 'Past 12 Months.'"

And just for good measure . . .

"Your search 'Meredith Falcone' did not match any documents under 'All Results Since 1851.'"

I fill my wineglass to the rim and then chug half of it down in one gulp.

I'm so sorry, Meredith. I don't care how much you seem to be enjoying your job blogging for Big Oatmeal, it can't compare to what should have been your future as a restaurant critic.

I take a few more healthy swallows before moving on.

Next victim? Jeremy Bloomquist, the mathstronaut who should be working for NASA.

Yet is actually working for *Nassau*.

As in the Nassau County Department of Storm Water Management. On the one hand, it's nice that he's helping to reduce pollutants in the New York State water table, but I'm guessing that his job as junior project administrator doesn't quite compare to that of captaining a space shuttle.

Sigh.

And drink.

Et tu, Jeremy, *et tu?*

I'm suddenly heartened when I see that Madonna/Robert is working in the fashion industry. But my hopes for him are dashed upon learning he does so in the men's shoe department at the Schaumburg JCPenney. Not that there's anything wrong with retail—it's just a long, long way from showing your line at Bryant Park.

The hits keep on coming.

No one is what they were supposed to be. Brooks Paddy isn't a big-time Hollywood player. This time around she still lives with her parents and has a part-time gig on the bookmobile. And, for the record, she has *not* been to Jenny.

As for sweet, easily influenced Kimmy, instead of working as a senior-level flight attendant on the glamorous Paris-to-Dubai hop, she's living in Cicero, Illinois, and married to Chet, who's actively cheating on her. At least, that's what I assume when I run across his Match.com profile.

I can't find any updates on April, Tammy, or Brian Murphy, and I don't know if I should be relieved or concerned. But if their presents are anything like everyone else's, I'm erring on the side of concerned.

I snap shut my laptop and pull out my phone.

> **Me:** will I see u on friday at the reunion?

> **Deva:** with balls on!

I'm not touching that statement.

> **Me:** things r seriously out of whack. need ur help

> **Deva:** will disco in person, looser roadway

> **Me:** discuss?

> **Deva:** no, disco! is a party, want 2 dance! also discuss a fix, but looking forward 2 doing the hustler and electric slit

Me: thx, see you then

Deva: ta-tas

Okay, so maybe I can put screwing up everyone's future to bed once I see Deva.

But first, family Thanksgiving.

I'm not sure which task is more daunting.

CHAPTER FIFTEEN

Watching Some Good Friends Scream, "Let Me Out"

"Let us never speak of this again."

That's my proclamation as Duke, Nicole, and I drive back to the city from La Grange after the tag-team wrestling match better known as the Beaulieu/Ryder family Thanksgiving. Mamma wanted us to stay over, but we live less than thirty minutes away.

Also, I was afraid someone would be stabbed in their sleep.

My mother, sensing my father's resoluteness about the whole retirement thing, has upped her normal level of vitriol to that of your garden-variety Axis power dictator. Imagine Mussolini, only clad in a Chanel suit with a penchant for saying "y'all."

To complicate matters, my mother called in reinforcements. Aunt Sissy and Cousin Gussie came up from Savannah to form the most unholy trinity in Christendom, with Gussie's five towheaded junior totalitarians providing enough scathing background commentary to make even the strongest among us crack.

But Daddy, bless his heart, stood up to them, for what I believe to be the first time in his life. He went so far as to tell Aunt Sissy that he'd be more prone to listen to her if she hadn't buried poor, overworked Uncle Jack last year and if Gussie's husband hadn't taken off with a Waffle House waitress. (Side note: What is it with powerful men and Waffle House waitresses? I'm sensing a disturbing trend.)

Anyway, that's right about when the first handful of sweet potato casserole went flying. Mamma claimed it came from one of the kids, but her orange palm told a different story.

Daddy eventually locked himself in his library, saying he wasn't coming out until it was time to go boat shopping on Sunday. As he has a couch, a bathroom, and a minifridge full of snacks, I'm inclined to believe him.

Then Mamma (and company) turned on *me*, claiming this was all *my* fault, and I was flabbergasted. Mamma said that everything she demanded from Daddy was for *my* benefit.

The old Lissy would have absolutely been on board, but the new Melissa in me just can't. I'll never forget the way Daddy spoke at lunch and I can't bear to take away anything else that he's earned.

That's right about when Duke's migraine started and we had to excuse ourselves from dinner.

We said good-bye to my father through the door and he promised to e-mail me a photo of his new boat as soon as he got it. And now we're on the way home, with Duke in the backseat, a cold washcloth pressed over his eyes.

Nicole's rocking a little in the passenger seat. "Eight years.

I spent eight years in the public school system and I've never seen more horrible children."

"They're worse than ChaCha?" I ask.

Nicole snorts. "Without a doubt. That girl is rough around the edges, but she's not incorrigible. Her manners are the problem, not her soul. As for your nieces and nephews? Sure, at a cursory glance, they're perfect little ladies and gents. They know which fork to use when and they call everyone 'ma'am' and 'sir.' Just because they're polite doesn't mean they're not the Children of the Corn, though. The young one? With the kitten smile and the adorable lisp? In the pink pinafore with the sideswept bangs secured by the big bow? She said, 'Was it your life's ambition to be a spinster, Miss Nicole?' What kind of kid says that? Suddenly I'm not quite so anxious to fill out the adoption paperwork."

Oh, great. First I screw up her ability to have kids, and now my family has made her not even want to adopt a needy one. Nice. What's my next trick? Maiming her? Letting Mr. Muffin go?

I absently pick some corn pudding out of my ear before I answer. "That was MaryKath, and yeah, Gussie's offspring are a special breed of vicious, aren't they? You know how some families are musical or they're great at languages or they can all fox-trot, which they show off at relatives' weddings? Our specialty is quiet, cutting cruelty. My mother's family crest would read, 'Aw, sugar, I simply asked if you were pregnant 'cause you have such a healthy glow.'"

"Sweet baby Ray! Is the whole family like that?" Nicole gasps.

"The Beaulieu side, yes. Grandmamma's big claim to fame is having once made Jackie Kennedy cry. She's still proud of that, too, like it's her crowning achievement. Also? She's over ninety years old and still driving herself. Not well, but no one's brave enough to say otherwise."

Duke comes to life in the backseat, adding, "That's because evil's impossible to kill. Like the Terminator. Only at a tea party."

He's not wrong.

I say, "You'd think because my mother's people are all so blond and pretty and pressed that they'd be nice, but that's the opposite of true. I caught Thomas—the gorgeous little boy in the plaid pants and the blue blazer—stealing all the cash out of my wallet, and when I busted him, he goes, 'Clearly you're just gonna spend this money on pizza pie, so I'm doin' you a favah, Auntie Melissa.' "

"Your poor father," says Nicole. "How has he put up with all this for so many years?"

While we ponder, Duke quietly comments, "The question isn't how. The question is *why*."

After that, we spend the rest of the drive home in silence.

Following yesterday's unpleasantness, I'm cautiously optimistic about the reunion. Even if I find that I negatively impacted every single LT grad's life, the night still won't be as bad as Thanksgiving à la Beaulieu.

Nicole and I arrived early at the Drake to take care of the last-minute details, with Duke to join later. Currently Nicole's busy with the bartenders, making sure they understand how to fix our signature cocktail called the Lion Tamer, a blend of Southern Comfort, lime juice, and powdered sugar. Sounds disgusting to me, but you can't beat it in terms of a clever name, right? (No wonder Nicole's in charge of MCPR's event planning.) We're also providing top-shelf liquor, craft beers, and an excellent assortment of wine, none of which comes in a box. I made sure of that. I kind of wish I'd been more cognizant of the company's finances *before* I wrote a corporate check to cover the open bar, but it's also possible that we weren't experiencing negative cash flow until I started writing corporate checks. Again, I'll think about that later.

As for me, I've been working with the deejay on the playlist, substituting Poison for Boys II Men and Lita Ford for Mariah Carey. Listen, with enough Lion Tamers in them, people *will* like the playlist and they *will* dance. Seriously, my dime, my decision.

Even though I'm practically walking distance from the Drake, Nicole and I got a room here so we could primp together before the party, exactly like we did in college. Out of everything I missed by springing ahead in time, I may be the sorriest to not remember our sorority days at IU. From what I understand, they were epic. Oh, well. We have our whole future ahead of us, right?

Satisfied that the ballroom is ready and all the players are in place in regard to bar service and catering, we dash upstairs to fix our hair and put on our dresses. Nicole's sleek and lovely in a short black number, while my pink tulle is an homage to my prom dress. For a minute I considered pairing it with Doc boots, but then I remembered exactly how stupid they look through contemporary eyes. Instead, I choose a strappy pair of silver Choos.

Dresses on, hair done, makeup refreshed, we're ready for action! Somehow Nicole's roped me into working the registration desk with her. I have no desire to be here, but she said she needs me and that's reason enough. A stream of recognizable faces begins to trickle in and we handily pair the right badge with the proper guest.

Turns out I was right the first time: People *can* read and

they *do* know what they look like. We're superfluous to the process, and yet I must admit to enjoying sitting here and having classmates not only recognize me, but also remember me fondly. I've been waiting to bask like this. So worth it!

When Steve-o arrives, he gives me a hug bordering on bad-touch but I let it go. Without Adam Levine in his life, my ass is the finest one he's likely to ever paw, accidentally or otherwise.

I recognize Elyse, Duke's former-life divorce attorney, the second she steps into the hallway. That bitch still looks incredible. I curtly hand her a name tag and she seems vaguely hurt at my snub. Sorry, honey, but you can't unring that bell.

Nicole and I are just about to pack it all in and join the party when I hear a gratingly familiar voice. "Ohmigod! It's the Belles, as I live and breathe." When I glance up, all I can see is a blur of red cannonballing at me. I'm hugged so hard I'm almost knocked from my seat.

"Lissy! Nic! You guys! This is so, so incredible! I missed you soooooo much! You totally suck for ditching me at UCI with no one but Kimmy and April! Spill! Spill! Tell me everything!"

Nicole and I trade a wary glance. "Hey, Tammy," I offer.

"How've you been?" Nicole politely queries. After the Amy Childs incident, I learned that the Belles didn't hang out like we had previously. We were all still friendly and cordial (keep your enemies close, as Mamma says) but we were never the same. After Nicole and I went to a different college from the rest of the girls, we lost touch on purpose.

Tammy starts to launch into a whole retrospective of her life, but Nicole quickly suggests that we catch up inside the party instead, as we still have tags to distribute.

"Then you'd better give one to my husband," Tammy demands, shoving a bald, slope-shouldered man in our direction. "Sugar bean, say hello to Lissy and Nicole."

"Hi, there," I offer, already scanning the few tags left on the table. "What's your name? Or did you RSVP as 'sugar bean'?"

He clears his throat. "Actually, it's Brian. Brian Murphy."

I immediately look up. "Brian? Across-the-street Brian?"

Because, no.

It can't be.

Before I went back in time, I finally unearthed Brian's photo in an archived issue of *Forbes* and he was handsome and ruddy and had filled into his frame. Also? He had hair. A lot of it, and not just coming from his ears and nose like this one. This grayish, shriveled creature is what supercutie Brian Murphy would look like having been trapped in a plaster cast from head to toe for a month.

"One and the same." The smile he offers is tired and doesn't quite reach his eyes.

I try not to let on my shock at his appearance. "Hey, Brian, so good to see you! I was just thinking about you when I heard the new album by Wildstreet. But I'm sure you're totally aware there's a whole third-gen glam-metal revival out there, a lot of it coming from Sweden, and—"

That's when it registers.

Brian Murphy is Tammy's *husband*. Tammy married Brian. *My* (not really, but still) *Brian*.

In what kind of bizzaro, fucked-up alternate universe is it possible for him to marry her?

Oh.

That's right.

The one I created.

That bad, bad feeling I've thus far avoided this evening is back with a vengeance.

Tammy shoves Brian out of the way. "He doesn't listen to that punk-rock garbage anymore. Tell Lissy how we saw Kelly Clarkson in concert last month!"

Numbly, Brian nods, affixes his name tag, and is summarily swept into the ballroom by the crimson tide that is Tammy.

Nicole merely shrugs as they retreat, while she sweeps up her clipboard and Lion Tamer. "I thought I'd heard they hooked up long ago. I guess I heard right."

Tammy and Brian and Kelly Clarkson. What happened?

My night's mission is to find out.

Well, here I go again, only this time I recognize the sleeping pit and I understand why I'm wearing a Central Asian Ikat robe.

So there's that.

At some point last night, I came to realize that not only are Lion Tamers *not* disgusting, but they are in fact the most delicious of all beverages. So I drank many. Many, many, many. I'm aware that there's a reason behind my consumption, but for this blissful moment, I'm simply enjoying the feel of yak pelt and the gift of not yet remembering.

"Namaste, Lissy Ryder! Was the sleeping pit to your comfort again?" Deva asks.

"I'ma get me one of these," I respond with a grin, and then I wince. Smiling hurts. Damn you, SoCo!

"Are you hungry?"

Oh, I've definitely been here before. "Pfft. Not for wheatgrass," I reply.

"Actually, I've become smitten with the cleverest concoction. They're little sticks of French toast and they come with a cup full of dipping syrup. So self-contained! So mobile!"

Now, that's a shock. "*You're* eating Burger King break-fast?"

Deva seems taken aback. "You haven't cornered the mar-ket on change, Lissy Ryder. Also, the food at the retreat? Blerg! Shaman Bob actually had us lick lichen off rocks one day. Even I have my limits. A couple of times I was able to sneak away from the forest reserve into the BK in Lahaina, and trust me, the French toast sticks were the best thing I ever tasted in that moment. So light! So golden! So not lichen! Here." She tosses me a bag and I dive in. There're hash browns, too! Woo!

"You're a lifesaver." The smell of hot grease and sugar fills the space around me.

"I'm more of an aura saver, but we can split the differ-ence."

Before I can even stuff the first hash brown mini in my mouth, I remember Nicole. "Hey, where's Nicole? Is she okay?"

Deva nods. "Nicole is perfectly fine. She left the party a little early with Steve Ramey."

I sit straight up and the whole room spins so hard I have to brace myself on a body pillow. "*What?* Do we need to find her?"

Deva's quick to calm me. "Fear not, Lissy Ryder. She's safe and sound. Steve Ramey has a lovely aura and she'll be per-fectly fine. I think they're back in your hotel room. I believe if you find a sock on the door, you might want to knock before you enter. He said something about rocking her like a hurri-cane?"

I shudder. I wonder if he takes off his jewelry to do that? Then I remember something else. "Wait, what about Duke?"

Um . . . is it weird that I should be more concerned about my friend than my husband?

And that's when the drinky-drinky portion of the night suddenly comes crashing into the front of my mind.

Last night I was waiting behind a privacy screen on the far side of the lounge to use the ladies' room. I quickly realized that Duke was deep in conversation with Elyse on the couch on the other side of the screen. They had no idea I was there, so they were completely unaware that I could eavesdrop on every single word.

At first, I thought he was hitting on her and I was ready to tear down the screen and confront him, but then I really started to grasp the content of his conversation, and frankly, that was way worse.

"She doesn't hear me," Duke started.

Oh, yes, I do, asshole. Loud and clear.

"I tell her what I want and what I need and I'm completely shut out, like I don't matter. Yesterday she was all upset over how her mom treats her dad and yet *that's exactly the way she acts with me*. She *is* her mother, minus the 'y'all.' "

I was really about to pop through the screen then, until I realized he wasn't exactly wrong.

"She bulldozes over everything and everyone. At least her father has some power, because he's the breadwinner. I'm just a fucking trophy husband and I'm sick of it."

"Have you tried to talk to her?" Elyse asked gently.

"Only a million times. She's incapable of understanding anyone's wants outside of her own."

Um, *ouch*. I honestly thought I'd gotten better about that.

"For example, I tell her how I'm feeling, I tell her what I need, and it's like I'm talking to a wall. I've been explaining how bored and lost I've felt since she had me retire and her response is always, 'Take a spa day!' or 'Go buy yourself something pretty!' as though that's what's going to make me feel like I have value."

Sweet Jesus. I'd rather he were hitting on her.

"For what it's worth, I'm really sorry," Elyse replied. "Are you prepared to take the next steps? Do you need representation? If so, here's my card."

He paused for not nearly enough time before he decided to completely explode our life together. "Yes. I want out. I can't take it anymore. And I don't need any of our marital assets."

Elyse was quick to jump in. "Whoa, hold on. Are you saying you don't even want your house? It's half yours. Duke, if you choose to hire me, I'm going to insist on a fair settlement; that's my job."

But Duke was resolute. "Don't want it. I've been kicking around in six thousand square feet when all I really need is a one-bedroom condo. The idea of being on my own and rebuilding my life is actually pretty exciting. I want to see what I can achieve in my professional life. I was great at my job and will be again. I need to rebuild on my own, for myself. I need a reminder that I have value, too."

That's when I slipped away from the screen, my business in the washroom forgotten.

"Deva, is it possible we're not meant to be together, Duke and me?" I ask. "I thought by changing the past, I'd guarantee us our future, but that's clearly not the case."

"Let me ask you something, Lissy Ryder—were you ever happy? Really, truly content and in the moment and so in love with Duke that you couldn't even believe your good fortune at being together?"

I toy with the fertility god perched on the table next to me. "That's a tough call. I can remember being really, truly happy in a lot of moments, like when I'd best him in an argument or when I could get him to see things from my perspective. But just day to day, do I feel an overwhelming outpouring of love, like I can't function without him in my world? I'm not—"

"Then no."

"Wait! I didn't say that!" I protest.

Maybe I thought it, but I didn't say it.

"Clearly, Lissy Ryder, you're in love with the control, not the man, and that's not fair to either of you. It's best you understand this now."

"Hold on, sister! You're putting words in my mouth!"

Deva helps herself to one of my untouched French toast sticks. She takes a bite and practically purrs. "Am I? Seems to me that if you were truly, madly, deeply in love, you'd not hesitate to have told me. Proclaiming your love for him would be as natural as breathing. Yet the first place you go is *winning*? That's not love, Lissy Ryder. Not by a long shot."

I'd argue but the shameful truth is, she's not wrong.

Didn't I want to change the past at first just so I could dump him on my terms? Our relationship was always about winning, my winning.

Now that I think about it, I didn't start dating him because I thought he was funny or nice or hot. I doggedly pursued him because I heard Elyse liked him and I was not about to let her have anything that should have rightfully been mine.

Whether or not I actually wanted him was beside the point.

I was aggressive; she was demure. I won.

Oh, Duke or Martin or however you want to be addressed, because I never really bothered to ask—I've done you a terrible, terrible disservice.

"You're saying I should let him go."

Deva chews, swallows, and shrugs. "I've not said any-thing, Lissy Ryder. All I suggest is that you examine the con-struct of your relationship. Is the foundation of your love built on sand or is it built on rock?"

As I reflect on our twenty-plus-year history, both in the first past and the present, I'm hit with a terrible realization. . . . The only thing we actually ever had in common was love.

More specifically, we were both in love with me. And that's not nearly enough. This realization is way too deep for this early in the morning.

"Do you mind if I cry for a while?" I ask.

"Knock yourself out, Lissy Ryder."

But I try and the tears won't come. Instead, I'm flooded with guilt because I don't have the depth of feeling for Duke that he deserves. Was the homecoming dance something spe-cial for us? Absolutely. But that's it. I think I was more swept up in all the events leading up to the dance than in actually being with him.

And I don't dare say this out loud, but I think I'm in love with my handbag more than my husband.

As I can't even properly cry for him, my only choice is to let him go without a fight. Were I to fight, it would be only so I could be victorious, and not because I really can't bear the idea of living without him. I hate myself a little for never hav-ing seen this before. He's too good a man to not be with a woman who worships him.

So, if we're not meant to be together, then do I wish for him to be with someone who cares about him?

You know what?

I think I might.

"Is he going to wind up with Elyse?"

Deva doesn't hesitate to answer. "Absolutely, even though

neither of them realizes it yet. Their chakras were lit up like Christmas trees, and the energy they radiated together was almost palpable! Plus, did you see her in that tight dress? My God, she looks exactly like Sofia Vergara! Va-voom! I don't swing that way, Lissy Ryder, but if I did, I'd be all up in that."

As I have no clue as to what else to do right now, I laugh.

Deva then leaves me to eat my breakfast, and when she returns, she has two big, steaming mugs.

"Coffee?" I say, all expectantly. I mean, she was just in Hawaii. Stands to reason she'd have brought back a nice Kona.

Deva sets my mug next to the naked dude on the table. "Yerba mate. It's a tea made from a variety of holly bush in subtropical South America."

Of course it is.

"Does it contain caffeine?"

"Yes."

"Good enough." I take a sip and it's not horrible.

Deva folds herself into a complicated pretzel twist across from me. "Tell me about the texts you sent, Lissy Ryder. You've experienced problems with the ripples in time?"

"Yes and no. Me? I'm great, except for the Duke business, which I guess was inevitable. I mean, I've got a cool life and good friends and a kick-ass business. Things couldn't be much better. You should see my house! Is MTV *Cribs* still on? Because I could totally star in an episode. I even drive a bitchin' whip."

But that's not the whole truth. Instead, that's what I've been telling myself. It's probably best to be completely honest with Deva, so I amend my previous statement. "Okay, I'm about to be sued by a fourteen-year-old named ChaCha. I kind of don't know how to do my job, because I never had this level of success before. I can handle the bare minimum, but beyond that, it gets complicated. Still, all of this is manageable and I'm one thousand percent happier than I was before."

"What aren't you telling me?"

I stare at the Ikat robe while I try to figure out the best way to explain what's happening. You know, the ancient people really did a bang-up job on dyeing these colors. The indigo and the fuchsia color bands are still unbelievably bright. I should find out what Deva washes this in and—

Deva's voice snaps me out of my reverie. "Lissy Ryder, I can't keep telling you that denial is not a river in Egypt. Although, interesting fact about the ancient Egyptians—they called the fertile deltas around the Nile 'black land' and . . . Damn it, now I'm doing it, too. Spill it."

I take a deep breath before I begin. "The problem is, though things are aces for me, life has become drastically worse for the people around me. Even Duke, now that I consider it. He was mad the first time around, but this time he was crushed."

Then I run through the litany of problems I've encountered with the lives I've influenced, sparing no detail.

Deva's unfazed. "I explained there would be ripples."

"Not like this," I argue. "A lot of these guys are stuck in lives that are awful compared to what they should have had. Nicole can't have kids! Steve-o makes minimum wage, not albums. Amy Childs is a big heartbreaking mess, as are so many others. What happened and how can we fix it?"

I don't add "without messing up my present," but I definitely think it.

Deva's still all nonchalant. "Again, Lissy Ryder, the nature of time is fluid. You make one change and everything around it is affected."

My greatest fear has been confirmed. "What you're telling

me is that by going back and making things right for myself, I absolutely messed it up for everyone else, beyond a shadow of a doubt?"

"I am."

"How? That's what I don't understand! I didn't do anything wrong! I was nice to everyone! I didn't inflict any emotional scars! I didn't engage in any verbal assaults! I was Lissy 2.0, new and improved, all the bugs worked out! No one's making videos now saying, 'High school was the worst time of my life, but it gets better.' Because it didn't have to get better for anyone, because I did the right thing from the start!"

Deva closes her eyes in concentration and places her face in her massive mitts. When she's finally worked out her thoughts, she looks back up at me. "Exactly."

The tenuous grasp I had on my patience has disappeared. "*Exactly?* That tells me *exactly* nothing! You're speaking in riddles! Are you saying that everyone should have had a terrible high school experience if they want to be successful later in life?"

"Exactly."

"*Argh!*"

"Shh, calm yourself; have a sip of tea." I comply, grudgingly. "Consider this, Lissy Ryder. It's possible that your peers went on to incredible accomplishments specifically because you were so awful to them. Perhaps that's your purpose. Maybe your future-fixing kindness has actually kept them from achieving their goals."

My mind is reeling. "You mean if I weren't there telling them they were talentless or fat or ugly, they wouldn't have tried so hard to prove themselves?"

"Exa—" Deva catches herself. "I mean, precisely."

"And there's nothing we can do about it."

"I never said that."

"You texted it."

She waves me off and creates a slight breeze with her great paw. "Oh, you can't go by those. Nothing comes out right. Just last week I texted Shaman Bob to please bring his 'big blue penis' to my tent, which is hilarious."

"Because you meant to type 'pen.'"

Deva creases her brow. "No, because I meant to type 'black.'"

Sometimes I wish I could unhear things.

"Back to the matter at hand. You said I couldn't just travel back to 2004 and convince Nicole not to quit; ergo I can't make sure she met her husband and thus fix her child-free situation." I stand up, rather unsteadily, and I begin to pace.

"Lissy Ryder, I learned a great many things about the tonic on this last retreat. Bob is just a font of information, truly. Although the man cannot stand on a surfboard to save his life. We were down on the Honolua Bay and—"

"Is this relevant?" I'm in no mood for courtesy right now . . . or another pornographic reference.

"Not really," Deva admits sheepishly. "Ahem, the tonic. Yes. When administered by someone other than the person who made it, the tonic takes that person where they *need* to go, rather than where they might want to go, so you can't pick or choose. The tonic does that for you."

"Did you not know that when you gave it to me?"

"Er . . ." Deva starts to dig in a giant basket next to the couch. "I should show you the piece of driftwood I found on the beach. I swear it's shaped exactly like Taylor Lautner's nose."

"*Deva*. Did you not know that was a possibility?"

She sticks her whole face in the basket. "It's almost un-canny, Lissy Ryder—there's flaring and everything."

I yank her back out of the basket by the hem of her caftan. "Damn it, Deva, you gave me a potion that had the potential to send me anywhere in time and you never mentioned it? Thank God I landed when and where I did! What if I'd ended up with the cavemen and a saber-toothed tiger ate me? What if I'd landed in Phuket right before the tsunami hit?"

Deva glances down at her bare wrist. "Hoo . . . is it getting late? Would you care for more tea?"

I'm about to go all HULK SMASH up in here. "You never sent anyone other than yourself, did you? I was your guinea pig! You're still pissed off about the corn dog incident!"

"No, Lissy Ryder, of course not!" She relents. "Well, okay, maybe a little. Mostly I figured if something happened to you, you were expendable."

"I can't believe you!"

Deva attempts to calm me. "But we're good now. I like you a lot more than I did when I brought you here the first time. I mean, you left Spanx strips all over my bathroom! Not cool. I'm a new age healer, not a maid, Lissy Ryder."

I say nothing, choosing instead to glare daggers.

"As I was saying, all is not lost. I believe there's a way for us to fix everyone else's situation."

"Finally!"

"But you're probably not going to like it."

CHAPTER SIXTEEN
She's Only Seventeen

Ever hear the expression that the cure is worse than the disease?

Welcome to my world.

Here I am, back in my childhood bedroom, under the shining visage of David Coverdale, faced with an impossible choice.

When I left Deva's yesterday, I started to walk home, but I ended up pacing the lakefront for hours. Nicole called, looking to commiserate about seriously regrettable decisions from the night before. Apparently she was *not* rocked like a hurricane. However, I told her I wasn't feeling well. I asked her to drop my stuff on the back porch on her way home. She readily agreed. I suspect she wasn't sad not to linger on the phone, as there was a Silkwood shower in her near future.

When Deva explained the only way out of this, my initial

thought was *No, no way, no how, never going to happen.* But as I walked and considered, I had to look deep inside myself and ask if I was ready to play God.

And, narcissistic as I am, it turns out I'm not.

Much as I want what I have, from the house to the Jag to the pending lunch date with David Coverdale, I can't be the one who keeps Nicole away from her rightful family. I can't keep Amy away from Oprah, and I can keep her from rehab. I can't keep Steve-o from all that mad naked ass. I can't let Brian end up a low-level functionary at an insurance company because he married the red menace. Brooks needs to win her Emmy for best drama. Meredith needs to go to French Laundry. Robert needs to go to Fashion Week, Charlotte needs to attend junior high, and Jeremy has to boldly go where no man has gone before. (Well, at least not very many men.)

Their futures are worth more than a Birkin bag . . . even one that's made out of ostrich skin.

Deva sent me packing with another vial of Incan fluid, this time about two weeks' worth. Unfortunately, when I traveled back in time the last time, the fluid I didn't drink was lost in space, because I didn't have it in my hand at the jump. She explained you can carry stuff between dimensions as long as it's touching you. That's why I was still dressed when I woke up the first time.

Deva was running low on the ingredients, so half a vial was the most she could provide. She's planning to fly to South America today in order to start gathering supplies to make more. Said she'll be back in about a month and she won't be available via phone, because the cell reception's terrible in Machu Picchu. Oddly enough, I'll miss her texts.

Deva explained the only way to fix the past was to jump back and do a full reset. She believes the fluid will take me to when and where I landed before, only this time my job is to do nothing.

That's a lot harder than it sounds.

I can restore everyone's life and livelihood and rosy future with one exception . . . my own. And all I have to do is be my old self. All those times I opted for kindness? No can do. When I chose to protect others, rather than denigrate them? Not this time. Will it be crooked and long and look like a schlong? Yep. Is Brooks's nickname about to stick? Uh-huh. Does Debbie do corn dogs? If I want everyone else to be happy, she does. Am I to break poor Brian Murphy's heart again? Abso-frigging-lutely.

And my big, shiny reward for having done all of the above? I wind up back in my parents' house, unemployed, friendless, and alone, lugging around thirty extra pounds.

Karma continues to be a bitch.

Deva says the only way to give my soul a blank slate is to sacrifice myself for the greater good of everyone else around me . . . and I picked a bad day to develop a conscience.

To facilitate the process, Deva thought I should make the jump in my parents' house. I was very relieved to find the place empty when I arrived earlier. The war between my folks is still raging, and that's the last thing I need to deal with right now.

I look around to make sure I'm not missing anything before I drink the fluid. I consider taking my high school journals with me, but their contents reflect the kinder, gentler Lissy and not the one from the first time around. Fortunately—or not—the memory of what I read the day after the reunion has stayed with me, and I'm clear on what I have to do and whom I have to do it to. And I am sorry.

I take one last lingering look at hot thirty-seven-year-old Lissy. I know I'm headed back to my smokin' high school bod, but that's only temporary. My big ass will be waiting for me when I get home. I'm temporarily cheered by the idea of cafeteria Tater Tots waiting for me and then I remember I won't be able to partake this time. Damn it!

I sit on the bed and open the vial, prying off the rubber stopper so I can get it over with faster. The fluid rockets through me just like last time and I can feel it actively lighten my mood, despite the heaviness of my heart. Once it's drained, I replace the stopper and the lid and shove it in my pocket. Then, right before I go under, I grab one more thing—my iPod. I'll make it so no one ever sees it, but I need at least one anchor to the real world and I can't take my Birkin. I slip in the earbuds and select SHUFFLE before hiding the unit in my bra.

Whitesnake begins to play and I tear up at the notion of never breaking bread with Mr. Coverdale.

"I don't know where I'm going, but I sure know where I've been."

Sing it, honey.

Sing it.

The yelling is what yanks me out of sleep. I can't quite make out the words, but the voices are definitely recognizable.

I open one tentative eye and it lands on Coverdale's crotch, which is currently illuminated by the morning light.

Okay, that covers where I am.

Now to figure out when.

I slide out of bed and scuttle over to the mirror. Judging from the clear skin and long, bouncy hair, I'm back in high school (whew, no saber-toothed tigers!) but I can't yet be sure of the date. I start searching my room for clues, but not before deciding to tape my iPod to the back of my dresser drawer for safekeeping.

Mission accomplished, I locate my purse and dump its contents on my bed. I find the usual detritus of a normal teen-age girl's bag—a few free-range pieces of Trident gum, passed notes, loose change, pressed powder, Clinique Rose Gold lip gloss, three scrunchies, mascara, a shitload of extra-slim tampons (aw, bless my not yet slutty heart), a couple of twenties, a credit card that's direct-billed to my dad, my shiny new driver's license, a BMW key, and a dime bag.

No, really, I was just holding it for a friend and—

Ahem.

Anyway—keys and a license. These are important. That means my birthday's already passed, because I didn't even bother trying for my license until I had my new car. I remember telling my parents I refused to drive anything I didn't personally own, so my folks had to cart me all over the place.

In retrospect, I probably would have benefited from a few spankings in my youth.

If I were to hazard a guess, this may be the Sunday after Duke yakked in my car. If there was only a way to know for sure. I poke my head out the bedroom door to see if my parents' fight offers any clues.

My father is as outraged as I've ever heard him. "Are you out of your mind, Ginny? You actually expect *me* to hose out the vomit in her brand-goddamned-new car? Do you have any idea how much it cost? The ridiculous paint job alone ran an extra two grand! And what do you think pink is going to do to the resale value? Not appreciate, that's for damn sure. Of course, *I* wanted to get her a used Honda and only if she improved her grades, but noooo—"

My mother cuts him off at the knees by saying, "Spare me the histrionics, George. Your opinion stopped bein' credible when you voted for Jimmy Carter—*twice*."

Yep.

It's Duke of Hurl Sunday.

It's also patently ridiculous that either my mother or I would expect my poor father to clean out my car after yet another week of sixteen-hour days. I throw on a comfy pair of LT-logo sweats and pull my hair into a ponytail, intent on doing the work myself, and then I stop in my tracks.

I can't.

I can't take care of the car myself.

I can't comfort my dad or tell him how much I appreciate his generosity. I can't do a damn thing that I didn't do the first time. I have to wait for my mother to work her "magic" and force him into the thankless and humiliating task of cleaning up what's rightfully my mess.

I climb back on my bed and curl into a ball, waiting for their argument to be over. Then I'll have to hang tight for another half an hour while my dad struggles with a scrub brush before he takes it to the car wash for professional detailing.

Daddy, why didn't you just do that in the first place? Or better yet, send *me* out to do it? Why did you let Mamma browbeat you so hard that you thought your only option was a bucket and some disinfectant? Why do you allow her to treat you like that? And why hasn't anyone ever said anything to her about her behavior? She's kind of awful. I used to find her overbearing nature charming, but now she's coming off as a shrew, and I hate that I've been mirroring her traits.

I pledge that as soon as I get back to the future, I'm going all Team Daddy. He's endured too much for too long to not have someone on his side. No one can fight Mamma alone, especially since she's always been about divide and conquer, but if we team up we may just best her.

Duke's going to show up at some point in the next hour or

so, furious because my doing doughnuts made him barf and then I played tonsil hockey with his friend, which means . . . today's the day he officially becomes Duke and I hook up with Brian for the first time.

I have no choice but to get together with young master Brian, and that feels all kinds of weird, statutory aspect aside. I know how it all plays out—Brian defends me, Lissy 1.0 gets all squishy at his courage, and we dash over to his house while our families aren't home. We roll around on Wookie sheets with some heavy over-the-shirt action until I see my mom return, whereupon I sneak home.

As I'm not sure what else to do, I brush and floss really thoroughly before hopping in the shower.

The doorbell rings just as I'm applying an edifying coat of Rose Gold gloss.

Okay.

Let's do this.

"And stay gone!" I add for good measure, kicking a tire to illustrate my point. I'm sorry that I have to make such a scene, but it's for the best.

What's so odd is that when Duke came to the door, I thought I'd be all shaken up from seeing him for the first time since the reunion. But the only stirrings I felt were those of sympathy and shame. I truly regret keeping him from being happy all these years. If the way Elyse looked at him at the first reunion is any indication, they're going to have a great life together, based not only on passion, but also mutual respect and a balance of power. He deserves that.

The newly minted Duke of Hurl peels out of my driveway while Brian stands next to me. Duke and I just had the fight that forced me into Brian's arms.

Which means I'm obligated to *get* into Brian's arms in the next hour.

I feel like I'm about to be featured on some parallel-universe episode of *To Catch a Predator*, like Chris Hansen is about to quaff his own Incan tonic specifically so he can come to 1991 and bust my Lolita-lovin' ass. (That's the thing about being a classic narcissist—it's always all about you, whatever the situation.)

Anyway, I have no choice right now. If I want to make Duke jealous and ensure Brian's Tammy-free, coupon-company future, I've got to do this.

Yet I feel so dirty.

"You want to come over?" Brian asks. He's not shy like I'd have expected. Then again, it's not as though we don't have history—we spent every minute together from when he moved here from Indiana in third grade until we went to LT South for ninth grade and our paths diverged. Not because I thought I was too cool for him then—mostly because that's the age when girls don't have boys as friends anymore, lest they be subject to an endless chorus of the Tammys of the world going, "Ooooooohh, he's your booooooooooyfriend." We stopped hanging out then because, frankly, it was easier than explaining that just because he was a boy and my friend that— Argh. See? I'm exhausted all over again just thinking about having to explain the nuance.

As my dad's taking care of my car before getting in a quick nine and my mom's off shopping, there's nothing stopping me from heading over to Brian's place.

I shrug. "I guess there's no present like time."

"What?"

"Nothing. Just a silly expression. Let's locomote."

When we enter his house, it's exactly as it was last time,

with all the toys and the dolls. But this time there's something missing.

"What's different?" I ask.

"What do you mean?" he replies. He steps over to the finger-painty fridge door. "Mountain Dew or Coke? Perhaps the lady would care for some SunnyD?"

"Coke's great," I absently reply. "But something doesn't feel right around here." Did I already screw this time-travel business up? Shit! If so, do I have to go back and reset again? I'm not sure how many times the universe is going to allow that before all parties involved wind up with flippers for hands or something. What's different around here, damn it?

Brian is the consummate gentleman. "Hey, Lissy, if you're not comfortable being here alone, we'll go back outside. It's just so rare that the place is completely empty that I like to enjoy the silence when I can."

Oh, the *chaos* is missing. No screaming rug rats. Duh. I quickly reply, "No, we're cool. I just couldn't figure out why it was so quiet."

He's quick to smile, and when he does so, his eyes crinkle and shine. "That's not a problem I have very often. Dad got passes for a preview screening of *Beauty and the Beast* and he took Mom and the kids, so I have a few noiseless hours. Honestly? I'm looking forward to college just for a little peace. Speaking of, where are you applying? I have to stay in state because of cost, but my first choice is U of I's computer science program. Northern and SIU at Carbondale are my safeties."

Noncommittally, I reply, "I haven't decided yet." Although I won't be in the past for it, I don't bother to submit any applications until my dad takes my keys away in the spring. Even then, I'm without my car only for the hour it takes me to work on the UCI app, which was pretty much one step above drawing a turtle on a cocktail napkin. (That's how long it took for Mamma to find out Daddy's plan and return the keys to me, FYI.)

Then I remember the Lissy Ryder I'm supposed to be right now and I add, "All this college talk is giving me boredom cancer. I want to *do* something. Maybe we should go up to your room."

Unclean! Unclean! I feel unclean!

Brian shrugs and leads the way up to the third floor. "You want to watch a video?" he asks once we get to his room.

"Depends. What have you got?"

He rifles through his VHS tapes and I suddenly recall how excited I was to see that he understood how to work his VCR. I mean, it wasn't even flashing twelve a.m.! He begins to pull tapes and read labels. "I have *Married with Children*, *In Living Color*, *The Fresh Prince of Bel-Air*, *Parker Lewis Can't Lose*, um . . . a couple of *Star Wars* movies, yeah, probably not your thing, um, *Headbanger's Ball*, but that wouldn't interest you, either, *Matlock*—my mom asked me to record that. Let me see what I have in this next box."

"Wait," I say, trying to sound nonchalant. "*Headbanger's Ball?* This week's?"

Brian acts like I just gave him his first puppy or hand job. "Really, Lissy? You watch the *Ball?*"

I try to play it off like I did the first time around. "Pfft, only because Riki Rachtman's cute."

He cues up the tape. "Then let's *Ball*." Then he realizes exactly what he's said and he blushes all the way down to the collar band of his Tesla concert tee and I'm utterly charmed.

Damn it, self, you need to *act* charmed, not *be* charmed.

He settles in on his bed and I sit down next to him. I haven't seen some of these videos for twenty years and I forgot exactly how much I've missed them. While I view the video for "Seventeen," I think to myself, *I have two words for you, Justin Bieber—Kip Winger.*

Brian offers running commentary as we watch. For example, he much prefers the Crüe's earlier work on *Theatre of Pain* versus *Girls, Girls, Girls* and David Lee Roth over Sammy Hagar. "Yeah, Sammy's talented, but he just doesn't embody the good-time rock-and-roll spirit that DLR brought to the table."

I'm telling you, it's all I can do not to stick my tongue in this kid's mouth right this second . . . even though that's exactly what I'm supposed to do. But that's the thing. He's a *kid*. And even though my tongue is seventeen, my brain is thirty-seven. I'm having so much trouble getting past that. Really, how did Edward not have this trouble with Bella? Before he ever set one icy lip upon her, he'd been a member of AARP for more than forty years! Or could he get past it because their love was written in the stars?

It's possible I'm putting too much thought into this. I shouldn't be having an internal jail-bait stalemate, yet here I am. If he were eighteen, things might feel different, because that way would be more Ashton and Demi. But as it stands, I'm Mrs. Robinson, coo-coo-ca-creepy-choo.

As we watch, we keep moving closer together and now our thighs are touching. On my last jump and this one, I can't get over how comfortable I am in Brian's presence. I can be *me* around him, probably because he doesn't put on airs or try to be something that he's not. And I don't feel like he sees me as Lissy Ryder, queen of the Belles. I feel like I'm more Lissy-let's-ride-bikes!

I mean, despite all the carnal knowledge Duke has of me, I bet he has no inkling that I'm Team Diamond Dave and not

Team Sammy. Duke wouldn't even know to know that I *had* a distinct preference. (Which is not his fault, but still.)

Of course, I spent twenty years calling him a name he didn't like, all of which makes me wonder, what did we even talk about for the past two decades? My hair?

Regardless, I need to fire up the old maker-outer, yet I feel more nervous now than when I was seventeen. The last time I was the one who threw the first move; ergo the onus is on me again, and yet the creep factor from our disparate ages keeps holding me back. So I look and don't touch; it's super-Mormon-feeling.

Midway through the episode, we both nod sadly when Riki updates viewers on the status of Tom Keifer's paresis of his vocal cords. Fortunately, I already know that Cinderella goes back to the studio in 1994 to record *Still Climbing*, but I can't say it. A Skid Row video comes on and Brian casually remarks, "I've been obsessed with these guys since my uncle sent me their album for my birthday."

I give him a playful (pedophile! stop touching!) shove. "I'm so sorry I missed your seventeenth birthday."

His eyes are fixed on the screen. "What? No. I turned eighteen."

I sit straight up. "How can that be? No one in our class is eighteen yet."

He shrugs. "I was born in Indy and they had different cutoff dates to start kindergarten. I was right on the line, so my mom held me back a year—figured I'd have more of an advantage being the oldest in the class instead of the youngest."

Oh, really?

I need to make doubly sure that I understand him. "What you're telling me is that you're old enough to vote?"

"Yep. My first presidential election is next year. So cool! There's this guy William Jefferson Clinton? Out of Arkansas? Very interesting guy. I just read that—"

"So you can buy cigarettes?"

"I guess so. You smoke, Lissy?"

"No."

(The occasional toke at parties doesn't count—just ask Cher Horowitz.)

(I mean, in 1995, when *Clueless* finally comes out.)

"Have you already filled out your Selective Service form?"

Brian seems awfully puzzled by my line of questioning. "Yeah. Back in August, I went to the post office and—"

But he can't complete his statement, what with my tongue in his mouth and all.

CHAPTER SEVENTEEN
Unspoken

*So that *happened*.

I didn't expect to enjoy kissing Brian, even after I made peace with the Demi and Ashton math.

But I did.

So much.

He does this thing where he holds my face in his hands and just looks at me and I feel like he's seeing into my soul or something. My thirty-seven-year-old brain has been neatly eclipsed by my seventeen-year-old hormones and it's all I can do not to scrawl *Mrs. Lissy Ryder-Murphy* on my notebook.

I'm deeply ashamed at the intensity of my feelings for an eighteen-year-old.

Yet I can't wait till the bell rings so I can cut cheerleading practice in favor of another mash session.

Our physical interaction isn't even the best part—he listens to everything I say and responds as if my thoughts are just as valuable as the package that holds them. If we were to grow up and have a life together, I have no doubt that we'd be a true partnership, with none of that trophy business on either side.

Brian challenges me like I've never been challenged (at least since the last time we were together). A couple of days ago I went off on a rant about how I hated Nirvana, and Kurt Cobain in particular. Brian insisted I back up my assertions and didn't allow me to make blanket statements like "He sucks." He helped me examine the roots of my anger at Cobain, which largely stem from his wearing a dress on *Headbanger's Ball*. I felt like he was mocking the glam rockers and not giving them credit for helping to define a genre. Although Brian didn't agree with my assessment of the band as a whole, I was pleased that he didn't feel he had to be on the same page. The whole conversation left me desperately wishing that Brian were in my adult life so we could discuss Cobain's legacy. (Had I understood his impact at the time, I'd have cut him a break.)

I wish I could talk to someone about Brian, but I kept everything under wraps last time, so I have to this time, too. I guess that's why I was always so into journaling. Too many secrets to not come out somewhere. Nicole senses that something's up, but she's not said or done anything beyond raising her eyebrows and hugging me for no reason.

Tammy, on the other hand, has no such compunction.

We're sitting at lunch, sipping Diet Coke and trying to quash the sounds of our audibly growling stomachs. Brian's across the cafeteria with his Dungeons and Dragons buds and it's all I can do not to run over and, like, lick him and then eat all his Tater Tots. (I would also consider reversing that order, but really, I'm good with either way.)

I've been stealing clandestine glances at him the whole lunch period, but I guess not clandestine enough. The Red Baron catches *everything*. "You're not, like, *with* dweeby Brian Murphy, right? I mean, slum much?" Tammy glances over to Kimmy and April for approval.

Yes! And I luff him! He's smart and compassionate and complex! When I'm with him, *I'm* smart and compassionate and complex, too! And because of him, Wookies will forever be erotic in my mind from this point forth!

But that's not what I say.

The best defense is a good offense, so I have to get offensive on her ass to deflect suspicion. "Tell me, Tammy, is it like a clown wig down there? Does it look like you've put Ronald McDonald in a leg-lock? Do you have some serious Fanta pants happening under your Hanes Her Way?" While I say this, I point at her lap. She tries to play off her shocked reaction with limited success.

I realize this sounds shitty, but I pretty much eviscerated her last time around when she grew nosy, so I have to bring out my big guns, and the hair thing's a huge issue for her. (Truthfully, her shade of red is lovely and chicks today pay big bucks for that look, and I imagine she eventually makes peace with it all, but I'm trying to win a war here, okay?)

"You wish" is her clever rejoinder. Clearly she received her master's degree from the School of Snappy Retorts.

To which I respond, "As if I'd dump Duke for Bill Gates."

"Who?"

Holy crap—does anyone who isn't Steve Jobs know who Bill Gates is in 1991? Deflect! Deflect!

My next statement belies the panic I feel at my future-knowing slipup. "God, Tammy, do you ever read anything other than the instructions on a pregnancy test? Maybe you should, like, look at a newspaper for once in your sad life. And by the way? Jaclyn Smith for Kmart called and she wants her sweater back."

For the record? No, I don't secretly regret being mean to Tammy. She's worse than I ever was, and that's really saying something.

Chastened but not quite finished, Tammy presses on. "Really? Then why did I see him getting out of your car this morning? And into it yesterday afternoon?"

I favor her with one of my trademark, perfectly glossed, raised-lip sneers. "Wow, Tammy, *Fatal Attraction* much? So you just, like, watch me all the time? What's next? Are you going to boil my bunny or something?"

Damn it, why doesn't *Single White Female* come out until next year? That would be such a better burn!

Tammy reddens but holds steadfast. "No, but you seem supershady about this whole Brian thing. Maybe you're not telling us the whole truth." Then she stands up, as if to prepare to pull a preemptive flounce.

I deliberately yawn and fake-stretch before answering. "Since it's soooo important for you to know, he's my neighbor and his mom's car is in the shop, so she can't drive him to school. But, like, forgive me for not running my good deeds past you first. And FYI? Your Designer Impostor perfume is making me queasy. Please excuse me while I go barf." Then I get up so quickly I knock over my chair and I saunter away without ever looking back. Kimmy and April give me the slow clap.

And that, my fellow Lions, is how you flounce.

As soon as I hit the hallway, I dash to the bathroom the farthest from the cafeteria, just in case Nicole tries to follow me. If she were to ask me what that was about, I'd be so inclined to spill everything.

Once inside the lavatory, I stand panting with my back against the door. Then I hear a flush and the creak of a metal back brace and Deva exits a stall. She doesn't say anything, instead motioning for me to look underneath the doors to make sure we're alone. (She's not so bendy in that thing.) We are.

I shout-whisper, "Holy crap, Deva, where have you been all week? Are you avoiding me pre–corn dog?" That's scheduled to go down (ha! pun intended!) tomorrow.

Even though the water's running while she washes her hands, Deva whispers back, "Absolutely, Lissy Ryder; it would not do for us to be seen conversing amiably."

"Actually, wait, why are you *here*? I thought you were on your way to South America."

"Right now in the present, it's only a couple of minutes after you drank the tonic. So I *am* headed to Machu Picchu, in a few hours of future time and a little over a week of 1991 time."

This is all so confusing. You know who could explain it all? Brian.

"Hey, real quick, I could use your advice. See, I'm falling for Brian and I don't know what to do about it," I admit.

"Go with it."

"Really?" I say in a loud, hopeful voice before catching myself.

Deva dries her hands, which is a three-towel job. "Indeed. It's imperative—if his future depends on your breaking his heart, then you must first capture it. That won't happen if you're not sincere."

I gush, "Well, that's awesome, because I feel so giddy when I'm around him, and he gets me, I mean, in ways that Duke never did and—"

She holds up a colossal digit. "Let me stop you right there."

I look left and right. "Why, is someone coming?"

"No, it's just that I don't want to hear about it."

"Why?"

"We're not girlfriends in *this* time period."

Ouch.

"Hold the phone, Deva—you're still not past the corn dog thing."

She snorts so hard it blows a paper towel off the sink ledge. "Damn skippy."

"That's not fair! You promised that we're pals now! And you told me CornDogGate was what caused you to dive head-first into the new age movement! You thanked me in front of God and your booby statues and everything!" Come on! She has to like me! I mean, having her on my side was the deciding factor for making the jump back again; I knew that this time in the future I'd have at least one friend.

Grudgingly, Deva admits, "Agreed. I appreciate who I am today because of you, and when we're both safely ensconced in the present, I hope to share French toast sticks with you. Yet that doesn't negate how you're going to make me feel tomorrow. You ruined corn dogs for me ad infinitum. And I loved corn dogs."

My chin begins to quiver, only I'm actually sincere and not just trying to get my way like when I usually bust out the waterworks. "Deva, I'm full of regret over the incident. If I could get away with not calling you out tomorrow, you know I would."

Deva's expression softens. "I understand, Lissy Ryder. Yet my dilemma is, if I don't piss you off, you won't be able to sell your performance tomorrow. So here goes—you're only smart enough to get into the worst college in America, your music taste is best suited to whoever's now appearing on the main stage, and you're a borderline perv for touching Brian's goodies. Also? Your Gucci bag is fake. You told everyone it was authentic but that was a lie."

I appreciate her effort. Maybe a little too much, because this bag is *totally* real. I inadvertently raise my voice. "Yeah? Well, *you* have man hands."

She gives my shoulder an affectionate squeeze. "Save it for tomorrow, Lissy Ryder. Save it for tomorrow."

"What is all this?"

"Brian, I think they're called 'stars.'"

Brian and I are at the old quarry about thirty miles out of town on this spectacularly crisp, clear October night. We're far enough away from downtown that there's no artificial ambient glow to lighten the black velvet sky and dull the millions of twinkling stars. The harvest moon is just beginning to rise, and in an hour it will be almost bright enough to read out here. (If I read, I mean.) We have a blanket spread out over the hood of my car and we're leaning against the windshield, with the boys from Poison playing quietly in the background.

Today's Thursday, which means tomorrow is homecoming Friday. It should also be home-going Friday, meaning I'll likely wake up back in the future once I go to sleep. I'm trying to savor every last minute, as tomorrow it all goes to hell at my hand.

Brian swings around to face me. "No, Liss. What's this? You and me. What are we doing? Is this just for fun or is this going somewhere? I know how I vote, but I want to hear your thoughts."

I'm as cagey now as I was the first time, only for different reasons. Last time it was about making Duke jealous so I could win the upper hand. That is, until it inadvertently turned into real feelings that I didn't know how to process. This time my emotions are so much more raw and I'm so pissed off at seventeen-year-old Lissy for not having the courage to act on them. How have I been so confident in my life that I welcomed having strange medical/aesthetic professionals renovate me from the neck down (bleaching, waxing, rejuvenating, lifting, etc.), and yet the idea of being seen in the halls with an attractive man who engaged both my head and heart was so repellent?

Yet my response is, "That's kind of a chick thing to ask."

"What am I to you, Lissy?"

What you are is the best guy I ever met, at seventeen or thirty-seven or any age in between. "Do we have to decide now? Can we just be in the moment, you know, Lissy and Brian, watching the sky and listening to music?"

"Of course." He takes my hand and begins to run his thumb back and forth across my palm, almost like he's reading it. "I just . . . You're really something special, Lissy. I don't mean to sound like one of your sycophants. God, not that. Never that." He laughs. "There's a soft side to you, a real depth that you rarely seem to show to anyone else."

This moment is almost too intense to breathe, so I keep quiet.

"Trust me, I'm aware of your reputation and I've seen you operate in the lunchroom. Your tongue should be registered as a deadly weapon. But I believe that under all your cutting remarks there's a real vulnerability to you. You're exceptionally protective of your inner self and you mask it with this badass attitude and all kinds of bravado. Don't forget, I knew you when you were the girl across the street who bought Good Humor bars for the kids from the other side of the railroad tracks who didn't have any money. Why are you so intent on hiding that side of yourself that's pure and selfless and light?"

I tell him the truth.

"Because it's easier."

He traces the designs on the sleeve of my sweatshirt. "If you keep hiding the woman you really are, whether that's 'Lissy' or 'Melissa' or whoever you wind up being, someday she may get lost amid all your bluster. For example, no one will care if you hate Nirvana, because you have well-considered reasons for feeling that way. Never be afraid to express yourself! People might even agree with you—not many, granted, because *Nevermind* really is a seminal piece of work and in twenty years, everyone's still going to talk about it. My point is, by keeping what makes you *you* quiet, you're doing yourself and the world a disservice. After all, you don't want to be like your parents."

Whoa, what? I don't remember this part from last time.

He continues, oblivious to how stiff I've become next to him. "I mean, your mom clearly loves your dad or they wouldn't have stayed together for so long. I don't understand why she's so intent on putting him down instead of building him up. Your mom is clearly not afraid to make demands—"

"Clearly," I interject. Seriously, this is homecoming week and I'm growing emaciated because of her. I'm well versed in her ability to make demands.

"See? Right. Because she's not afraid to say and do and demand what she wants, if she didn't care to be married to your father, she'd be on the first plane back to Atlanta—"

"Savannah."

"Eh, potato, po*tah*to. So—"

I practically bark with laughter. "Don't let her hear you say that!"

"Lissy." He angles my face toward him with his palms. I can see the harvest moon reflected in his eyes, and if he weren't so busy telling me something I didn't want to hear right now, this would suddenly become the best night of his life, if you know what I mean.

(I mean sex.)

"My point is, your mom wants to be with your dad, and if she didn't, she wouldn't. But she's on some bizarre power trip where she absolutely refuses to allow herself to be vulnerable to him, because it gives her the upper hand. Don't do that. Don't be that way. Open up."

I'm not sure what to say, so I opt to tell him the truth again. "I promise to try."

Yet I'm destined to fail.

And I couldn't be sorrier.

'm at my locker when I hear a familiar voice behind me.

"Yo, Listerine."

I needn't look to see who's speaking. "Don't call me that, Duke."

"Then don't call me Duke!"

I turn around and lean back against the bank of lockers. "Do you want something from me?" I mean, other than for me to be a raging bitch to you for no good reason?

"What's the deal with you and Murphy?" The jealousy's written all over his face. Last time I felt like I won the lottery, but this time I just want to hug him and tell him to call Elyse now and not make her wait twenty years.

"Pfft, wouldn't you like to know?" Seriously? Would he like to know? Because I want to shout about my feelings from rooftops! No matter what it takes, I'm going to find Brian in the future and I'll spend the rest of my days trying to win him back. If that means giving up Tater Tots and taking the bus and living in a one-bedroom apartment with roommates while I rebuild myself into a person who's worthy of him, that's what I'll do. But don't worry, Martin/Duke! You're going to end up with a chick even straight women want to bang! It's all good!

"Do you like him?"

Yes, yes, yes, oh, yesly yes!

I scowl. "What if I did? You and I aren't together. What do you think I am, Duke? A toy you can put on the shelf and pull out when you get bored? Doesn't work that way. We're on or we're off. Period. Make a decision."

I desperately want him to say we're off so I can have one more night with Brian, but I can't rewrite history. (I know; I've tried.) Instead, my browbeating works exactly as well as it did twenty years ago and Duke grudgingly agrees that we should attend the dance together.

Aces.

I muddle through the rest of the school day and the pep rally, and when I arrive at my car afterward, Brian's waiting exactly where I expected him to be.

I hate my life so much right now.

We get in the car and he squeezes my knee. This is the kind of guy he is. Here I am in my cheerleading outfit, which is pretty much every guy's fantasy, and he has so much respect for me that his only action is a brotherly touch because we're in public. "Are you ready for tonight? Big game!"

"Yeah, so excited," I lament.

Brian smoothes back the blond strands that have escaped from my ponytail. "Lissy, what's wrong?" Please stop being so nice to me. I do not deserve you, even for the next ten minutes.

He peers at me for a couple of seconds and then remarks,

"You seem a little pale and gaunt. What have you eaten today?"

"A couple of Mentos and four Diet Cokes." And, yes, my stomach feels like all those explosion videos on YouTube right about now. I start the car and I begin to drive out of the lot.

Brian's a bit exasperated. "Lissy, that's ridiculous. You're going to pass out at the game. You can't live on zero calories a day. Will you at least eat something when you get home?"

I shake my head. "Not if my mom's there." Seriously. If so much as a single Apple Jack passes my lips before I have to squeeze into that stupid dress, it would be World War III up in here.

"Lissy, turn down South La Grange Road."

No. Nooooooo.

I grip the wheel to brace myself. "Why?"

But I know why.

"Because we need to get you something to eat. We can go to the frozen yogurt shop on the corner. Between the sugar, the protein, and the vitamin D, you just might last the night without blacking out when you shout, 'Lion pride!' "

I keep my gaze fixed on the road. "I don't think so. I don't have time."

Brian is a paragon of reason. "Lissy, getting yogurt will take five minutes and make all the difference in the world." Wait for it . . . wait for it. "Plus, my mom gave me a coupon—we can get two-for-one waffle cones."

And here it comes.

"I don't have time for coupons, Brian," I hiss.

Brian is taken aback—of course he is, because I practically spit at him for being kind and gentlemanly and more concerned about my welfare than what's underneath my pleated skirt. "Excuse me?"

"I said I don't have time for coupons, *Brian*. God, what are you, deaf?"

"Whoa, Lissy, who are you right now?"

"I'm Lissy fucking Ryder, okay? Do you really think I'm going to A) make my public debut with you at a *yogurt store*, and B) use a fucking *coupon*? Are you mental? Do you mean for me to commit social suicide? Because that's what you're asking me to do."

I can't even look at him.

Brian takes a couple of deep breaths before responding. "I'm going to attribute this to your brain being in starvation mode right now. Let's get some food in you and—"

The only thing that's getting me through this right now is the conversation we had at the reunion. I've been in denial about it for two weeks, but the simple fact is that his current life is almost unbearable. Brian seemed like a fraction of his former self when we talked. He told me he spends fifteen hours a day in a tiny cubicle in a damp basement, writing code for a cut-rate insurance company for very little money. He has no outside interests or hobbies and seems so resigned to his fate. He doesn't even give a shit about music anymore, and that was his passion. I mean, really? *Kelly Clarkson?* And we didn't lose a war or anything? He even said, "I guess not everyone's allowed a happy ending." He hates his life and his wife, who swooped in on him last time solely because I let him down gently and didn't scar him so badly that he barely even thought about dating until he finished college.

So I have to sell this. For him.

I slam on the brakes and pull over to the side of the road. "What part of 'I don't have time for coupons' do you not get, Brian? Did I stutter? Was I not perfectly clear? Do I need to enunciate? My God, Brian, it's like you don't even know who I am."

Actually, it's like I can literally see his heart break.

He grips the door handle. "You're right about that. I thought I knew, but as it turns out, you actually *are* your mother. I'll walk home from here."

My job isn't done, though. "Of course you're going to walk!" I shout after him. "You don't have a car, because the Murphys breed like rabbits! You shouldn't even be allowed to live in my neighborhood if your family can't maintain standards! And do you really think I could ever date someone who liked Nirvana?"

He heads down the street without ever turning back to look at me.

Which is good, because then he can't see me cry.

CHAPTER EIGHTEEN

Sorry Seems to Be the Hardest Word

"You again."

For the first time ever, my poster of David Coverdale doesn't fill me with delight. Seeing him means I'm back exactly where I should be, whether or not I like it. The raised voices and slamming doors confirm it—I'm home again.

I don't even bother to look in the mirror this time, because I know what I'm going to see.

As I change out of my pajamas, my iPod and the empty vial fall onto the floor. I'm glad I had the presence of mind to bring them back, because this way there are no loose ends.

I'm not sure what to do right now. As I've reverted back to post(apocalyptic)reunion Lissy, I'm surely still living at home and I have few professional prospects. But at least I have some self-awareness that I previously lacked, and I look forward to being able to sit down with Daddy and show him my full support.

Actually, that makes me feel a bit better, so I head down the stairs to say good morning to him, but I guess the slamming doors means they both left, because the house is empty. According to the note, my mom's provided breakfast in the fridge and there's coffee in the pot. You know what? That's shameful. I'm thirty-seven years old and it's time I learned to cook a meal for myself.

I wonder where my parents went. Technically, this is the Sunday after Thanksgiving—is it possible they're still boat shopping, or was that only the case the last time I came back to the future? Being the same sad sack that I was the first time around, does that mean Daddy's not thinking about boats and retirement? For his sake, I truly hope he is.

I guess my main priority should be to figure out what's next for me. What I *want* is to find Brian right this minute and go to him, but if he still thinks of me at all, it's not fondly. I need to be a better Lissy before I come back into his life, in all aspects.

It sounds shallow, but I'll have to diet and exercise first, not because he's someone who doesn't accept a person as she is, but because I'll feel better about myself if I get back on track. I don't have to be who I was, but I need to find a happy medium between gluttony and starvation. I never considered myself someone "normal" or "average," but that would be an excellent goal right about now. I can't be good to anyone else until I feel better about me.

What else? I need to get my shit together professionally. You know, some schooling wouldn't be the worst thing in the world. Maybe if I went back and took some classes, this time around I'd actually pay attention and garner enough knowledge that I *could* run a successful PR firm, possibly even with a music specialty. It's not too late. Maybe I'd pick up the kind of skills that would help me land new clients, ones who weren't doing my parents a favor, or feeling obligated because I tried to twist fate.

I should also work on who I am as a person. The time has come to make amends. Rather, I *want* to make amends, and not because there's any personal gain attached. No one's going to hire me because I said I'm sorry, and I wouldn't expect them to. Actually, until I have a better grip on how to run publicity campaigns, I wouldn't let them work with me. (Note to self: Send the electrical plating company back three hundred and fifty of their four hundred dollars.)

This time when I apologize, I'll be able to do so with an entirely new perspective. I don't expect anyone to forgive me, but for my own sake, I must officially own up to my behavior.

To begin, I'd better verify that everyone's exactly where they should be in the present.

Oh, please, oh, please let this have worked.

I sit down at the computer my mother keeps on her kitchen desk and begin to Google.

I search for Robert and the first link takes me to PerezHilton .com. Apparently Robert, whom critics are calling the second coming of Alexander McQueen, has just been romantically linked with Adam Lambert. There's a photo of them coming out of Nobu together holding hands. Perez has drawn big white hearts around both of them, and I feel a rush of pride for which I have no rightful claim.

I can't help grinning over how much better it got for him.

After some clicking I find a Contact Me! box on his design Web site and I input the following:

Robert ,
You probably don't remember me.

Actually, I'm sure you do. I'm writing to tell you how sorry I am for everything that happened to you twenty-one years ago. You had your ass handed to you that day because of me.

The whole truth is, you made a better Madonna than Madge herself and I was jealous of the reaction you caused when everyone thought you were some new, hot girl. Granted, the boys are the ones who attacked you, but it was me who incited them.

I did the equivalent of shouting "fire" in a crowded theater.

The guys were appropriately punished by being kicked off the team, but I wasn't and now I have to live with what they did to you, knowing there're no amends I can make that would be commensurate. I am truly and profoundly sorry.

Wishing you the best,
Lissy Ryder

You know what?

Catharsis is better than carbs.

I send similar e-mails/Facebook messages to Meredith, Kimmy, April, Steve, Jeremy, and even Tammy. I tell Meredith how much I regret not respecting her unique taste and honed palate. I explain to Kimmy that my ends didn't justify my means. April is briefed on exactly why my insensitivity was so out of line, and I compliment Jeremy for being un-apologetically smart, even when people like me tried to drag him down. I tell Tammy how contrite I am for making her big day all about me. As for Steve, I praise him for the strength of his convictions. I tell him how much I admire his not compromising because of what some arbitrary asshole like me deemed cool, especially when I wasn't even honest about my taste. How dared I mock *him* for digging Gershwin over Pearl Jam?

In each note, I'm forthcoming about my culpability. I don't ask for forgiveness, because I don't deserve it. Even though my bad deeds helped spur their success, I don't exactly merit a trophy for being my unpleasant self from the get-go.

(By the way? Ten bucks every single e-mail recipient thinks I'm in AA now, working through the steps.)

The next letters are the ones that especially count.

To Brooks I write:

> *Dear Brooks,*
> *Despite my best efforts, I can't change the past, and if I told you I tried, you'd believe I was crazy.*
>
> *My behavior at the reunion was inappropriate and my performance in high school was unconscionable. I realize I'm in no position to ask you for a favor, but if I were, I'd implore you to keep recounting tales of my abhorrent behavior. Your words will have an impact on the younger generation and they'll be less likely to abuse their peers like I abused you.*

*I wish you nothing but the best, as that's
what you've always deserved.*

Lissy Ryder

Before I contact Duke, I take a quick peek at his Facebook page, but it's locked down, at least to me. I could easily hack into his account if I wanted to see it—he's been using the password "lionpride" now for years. However, his profile photo tells me everything I need to know; it's a shot of him and Elyse at the reunion. He's busting some goofy boy-band dance move, and she has such a smitten expression on her face that I feel like I'm intruding on a private moment just looking at it.

Dear Martin,
I've finally come to realize that you've always
deserved better. I'm sorry it took me so long.
I promise you won't hear from my attorney
again, save to agree to all your requests.
I wish you and Elyse every happiness.

All the best,
Lissy

I struggle for the right words to say to Amy Childs for a long time. I decide simplicity is best.

Amy,
I've blown any chance to apologize to you, so
I won't insult you by trying. Instead, let me
say this—living well is the best revenge, so I

*hope that you're able to exact that revenge
every single day.*

*Namaste,
Lissy Ryder*

Finally, it's time to write the one letter that counts more than any of them.

*Dear Nicole,
Thirty years ago I tried to buy your affection
with Good Humor bars. That was probably my
last selfless act, and even then I might doubt my
motives. Since that time, I've never lived up to
the promise of what I should be as a friend.
    I don't deserve to have someone as kind
and pure and good as you in my life, but if
you'd consider giving me another shot, I
promise to show you everything I've learned
in the last month about truly—and for the
first time—putting someone else's needs
above my own.
    Please allow me to be your second.*

Liss

Before I can even finish my next Google search, I receive a note back from Nicole.

*Liss,
I'm sorry. I just can't.*

Nic

Somehow, this feels even worse than having to break Brian's heart.

The old Lissy would have gone to her house bearing gifts and demanding that she allow me back into her life. I wouldn't take no for an answer. I'd do my usual bulldozing act where no one else's feelings or wants took precedence over mine. But at this point I realize that I love Nicole enough to respect her wishes.

If and when she ever comes around, I'll be waiting for her.

I'm so thrown by Nicole's note that I almost forget what I'd been doing, which was searching for current news on Brian. The last time I pulled up only his professional credentials, but now I'm very interested in his personal life.

I scroll through pages and pages of press releases and company profiles. Looks like his IPO is progressing, which is wonderful for him, but how is he outside of work? Who are his friends? What does he do to relax? Is he even able to have any fun, given the intensity of what's about to happen professionally?

I still can't find any obvious telling information about him, save for a sterile bio on NoCoup.com's Web site, where it states that he "likes music." What *kind* of music? Good music or Kelly Clarkson music?

I can't find a thing about him on Facebook, possibly because there are too damn many Brian Murphys in the United States. However, I do find a Twitter feed titled NoCoupCom-Prez, so I click over there.

I start at the bottom and work my way up so I can read his story chronologically. His early messages are pretty generic, regarding whatever the daily offer is, whether it's 50 percent off a night at the Brew & View in Lakeview or a discount blowout at the Ruby Room in Wicker Park. Everything seems so professional that I'm convinced he's using an outside publicist. (Not that there's anything wrong with that.)

Yet what catches my attention is the spate of replies he's been sending out over the past few weeks.

>   *@AddyMcAdams—Thanks! So happy!*

>   *@RolfGustavson—Agreed! Very exciting
>   times, my friend.*

Aw, he has a friend. It's not like he never had them before, but that makes me happy to know there's someone out there pulling for him.

>   *@Yello_submachine—I can't believe it either.
>   Finally, right?*

>   *@iamcoltonbolton—Twelve years, but who's
>   counting?* ☺

Is that how long he's been trying to take this thing public? That makes total sense. That'd put his start date right around the dot-com crash. He probably had a devil of a time trying to round up venture capital back then. I'm so proud that he finally got it together. He deserves this. He deserves to be happy.

>   *@cest-parfait-okay—You deserve to be happy!*

See? C'est Parfait Okay feels me.

>   *@DokkenStillRocken—We wish you could
>   have made it, too.*

@red-man-walking—Mazel back at you!
Thanks so much for your generous gift—note
and stories to follow!

Um . . . made it to what? Gift for what?

@FIJIGardenOasis—Oh, we'll be back, bank
on it.

We?
And what's the Fiji Garden Oasis? I open another window
and input that search criteria.

I'm taken to a page that looks like someone pulled it right
out of a screen saver. I'm talking little huts with thatched
roofs underneath the bluest sky I've ever seen. Although the
cabins appear primitive at first, each open-air unit comes
with a minikitchen and top-of-the-line Grohe bathroom fit-
tings. The private bungalows are built out on docks that jut
over crystal-clear blue water and they all have small, private
pools.

"The Fiji Garden Oasis Resort offers five-star lodging and
amenities on one of Fiji's most pristine beaches."

A slide show of stunning scenery begins to cycle as a nar-
rator begins his pitch.

"Built on the site of a former pineapple plantation . . ."

But I'm not really listening, because I'm trying really hard
to convince myself that this was the site of a corporate retreat.
Because why else would Brian go to a vacation in paradise?

I tab back to Twitter.

@TheNewMrsMurphy—I think you were
worth the wait, too.

No. No, no.

That's not from his wife.

That's from his sister-in-law.

Or his mom. Or his aunt. Because Brian did not just get married.

Karma can't possibly be that much of a bitch.

I click over to the New Mrs. Murphy's feed and I find the link to her Facebook page.

Unless someone is very skilled at Photoshop, it would appear that Brian and Joy were married on the weekend of our twentieth class reunion. I guess that's why he couldn't come.

Joy.

Her name is Joy.

I do a search on the *Chicago Tribune* Web site and I find the following announcement:

Grant/Murphy

Warren and Beatrice Grant, of Western Springs, IL, are happy to announce the marriage of their daughter, Joy Marie, of Chicago, IL, to Brian John Murphy, also of Chicago, IL.

Mr. Murphy's parents are William and Priscilla Murphy, of La Grange, IL. The wedding took place on October 20, 2012, at the Bond Chapel, University of Chicago, with Deacon Rolf Gustavson officiating. Dinner and dancing followed at the Metropolitan Club.

Miss Grant is a 1995 graduate of Lyons Township High School, La Grange, IL, and University of Illinois, Champaign-Urbana, IL, where she obtained her bachelor of science and master's in computer science. She is currently employed at Google in Chicago, IL.

Mr. Murphy is a 1992 graduate of Lyons Township

High School. He also obtained a bachelor of science degree in computer science from University of Illinois, and a master's in computer science at University of Chicago, Chicago, IL. He is currently employed as president and CEO of I Don't Have Time for Coupons™ in Chicago, IL.

The couple honeymooned in Fiji following the wedding.

I feel very detached as I toggle back to her Facebook page. I'm not sure the magnitude of this has hit me yet. Until it does, I plan to glean every tidbit I can about her life, starting with her photographs.

First, it has to be said that she's cute. I'm not being critical when I say she's not beautiful (okay, maybe a little), but she is cute in a girl-next-door kind of way. She has a pointy chin and round blue eyes and a bunch of corkscrew curls. She reminds me of Meg Ryan before All the Unpleasantness. She's not particularly tall or thin but her wedding gown fits impeccably.

I wonder if *her* mom didn't let her eat for a month before the ceremony.

Looks like she owns a cocker spaniel named Cerberus. Really? Like the hound from hell? She's funny, too?

Here's a photo of her at LT with the caption, *Scene of the crime!* Further investigation reveals that she and Brian met while working a computer science booth at Career Day shortly after she finished grad school.

Hey, how about a volunteer outing with her little sister, LaTonya?

Damn it, Joy, I'm having a very hard time finding reasons to dislike you.

Of course she dressed as Princess Leia for Halloween last

year. At least she's in the white robe and not the stupid gold bikini.

And here's the happy couple at the Guns N' Roses show at the Allstate Arena in 2011. She's throwing the horns in the photo.

This really happened.

Brian's with her. And she's exactly like him.

Game over.

I lose.

I can barely even begin to feel sorry for myself when the house phone rings. Who calls a landline? I'm in no mood for a conversation, so I ignore it. But it continues to ring, so I finally pick up on its millionth ring.

"What?"

I don't say this nicely, either.

I'm having a crisis, okay? I think I'm allowed to be curt.

"Hello? Who is this?" The static on the other end of the line is so intense I can barely hear anything.

Right before I'm about to hang up, I hear my mother's voice. "Lissy, come to Methodist General Hospital right now. There's been an accident."

CHAPTER NINETEEN
Empty

"This is all my fault."

My mother has aged forty years in the course of three days. Sitting huddled on one of the unyielding chairs in the ICU waiting room, she's fragile in a way I've never seen before. The shadows below her eyes are deep and dark, and her hair is matted and lank, as she's yet to leave the hospital.

After all the time travel and alternate realities I experienced in the last month, being here is the most surreal experience of all. We're the only family in this artificially sterile place, with its stiff, upright chairs and silk plants. The area is almost eerily silent, save for the occasional muffled squeak of the nurses efficiently whisking past us in their rubber-soled Danskos. There's a television in here, and when I arrived this morning *The Price is Right* was playing. Hearing the audience cheer and Drew Carey cackle seemed almost obscene, so I yanked the cord. No one's been by to plug it back in. So we're waiting in the quiet until eleven a.m., when we're permitted in to see Daddy.

"Mamma, this is not your fault," I try to reassure her, holding on to her hand.

And yet I'm not entirely sure that's the truth.

From what I've pieced together from eyewitness accounts, the police, and my mother's own words, my parents were on I-55 on their way back from brunch with friends in Burr Ridge. They were arguing about the possibility of retirement and suddenly my father began to experience severe chest pains. Yet he wasn't having a heart attack so much as terrible indigestion from too many horseradish-covered oysters from the raw bar.

However, when he took his hands off the wheel for a moment, my mother freaked out, grabbed it herself, completely overcorrected, and clipped the car next to them, which caused them to veer left and plow into an embankment on the driver's side.

The great irony here is that Daddy would be in much better shape had the incident proven to be a heart attack and had Mamma kept her hands from the wheel.

As it stands, he's in a medically induced coma to reduce the swelling around his brain, as he hasn't responded to other treatments. He suffered severe head trauma and he's covered in lacerations. His left arm and collarbone were broken and his pelvis and femur were shattered when his side-curtain air bag didn't deploy. His firm partners are already poised to take action against the car's manufacturer, but that's of little comfort at a time like this. If my father recovers—and that is a big "if" at this point—his road to recovery will be difficult and he'll likely not be mobile without assistance.

My mother doesn't have a scratch on her.

I didn't even recognize Daddy when I saw him yesterday, with all the cuts and bruising and bandages. He's hooked up to a dozen machines and all of them ping and beep at different times. If he were awake, he'd never be able to rest with the noise of the machines that are keeping him alive.

"Why'd I have to start after him again?" my mother asks no one in particular. "Why couldn't I just let him be? All he wanted was to quit working so hard, maybe travel or buy a boat, and definitely spend some more time with me. Why couldn't I have accepted that? Now that dear, sweet man has spent his whole adult life givin' to us and what does he have in return?"

In the past forty-eight hours, my mother has fallen desperately in love with my father. Or maybe she always was and is just now figuring it out. She hasn't eaten or slept since the accident, and she refuses to leave the hospital, even for the briefest shower or nap. Daddy would be so overwhelmed with this show of emotion. Actually, he might even doubt its veracity. "What are you angling for, Ginny?" he'd likely ask.

My mother wraps her arms around herself tightly, as though she were freezing, even though it's warm to the point of suffocating in here. I always wondered if people wouldn't feel a little better in hospitals if they could just catch a breath or two of fresh air.

"Don't make the same mistakes I've made, Lissy. Don't let Duke go without a fight. Tell him how much you love him and show him every day."

I can't argue with her right now. This is neither the time nor the place to explain to her that Duke—I mean *Martin*—is head over heels for someone else. He actually called me after his parents told him about the accident and tried to come and lend his support. I urged him not to, explaining that would only complicate matters. And when he sounded relieved, I didn't hold it against him.

"I have so many regrets," my mother laments. "Why couldn't I appreciate all the little moments? Why was I so obsessed with havin' the biggest and the best of everything? We could have been happy with less. But I drove him and drove him to do more and more and more and now what? I'll be able to wear all my diamonds to his funeral?" She begins to sob.

"Don't talk like that, Mamma—we don't know anything yet." Then I hold her until she stops.

At eleven o'clock on the dot, Rosa, my favorite nurse on staff, comes to tell us that one of us can see him now. "You go first, Mamma."

Without even looking back, she races down the hallway to the ICU.

When she's gone, I rush outside to check my phone. I've always tacitly ignored places with cell phone bans, assuming those rules didn't apply to me. Yet now, knowing there's an off chance that the radio waves could somehow interfere with the machines helping my father breathe? I am all about following the rules, and woe be to anyone who doesn't. There was a pharmaceutical rep in here yesterday who made a motion toward the BlackBerry clipped to his belt, and when he saw the daggers I was staring at him, he apologized before hurrying off.

I've been sending Deva dozens of 911 texts since she's been away on the hope that she may have reception. I'm not sure what she might be able to do, exactly, but for crying out loud, she can bend the space-time continuum. Stands to reason there's some way she might help fix a critically injured old man. But I don't hear back from her, much as I feared.

I head back to the waiting area and thumb through a dec-orating magazine, looking at but never actually seeing any of the brightly colored couches or funky knickknacks on the pages.

When my mother finally comes out to tag me in, she's even paler and more gaunt than when she went in. All she can say is "No change."

So I take my turn with my dad. I walk into his room, which is a shock each time I see it. Dad's bed is on the end of the row, curtained off from the others in the unit, which means he has a solid wall on one side where a hopeful painting of a rainbow hangs. If my mother were in her right mind, that thing would have been placed on a gurney and wheeled out of her line of sight in the first five minutes.

Daddy's propped in his bed at a thirty-five-degree angle. He's covered with wires monitoring his vital signs, and there's a ventilator doing his breathing for him. All I want to do when I see him is cry, but on the chance that he can hear me, I opt to deliver a message he'll want to hear.

"Daddy, hi, it's Liss. I hope you're not too uncomfortable. The doctors are taking great care of you and they tell us you're doing so well!" That's a bald-faced lie, but it's best he not understand how grave his condition is. I place my hand on his unbroken shin, as it's one of the only areas that's not hooked up to something or another.

"Hey, I was in your library yesterday. I found your notes for your manuscript! I can't believe you don't have arthritis from writing everything out longhand. You really are old-school, aren't you? So I have a little surprise for you once you recover. I've been putting everything into a Word document for you; that way you'll have an easier time when you're ready to edit. And, Daddy? Your story is really good."

That? Not a lie at all. His book is a legal thriller in the same vein as Steve Martini or John Grisham, but there's a certain underlying sweetness to his long-suffering protagonist that's uniquely Daddy. I felt like I'd won the lottery when I ran across the big box of yellow lined legal paper, covered in Daddy's tidy handwriting. I guess he must have been taking notes for years in down moments between meetings and trials. He wasn't going to write his book when he retired so much as simply type up what he'd already penned.

"Anyway, I also found your recipe for that special Bolognese sauce that you love. I stopped by the market last night on my way home and I'm going to teach myself to cook by making it and freezing some for you."

I continue with my cheerful monologue for half an hour. After I've talked myself out, I sit with him for a while and watch the rise and fall of his chest. I wish there were something else I could do for him. I wish he could understand how both Mamma and I have come around to being on Team Daddy and, when he pulls out of this, everything's going to change for the better.

When it's time to switch again, I see that Mamma's not alone in the waiting area. I recognize the people who are with her, but not in this context. One of them has dark hair and the other is slight and blond. As I come closer, I almost feel like I can't believe my eyes.

"Nicole?"

She springs up when she sees me and wraps herself around me. "Oh, Liss, we came as soon as we heard about George." Normally I'd be none too pleased about Charlotte's presence, but just spotting her here in this waiting room wearing a loose pair of cargo pants and a T-shirt that's neither tight nor covered in obscene language is one of the greatest gifts that I could receive. Nicole's life is truly back as it should be, and that brings me tremendous comfort.

Nicole smoothes my hair as she speaks. "I know everything's weird right now, Liss, but you're my oldest friend and I have to be here for you. Whatever else has happened, I can't turn my back on you. How can I help?"

She's shocked by my answer, yet she willingly complies.

I spent the afternoon in the cafeteria with Nicole and Charlotte. Charlotte, of course, never once looked up from her (non)blingy ringy-dingy, but Nicole's eyes danced as I demanded she tell me everything about each one of her children. We looked at a million candids, and at this point, I can grudgingly admit the little ones are cute. As for Charlotte, apparently Nicole and Bobby have been paying for her to see a voice coach, because she really wants to try out for *American Idol* next year. I wish her the best, and when it's time for her to find a music publicist, I'll be right there . . . with a referral. Nicole and I are okay now. No matter what else happens, we're okay, and that's the only reason I'm not completely out of my mind at the moment.

When visiting hours ended, Mamma insisted I go home and get some rest. I insisted she do the same, but come on: This is my mother we're talking about. She said she didn't plan on going anywhere until his condition improved.

I wasn't being truthful with Daddy when I said I'd make his sauce, but after I thought about it, I figured, why not? I've read the recipe enough times to memorize it, so on my way home, I stop at the Jewel to pick up mortadella and parsley, as we have everything else.

I'm making adequate progress with the preparation. I was able to chop everything without incident and things are moving along exactly as the recipe promises they will. The process is long and labor-intensive, so I understand why my dad never had the two spare hours it would have taken to properly cook it. He'd be so pleased at my effort, though. My onion really did turn golden brown and translucent, exactly as the recipe promised. My sauce actually reduced to the consistency it was supposed to once I added the beef stock and boiled it down. It's such a minor victory, yet I feel like Daddy would be proud of me for having made the effort.

I'm just about to add the cognac—the part of the recipe that says "just a drop is enough to make all the difference"— when the phone rings.

"Hello?"

My mother is sobbing on the other end. "Lissy, baby girl . . . Daddy . . . Daddy didn't make it."

In the end, Daddy's body couldn't sustain his injuries and his heart gave out.

His wasn't the only one.

Mamma is home now, under heavy sedation. She had a breakdown at the hospital and couldn't make any of the decisions that needed to be made next. I didn't think I could either, but I realized I owed it to my father to step up and be an adult for the first time in my life.

The great irony is that I wish he could have been here to see it.

I don't know how to deal with my grief and my anger right now. Nicole told me to call her at any hour of the day, but I think I need time to process this myself. I just want to be alone with my thoughts of him as he was.

I'm too full of bitter hospital coffee and adrenaline to get any sort of rest, and I refused the offer of a sedative. One of us needs to be in her right mind around here. I've spent the morning walking through the rooms of the house and I'm furious at how few traces there are of my father. There's nothing of his personality or his taste in the living room or the sitting room or the four-season room. The dining room is more suited to an eighteenth-century French viscount than a sixty-something patent attorney who specialized in civil engineering cases.

I'm so angry right now, and I'm not sure where to direct it. I'm furious at my mother for never cutting him a break and placing such demands on him, especially in regard to me. How fair is it that he had to slave away in the office so that seventeen-year-old Lissy could drive around in a big, pink status symbol? How much extra work did he have to bear to pay my five-figure American Express bill? Don't even start me on the six-figure circus that was my wedding. And what does he have to show for all his sacrifices now? With the way he planned his estate, Mamma and I are going to be set for a long time, but neither one of us wants anything except for him to be here with us.

The guilt I feel is almost unbearable, because I'm furious with him, too. Why did he allow us to call the shots? Why didn't he ever say no?

But mostly I'm livid with myself. I had the unique opportunity to go back in time and do absolutely anything, and I was so selfish and self-absorbed that I altered my history just enough to buy a stupid purse and a big house. If I'd possessed the maturity to suck it up in the first place, to figure out how to live on my own, I'd never have time-traveled once, let alone twice. Then there would still be enough Incan tonic for me to go back and do the only thing that was important—saving my dad.

I want to hit someone. I want to throw something. I want
to scream until I lose my voice. But I feel like engaging in such
behavior would disrespect my father's memory. I have to do
something productive right now, no matter how small or in-
significant. I need to feel like I've accomplished one tiny thing
so I don't go completely out of my mind.

I walk into the kitchen and I find all the mess from the
Bolognese sauce right where I left it yesterday. My iPod is
there, too. I planned on listening to music while I cooked, but
some instinct told me I might want to listen for the phone. I so
hate that I was right.

But I'm tired of hearing all the voices in my head, so I put
in the earbuds. I press SHUFFLE and the song that comes on is
Whitesnake's "Give Me More Time." Although technically a
song about a breakup, the chorus hits home and the tears pour
down my face and splash onto the countertop. I can't stop
thinking, *If only, if only, if only.*

In a daze, I dump the pot contents and all of the ingredients into the garbage disposal and I flip the switch. I feel an
odd sense of satisfaction as a sink full of meat and vegetables
disappears into the black hole of the disposal. Once the sink's
cleaned out, I load the dishwasher and I scour the Dutch
oven. Hey, look at me, Daddy—doing dishes without being
asked!

After I complete this task, I tackle all the tomato sauce and
grease splatters on the range top before giving the counters a
once-over with Fantastik. Then, with clean hands and much
care, I retrieve the recipe to put back in Daddy's file. I know
he's not coming back for it, but I just want to show him that
I'm finally capable of respecting what was his.

Before I close the manila folder, my eye catches the line
toward the bottom of the page.

It doesn't take much more than a drop, but a drop is enough to make all the difference.

That phrase has been running through my head all morning and I don't know why. It's just a garden-variety word obsession, like that time Martin was watching some show on World War II and for the next three days I had the German term for submarine stuck in my head—*unterwasserboot.*

I decide to head upstairs for a shower, for lack of anything better to do. Once the word spreads about what's happened, the house is going to be flooded with well-wishers and family and I probably should try to pull myself together by then.

Before I go to my room, I crack the door to check on my mother. She's curled up on the bed with a pair of my father's hideous golf pants—the ones she said made him look like Santa Claus on casual Friday.

Just when I think my heart can't break any more, here I go again.

When I walk into my room, my toe connects with something that skitters underneath the bed. My mother's always wearing—and subsequently losing—precious-gemstone earrings, and today doesn't seem like the kind of day to discover she's lost an emerald, so I squat down to grab it from under the bed.

But it's not an earring I kicked. Rather, it's the empty bottle of Incan fluid. I'm about to toss it in the trash when the phrase from the recipe runs through my mind again.

It doesn't take much more than a drop, but a drop is enough to make all the difference.

I examine the vial but it's clearly empty.

Emptyish, at least.

I mean, there's a tiny, tiny bit of the viscous fluid clinging to the sides, but it probably wouldn't even amount to fifteen minutes in the past, and what good would that do?

It doesn't take much more than a drop, but a drop is enough to make all the difference.

But what if it did?

CHAPTER TWENTY

Through the Looking Glass

No.

    A drop is enough to make all the difference.

    This is crazy.

    A drop is enough to make all the difference.

    It can't work.

    A drop is enough to make all the difference. Okay, even if I were to somehow lick the drops off the side of the vial, I have no idea when or where I'd end up. I don't know where the universe thinks I'm supposed to be right now. As bad off as I am right now, what if this takes me somewhere worse? What if this puts me in the backseat of their car during the accident? I don't care about myself right now, but if something happens to me, it will likely kill my mom. I can't take any unnecessary risks.

    I leave the bottle on my desk while I shower. I'm actually

a little relieved to have something to deter my focus, because otherwise I'd be crushed with overwhelming sadness.

A drop is enough to make all the difference.

I throw my damp hair into a ponytail and ignore my overflowing collection of lotions, potions, and unguents, because I could not give a shit about my appearance.

A drop is enough to make all the difference.

I pull on an old pair of sweatpants and one of my dad's ancient UGA T-shirts and I sit down on my bed in full view of the vial.

A drop is enough to make all the difference.

I pick it up and turn it over and over again in my hands. Then I unscrew the top and pick at the stopper. This is crazy, because this thing is definitely empty.

Emptyish.

As I consider how to get tonic out of an empty bottle, I flash to last night, when I was making the sauce. When I dumped the tomato paste into the pan, there was a little bit left clinging to the sides. I remembered when I was a kid and my mom would be in Savannah on the rare trip without me, Daddy would make me spaghetti with jarred sauce. This was a huge treat, because we never got processed foods when Mamma was around. Anyway, once he poured the contents into the pan, he'd always swish a little red wine around in the jar to catch the stubborn bits.

Could it really be that easy?

(Easyish?)

And can I live with myself if I don't at least try?

I very cautiously make my way to the bathroom, holding the vial as though it contained nitroglycerine and will blow the roof clean off with the slightest misstep. Once in the bath, I turn on the tap to a trickle. Very, very gingerly I place the vial under the stream of water and I fill the bottle three-quarters full. Then I replace the stopper, screw the lid back on, and shake it as though my life depends on it. Or *a* life, anyway.

After I've finished, I pry the stopper back out and there are microscopic oily blobs floating in the water. So this part worked, but I have no clue if the next part will.

I take a deep breath and turn to David Coverdale. "Wish me luck."

I quaff it and . . . nothing happens.

I wait.

And wait.

Nothing.

I thought this might work a little bit.

Maybe this stuff loses its power when diluted, or maybe you have to meet a minimum amount of the fluid, kind of like you have to spend ten dollars before you're allowed to use a credit card.

I slump back against the wall.

Oh, Daddy, I'm so sorry. I wish I—

That's when I feel the initial tingle, followed by a wave of endorphins, and I'm flooded with happiness. The joy starts in the back of my mouth and travels down to my stomach, a lot like the feeling when I have my first cup of coffee. The warming sensation is the same, too. Then I'm hit with another wave, only this time it makes me tired. I wait to see if I feel it again, and seconds later I do. The exhaustion is the tide pulling me away from consciousness. Sleep beckons to me and I stop fighting it and close my eyes.

Okay. Here I go again.

'm afraid to open my eyes.

The place I'm in is silent and motionless, so at least I

know I'm not speeding toward an embankment. And I'm lying somewhere comfortable, which I hope against hope to be my bed. But I'm too scared to see for myself.

I've never been a religious person—largely due to the Sunday-morning inconvenience factor and a flexible moral compass—but now seems like an excellent time to start praying.

> *Dear God,*
> *Hi, it's Lissy. I mean, Lissy Ryder? But You*
> *probably figured that out, because I can't*
> *imagine You know many Lissys.*
> *Okay, wait, that sounded superbraggy.*
> *Let's start again—dear God, please be*
> *with me. I'm not sure what to ask for, be-*
> *cause I don't know what needs to happen, so*
> *if You could maybe have my back while I fig-*
> *ure it out, that would be great.*
> *I'm really not good at this prayer thing,*
> *am I?*
> *Sorry about that.*
> *Please, Lord, if there's any way for me to*
> *fix things, please help me find it. I'll make*
> *any sacrifice. I'll do whatever You want.*
> *Within reason.*
> *Again, I'm sorry. Prayer is not my forte,*
> *and I don't want to sound like the kind of*
> *asshole who believes she can bargain with*
> *God.*
> *Argh, I'm sorry I just swore at You, God.*
> *No one will blame You if you smite me. So*
> *what I'm trying—and failing—to say is to*
> *please just put me down for anything within*

Your will and I'm all over it if I can please,
please, please somehow help my mom and
dad. Thank You and sincerely Yours, Lissy
Ryder.
That didn't sound right, either.
In Your name, Amen.

Love,
Lissy

That's when I feel an almost psychic flash and I hear a vaguely British voice saying, "Open your eyes and get out of bed, dumb ass."

They say the Lord works in mysterious ways. If one of those ways is talking to me in language I understand, then I'd best do what He says.

Oh, so gingerly, I ease my eyes open.

I guess He wants me to see David Coverdale.

The sun beams down, making David seem all the more beatific in the poster. I want to take a look around and get my bearings, but I don't know how long the tonic will last and I cannot blow this shot.

I stumble out of bed right when the yelling begins downstairs.

Yes!

They're fighting!

Both of them!

Which means *Daddy is alive*!

My heart in my throat, I run down the stairs so fast that I miss the final couple of steps and pretty much fly into the foyer. But midflight, I notice something twinkling. When I land, I pause for a second to take everything in. I'm standing beneath a ball of mistletoe and there are swags of greenery everywhere. Across from me in the living room, a massive Fraser fir fills the entire bay window, and it's a monochromatic monster, decorated solely in hot-pink lights and hot-pink ribbons.

Wait. I know this scheme—this is how we decorated the tree in 1991.

Even though I'm so glad to be here, I don't understand why I landed on this particular date. As I hustle toward the sounds of yelling, my mind races through the possibilities. If we're in December, that means I already inflicted all the damage I was supposed to do back in October. So this isn't about changing anyone's past except for that of my family.

I linger in the doorway, taking in all the life in my father's face. Seeing him leaves me breathless. Daddy's wearing a warm plaid robe and pajamas with little sailboats printed on them. He and Mamma are sitting in the atrium breakfast area with a plate of fruit and a pot of coffee between them. Daddy has an array of credit card statements at his side and he's gesturing at my mother with the checkbook. They're bathed in sunlight and surrounded by greenery and it's pretty much the best thing I've ever seen.

"She already got a BMW for her birthday—now you bought her a *mink*? For how much? This statement must be a mistake, because no one would spend that much money on a child. And what's wrong with the three winter coats she already received this year? I don't understand, Ginny. Help me understand."

Mamma rolls her eyes. "That's because you understand nothin', George! Sissy bought Gussie her first fur when she was sixteen! We are so far behind the curve raht now it's not even funny!"

"*Au contraire*, Ginny, it's very funny. I'm laughing all the way home from the bank."

And that's when, for the first time ever, I interject myself into one of their arguments.

"Stop it! Both of you!"

They both turn to me, openmouthed with shock.

"I don't have much time, so do not interrupt me right now. This? What you're doing right now? Has to stop. Do you understand me? Because you know what happens when parents don't get along? Their daughters act out. As it stands, I'm not due to turn slutty until college, but if you keep it up, I'm going to get started now instead. So unless you're looking to be the youngest grandparents at the country club, or hearing 'Let's welcome Lissy Ryder to the main stage,' knock that shit off. Because FYI, if I get knocked up, I'm staying here for *you* to raise the baby."

Mamma visibly shudders and Daddy leans forward in his seat. I can't tell if he's enthralled or enraged, yet I haven't time to worry about that right now.

I point at my mother. "You. Cut it the fuck out with the sibling rivalry. And yes, I said *fuck* and I don't care if it's not ladylike. See? I'm already halfway to the stripper pole. Keep it up with the crazy possession-based arms race with Aunt Sissy and you're both going to bury your husbands before they can even retire. So unless you're competing over who gets to be a widow first and which of you wears the most gemstones to the funeral, cool your damn jets."

"Melissa Belle Ryder, I would nevah—" she starts.

"*Zip it*, I'm not done with you. Next, you have to get over your mother issues, okay? You're what, almost forty years old? It's time to put that shit to bed. Why don't you start by taking one day a week to go to therapy instead of the mall?"

Daddy tries to suppress a snicker. He fails and I give him the whale eye. Duly chastened, he does his best to stop smiling.

He fails.

"You refuse to treat Daddy well because Grandmamma never approved of him, even though you claim she *made* you marry him. Did she have an actual shotgun? Were there real death threats? No. Could you have asserted yourself if you didn't want it to happen? Yes. So you married him and you stayed married, not because you *had* to, but because you *wanted* to. You love him and you need to show him. This endless power struggle has to stop. Nothing bad is going to happen if you finally allow him to see that he's half the equation. It's not all about winning, Mamma."

Mutely, my mother nods. I may just be getting through to her, possibly because she fears I might follow through on my threat to become an exotic dancer. Or a teen mom. But it doesn't matter *why* I'm reaching her; it only matters *that* I'm reaching her.

"From this day forward, your job is to treat him like the wonderful, kind, compassionate, endlessly patient man he is, and not like some barnacle you can't quite scrape from your hull. Got that? And speaking of, Daddy's buying a boat."

Daddy cocks his head as though I were speaking in Swahili. "I am?"

I whip around to point at him. "Not your turn!" I refocus on my mother. "So, you, Mamma, first up—return the frigging coat. What am I going to be, seventeen and running around in a fur? I'll look like a Russian prostitute, which, correct me if I'm wrong, is not the image you want to cultivate. Also, I am not your status symbol. My achievements, or lack thereof, are no reflection on you. Do something with yourself, for yourself! Play to your strengths! Become an interior designer or a personal shopper or a pageant coach!"

My mother smiles her first genuine smile in a very long time upon hearing this. Sometimes the solution has been right in front of you and you need the threat of your daughter removing her clothing for strangers' money to finally recognize it.

"You're going to be so much happier if you can base your self-esteem on something other than where you vacation and what your kid drives. Also? I'm starving. I'm hungry all the time and I suspect you are, too. We need something other than lettuce and melon cubes in this house. I don't want to wait until I'm married; I want to eat now. People have to consume protein and carbohydrates every day or they get super, super-bitchy. We need to fix that. Make some damn spaghetti. Daddy will teach you how if you're unfamiliar."

I feel the first pull of exhaustion from the tonic wearing off, but I can't stop until I'm done. I press on.

"Now, Daddy, here's what you need to do: Learn to say no and mean it. Put your foot down. Don't let her run roughshod over you. I think part of why she's been so overbearing is that she's looking for the limits on your patience. If you keep showing her you have no limits, then nothing is ever going to change."

Daddy slowly nods and I believe what I'm saying makes sense to him, too. I soften my tone. "Daddy, I love you so much, and so does Mamma, and we're both about to start showing you that, aren't we? But you need to show us you're the man of the house. Be our pack leader."

I shoot Mamma a look and she quickly nods in agreement.

"Now, wait one second." I run into the kitchen and find my keys hanging on the hook by the garage door. I hand them to my dad. "You are going to take these and you're going to sell this car."

Mamma blanches. "Lissy, sugar, what are you—"

"*Zip. It.* You, Daddy, talk to my friend Tammy's parents, because she's been dying over this thing and they're probably the only people you can unload a pink convertible on without taking a massive loss. Then I want you to use that money *that you earned* and do something for yourself with it—buy your boat or maybe take a six-month sabbatical to work on your book."

Daddy's reeling as if I've just delivered a punishing upper-cut. He's shaking his head like a boxer who barely made it off the ground before the count.

A wave of fatigue hits me so hard that I have to brace myself on the table. "I know stuff about you, Daddy. We do live under the same roof. What *you* don't know is that you're a great writer—really, you are. You could make something of it. You don't have to be imprisoned in your office for fifteen hours a day. There's another way. Take that path, Daddy. Please. For all of us."

My knees buckle, and if I don't go upstairs to lie down right now, I'm not going to make it. "So that's it. That's your food for thought. Right now, you two need to figure out how you're going to be with each other. Mamma, let your guard down. Daddy, sac up. Get this done. Make out if you need to. I'll be upstairs." Then I hug my mother and I plant a kiss on my dad's forehead. I can barely tear myself away from him.

With much effort I'm able to haul myself up the stairs, and the last sound I hear before I shut my door is that of their laughter.

My bed has never seemed more inviting, and David Cover-dale beckons for me to rest my weary head. I look out of my window and I see the Murphy family piling out of their station wagon in their Sunday best. They must be coming home from church.

That's when I hear that little voice again, and He tells me I'm not quite finished. I have to think quickly.

I grab a thick Magic Marker and a piece of poster board left over from some silly pep rally. In the biggest letters I can fit on the board I write a quick message and stick it in my window.

And then I'm out.

CHAPTER TWENTY-ONE
Karma Chameleon

And now I'm back.

Whether I'm back in black is yet to be discovered.

The benevolent figure of David Coverdale watches down over me as I try to figure out my next move.

One time when Brian and I were hanging out, he explained the concept of Schrödinger's cat in regard to my deep and abiding love of denial. He said that some weird (my words, not his) Austrian dude tried to explain what a paradox was by coming up with a scenario wherein a cat was stuck in a box with radiation or something. I didn't really understand what he was saying, but the crux of it was that until someone actually looked in the box, the cat could be considered both dead and alive, but nothing was official until the box was opened.

So right now my world is one big, unopened box that may or may not contain a dead cat.

Disconcerting, right?

If I get up and go through the rest of the house, then I'll know for sure what happened to my dad. I'll either find out that my past-fix worked, or that it didn't, and then I'm going to be paralyzed with grief. As hopeful as I am that he's here, I'm equally dreading that he's not.

So my plan right now is to hover in the in-between. Box-o'-cat territory. I'm just going to stay here in my room and avoid stuff until I can't anymore.

No matter what happens next, and whenever I choose to open the box, I believe I'll have come through this experience a better me. I'm not so enamored of the whole Lissy Ryder persona I've been putting on for so long. She was shallow and mean and self-involved. She wasn't someone anyone (outside of a villain in a teen movie) would aspire to be.

Melissa Connor was better, yet she was a different kind of self-involved, overly controlling and equally dismissive. She may have been a little nicer (at least to your face) and far more successful, but she didn't quite get it right either. She was unable to unclench.

I don't think I want to be either of them anymore, at least not entirely. Although . . . they both had a few decent qualities. For example, I kind of want to be the Lissy who gave a young Nicole Good Humor bars and who made Madonna scrub her face to keep her safe.

I wouldn't mind being the Melissa who wrote a check to send Amy to rehab, but not because she felt guilty. Rather, I'd want to write that check because it was the right thing to do. I want my first thought not to be "What's in it for me?" but "What can I do for you?"

I want to be someone who's there for my family and my friends, and not just when it dovetails into my own needs.

I want to work for a company whose goals I support, and I want to give them my all, and not the bare minimum. I'm not saying I should give more than I get, because corporate America can be pretty Lissy Ryder in its own right if you let it. I'm just saying three hours of tanning and treadmilling on company time is bullshit. I accept that now. I was in the wrong.

I want to be more comfortable when things aren't perfect. Perfection is overrated, and also, it makes you superhungry. If I could not launch into absolutely apoplexy at a gray hair or a tiny line or a cellulite dimple, that'd be great, because I want to be someone who's not a slave to her appearance. I've come to realize that the package doesn't matter nearly as much as the contents.

I want to worry more about what's important and less about what others think.

Not to go all Dorothy at the end of *The Wizard of Oz*, but I have come to understand that the only person who's in charge of my destiny is me. If I want all of the above, then the onus is on me to make those things happen. I may be unemployed and living at home, but I can change that with a little hard work.

I decide I can start the process of becoming more me by looking the part. I strip down and then re-dress in some silly but flattering mom jeans and a still pristine Whitesnake baseball-sleeve concert T-shirt. I never once wore it outside of the house. Well, that changes today. This is who I am, like it or lump it.

While I'm bent over tying my sneaker, I spy the end of the poster board sticking out from underneath my bed. I cautiously pull it out and use the sweatpants I just took off to dust the top of it, revealing the words "LION PRIDE" in big letters, topped with glitter. But that wasn't the important message on

this board. I flip it over to see what I wrote twenty-one years/
twenty-one minutes ago.

BRIAN, YOU WERE RIGHT ABOUT KURT COBAIN (AND EVERY-
THING ELSE).

I can't help but smile.

Brian really was right.

Nirvana *was* groundbreaking, and their music is as relevant now as it was back then. I get it now. Finally. Maybe they
weren't to my taste back then, but that doesn't mean they
didn't change everything two decades ago. And maybe that
was my problem with them—they represented a new age and
a new era, and that scared me because I thought I'd be left
behind, like so many eyeliner-wearing, spandex-clad, Aqua
Net–using icons whose packaging was just as important as
their contents.

Nirvana was all about sound without any glam-rock theatrics, without any distractions or gimmicks, and that had to
have terrified me, as I was made of the sum parts of my own
personal stage show. Nirvana was just who they were, take it
or leave it. When Cobain made the tragic decision to neither
burn out nor fade away, he cemented his position as a music
legend. I can't deny that.

A denial, a denial, a denial keeps running through my head.

You know what?

It's probably time I download *Nevermind*.

It's also time to check on that cat.

I slowly open my door and make my way down the hallway to my parents' bedroom. The bed is unmade and there's
a pair of Daddy's plaid pants on his side. But I don't allow
myself to break down over what this might mean. This isn't
over until it's over, and I'm going to have some faith, for the
first time in my life.

When I'm down the stairs, I slip into Daddy's library. I'm instantly enveloped in the scent of Royall Lyme and Wint-O-Green Lifesaver. I inhale deeply and just stand there for a minute, imagining how it felt when Daddy would hug me.

Eventually, I open my eyes again. At first glance, all is how I left it after I came home from the hospital, only his file folder of boats is missing. Then I spot an anomaly on his shelf. There are rows and rows of books, and each individual row contains books with the same covers. I pull one out and look at it.

A Civil Affair by George Ryder.

Oh, Daddy, you did it!

His other titles all include some play on the word "civil," like *The Civil Warriors*, *A Civil Tongue*, and *Civil Wrongs*. I quickly scan the back of one of them and it looks to be a legal thriller from the perspective of a patent attorney whose specialty involves civil engineering. This makes total sense, because Daddy's undergraduate degree was in civil engineering, which is one of the prerequisites for practicing his type of patent law.

I'm so proud of him.

No matter what happens next, Daddy had the chance to live his dream, and my job here is done.

I peek out the front door and I notice a couple of unfamiliar cars in the driveway. Who would be here? And why? Please tell me they aren't paying their respects or dropping off casseroles. I hear murmurs toward the back of the house and I'm drawn to them like a moth to a flame. The fate of the cat is about to be revealed.

My knees buckle when I see the cat is alive, well, and sharing a plate of bacon with Mamma.

My mother frowns. "Good Lord, sugar, what's a matter with you? Look lahk you've seen a ghost!"

Okay, do not even get me started on the irony of that statement.

"Hi, honey, would you like some breakfast? Your mother made biscuits that are out of this world. Please eat some so I stop," Daddy implores me.

I'm so overcome with emotion that I can't say anything, instead choosing to hug him again and again and again.

"No need to cry, sugar. The biscuits aren't really that good. I don't make 'em with lard anymore, because your daddy and I are gittin' fat." Then she pinches him, but gently.

My dad grins at my mother. "I don't know; you still look pretty good to me." Then he grabs her for a prolonged kiss.

Clearly I have landed in the Twilight Zone.

I don't mind one bit.

I'm not entirely sure what else to do, so I pull up a chair and I help myself to a couple of biscuits with jam and butter, and they're seriously the best thing I've ever put in my mouth.

I'm one sip into a glass of fresh-squeezed orange juice when my father asks, "Are you excited to go back?"

That's when I begin to choke. Go back? Where? In time? In space? What's happening? I hack and sputter into my napkin while Daddy whacks me on the back.

"Judging from your reaction, you must be excited. Prolly tard of seeing me and your daddy snugglin' all the time."

I tell her, "Trust me when I say I will never be tired of that."

"I imagine the varnish should be dry by now, right?" Daddy asks.

"I'm sorry?"

"Sugar, did you not sleep well? You're all over the map today," my mother says.

"I'm a little groggy," I admit.

"You'll be glad to be home," Daddy decrees. "You'll be back in your own home and you'll have those beautiful new floors."

I have a home?! But before I can even ponder what that means, my mother says, "We don't mean to kick you out, darlin', but your daddy and I sure could use some quiet time. This has been truly lovely, but it's a bit much."

What's a bit much?

"Plus, honey bunny, we're leaving for Canyon Ranch tomorrow." She gives Daddy an affectionate poke. "I mean, someone's got to play all that golf while I redesign their spa."

That's when I notice the huge stacks of wallpaper and fabric samples behind her, all adorned with a Ginny Ryder Designs logo.

Oh, my God, she did it, too! She actually listened to me! She found her calling as an interior designer! And she must be great at it, if she landed a project like Canyon Ranch.

My mother begins to herd me to the front door and says, "I see you have all your stuff already. All righty, sugar! See you soon!" Then she plants a kiss on me, hands me a purse, and sends me out the door with a small whack on my bottom.

I have no idea what's happening here, but I hope it never ends.

So I'm ready to go home, I guess. I just need to figure out where that might be. I open the purse—not a Birkin, but who cares?—and the first thing I stumble upon is my iPhone.

I have one waiting text.

> **Deva:** lassie rodeo, do you require my hope?

I text Deva back.

> **ME:** no thx, i'm full up on hope right
> now

My heart swells to nearly bursting when I notice that one of the cars is covered with boating bumper stickers and I see a parking permit for Diversey Harbor. Way to go, Daddy and Mamma, I mean, *Mom and Dad.* If I'm going to be a better, newer, different me, I should probably start addressing my parents like an adult.

Seriously? Everything is perfect right now.

Except . . . I have no idea where I live. But I can figure that out from my driver's license. I start to dig around in my handbag, which is really kind of massive.

Why do I carry so much shit in my purse? I dig and dig and dig, but I still don't unearth a wallet.

Really, what the hell?

I have all the usual stuff, like tampons and elastic bands and an iPod. I've got one of those small e-readers. (I read now?) (Wait, Daddy's a writer; I guess I must.) There's Kleenex and granola bars and a bunch of weird plastic items that I don't even recognize. I have three kinds of hand sanitizer! What's my obsession with antibacterials? Am I a germaphobe now? Do I live in a bubble?

Okay, this is a little ridiculous—there's a frigging banana in this bag. I would never carry a stupid banana around with me . . . except I guess I would and I have and I do.

I am very interested to get to know the new me. What do I call myself? Am I Lissy? Am I Melissa? Neither one of those names feels quite right anymore.

I should probably call myself "disorganized," because this

purse is a holy mess. I finally dump the whole kit and caboodle onto the porch. Okay, cool, here's a gas bill. Where's the address on this thing? Ah, looks like I live on . . .

"Belle?"

. . . Washington Street in Hinsdale. Huh.

"Belle?"

The suburbs. I never really thought of myself as a suburban-dwelling adult, yet here I am. What else don't I know about myself?

"Belle. Belle. Melissa Belle Murphy, what are you doing with all that stuff?"

I look up and the entire universe feels like it's shifted. "Brian? What are you doing here?"

"I was across the street saying good-bye to my parents."

"Oh." I can't take my eyes off him. He's so ruddy and vibrant and has hair in all the right places.

"Did you hit your head or something?" Brian's staring at me like I have three noses or an unfortunate piercing, yet he's holding out his hand to help me up.

I'm not sure what else to say, so I respond, "I think so."

"Well, we'd better get you checked out before we go home."

"No, no, I'm okay. But are we going to the same home? Together?"

"That's kind of how it works, Belle," he says with an amused expression on his beautiful, beautiful face. That's when I spot his simple gold band. I glance down at my hand and I'm wearing one, too.

"We're married? I mean, we're married! Woo!"

Brian grows more concerned. "How hard would you say you hit your head?"

"No, no, I'm fine . . . honey." I try out a term of endearment, just to see if it sticks.

He grabs me and gives me a quick kiss. "All right, then. Let's go home." Then he helps me scoop all the crap back into my purse and we walk hand in hand down the driveway.

I'd say I didn't know how this happened, but I do. The key to everything was helping my parents fix themselves.

Certainly I want to catch up with everyone from my past, but I have a feeling that everything has fallen into place exactly like I hoped it would.

When we get to the end of the driveway, I try to open the door of the ultra-high-end luxury sedan parked there.

"Um, Belle, what are you doing?"

Okay, can I tell you how much I love being called by my middle name? That's the perfect antidote to both Lissy and Melissa. It feels so right, harkening to my past but also speaking to my future.

Everything is perfect.

"Um, we're not driving your mom's car, Hell's Bells. Come on; let's get out of here." Brian clicks a button on the remote and there's a weird chirping that triggers the door sliding open on a shiny new beige minivan.

Okay, that's not mine.

Yet the Brian who's climbing into the driver's seat begs to differ.

And that's when I see something that knocks the wind right out of me.

There are two captain chairs in the middle of the van and a big bench seat in the back. The chairs contain two smaller versions of Brian with my coloring, in deft concentration over their Nintendos.

They're probably his nephews, right?

Then movement in the backseat captures my attention and I come face-to-face with a fourteen-year-old version of myself—

blond hair, eyes that switch from blue to green depending on the outfit and mood, and the strong jawline capped off with a determined little chin. She's clad in skinny jeans and a *Bieber Fever* T-shirt, and she's holding one blingy ringy-dingy of a cell phone.

This person looks me up and down with more than a modicum of contempt. "Are you seriously wearing that heinous outfit, Mamma? You look like you got dressed at a garage sale. Or that you're homeless and have really atrocious taste." Then she rolls her eyes, huffs loudly, and returns to her texting.

Mamma.

Mamma?

Whoa.

Karma really *is* a bitch.

ACKNOWLEDGMENTS

They say a change will do you good and nowhere is that aphorism more evident than in this book. So I'd like to offer a million thanks to Scott Miller and the rest of the team at Trident. You've yet to be wrong, and I am so appreciative.

Also leading the change management team is Tracy Bernstein, who encouraged me to stretch, grow, and finally not base a heroine on my own life. I'm really proud of what we've accomplished here. And I'd be nowhere without the wisdom and skills of Kara Welsh and Claire Zion. Thank you for being so firmly Team Jen. Craig Burke, you rock, and Melissa Broder, you complete me. (By which I mean you humor and take care of me, which is the same damn thing. What Would Dick Cheney Do? indeed).

Extra big props go to my girls, starting with Stacey Ballis, who altered my future by saying, "But what if Lissy did this, instead?" Spot-freaking-on you were. I am so lucky to have you!

I'm equally fortunate to be surrounded by all of my family of choice—Tracy Stone, Gina Barge, Joanna Schiferl, Angie Felton, Wendy Hainey, Poppy Buxom, and Blackbird. Extra-special thanks with sugar on top goes to those who were kind enough to give me (and Lissy) an early read—Karyn Bosnak, Caprice Crane, Laurie Dolan, Benjamin Kissell, Lisa Lampanelli, and Sarah Pekkanen. How lucky am I to have so many talented women behind me? (Very lucky, in case that wasn't clear.)

I'm equally grateful to those behind the scenes at New American Library—production, sales, marketing, etc. Your efforts are deeply appreciated, so thank you. And, of course, the booksellers and readers have rocked my world since 2006. I do this for you, so thank you times infinity.

The most thanks go to the long-suffering Fletch, the folder of the laundry and the cooker of fish dinners. You complete me even more than Melissa. Thank you for my hair metal education and for not laughing (too hard) when you'd catch me watching Kix and Ratt videos on YouTube. You're right—those guys were WAY more masculine than the boys in WHAM. Who knew?

Finally, to Mr. David Coverdale, I throw the horns for you. You've still got it, sir. Indeed, you do.

ABOUT THE AUTHOR

Jen Lancaster is the *New York Times* bestselling author of eight books. She has appeared on *Today*, *The Joy Behar Show*, and NPR's *All Things Considered*. She resides in the suburbs of Chicago with her husband and their ever-expanding menagerie of ill-behaved pets.

CONNECT ONLINE

www.jennsylvania.com
facebook.com/authorjenlancaster
twitter.com/altgeldshrugged

JEN LANCASTER

Here I Go Again

Questions
for Discussion

1. *Here I Go Again* deals with the ways in which our high school experiences can influence our futures. Given the opportunity, would you go back in time to make changes to your teenage self? If so, in what ways?

2. What are five things you wish the adult you could have told the high school you?

3. Lissy Ryder is a prototypical bully—or is she? In what ways does her relationship with her family influence how she treats the rest of the world? Discuss how the women in this book react against their mothers in their life choices.

4. Why is having "frenemies" so much more prevalent in female relationships than with men?

5. *Here I Go Again* is an homage to movies such as *Mean Girls*, *Back to the Future*, and *13 Going on 30*—what other tributes or nods to pop culture can you find?

6. At what point in the story do you believe Lissy begins to fully grasp the consequences of her actions?

7. In what ways are Lissy and Deva different? In what ways are they similar? How would this tale unfold from Deva's perspective?

8. How does Lissy's relationship with her father impact her choice of men?

9. What does Lissy's choice of music say about who she really is?

10. In your own life, how are the "class losers" and those "most likely to succeed" doing now in comparison to expectations? (And really, isn't the process of investigating why Facebook exists?)

Read on for a sneak peek of
Jen Lancaster's hilarious new novel,

TWISTED SISTERS

Available from New American Library in February 2014.

"Do I know you?"

The well-appointed woman peers at me over her Whole Foods shopping cart, brimming with free-range chicken, organic fruit, and glass-bottled Kombucha.

I'm not surprised she's finally asking. She *seems* like someone who'd recognize me, clad in the unofficial Lincoln Park Trader's Wife uniform of perfectly buttery blond ponytail, high-speed sneakers, Lululemon, and more ice than you'd find in your garden-variety cocktail. I noticed her watching me while I debated between frisée and spring-mix greens and then later when I perused wild-caught salmon. (Naturally, I buy only seafood approved by the Monterey Bay Aquarium's Seafood Watch Program. And who wouldn't? Sustainability *matters*.)

She continues. "I'm so sorry—this is weird, right? But I

feel like I know you somehow." She taps a couple of expertly manicured fingers on her artificially enhanced lips as she tries to piece together our connection.

I smile beatifically, as this sort of thing happens to me *all the time*; it's one of the complications of being a local celebrity. I find that people have a lot more fun when they finally determine who I am on their own, so I opt not to offer any clues.

"Did you graduate from Maine South High School?"

Public school? Oh, honey. No. But bless your heart for marrying up.

I shake my head. "I attended Taylor Park Academy." I don't mention that this is Chicago's most infamous Ivy League feeder school, as anyone who cares is already familiar with their commitment to academics.

She furrows her brow and searches my face. "Hmm . . . did you go to Northern?"

Again, a great big *no* here. I attended the University of Chicago for undergrad and master's, even though I was accepted to Yale and Stanford, too. Clearly, Taylor Park Academy is no joke. Had Obama not been elected for a second term, this is where his kids would matriculate. However, I'm a public figure, so I'm loath to make this potential fan feel bad about her subpar education.

"No, I'm afraid not."

It's irrelevant to mention that my older sister, Mary Magdalene, attended Northern. Of course, she was there for only a year before she dropped out to marry her high school boyfriend.

(Ahem, *shotgun wedding*, ahem.)

Presently, Mary Mac—that's what we call her for short—has churned out more kids than I can count. It's like she's a hoarder, only for children. In terms of personal achievement, she's pretty much the patron saint of minivans and stretch marks. What is that meme I've seen about the prolific *19 Kids and Counting* mother? Ah, yes. "It's a vagina, not a clown car." Add one persecution complex, stir, and boom! Meet my older sister.

Among numerous others, Mary Mac and her contractor husband, Mickey, have a couple of identical ginger daughters named Kacey Irelyn and Kiley. I can't tell them apart for the life of me, so I generally just refer to both of them as Kiley Irelyn. Perhaps if the little ingrates sent thank-you notes when I gave them birthday presents, I'd be better able to determine who's who. But apparently American Girl dolls grow on trees in that house, so my efforts are thus unrecognized.

Anyway.

I still have to pick up pasture-raised eggs and a probiotic supplement, then bring everything home to refrigerate before my call time, so I need to move this along. I volunteer, "Perhaps we met at Pepperdine?"

Before I can even mention their doctorate program, I see a flash of recognition in her face and I steel myself for the inevitable, ready to tell her, no, I did *not* major in *Battle of the Network Stars*. Because that joke wasn't already old the second my younger sister, Geri, first uttered it a decade ago.

Let me ask you: how is it a negative that my college campus, situated on a Malibu bluff overlooking the Pacific, was so bucolic that ABC simply had to film their campy television battles there in the seventies and eighties? I chose Pepperdine *not* because Scott Baio ever pitched a javelin there, but because they have one of the top psychology programs in the country.

I mean, there I was, paying for my PsyD with grants and loans I'd garnered on my own, on my way to becoming Dr.

Reagan Bishop, and did anyone in my family give me the credit I deserved? No! Instead, they all brayed like jackasses, congratulating bratty teenage Geri on her hilarious quips.

Bah-ha-ha! Battle of the Network Stars! Hey, Reagan, will you take Greg Evigan's classes on potato-sack races or will it be obstacle courses with William Shatner?

Seriously?

I'm a licensed psychologist; Geri's a licensed *cosmetologist*.

I deal with what's inside the human head; she concentrates on what's on top of it.

Plus, Geri was barely three years old when the iconic TV battles ended back in 1988. In theory, she's not capable of discerning a Charlene Tilton from a Tina Yothers. I suspect long-suffering Mary Mac fed her that line. Mary Mac and Geri are a decade apart and haven't a thing in common, save for a love of pop culture, a lack of ambition . . . and a grudge against me.

I've counseled my fair share of families in which the siblings' alliances are constantly realigning. Most often, this is due to the perception of the parents' having picked a favorite, regardless of how inadvertent the choice may be. The other siblings get caught up in the injustice of not being in the spotlight. As the spotlight shifts, so do alliances.

Of course, this has never been the case with the Bishop girls. Those two have been Team NotReagan since day one. From choosing what TV show to watch to deciding what color to paint our bedroom, Geri and Mary Mac have always cast their votes together, neatly eclipsing any opinion I might have had. Of course, I'd get them back come birthday time, requesting mile-high peanut butter pie for my dessert because of Geri's nut allergy. Ha! No pie for you!

(Side note? It's my professional opinion that Geri's been faking her supposed nut sensitivity ever since there were fixings enough for only one ham sandwich for our packed school lunches.)

Anyway, since my family never seems to appreciate what I've accomplished, please allow me to blow my own horn for a minute. (I try to practice self-validation whenever possible because it's an important ingredient in cultivating positive self-esteem.) Not only did I skip a grade in elementary school, graduate from Taylor Park, and garner two degrees at U of C in four and a half years, but I also received my PsyD with highest honors. While my classmates were still muddling through their clinical training, I was already in private practice, being named one of Chicago's Top Doctors by *Chicago* magazine. And that's how Wendy Winsberg found me.

Yes, *that* Wendy Winsberg, grande dame of daytime talk television for almost three decades and, according to *Forbes*, the number one entry on their 100 Most Powerful Women list. When she finally burned out on hosting a daily show herself, she formed the WeWIN cable network with a plethora of what she calls "fempowering" television for women.

The crown jewel in her lineup is the breakout show *I Need a Push*, in which participants learn to become their best selves by overcoming obstacles and changing behaviors. They also receive sassy haircuts and wardrobe makeovers, but that's really not my department.

As for my role?

To quote Tina Fey, I'm a pusher, meaning I'm the one who manifests the push.

Two and a half years ago, I put my practice on hold and became one of the show's lead psychologists. Although I miss taking private patients, I excel equally at working in depth with the participants. In my old practice, I spent an hour a week with my clients. That's barely enough time to scratch the surface on someone's latent daddy issues, let alone his or her present-day problems with work, finances, relationships, et cetera.

But with *I Need a Push*, I have the luxury of almost un-limited time. In some cases, I'm able to spend up to two months administering daily one-on-one cognitive therapy, so by the time pushees have their tips frosted (or whatever it is *Push*'s hairdressers do), they're returning to their lives able to face challenges with a new and improved set of behaviors.

I'd like to see you fix someone's life armed with nothing but a flatiron, *Geri.*

I glance down at my watch as an indication that we need to wrap this whole how-do-I-know-you business soon. Things to do, groceries to shelve, lives to touch, et cetera.

The shopper gives a self-conscious laugh. "I'm keeping you—I apologize. But this'll drive me crazy until I figure out our connection, and then in the middle of the night, I'll wake my husband up by shouting '*Spin class!*' or something. Wait, are you in my spin class?"

I shrug. "I'm more of a runner than a spinner." Time at last year's Chicago Marathon? Four hours, twenty-nine min-utes. Personal best, thank you very much. Working to get my pace down to less than ten minutes per mile, though. (I *believe* in me; I can do it!)

Of course, Geri's decided she's an athlete now, too, having just walked a 5K. Not ran, *walked.* Took her over an hour and required the whole damn family waiting for her at the finish line, holding banners and balloons. From the way everyone was celebrating, I thought they were going to carry her off on their shoulders Cleopatra-style, chanting, *Hail the conquering hero!*

Yes, Geri, hurrah for the bare minimum!

Yet when I crossed the finish line at my first *marathon* after having run 26.2 miles? My family members were all whooping it up in the beer tent and they missed *everything*. Where were my banners? What of my balloons? Who was carrying me off on their shoulders? (Trust? I'm a lot lighter.) There I was, wrapped up in the Mylar blanket, all alone searching for my missing cheering section. Typical. Later, Geri admitted, "We didn't figure you'd be done so soon. Hell, it takes me that long to drive 26.2 miles!" I scowl remembering the incident.

The shopper becomes apologetic. "You know what? I'm being a pest. I guess I'll just wake my husband when I figure it out. Thanks for indulging me." She gives me an awkward little bow and begins to circle her cart over to the cheese counter.

Okay, game's over. Feeling magnanimous (largely because I am magnanimous), I draw a breath to tell her that, yes, *I'm* the one she saw in all the magazines, and in the *Tribune*, and on WeWIN. I've lectured at colleges across the country and I've been on morning shows, on all the cable news networks, and one week last fall, I cohosted with Dr. Drew. And once in a while, the paparazzi publish a shot of me with my überfamous mentor, Wendy.

But before I can share the highlights of my CV, she spins back around and snaps her fingers, face wreathed in a smile. "Oh, my God!"

I know what's coming next and I can't help but swell with pride. Indeed, I've accomplished so much already in my career and my life.

"You're Geri's sister!"

Of course I'm the hairdresser's sister.

Of course I am.

*   *   *

"**A**re you still in love with Lorenzo?" I ask.

Dina's kohl-lined eyes are rimmed with tears as she contemplates her answer. With dozens of sessions under our belts over the past month, we've come so far. She's finally let down her guard and lately her insights have been coming rapid-fire. I'm so proud of her progress and I'm confident Wendy Winsberg will be thrilled with this episode. This is the exact kind of positive change we want *I Need a Push* to manifest.

And if highlighting positive change wins us a Daytime Emmy?

All the better.

Dina unfastens the white plastic claw clip holding back torrents of black hair and rakes inch-long, French-manicured tips through her mane. Somewhere, underneath the spandex leggings, the bronzer, and all the bravado, lives a wounded little girl . . . with a serious penchant for leopard print.

But my job is not to judge.

Although as I'm an expert in human behavior, I'd be particularly adept at doing so.

Take Dina, for example. Here she is, a bright, attractive—albeit somewhat flashy—girl with her entire future ahead of her. Maybe she won't become secretary of state with her liberal arts degree from Rutgers, but still. Her life is rife with possibility. (Again, save for cabinet-level work.) But surely there are accounts she can manage, minor projects she can spearhead, cell phones she can market, or memos she can draft to other entry-level managers. I fail to understand why she's willing to jeopardize her potential for some oily Pauly D wannabe club DJ/bouncer. *Push* intervened at the insistence of both her parents and the family court judge. If she can't curb her behavior and ends up saddled with a restraining order, she may as well buy some clear heels and prepare for her debut on the main stage.

I take in her artfully shredded racer-back tank and visible bra and realize it's possible she already owns stripper shoes.

"I am, but I'm trying so hard not to be. Oh, Dr. Reagan, it's like, whenever I think about him I feel so frigging . . ." She scans the horizon, where a few brave boaters are navigating the sun-dappled water, taking their first sail of the season.

In therapy, deliberate silences are as important as actual conversation. I nod encouragingly as she chooses her words. Sometimes when they take too long to find the words, I use the opportunity to jot down my shopping list.

What? It's called "time management" and that's why I'm a pro.

Dina and I are discussing her abandonment issues while we stroll the path by Lake Michigan. With blue skies and balmy breezes, summer's come particularly early to Chicago, so Craig, our nebbishy director, wanted to provide a more visually stimulating backdrop than the studio. Mind you, the presence of two cameramen, a couple of sound and lighting guys, Craig, a hair and makeup stylist, and one hapless production assistant who keeps spilling my tea isn't exactly conducive to unfettered communication at first, but after a while, even the most self-conscious forget we're rolling.

Earlier, I noticed a couple of college girls wearing bikini tops paired with their shorty-shorts as our broadcast team made our way past Oak Street Beach. Our secondary cameraman noticed the coeds, too. After enough time passed that his filming the nubile sorority girls morphed from "collecting B-roll" to "peeping Tom," I had to remind him that *I Need a Push* is not about titillation, okay?

Again, unless titillation wins us an Emmy; I can't stress that enough.

Although, technically, I imagine Wendy would be the one who kept the Emmy, but surely I'd have a chance to pose for photographs with it, as I would have done the lion's share of earning it. Without me, and to a lesser extent Dr. Karen, there is no show. What separates us from makeover programs like *What Not to Wear* is the psychotherapeutic element. At least once an episode, I will bring viewers to tears with my innate understanding and ability to facilitate change. Bank on that.

Regardless, after filming for three hours today, we may end up with two minutes of usable footage, so I don't come down too hard on the second cameraman for his lasciviousness. Everything's digital, so he's not exactly wasting tape.

Currently, we're heading down the path to where the volleyball nets have been set up on North Avenue Beach. I've spent a lot of time in this spot over the years, so I'm familiar with many of the league players here. The idea was mine to come this way; I figured if it's imperative we have eye candy on-screen, we may as well include some cute guys in the shots as well. Worked in the movie *Top Gun*, yes?

(Related note: What exactly happened to Val Kilmer? He used to be Channing Tatum's level of attractive. From Batman to fat man he went. Mark my words: He's an emotional eater.)

Of course, my focus ought to be on Dina, so I circle around and stand in front of her. I maintain intense face-to-face contact so she understands that I'm really hearing her.

Also, my left side is more photogenic. Ask anyone.

"Dina, I understand you want to be strong, yet I'm hearing there's more. What aren't you telling me? When you say 'I'm so frigging . . .' and then trail off, I'm sensing something unsaid."

Spill it, Jersey. I need my aha moment.

She bows her head in shame. "I . . . Dr. Reagan, I went to his frigging Facebook page."

Damn it, I thought we were past this behavior. I can't let her witness my aggravation, because this is not about me. Instead I calmly ask, "Dina, what did I tell you about Facebook?"

(Seriously? Sometimes I'm overwhelmed at my level of competency.)

She sighs and bats her false eyelashes as she repeats my sage advice. "Facebook is the devil's playground."

"And what do I mean by that?"

"You mean that I'm never going to get over him if I keep spying on his activities."

"Consider this: A scab can't heal if one keeps picking at it and reinjuring the wound." I place a hand on my hip and cheat my face toward the camera, as there's nothing inherently unethical about capturing my best angle while doling out life-altering advice. "I have to be firm here, starting with the advice I've given you. Are those the exact words I chose? To 'not spy on his activities'?"

She shrugs her delicate shoulders. "Basically."

"Dina, tell me what I say."

Sotto voce she says, "Don't stalk your ex."

Boom. There we go. That's the moment we'll use in the show's promo. The whole crew smiles and the secondary cameraman tries to hide his smirk, but I ignore them, this being a therapeutic milieu and all.

"Thank you. Sounds like a brief refresher course is in order, so let's discuss Dr. Reagan's Rules again." At some point I'd like to write a book, possibly called *Dr. Reagan's Rules*, so it doesn't hurt to start branding early and often.

Dina stops walking and slouches onto one of the hard

wooden benches across from the volleyball nets. Craig motions for her to face me so she catches the light and then he films us from the back side in order to frame the players in the distance. She fiddles with a neon zebra-stripe bra strap (oh, honey) and stares down at her lap.

"Dr. Reagan's Rules, please, Dina."

With much hesitation, she finally begins to recount my rules. "Um . . . don't check in on Lorenzo's Facebook. Ignore his Twitter feed. Stop texting him at all hours. No more following his Instagram account. Don't drive by his house. Don't drive by his brother's house. Don't drive by his mother's house. Don't steal the trash from the frigging cans outside his house. Don't go to the club on the nights he works there. Stop asking his friends about him. Throw away stuff that reminds me of him." She sighs wearily. "Did I name 'em all, Dr. Reagan? Or was there one more?"

I hold my hand to my ear, middle fingers cupped with my thumb and pinky extended. Sometimes I use gestures to emphasize my point, and also to remind the camera that I'm still here.

"Oh, yeah, don't call his cell phone no more just to listen to his outgoing message. But I haven't done that in a long time, I swear to God."

We're both aware that "a long time" means "a week" but it's a far sight better than the thirty times a day she'd been doing it. Why Lorenzo didn't just change his phone number after the first hundred hang-ups, I don't know, but he's not my patient/not my problem. I strongly suspect some narcissistic tendencies on his part, though. Who tattoos *his own name* on himself? Also, I had no idea Chevrolet was still making Camaros. I figured they disappeared around the time that *Saved by the Bell*'s Zack Morris finally had his testicles drop.

I smile encouragingly at Dina. "Excellent."

She nods and attempts to put on a happy face, but it's clear there's more troubling her.

"It's just on Facebook—," she begins.

I'm resolute here. "Devil's playground."

She exhales so hard that she appears completely deflated. "Believe me, I get it. I've seen frigging Lucifer on the jungle gym and I wish I hadn't, you know? But I noticed he has a new girlfriend and she's not even cute."

I start to say, *They never are,* but I catch myself. I'm careful not to insert any personal commentary into our sessions because it's not appropriate.

Besides, this is not *my* time to complain.

But believe me, I could complain about plenty.

Plenty.

Just this morning I had a voice mail from my mother telling me how Geri placed third in some White Sox bar's karaoke contest. Which . . . whatever. Perhaps once she dusts all the stray hairs off herself at the end of the day, she needs an alternative creative outlet.

However, today's about Dina, not me.

". . . and the more I flipped through his photos . . ."

Ultimately, though, I don't care how Geri occupies her free time. Although I'm surprised she has any, what with her busy sponging-off-my-parents schedule.

And I need to be present here because Dina's so close to another breakthrough.

". . . like I'm standing all by myself on a desert island, without makeup or nothing and . . ."

Yet all I'm saying is maybe it would have been nice for my mother to express this kind of maternal pride when I was on *Good Morning America* last week. Of course, she didn't even watch the episode—she said she'd forgotten to program her DVR. Way to demonstrate familial pride, Ma, especially since on this particular visit? George Stephanopoulos was flirting with me.

Well, I can't say he was flirting for sure, but what heterosexual male wouldn't with my co-commitments to diet, exercise, and clean living?

I heard from all the interns afterward about how fantastic I looked. "Oh, Dr. Reagan, you should always wear emerald green! What was that, a Diane von Furstenberg wrap dress? Amazeballs!"

And yet when Geri does the most innocuous thing, like sing in a karaoke contest, my parents reach Amber-Alert levels of word spreading. One time in fourth grade, Geri earned an A for some stupid poem she'd written about a bird who flew through the air like he just didn't care. You'd have thought Ma and Dad were going to contact the Globe Theatre, as clearly she was Shakespeare reincarnate.

Do I even need to mention that I entirely tested out of the fourth grade? Their response? "Nice job, but that doesn't get you out of doing the dishes."

". . . the same thing happened with my dad . . ."

Focus, self. Focus. Dina needs you. The *show* needs you.

Was the bar even crowded the night Geri won her Major Award? Or were there only, say, three people performing? What, she came in third? What if third means last? The people who graduated last in my program at Pepperdine are still technically doctors of psychology. Terrible doctors, no doubt, but doctors nonetheless. And are any of them on television? I think not.

". . . what if this is it for me? What if I never find happiness? How will I . . ."

Sure, sure, you're a national hero, singing "Total Eclipse of the Heart" like you meant it, Geri. You're a champion. Someone should pin a damn medal on your chest. And then maybe our parents could put your medal on the mantel, right next to the photo of me with my Emmy. You know, the one that I *actually will have earned someday very soon.*

That's when I notice that Dina and the entire crew are staring at me, waiting for me to comment. Crap, I must have really drifted off there. But let's tell the truth here: Sometimes therapy can be boring. It's all "me, me, me." Well, what about *my* thoughts and dreams for once?

I have all kinds of issues and dilemmas right now, largely due to Sebastian. We're technically on a break, but then he'll still come over. Yet afterward, he's hesitant to call me his girlfriend (not that I need labels) and he doesn't invite me to his work gatherings. It's confusing and distracting. My romantic life was decidedly easier when I was with Boyd back in California, but what was I going to do? Follow Geri's advice to drop out of my doctoral program and marry an amateur surfer? Not in this lifetime.

So while everyone awaits my input, I pull out the ultimate old chestnut, the one that every mental health professional relies on when she's grown bored/distracted or plain old fallen asleep. (Listen, it happens.)

"How does that make you feel?"

Actually, this is a phrase that's much more in line with Freudian psychoanalysis, where a patient's drives are largely unconscious and rooted in childhood. Seriously, Sigmund? Give me a break. If my psyche were truly formed in my childhood, then I'd be a hypercontrolling, tightly wound, empathy-lacking basket case from everyone ganging up on me and being jealous all the time. I'd say I turned out pretty damn well, if for no reason other than I don't have to shake strangers' hair out of my underpants every night, *Geri*.

Anyway, I practice cognitive behavior–based therapy, which is more about how patients' actions influence the way they see themselves, rather than how they feel. Regardless, my red-herring question puts us back on track.

Dina surreptitiously adjusts her silicone parts while she ponders her reply. I'm on the fence in terms of surgical enhancement. On the one hand, I'd look fantastic if I went up a cup size (especially according to Sebastian). On the other, gravity's been kind and I can't say I'm a fan of elective surgery and the resulting onslaught of pharmaceuticals.

I tune back in when Dina says, "I feel like . . . I need to understand what he sees in her. I wanna hear what he says to her. Like, how is it different with her than it was with me? So I didn't only visit his page—I went to hers, too."

I grimace. "Devil's. Playground."

I wonder if Geri actually received, what? A certificate of merit? Did the audience clap? Did she have all her south side cohorts there to lull her into a false sense of security? I'm sure Celine Dion need not watch her back.

Then I feel a flash of guilt for not giving Dina my undivided attention.

All right, I'm listening now.

"This is dumb, but I wish . . ." Dina tends to trail off a lot. When I'm quiet (and actually paying attention), I draw more out of her. People are generally far too reticent to allow prolonged gaps of stillness, rushing to fill the awkward silences with nervous, self-revelatory chatter.

But if Geri did receive a tangible artifact of some sort, I guarantee my parents will put the damn thing on display with all her old soccer participation trophies on the shelves next to the fireplace.

This? Right here?

Is why *Push* needs to win that Emmy.

I slap my thighs a couple of times to refocus. I'm not letting the world's lamest little sister throw me off my game. Dina interprets this gesture as a demand that she start getting real.

". . . I wish that I could, like, insert myself into her body." Suddenly, the whole crew snaps to attention, particularly the second cameraman. He's fresh off a stint filming MTV's *The Real World: Logan Square* and he's desperately disappointed that no one's having threesomes in hot tubs on this show. Of course, he won't catch hepatitis C on this particular job, so I guess that's the trade-off.

Whoa, I just had a brainstorm! Seven strangers and one shrink (read: PsyD) picked to live in a loft and have their lives taped to find out what happens when people stop being polite . . . and start getting therapy! I make a mental note to run this idea past Wendy later.

I would kill it in my own spin-off.

Kill. It.

I notice Dina blinking at me again and it's on me to pick up the conversational thread. "So I understand what you're communicating. Do you mean you want to insert yourself *biblically*?" I query. Funny, but on the spectrum between heterosexuality and homosexuality, I'd have placed her firmly on the "Team Nope, Not Once, Not Even at Camp That Summer" end of the continuum.

Dina's immediately flustered. "God, no, I'm not attracted to her, nothing like that. Alls I'm saying is I wish I could trade places with her for a day. You know, ride around in her head or something. Or swap bodies to see how Lorenzo reacts to me as her. Like in the movie *Freaky Friday*."

Unfortunately—or not—I spent most of Lindsay Lohan's career in Drescher Library and I'm largely unfamiliar with her oeuvre. Although, frankly, I'd welcome the opportunity to sit that child down with the DSM-IV. So troubled. Her neuroses are buying someone a beach house—I guarantee that. And if I could get my hands on Charlie Sheen? Hello, early retirement!

"Are you referring to astral projection?" I ask. Dina blinks three times in rapid succession and the entire crew seems confused, so I'm obligated to explain the concept. "Astral projection is a kind of out-of-body experience. Your mind separates from your physical body and your consciousness is able to travel outside of your corporeal self."

"Yes! Like, body swapping and stuff! That! I want to do that."

I give Dina a wry smile. "I'm afraid that's a little outside of my area of expertise."

Also?

The concept of astral projection is utter and complete horseshit, but I dare not say this out loud at work. Wendy Winsberg has a huge mystical/spiritual bent, so much so that last season she hired a ridiculous New Age healer named Deva for the show. I avoid her whenever possible. I guarantee whatever ails my patients can't be cured with some gewgaw or artifact from Deva's oddball little boutique, even if it is across the street from Prada.

But, if it were possible to astral project, particularly if I were to be able to swap bodies and not just rattle around a different dimension, I know exactly where I'd go. I'd head straight for Geri's meatball-shaped vessel because I'm desperate to understand why everyone falls all over her. She's not particularly smart or terribly driven or even that cute, yet you'd think she hung the moon. There's a reason she has a Svengali-like hold on the rest of the world, and I'd make it my job to discover what it is.

I'd also prove she's not allergic to nuts. (That was *my* ham sandwich, damn it!)

I stand and gesture toward the walking path, largely because it's the golden hour, which is the most flattering lighting of the day. I make sure I'm on the left side for maximum sunset benefit.

"Dina, why don't we address the issues within our locus of control before branching into metaphysics?"

She quickly falls into step next to me, the crew clattering along in front of us. When we're on the move, they have to walk backward in order to film our faces.

Here we go, money shot! Clear a space on the mantel, Ma!

"Dina, take out your phone."

She blanches beneath all her bronzer and blush. "No, Dr. R, please. Not that."

"It's time," I say in my most authoritative voice. The primary cameraman circles behind us and pans in over Dina's shoulder. "Strong, Dina. You can do it." With a hand trembling so profoundly that her bracelets clatter, Dina extends a shaky finger and pulls up her Facebook account. I instruct her, "On the count of five, Dina. This is what we've been working toward. Let's go. Five . . . four . . . three . . . two . . . one."

Everyone gathers around to watch Dina finally, blessedly, delete her (frigging) Facebook account. The crew can't help but let out a rousing cheer.

"You did it, Dina!"

I'm so overcome with pride that I hug her to me. Wow. Those are like a couple of kettlebells in there. So not a surgical selling point. Is that what happens when you cheap out on the augmentation? They get hard? Wouldn't they hurt? Like, all the time? Would I even be able to sleep on my stomach? And how would I run any kind of distance with them? I'd need three bras! Plus, for all of Sebastian's enthusiasm, I can't imagine he'd appreciate a handful of concrete. Besides, what I have going on is far better than Geri and her ridiculous rack. She claims they're homegrown, but she was flat when I left for my doctorate and stacked when I came home. And everyone else in the family is small to mid-busted, save for Great-Aunt Helen and her uniboob. I mean, Geri's already proved herself a liar with the nut business and— Ahem, Dina.

Focus, self, focus.

I say, "Tell me what feeling you have now that you're rid of that temptation."

Dina lifts her head, and it's almost like she's taking in the scenery for the first time. The sun, the lake, the after-work crowd, released from long days in the office and confining business garb, filtering onto the walking path. Then she shows me the brightest smile in all of New Jersey.

"I feel . . . free. I feel like I can breathe again for the first time in a very long while."

Damn, it feels good to be a gangsta.

A few more days like this and I'll have the confidence to turn her over to the makeover team. I find once I figure out our pushee's insides, working on the outside is pure gravy.

Before Dina can further express her joy, a Lycra-clad biker whizzes perilously close to us, causing the production assistant to drop my beverage, which splashes all over Dina's leggings.

"Yo! *Yo!* Yeah, I'm talking to you, you frigging Lance

Armstrong wannabe. *This* is the walking path." She gestures with talon-tipped fingers. "*That* is the bike path. Follow me here—walkers go on walking path; bikers go on bike path. But maybe they need to post a big, frigging sign that says 'Bikes *and* Douchebags' so you understand that this means you ride there. Oh, you're riding away from me? Really? Big man! Get your narrow ass back here, ya frigging pussy!"

Two points to make here:

This is likely not the episode to earn me a spot on my parents' mantel.

Also, I may need to touch upon anger-management skills before sending Dina back to Perth Amboy.